Will they surrender to their hidden desires?

"I have to know your scent."

She rubbed her nose against his shirt. "Lean over, please."

He leaned forward slightly, and she buried her nose in the crook of his neck.

"I can't track down any old vampire I might detect," she whispered against his neck. "It has to be you."

His hands tightened on her arms. How on earth was he going to work with this woman when he longed to hold her in his arms?

Her breath was warm and sweet against his neck. All he had to do was turn his head and he could kiss her. Would she let him? Would she curl up against him like a tiger kitten and purr?

He shoved that thought away. This was business. Only business.

"I'm ready." She glanced up at him, smiling.

I'm screwed. His dead heart squeezed in his chest. Her smile was the most beautiful thing he'd seen in ages. He gathered her close so he could teleport, trying not to think about how good her body felt pressed against his own.

By Kerrelyn Sparks

CROUCHING TIGER, FORBIDDEN VAMPIRE
HOW TO SEDUCE A VAMPIRE (WITHOUT REALLY TRYING)
THE VAMPIRE WITH THE DRAGON TATTOO
WILD ABOUT YOU
WANTED: UNDEAD OR ALIVE
SEXIEST VAMPIRE ALIVE
VAMPIRE MINE
EAT PREY LOVE
THE VAMPIRE AND THE VIRGIN
FORBIDDEN NIGHTS WITH A VAMPIRE
SECRET LIFE OF A VAMPIRE
ALL I WANT FOR CHRISTMAS IS A VAMPIRE
THE UNDEAD NEXT DOOR
BE STILL MY VAMPIRE HEART
VAMPS AND THE CITY
HOW TO MARRY A MILLIONAIRE VAMPIRE

Available from Avon Impulse

LESS THAN A GENTLEMAN
THE FORBIDDEN LADY

CROUCHING TIGER FORBIDDEN VAMPIRE

KERRELYN SPARKS

AVON
An Imprint of HarperCollins*Publishers*

This is a work of fiction. Names, characters, places, and incidents are products of the author's imagination or are used fictitiously and are not to be construed as real. Any resemblance to actual events, locales, organizations, or persons, living or dead, is entirely coincidental.

AVON BOOKS
An Imprint of HarperCollins*Publishers*
195 Broadway
New York, New York 10007

ISBN 978-0-06-210777-0
www.avonromance.com

First Avon Books mass market printing: January 2015

Printed in the U.S.A.

10 9 8 7 6 5 4 3 2 1

To the friends who have blessed my life,
and the best critique partners an author could ever wish for,
M. J. Selle, Sandy Weider, and Vicky Yelton

CROUCHING TIGER FORBIDDEN VAMPIRE

Chapter One

Shrouded in the dark, and half hidden behind the thick trunk of an oak tree, Russell Ryan Hankelburg carefully aligned the trajectory of his arrow to the exposed neck of Master Han. *Steady,* Russell reminded himself in response to the adrenaline pounding through his veins. No point in acting like a human. He wasn't one. Han had made sure of that, and now the bastard would die for it.

For over two years, through hot, humid jungle and over cold, windblown hills, Russell had tracked his prey. Finally, in the next few seconds it would all be over. His quest for revenge. The culmination of all his rage, the vindication for all he had lost, and the sole purpose for his sorry undead existence.

The clearing where Han stood was about fifty yards away, and a dozen guards stood around the perimeter, four of them holding torches. The flames licked at the overcast night sky and flickered off the polished gold of Master Han's mask.

How many times had Russell envisioned ripping the ridiculous piece of metal off the evil vampire's head? In the best-case scenario, he imagined tearing it off before delivering the final blow so he could watch Han's face as the Master Bastard realized death was only seconds away.

What good was revenge if it wasn't acknowledged? Han needed to know that it was Russell who would end his life and turn him to dust.

Han stood at the far side of the clearing, outside the wooden palisade of a camp in northern Myanmar. He was wearing a black Kevlar vest over his red silk robe to protect his heart. If Russell's arrow failed to pierce the vest enough to kill Han, the bastard would simply teleport away.

Fortunately there was more than one way to kill a vampire. So Russell aimed at the neck instead of the heart, hoping that a ripped carotid artery would incapacitate Han enough to keep him from escaping. Then Russell could teleport straight to him, rip off the mask, and sever Han's head with one final swing of his sword.

The dozen armed guards were probably supersoldiers, mutated by Han's demon buddy, Darafer, and they were going to be a problem. Even so, Russell couldn't take them out first. Their deaths would alert Han, and the cowardly cretin would teleport away like the last few times Russell had come close to killing him.

Russell gritted his teeth with impatience. So close, but still unable to shoot. Han was standing next to the kidnapped dragon shifter, practically hugging him as he taught the young captive the proper stance for drawing back a bow. With a silent curse, Russell lifted his finger off the trigger of his crossbow.

He'd seen the boy once before, so he recognized him. Since dragon shifters aged twice as fast as mortals, Xiao Fang looked about twelve years old. In mortal years, he was only six. Russell wasn't sure what the kid's mental age was, but he was certainly young enough to have been traumatized by recent events. Darafer had captured the dragon boy over two months ago and delivered him to Han. Since then, Russell had been spying on all thirty of Han's camps, hoping to catch a glimpse of Han and the boy.

It was extremely rare to see Han outside one of his encampments, but apparently he'd made an exception for the boy. He was giving Xiao Fang an archery lesson and playing the role of a father figure, no doubt to win the young dragon shifter to his side.

The sad reality was that the strategy might work. Away from his home for over two months, the boy could have fallen prey to the Stockholm syndrome, so that he was now identifying with one of his captors. Master Han probably seemed the safer choice. Safer than the demon Darafer, for sure. And here was Han patting the kid on the back and giving him words of encouragement.

It made Russell's stomach churn with disgust. For a second, he considered teleporting straight to the boy, nabbing him, and taking him to Tiger Town, where he would be safe. The good Vamps were gathered there with their allies, the were-tigers, anxiously awaiting their chance to rescue the dragon boy and defeat Master Han. One phone call and Russell could have a dozen Vamps and shifters by his side.

But wait. Han was stepping back to let Xiao Fang take his shot. It might be another two years before Russell got a chance like this. His first priority had to be killing Han. In the ensuing chaos, the boy could easily be rescued. And this situation was ideal, since Han and his supersoldiers were all standing perfectly still so as not to disturb the boy's concentration.

Russell eased his finger back onto the trigger. *Die, you bastard.*

One of the guards jerked suddenly. As he fell forward onto his face, the soldier next to him stiffened with a cry, then crumbled to his knees.

What the hell? Russell barely had time to spot the knives protruding from the fallen soldiers' backs when Han jumped on the boy, pushing him down onto the ground. A third knife whizzed past where Han had been standing, embedding itself with a thunk in a tree.

The remaining soldiers shouted, immediately drawing their swords. Han vanished, taking the dragon boy with him.

Damn it to hell! Russell fumed silently. Who were these assholes who had ruined his plans? From the speed and accuracy of the attack, he assumed there were two knife throwers. Maybe three. Whoever they were, they might have trouble escaping the superfast soldiers who were giving chase.

Not my problem, he told himself. The attackers had destroyed the best chance he'd had in a long time. If they were all murdered in the next few minutes, they would never have a chance to interfere with him again.

With a groan, he rested his head against the tree trunk. When had he become such an uncaring prick? Even though he'd been stripped of his humanity, did that mean he had to act like a heartless monster? The attackers were clearly on the same side he was. That made them allies in the war against Master Han.

Damn, but he hated having allies. As long as he was alone, he had nothing to lose.

Maybe the attackers were guys he knew, like J.L. Wang and Rajiv, and in that case, vampire J.L. would have teleported his were-tiger buddy out of danger. But knife throwing was not J.L.'s style. He would have used a rifle or handgun. And he would have wounded the soldiers instead of killing them.

If the attackers were mortal, they wouldn't stand a chance against ten supersoldiers. An old vestige of Marine honor pricked at Russell's undead heart. *You don't leave men behind.*

"Dammit," he muttered, hitching the leather sling of the crossbow onto his shoulder.

He levitated to the top of the tree. The soldiers were easy to spot, since four of them were still carrying torches. The four flames of light were weaving through the forest at a speed faster than any mortal could achieve.

He focused on the tree line ahead of the lights,

then teleported there. Perched high in a tree, he searched the ground below for movement. Even though the sky was dark and overcast, his superior night vision spotted a runner, lean and lithe, maintaining a fast pace, but not quick enough to outdistance the soldiers.

Only one? He scanned a wide area in case the attackers had fanned out. No, only one was running. Had the others hidden themselves, leaving this one to draw away the heat? A quick glance back verified that the soldiers were gaining on him. Ten against one. It would be a slaughter.

He teleported again to get a closer look at the runner and nearly fell off the tree branch. It was a woman. Her tunic-length top was cinched tightly around her narrow waist. A thick braid of long black hair swayed back and forth as she ran.

Was she one of the warrior women of Beyul-La? They all possessed long black hair and were lean and athletic, like this woman. The warriors of Beyul-La were the guardians of the dragon shifters and had kept them hidden for centuries in a secret valley in the Himalayas. After a battle with Master Han, their valley had been destroyed. Fortunately, the remaining dragon children and eggs had been safely whisked away before the battle. No doubt the women were eager to rescue the captured boy, Xiao Fang. Russell had fought alongside the women before, so he knew how fierce they could be. This one definitely had balls, for it looked like she'd attacked Han single-handedly.

He glanced back. The ten supersoldiers were

closing in. Time to slow them down. He shot an arrow at one holding a torch, and the soldier let out a yelp and fell over, his torch tumbling to the ground.

The flames quickly spread, drawing the attention of the other guards. One of them kicked the fallen soldier into the flames to smother them.

What a shithead. Russell notched another arrow into his crossbow as the fallen soldier thrashed and screamed. A second later, his arrow put the burning soldier out of his misery, and three seconds later, another arrow took out the shithead.

"It's an ambush!" one of the supersoldiers yelled as he dove behind a tree.

The other soldiers scrambled for cover and quickly extinguished the torches. A dark, tense silence fell over the forest.

Russell readied another arrow, waiting for one of the eight remaining soldiers to venture out. A quick glance toward the woman, and he groaned inwardly. Instead of running, she'd crouched behind some bushes. His sudden appearance must have confused her. She was breathing heavily, twisting this way and that in a frantic attempt to discern his location.

Just run away, he pleaded with her silently. *I have this covered.*

From her belt, she pulled out a knife. Apparently she was afraid to trust him. He couldn't blame her. If you trusted no one, you tended to live longer.

He turned his attention back to the eight soldiers. On the far left, one darted to the cover of another tree, too quickly for Russell to take him out. He aimed an arrow at him, waiting for him to make another move. Meanwhile, to the right, another soldier dashed to a tree. The group was obviously trying to surround the woman, and eventually they would if she didn't make a run for it.

The guy to the far left made another move, and this time, Russell wounded him in the shoulder. He was still alive, but his sword arm would be useless.

Rustling sounds emanated from bushes and trees as the remaining seven soldiers attempted to encircle their prey. The woman slipped her knife back into its sheath, then leaped from her crouch into a full sprint. Russell paused a second, amazed by her speed and grace, but quickly came to when he realized the soldiers were dashing after her. He shot one with an arrow, then noticed another aiming a pistol in his direction. Just as the sound of gunfire echoed through the woods, he teleported away and landed in a tree ahead of the woman.

The six remaining soldiers were gaining on her fast. *Enough of this nonsense. Just get her out of here.*

He jumped down to the base of the tree. Hidden behind it, he could hear her approaching. Her steps were light, as if she barely needed the ground, but her breathing was louder and tinged with panic. He stepped out, directly into her path.

Her night vision was excellent, for she spotted him immediately and skidded to a stop so fast that she fell back onto her rump.

Russell lifted his empty hands to show her he meant no harm, but within a second, she was back on her feet with her knife drawn and pointed at him. Once again, he was amazed by her speed and gracefulness.

"Friend," he whispered in Chinese. Her face was partially blocked by her raised knife, and he tilted his head to get a better look.

She pivoted to check on the soldiers behind her. When Russell stepped closer, she whipped around to face him.

He blinked. She was stunning. And not one of the warrior women of Beyul-La. If he'd ever met this woman before, he would have remembered her.

Her golden eyes widened as she looked him over.

Who the hell was she? "Friend," he repeated and motioned to the crossbow on his shoulder. "I helped you."

She sheathed her knife but retained her grip on the handle. Apparently she wasn't ready to completely trust him. Smart girl. He was still tempted to wring her neck.

The glint of metal behind a bush caught his eye and he grabbed her, pulling her behind the tree with vampire speed as a knife whooshed toward them. With his back pressed against the trunk, he felt the tree shudder with the knife's impact.

"Let me go," the woman whispered, tugging at his grip.

He considered complying. After all, she wasn't his problem. And she'd destroyed the best chance he'd had at killing Han in over two years.

I am not responsible for her, he thought, but he made the mistake of looking at her. Big, golden eyes, flickering with emotion. A beautiful face, vibrant and alive. Delicate, but determined. He had a feeling she was near panic but holding it together with sheer willpower and courage. Something twisted in his undead heart.

I'm going to regret this. He tightened his hold on her, then teleported, taking her with him.

As soon as Jia felt solid ground beneath her feet, she pulled away from the man's grip. It was dark, too dark to see, even with her excellent night vision.

"Careful," the man said in Chinese. His accent was odd and his voice gruff, as if he didn't speak often.

She pulled her knife from its sheath, ready to strike if he attacked her. From his scent and the fact that he'd teleported, she knew he was a vampire, but he might be a good one, like her friends Jin Long and Dou Gal. This man seemed to be on her side, but when it came to vampires, appearances could be deceiving. Until she'd met the good Vamps, she'd thought they were all evil.

"Don't move," the man grumbled. "I'll light up the place so you can see."

The decreasing volume of his voice indicated he was moving away from her. Jia took a deep breath, attempting to quell the panic that had seized her when the two soldiers had fallen dead from her knives. *They were the enemy,* she reminded herself. Anyone who stood in the way of her mission had to be removed. Nothing could stop her from killing Han.

She'd trained since the age of eight, learning martial arts with the boys of Tiger Town and then in private, throwing countless knives at straw targets until her speed and accuracy had become as good as any man's. But bundles of straw never cried out in pain and bled to death. Thirteen years of practice had not prepared her for the grim reality of war.

She had thought she was ready for death, even her own. As a were-tiger, she had nine lives, and advancing on to her second life would give her a much-needed strategic advantage. It would allow her to shift any time and anywhere. If she'd been able to shift tonight, she could have easily defeated her foe.

But once the soldiers had charged after her, the prospect of dying at their hands had terrified her. What if they chopped up her dead body, so she couldn't come back? That was what Han had done to her parents and brother.

A vision of her mutilated family swept across her mind, followed by the memory of the two soldiers she'd killed tonight. With a shudder, she shoved the images aside. She needed to get a hold of herself and focus on her current situation.

Location unknown. Vampire captor unknown.

She flexed her hand on the knife handle. "Who are you?"

He didn't answer.

Since she couldn't see, she used her other heightened senses to detect her location. A strong, earthy smell surrounded her. The air was warm and humid, similar to the Yunnan province where Tiger Town was located. Water was moving nearby, the trickling sound pleasant to her ears. She picked up the warbling call of a bird, muffled and distant. Outdoors, but no sky overhead. A cave?

Why had the vampire brought her here?

Two months ago, when the good Vamps had gone to battle to defend the valley of Beyul-La, they had all traveled through Tiger Town, and they had returned there each day to do their death-sleep. Her cousin Rajiv, the Grand Tiger, had gone to battle, too, along with her uncles Rinzen and Tenzen. She'd been left behind to rule in her cousin's stead, so while she'd played princess of Tiger Town, she'd met dozens of good Vamps.

This vampire had not been with them.

"Who are you?" Jia asked again, taking another step back.

"Don't move," he repeated. A flame appeared at the end of a pistol-looking device, and then the wick of a camping-style oil lamp lit up.

A golden circle of light shone around the lamp, illuminating the profile of the man leaning over it. Whoever this vampire was, he was certainly handsome. She'd noticed that before in the forest. Strong features, strong body. All the good Vamps she'd met were strong and good looking, but this man was different. The good Vamps were usually well dressed, well groomed, and well behaved. Polite, friendly, and respectful. She doubted any of them would kidnap a young woman and take her to a dark cave.

This vampire had a rough, primitive look about

him. His khaki pants were torn in a few places. His knee-length brown coat was old and shabby. Dark stubble shaded his square jaw. Some of his hair had come loose from his short ponytail, and he'd hooked the strands behind his ears. At first, his hair appeared brown, but the longer she stared, the more she detected light copper streaks that gleamed in the golden lamplight. American, maybe? Or British?

Why was he in China? What did he want from her? Was he hungry and expected to feed from her? She lifted her knife and took another step back.

"Don't—"

Kerplunk. Her foot plopped into cool water up to her shin. She quickly regained her balance and moved her foot back onto dry land. Unfortunately, some water had seeped into her ankle-high hiking boot. Damn, she hated wet socks.

"Told you not to move," he muttered.

She glared at him. "You could have warned me about the lake."

"It's not a lake. And I don't explain myself." He gave her an annoyed look that made her blink at the intensity of it.

He was angry with her? More than angry. His brown eyes seethed with controlled rage. Great. She'd been kidnapped by a pissed-off vampire.

He moved away from the light, and soon, he'd lit two more lamps.

She pivoted to look around, her sodden leather boot squishing as she moved. They were definitely underground. The walls were solid rock, and part of the ceiling high overhead was stone. The rest of the ceiling was a tangled mass of earth and tree roots. In places, long strands of green ivy dangled down into the cave.

As far as she could tell, they were just below the surface. Tiny cracks here and there let in damp, fresh air, and brilliant green moss clung to the tree roots and rock ceiling.

She was standing on the sandy shore of an underground stream. On the far side of the stream, she spotted a narrow strand of sand, then a smooth wall of rock. No exit there. The cave was narrow and long, following the path of the stream. It was a beautiful place, what with the green moss and tendrils of ivy overhead, and the soothing sound of moving water.

To the right, where the cave's ceiling was solid rock, she spotted a dark alcove. Inside were some wooden crates, set side by side to form a rectangle. Stacked on top were several open sleeping bags and a blanket. His bed.

This was his home. She glanced back at him. He was levitating up to a tree root with gnarly stems that protruded like fingers. There, he hooked the leather slings of his crossbow and quiver of arrows. He dropped neatly to the ground, then walked a few steps to a foldout camp table.

He emptied the deep pockets of his coat, placing four knives, a phone, two handguns, and extra ammunition on the table. Then he unbuckled a sword belt and set his sheathed sword on the table. Apparently he wasn't worried about her attacking, for he was completely disarming himself.

She pivoted once more to examine his home. He had quite a collection of camping gear: oil lanterns, two ice chests, two foldout tables. He'd built a makeshift bookcase with cinder blocks and planks of wood. Neatly folded clothing was stacked on the bottom two shelves. The top shelf held an assortment of books and electronic gadgets. How did he power them? A thick wire snaked up the rock wall and disappeared among some tree roots. Interesting. His cave might not be as primitive as she'd first thought.

Far to the right, past his bedroom, the underground stream disappeared into a rock tunnel. He'd situated an old-fashioned tin bathtub on the sandy shore with a spigot that extended over the water. Hanging from a hook rammed into the rock ceiling was a large bucket with a long chain. His version of a shower, she assumed. Close by there was a foldout wooden rack where he'd stretched out his laundry to dry. For a guy who lived in a cave, he appeared to be rather neat and tidy.

"Who are you?" His deep voice rumbled behind her, tingling the skin at the back of her neck.

She turned and her jaw dropped. He'd taken off his bulky coat and tossed it on the table. That one move had transformed him from an anonymous hobo into a gorgeous superhero. His dark green T-shirt stretched over incredibly wide shoulders. The worn, faded material clung to every contour of his muscled chest and abdomen before tapering to his narrow hips. He folded his arms over his chest, and she thought his sleeves might rip from failing to accommodate the size of his biceps.

The tingle on her neck skittered down her spine. It wasn't just his muscles that were affecting her. It was something more. His presence. It seemed to fill the cave and, worse, fill her senses, leaving her with no doubt that this man was powerful, intelligent, and perhaps even dangerous.

She swallowed hard. "Who are you?"

"You know what I am."

"A vampire, yes. But I haven't figured out yet if you're one of the good ones."

"Neither have I." His mouth twisted with a wry look. "I take it you've met the good ones?"

She nodded. "Jin Long, Dou Gal, Angus, and some others. Do you know them?"

"Yes. How do you know them?"

She ignored his question. "Then you're on their side?"

"Only when it suits me." He pulled a bottle of blood from an ice chest and opened it. "I won't feed from you, if that's what you're worried about." He took a long drink.

That was good news. She sheathed her knife.

He set the bottle down and frowned at her. "You pissed me off."

Her hand shot back to the handle of her knife.

He snorted. "I'm not going to hurt you. Not after going to the trouble of saving your pretty ass."

She narrowed her eyes. "I have excellent aim, so I suggest you rephrase that."

He finished his bottle, then wiped his mouth with the back of his hand. "You're right. 'Pretty' was an insult. I'd say your ass is damned beautiful—" When she pulled her knife from its sheath, he scoffed. "I rescued you, and you're going to kill me? You should be thanking me."

She pointed the weapon at him. "You brought me here against my will."

"Would you prefer I take you back? I could drop you off at Han's camp and let them capture you." He took a step toward her, his scowl deepening. "What the hell were you thinking, taking on a dozen supersoldiers single-handedly? Are you trying to get yourself killed? Don't you have family somewhere worried about you?"

The vision of her mutilated family flitted through her mind once more. With an inward groan, she lowered her arm. "Just tell me where the exit is, and I'll be on my way."

"There is no exit. I teleport you in or out."

And he would control where they went? She motioned to the stream. "I'll follow the water. I'm sure it surfaces at some point."

"Yes, after going through a rock tunnel for a mile or so. Your body would emerge eventually. Dead."

Jia bit her lip, her gaze wandering to the stream where it disappeared into the tunnel. If she drowned, she wouldn't have to worry about being hacked to pieces. Her skin pebbled with goose bumps as she imagined those last terrifying moments when she would run out of air—

"What the hell?" he whispered, and she turned to face him. "You're considering it, aren't you? You're suicidal." He strode toward her.

She lifted her knife. "Stay back!"

He vanished. Before she could even react, he

grabbed her from behind. His left arm encircled her rib cage and pulled her hard against his chest. His right hand wrenched the knife from her hand and tossed it aside.

So incredibly fast. And strong. Self-doubt crept into her mind once again, reminding her how difficult it was going to be to kill Master Han on her own. As a vampire, Han was just as strong and fast as this one who was pinning her against his rock-hard chest.

"Release me." Her breath caught as his hand groped along her belted waist.

"Any more knives? Do I need to frisk you?"

"Let me go!"

"I will. Eventually." His chin grazed the top of her head. "I haven't decided yet what to do with you."

She swallowed hard. There was no way she could overpower this man. And even if she did, where could she go? The only way out of this cave was the stream. And death.

His cheek slid along her hair till she felt his breath, hot against her ear. Hot? Shouldn't a vampire be cold? His whiskered jaw scraped across her cheek. She tilted her head away from him, but that only served to give him better access to her throat. He buried his nose in the crook of her neck, and she shuddered.

"You have the scent of a shifter." With his right hand, he took hold of her jaw and turned her face toward him. "And the golden eyes of a tiger."

Her gaze met his, and for a few seconds she forgot to breathe. His stare was bold and fierce, as if he was trying to look into her soul. His eyes were not solid brown, as she'd thought, but hazel, with shards of gold and green shimmering among the brown.

There was something so . . . sincere about his eyes and expression. Instinctively, she felt he was solid and honest. A man who said and did what he felt was right and never apologized for it.

His gaze lowered to her mouth, then returned to her eyes. "Shall I teleport you back to Tiger Town?"

"No!" She pulled away, surprised for a second that he let her go. "I can't go back there. Anywhere but there."

He smirked. "So you admit that is your home."

"Yes, but I can't go back before my mission is done."

"Your family must be worried sick—"

"My family is *dead*! My parents and brother, hacked to pieces by Master Han. I won't stop until I've killed him."

The vampire stiffened. "You will not kill Han."

"I will! I swore I would avenge my family—"

"You're not killing Han!" the vampire yelled. *"I am!"*

Jia paused a moment, stunned by the vampire's words and the ferocious look on his face. "Why do you want—"

"I don't explain myself," he growled and took a step toward her. "I was so close to killing Han tonight. I had a clear shot at his neck, and you ruined it."

She stepped back. "You—"

"Two years of tracking that bastard, and you screwed it up!"

She winced. No wonder he was pissed. "I didn't know."

"You know nothing about warfare! You can't attack his guards first. He just teleports away."

"I realize that now. I'll do better next—"

"There is no next time for you. Killing Han is *my* job, and *you* will stay out of it!"

Jia's breath caught when she realized who this vampire must be. How many times had she heard Jin Long and her cousin complain about him? Angus kept sending them on missions to find him, and somehow, he always eluded them.

What was his name? He seemed like a legend, the way people gossiped about him. Some said he was dangerous; others called him a hero. According to her cousin, he'd cut the tracking chip out of his arm and disappeared two years ago, vowing to kill Master Han. A few times, when Rajiv and Jin Long had found themselves surrounded by Han's soldiers, this vampire had miraculously appeared and rescued them.

Just like he'd rescued her tonight. "I know who you are. You're the—the—"

"The deserter?" he growled. "Do they say I'm crazy?"

"No! Of course not." She winced inwardly. This was not the time to admit that Rajiv called him "The Crazy One." And Jin Long claimed he was a loose cannon. She searched her mind for something good they'd said about him. "They say you're the best tracker in the world."

He stared at her a moment, then looked away, shifting his weight as if he didn't know how to respond.

He's not used to compliments, she thought, and

her heart softened. What a lonesome man he had to be. But so wonderfully dedicated to his cause. She inhaled sharply as an idea popped into her mind. "I know what to do. We'll work together!"

He blinked. "No."

"Yes!" It was a brilliant solution, so brilliant that she felt a surge of confidence that she could easily convince him. "It's perfect! We have the same goal, so all we have to do is team up to defeat our common foe."

"Hell, no."

"In fact, I think fate has brought us together for this purpose."

He hesitated, a stunned look on his face.

Yes! He was coming around. The more she thought about this new idea, the more excited she became. She'd always known it would be difficult to kill Han, but when she'd asked her uncles, Rinzen and Tenzen, to help her, they had refused. And then, to make matters worse, they'd reported her plan to her cousin, and Rajiv had forbidden her to go. Vengeance should be left to the male were-tigers, Rajiv had told her. As the resident princess in Tiger Town, it was her job to play hostess and perform the tea ceremony for their visitors. She'd been sorely tempted to tell Rajiv what he could do with the ceremonial teapot.

"As a vampire, you can do all the levitating and teleporting," she continued. "And I'll do whatever needs to be done during the day. I can even guard you while you're in your death-sleep."

He shook his head. "I don't need a guard. No one knows about this place."

"I know."

He snorted. "You have no idea where we are."

"That's even better! No one should know the location of our secret hideout."

"*Our* hideout?"

"Yes!" She grinned, delighted that he was agreeing. "And you needn't worry that I won't pull my weight. I know martial arts, and you've seen how well I throw knives."

"I work alone."

She waved a dismissive hand. "I realize you're stuck in a rut over that, but it's time for you to be daring enough to try something new. We have to be bold in order to succeed."

He gave her an incredulous look. "Are you calling me a coward?"

"Of course not. I'm just saying we'll be more efficient as a team. Take tonight, for example. If I had known your plans ahead of time, I wouldn't have interfered." She gave him an encouraging smile. "We should start right now tracking down Master Han. You know where his camps are, right? Let's go!"

"I think we should go." The vampire grabbed hold of her arms.

Yes! They were a team! "Shouldn't you arm yourself—" She stopped when everything went black.

When her feet hit solid ground, she pulled away from him and looked around her. *Oh, God, no.*

They were in the courtyard of Tiger Town. Torches lit up the perimeter, and dozens of armed male were-tigers were standing nearby. They all stared at her in shock. Her heart sank in dismay.

"Jia!" Rajiv ran toward her. "Where have you been?"

"What have you done?" she hissed at the vampire. "I told you not to bring me here."

Rajiv stopped in front of her. "Jia, what happened? You left seven days ago to see my brother in Thailand, and then today I get a call from him that you never arrived! I was about to send out search parties for you."

The vampire smirked. "I thought you might be worried about her."

"Russell!" Rajiv shook his hand. "Thank you for bringing back my cousin."

Russell? So that was the vampire's name. Jia glared at him. It could take her weeks to find Han again. And now that Rajiv knew what she was up to, she'd have a hard time escaping Tiger Town.

"Cousin?" Russell gave her a wary look. "You're in the royal family?"

She was royally pissed. Before she could answer, Rajiv cut in.

"She's our resident princess," he explained. "We are indebted to you for bringing her back safely."

Russell's face went cold. Without looking at her, he muttered, "I'll be going then."

"You're leaving me here?" Anger spiked in her chest. "We have the same goal. I thought you understood me. I thought I could trust you."

His mouth thinned. "You thought wrong."

She pulled her arm back and slapped him hard across the face.

Chapter Two

Russell shifted his jaw to make sure it still worked. She was damned strong for a princess. And damned angry.

He turned away from her accusing glare. No matter what she thought, he'd done the right thing. The woman had family, *royal* family, and they were relieved to have her safely home. Her plan to go after Han was clearly suicidal. The bastard had hundreds of supersoldiers. She'd never manage to kill him on her own.

That's why she wanted to team up with you. With a dismissive snort, he ignored the inner voice. No doubt it had hurt like hell when she'd lost her parents and brother, but her need for vengeance could never take precedence over his. Vengeance was all that he had left. She still had family. And friends. Still had a home and a future. There was no need for her to suffer anymore.

And that was the big difference between them. He didn't give a shit if he suffered or died. He'd endured enough pain that his cold, undead heart had grown immune to it.

When Angus and his buddies had found him three years ago in Master Han's cave in Thailand, they'd wakened him from a vampire coma. It had been unnerving to discover he'd joined the ranks of the Undead, but he'd adjusted quickly. After all, being a vampire put him on equal footing with the villain who had attacked him. It made revenge possible. And that gave him a reason to live.

Russell had no memory of how he'd ended up in a vampire coma, but he'd been found in Han's cave with Han's tattoo of ownership on his right wrist. It could only mean that Han had attacked him, sucked him dry, then stashed him away for thirty-nine freakin' years.

Russell's theory had been confirmed when he'd met Han and the bastard had declared that Russell belonged to him. Russell had known then and there that Han had to die. But if possible, he had one question to ask Master Han before killing him. *Why? Why did you leave me there for thirty-nine years?*

During that time, Russell had lost everything. Unlike Jia, he had nothing left to lose. There was no family, no home, no future. Nothing and no one.

That was the way it needed to stay. He had to work alone. A partner would slow him down. Make him feel responsible. Make him . . . feel. Feelings would make him weak. And weakness would make him fail.

"Tenzen!" Rajiv called over one of his uncles. "Will you take Jia to her room?"

The princess's eyes blazed with anger, and she aimed a molten-gold glare at Russell. "See what you've done? I'll be a prisoner!"

Tenzen took hold of her arm, and she shook him off. "I know the way." With a lift of her chin, she started across the courtyard.

Her dignified exit was somewhat marred by the squishing sound of her wet boot, but even so, Russell was impressed by her refusal to appear defeated. Was she really a prisoner? He winced at the sight of her uncle and two guards following close behind her.

"Jia, thank God you're back!" J.L. Wang grinned at her as he approached. "Are you all right?"

Russell's eyes narrowed. J.L. was the vampire she'd called her friend, using his full name, Jin Long. As a former special agent for the FBI, J.L. had fit right into MacKay Security and Investigation. Officially, he was head of security for the West Coast Coven, headquartered in his hometown of San Francisco. But recently, he spent most of his time in China, where his knowledge of Chinese was helping the good Vamps in their fight against Master Han.

Jia lifted a hand in greeting, then marched right past J.L. without a word. As J.L.'s smile faded, a pang of satisfaction reverberated in Russell's chest.

J.L. jogged over to Rajiv and Russell. "What happened?"

"Russell found her and brought her back," Rajiv replied.

"Thank you." J.L. gave Russell a quick smile. "We were worried about her."

Russell's hands curled into fists. "Then why weren't you with her? You call yourself her friend but leave her alone to face danger?"

J.L. stiffened. "What's gotten into you?"

"She wasn't alone," Rajiv explained. "At least not at first. My brother's wife has recently given birth to twins. Jia offered to be our emissary to deliver gifts and assist with the care of the babies. She set off a week ago with a small caravan. Five guards. Just across the border in Thailand, she managed to sneak away in the middle of the night. The guards searched for her but couldn't find her. So they rushed on to my brother's village, and he called tonight with the news that she was missing."

"We were about to search for her," J.L. added. "Where did you find her?"

Russell shifted his weight. He wasn't sure if these guys knew about Jia's plan to assassinate Master Han. Even though he should warn them, he found himself strangely reluctant to tattle on her. "I'm not sure. Someplace in northern Myanmar."

J.L.'s eyes narrowed with suspicion. "Master Han has a camp there."

Russell shrugged. "He has camps all over."

"Was Han there?" Rajiv demanded. "Was she trying to kill him?"

So they knew. Russell sighed. "Yes, she tried and came damned close to succeeding."

J.L. sucked in a hissing breath.

Rajiv grimaced. "I strictly forbade her to go anywhere near Han or his camps."

J.L. shook his head. "She's too impetuous. She'll get herself killed."

A surge of anger shot through Russell. "At least she's doing something! She had the courage to go after him, which is more than I can say for the two of you!"

Rajiv's eyes flashed with anger. "If you know where Han is, tell me and I'll gladly kill him. I promised Jia I would avenge her family. And since you found her, you must have been near Han, too. Why didn't *you* kill him?"

Russell's jaw shifted as he ground his teeth.

"Do you think we're doing nothing here?" J.L. glared at him. "In the last two months, we've attacked six of Han's camps and taken his supersoldiers. They're in the clinic now, being changed back to normal."

"We've whittled Han's army down to three hundred and twenty," Rajiv added.

Russell scoffed. "Instead of saving soldiers, we need to kill Han. Once the head is dead, the body will wither away."

"Then the next time you see Han, call us," J.L. growled. "We're on the same side, dammit."

Russell stepped back to teleport away. "Later."

"Wait!" J.L. held up a hand. "We need to know more. Is Han still in Myanmar?"

"He left." Russell scowled. "There's no telling where he is now. And he had the dragon boy with him."

"Xiao Fang?" Rajiv asked. "Is he all right?"

"He appeared to be."

"Let me get you a sat phone," J.L. said. "The next time you see Han—"

"I have a phone."

"But the charge—"

"It's fine." Russell visualized his underground lair, ready to teleport there. *Our secret hideout,* the princess had called it. Was it true what she had said? "Is she really a prisoner?"

Rajiv glanced in the direction of the houses next to the courtyard. Jia had disappeared down one of the narrow alleys. "She's exaggerating. She's free to go about Tiger Town as she wishes."

Tiger Town was small. Russell tamped down on the anger that still sizzled inside him. How dare they keep down a fighting spirit like hers?

"If she still wants to visit the were-tigers in Thailand, I'll teleport her there," J.L. offered.

Russell snorted. Did the fools think she wanted to babysit? She was probably sharpening her knives right now and planning her escape. She had one thing on her mind—killing Han.

And he needed to beat her to it. Russell teleported away.

Jia slid the bolt across her door. The last thing she needed now was someone barging in while she checked on her hidden stash of weapons. She dashed across the dark room and opened the shutters to the back window. It had been overcast in Myanmar, but here in the Yunnan province of China, the sky was clear. Countless stars and a quarter-moon shone through the window. With her excellent night vision, there was enough light for her to see.

As the granddaughter of the late Grand Tiger, she'd lived in Tiger Town since the age of eight, moving there after the deaths of her parents and brother. She'd been trained in all the intricacies of courtly life and its elaborate ceremonies, but here in the privacy of her room, she'd always maintained a Spartan existence. As long as her family cried out for vengeance, she couldn't afford to grow soft.

Her room took up half of a building situated on the bluff overlooking the beach and Mekong River. Down by the river, she could see lights in the windows of houses and stores built up on stilts. Most of the villagers of Tiger Town lived along the river and worked as fishermen or merchants. Up here on the bluff, the royal residences and guesthouses sat next to the courtyard and palace.

Her sensitive hearing caught the sound of a boot scraping along the stone alleyway outside her door. The guards were still there. Dammit. How dare that vampire bring her back to Tiger Town? She'd clearly told him anywhere but here.

She darted over to her wooden chest and dug beneath the embroidery supplies to find her hidden stash of knives. Still there, thank God. Apparently Rajiv hadn't ordered her room to be searched when he'd learned she was missing.

After pulling out the leather parcel, she untied the strings to unroll it on the floor. Ten perfectly balanced knives lay in a row, their handles nestled into narrow pockets, their blades gleaming in the moonlight. She retrieved a knife from each of her boots and a third one that was lashed to her calf underneath her trousers. She lifted her baggy pants higher to uncover the short, emergency dagger strapped to her thigh.

With a snort, she added the four knives to her collection. The vampire had made a mistake not searching her for more weapons, although the thought of his hands roaming up her legs made her pause. Such strong hands. She only had to close her eyes to remember his rock-hard chest against her back, the scrape of his whiskers along her cheek, and the bold way he had stared into her eyes. What an intense, exciting . . .

"Bastard." It didn't matter how strong or handsome he was. He'd betrayed her. And then he'd turned away from her like he didn't care. The cold, heartless worm. He was definitely not one of the good Vamps.

She hurried over to the delicate folding screen that partitioned off the section of the room she used for her bedroom. A gift from her grandfather, the screen was comprised of squares that each showed a different landscape painting. She folded it to the side to make the back wall visible. A length of white silk was rolled up like a shade near the ceiling. She untied the cord, and with a whoosh, the silk unfurled down the wall. The outline of a man had been painted in black on the white silk. She planted a few books along the hem to keep the silk banner stretched taut against the wooden wall.

After a quick run back to her stash of knives,

she grabbed one and twisted toward the silk banner, letting the knife fly. *Thunk.* A direct hit to the man's heart.

"Try to stop me again, vampire, and this one will be for you." She hurled another knife, and it lodged in the man's head.

She winced. *Not his handsome face.* With a groan, she turned away from the silk banner. His name was Russell. The best tracker in the world. *Don't think about him.* But what if he was searching for Han right now? What if he found Han and killed him, stealing the vengeance she'd promised her family? How could she live with herself if she failed the mission she'd spent thirteen years preparing for?

Dammit, he needed to let her work with him. It didn't matter if he was a cold, heartless worm of a vampire, not when he represented her best chance at actually completing her mission. And surviving it.

She shuddered as the memory of tonight's fiasco flooded her mind. Not only had she failed to kill Han but she'd also panicked when the soldiers had come after her. Never had she experienced so many men intent on killing her. And how could she blame them? She'd killed two of them.

Her knees buckled, and she collapsed on the floor next to the trunk. For more than half of her life she'd dreamed of avenging her family. In her mind she'd always envisioned it as a lofty, noble quest and imagined herself a noble warrior.

But because of her, two men had died. They had families.

Tears stung her eyes. *I had family, too!* She reached into the trunk for the red silk bag that held her most prized possession. Carefully she removed the two ornate, cufflike bracelets made of hammered gold and decorated with inlaid jade. Her father had given them to her mother as a wedding present. They were all she had left of her parents.

Taking a deep breath, she clasped the bracelets onto her wrists. "I will avenge you, I promise." She would kill Han. Even if he had a hundred soldiers guarding him, she would plow right through them. Nothing would stop her.

Not even Russell.

A knock sounded at her door, and she leaped to her feet.

"Jia!" Rajiv called out. "Can we talk a moment?"

"Just a second!" She grabbed the knives and jammed them into the chest, hurriedly throwing a half-finished embroidery project on top, then closing the lid. She ran to the screen and stretched it out across the room to cover up the silk banner she'd used for target practice.

She unbolted the door and cracked it. "Yes?"

Rajiv pushed the door open and entered. "We didn't get a chance to talk earlier. And I thought you might be hungry."

She was starving. For the last few days her rations had been a pouch of dried beef, nuts, and berries. Her mouth watered as she watched a maidservant enter, carrying a tray of rice, soup, and fresh steamed buns. Another servant brought a tray containing a teapot and two small porcelain cups.

The servants set the trays on a low table, then bowed.

"Thank you," Rajiv told the women. "Could you light the candles, please? And bring the gifts that came today."

"Yes, Your Eminence," the women murmured and left.

"Gifts?" Jia asked.

"I'll explain later." Rajiv looked her over. "Are you all right? Did any harm come to you?"

"I'm fine."

He frowned at her. "Do I have to tell you how much you frightened us? And how angry I am that you disobeyed—" He halted when one of the servants returned with a lantern and long narrow stick.

Jia was grateful her cousin wasn't going to reprimand her in front of a servant, but even so, it irked her that she should be in trouble at all. If a male were-tiger had taken off like she had to accomplish a dangerous mission, he would have been commended for his bravery.

"Let's have some tea." She sat cross-legged on one side of the low table and poured tea into the two small cups. She held one out to her cousin. "Please enjoy."

Rajiv sat and took a sip, remaining silent as the servant went about the room, using the long stick to light all four candles. "Thank you." He nodded at the servant as she bowed and left.

The guards outside closed the door.

"How long will I have guards?" Jia asked.

"That's up to you." Rajiv gave her an annoyed

look. "How long will you persist in this foolish notion that you can single-handedly avenge your family?"

Jia dug her spoon into the bowl of rice. "My parents and brother deserve to be avenged."

"I'm not arguing that." Rajiv refilled his cup with tea. "They're my family, too. And I understand how you feel. Lord Qing killed my parents—"

"And you got your vengeance. I helped you, remember?" Jia stuffed some rice into her mouth. "If you don't want me doing this on my own, then help me!"

Rajiv sighed. "I promised Grandfather I would keep you safe."

"I have nine lives. I'm prepared to lose a few to see justice done."

"Are you?" Rajiv gave her a wry look. "Just because we can come back from eight deaths, it doesn't make each of those deaths less painful. I know this from experience."

Jia winced. No doubt Rajiv was telling the truth. He was on his second life after dying from a fatal cobra bite as a teenager. She recalled the panic she'd felt earlier when the soldiers had chased after her. The possibility of multiple stab and gunshot wounds had terrified her.

She pulled a steamed bun apart and handed half of it to her cousin. "I'm sorry I made you worry."

Rajiv nodded and took a bite out of the bun. "You're wearing your mother's bracelets. I always liked those."

"They help to keep me motivated."

He groaned. "How can I convince you to give this up? I promised you I would avenge your family. Tenzen and Rinzen have also promised. Your father was their brother."

"Then what are we waiting for?" She stuffed her half of the bun into her mouth. "Let's go!"

"When we go, you will not be with us. I will not risk your life."

She swallowed hard. "That should be my choice. I'm fully prepared for this, Rajiv. I have trained for years. Lend me a few soldiers so I can get on with it."

He sighed. "I've explained this before. Han has thirty camps, and he teleports from one to another. He can change location in a second. Meanwhile, it would take you a week to move to the next one, with no guarantee that he would be there—"

"I found him tonight."

"A lucky break. He just happened to be at the camp you found." Rajiv gave her a curious look. "How did you find his camp?"

"Before we left for your brother's village in Thailand, you showed me the way on the giant map in your office. And you have all of Han's campsites marked. When I saw how close I would be to his camp in Myanmar, I knew I had to try it. Once I was close, I caught his vampire scent, and it led me straight to his camp."

Rajiv shook his head. "I hate to think what could have happened to you if Russell hadn't been there."

Jia made a sour face. "I don't need his help."

"We do need his help. He can find Han faster than any of us."

Jia shrugged and ate some soup. Her sense of smell was excellent. She'd find Han by herself.

Rajiv watched her, frowning. "How am I going to keep you out of trouble?"

A knock sounded at the door, then a maidservant slipped inside. "I brought the gifts, Your Eminence."

"Set them down by Lady Jia, please." Rajiv motioned to the floor.

Jia smoothed her hand over the two bolts of beautifully embroidered silk, one red and one gold. "Who sent these?" She fingered the ornately carved wooden box that sat on top of the bolts of fabric. When she lifted the lid and peered inside, she gasped at the sight of an antique gold and jade hair ornament. It was worth a small fortune. "Why was this sent here?"

The maidservant smiled. "They are lovely betrothal gifts, don't you think?"

"Wh-what?"

"Your betrothed must be very wealthy," she added.

"My *what*?" Jia slammed the box shut.

"You may leave us now," Rajiv told the maidservant. As she hurried out the door, he gave Jia a sheepish look. "I can explain—"

"Is this how you plan to keep me out of trouble?" Jia demanded, her voice rising. "Am I a problem you can solve by marrying me off?"

Rajiv winced. "I would never make you do anything you didn't want to—"

"Oh, that's big of you!" She jumped to her feet. "How dare you!"

"Sit down and let me explain." When she remained standing, he scowled at her. "Sit!"

She sat with a huff, glaring at him.

"I was as shocked as you are when the packages arrived," Rajiv began. "I had no idea Grandfather had arranged your betrothal. He died so suddenly, he never had a chance to tell me—"

"He never told *me*!" Jia clenched her hands into fists. "Why would he do this and not tell me?"

"He may have thought you were too young at the time." Rajiv sighed. "I looked through the correspondence this afternoon, and apparently, Grandfather made the arrangements eleven years ago."

"I was only ten!"

"Exactly. But since you had lost your parents, I'm sure he considered it his responsibility to provide a good future for you. You grew up here in the palace, so no doubt he wanted to make sure you maintained the lifestyle to which you are accustomed. Now that you're twenty-one, it looks like your betrothed is moving forward with—"

"Who is he?" She motioned to the presents. "Who sent these?"

"The Grand Tiger of South Korea. You're engaged to his oldest son and heir."

Jia gasped. South Korea was so far away. It was a different culture, a different language. She didn't know anyone there. "How could Grandfather do this to me?"

"It's not uncommon," Rajiv assured her. "If you

recall, Grandfather married two of his daughters to distant were-tiger princes. One of our aunts is now the queen in Sri Lanka; the other, the queen of Cambodia. It makes for good public relations—"

"I am not a political tool!" Jia rose to her feet and paced across the room.

"I don't expect you to be." Rajiv turned to face her. "But look at it this way. You want to marry someday, don't you?"

"I could live hundreds of years. What's the hurry?" She paused in front of the window and gazed out at the stars.

"You could marry a villager and live in a shack. Or marry a prince and live in a palace. Which sounds better to you?"

The vision of a cave with an underground stream flitted through her mind. Could a were-tiger prince be anywhere as handsome as Russell? What was she thinking? The heartless worm was a vampire. With a shake of her head, she paced away from the window.

"What's the harm in meeting this prince?" Rajiv continued. "You might like him."

"I might hate him."

"He might hate you."

She snorted and affected an injured look. "How could anyone hate me?"

Rajiv's mouth twitched. "Well, let me count the ways." He ticked off his fingers. "You're disobedient."

"I obey if the order makes sense."

"Argumentative—"

"I am not!"

"Childish—"

She stomped a foot.

He grinned.

She blushed and looked away. "If I'm such a terrible catch, you should warn off the prince."

"He'll be able to judge for himself whether he's interested in you."

Jia turned back to her cousin. "What do you mean?"

Rajiv rose to his feet. "He's coming here in two weeks."

She stiffened with a gasp.

Rajiv motioned to her food. "You should eat before it gets cold. We'll talk again in the morning."

Jia remained still as her cousin let himself out and closed the door. She heard low whispers as he talked to the guards. No doubt he was making sure she stayed put for the night.

Her gaze wandered to the gifts on the floor. Two weeks? A were-tiger prince was coming for her in fourteen days. If she married him, she would spend the rest of her life far away. Far from her family and friends. Far from the quest she'd worked on for the past thirteen years.

She took a deep breath. Once the prince arrived, she would be immersed in endless ceremonial duties. There was no time to waste. She had less than two weeks to escape from Tiger Town and kill Master Han.

Chapter Three

The following evening Russell was perched high in a tree, aiming his binoculars at the interior of one of Han's encampments. He'd counted only a dozen soldiers so far. Half of them were immersed in a dice game, gambling away what little money they had. Others were dozing or drinking. Only one was gazing over the battlements occasionally in a halfhearted attempt at guard duty. Clearly, Han wasn't here. Nor were any of his high-ranking officers.

With a sigh, Russell lowered his binoculars. As much as he enjoyed the thought that last night's assassination attempt must have scared the crap out of Han, the result was damned annoying. The coward was hiding so well now that Russell couldn't find him anywhere.

Last night, after delivering the princess to Tiger Town, he'd visited each of Han's thirty camps, searching for the bastard. No luck. After finding two of Han's officers, Russell had hidden on the roof to listen in on the conversation, hoping they would mention Han or even the location of a new camp.

Nothing. He'd considered kidnapping one of the officers and trying vampire mind control on him to acquire more information, but it probably wouldn't have worked. Russell was able to erase memories, but all of his attempts to control supersoldiers had failed. As far as he could tell, the demon Darafer had programmed their minds to obey only him and Master Han.

With dawn approaching, Russell had been forced to call it quits and return to his lair. Lying on his bed as death-sleep had stolen over him, he'd imagined the same scene he'd daydreamed for the last two years. The final battle where he beat the hell out of Master Han, ripped off his mask, and then killed him. If he envisioned it enough, it would eventually happen. It had to.

But then something odd had happened. For the first time ever, the dream hadn't stopped with his victory. He'd seen himself teleport to Tiger Town after the battle and, on bended knee, present Han's mask to the princess. She'd been dressed in a golden gown with a sparkling tiara on her head. The air around her had shimmered with candlelight, so she'd been surrounded by a golden nimbus, and he'd thought she'd looked more like an angel than a tigress.

"My lady, I have avenged your family for you."

She'd clutched the mask to her chest as tears had glistened in her golden eyes. "Truly, you are the bravest, most noble man in the world! Nay, in the entire universe!"

With his eyes closed and his mind drowsy, Russell had still managed a derisive snort. Well, if he was going to dream, he might as well dream big.

"How will I ever repay you?" she'd continued, a tear slipping down her soft cheek.

"I'll think of something." He'd stepped close and wiped the tear away with his thumb.

"How dare you touch a princess!" She'd pulled her hand back and slapped the hell out of him.

"Shit," Russell had muttered. Even his dreams turned on him. And with that final thought, he'd plummeted deep into the dark abyss of death-sleep.

Now he leaned against the tree trunk, stifling a groan. Tonight was looking like a repeat of last night's failure but even worse, for tonight he was constantly plagued with the memory of that stupid dream.

Why did he keep thinking about her? So he found a beautiful woman attractive. Big deal. It just proved he wasn't completely dead. Only fifty percent dead.

He snorted. How could a were-tiger princess ever be interested in a vampire vagabond who lived in a cave down by the river?

Perhaps the oddest thing about the dream was that it hadn't ended as usual with Han's death. For the past few years, Russell had been so intent on reaching his goal that he had never thought past it. What would he do once the villain was dead?

His chest tightened as an insidious, dark cloud crept over him, threatening to overwhelm him with despair. There was nothing for him to do. No family, no home to return to. Nothing.

Was that why he'd let this mission drag on for so long? Because it was the only reason he had to live?

For a moment, he recalled the way Jia had talked to him in the cave. So alive and animated as she'd tried to convince him to team up with her. Even now, the memory of her excitement made him feel lighter inside. What was she doing now? Was she planning her escape? Did she still have those knives strapped to her calf and thigh? He'd been tempted to remove them just as an excuse to touch her soft skin.

He shoved that thought aside and teleported to the last camp. High on a bluff, he studied the soldiers. They looked bored. Disinterested. If Han was here, they'd be on their toes, for he had a nasty habit of murdering any soldier he was displeased with.

No Han in sight. Another night down the drain.

Russell teleported back to his underground lair. The bat cave, he liked to call it. After lighting a few lamps, his gaze drifted to the spot by the river where Jia had stood the night before. She was the only one who had ever seen his secret hideout. *Our secret hideout.*

He shook away the memory of her voice as he unloaded the pockets of his coat. He adjusted his watch and caught a glimpse of the tattoo on the inside of his right wrist. *Slave,* it said. Whenever he needed a reminder of how much he hated Han, he only had to look at the damned mark.

"Why, you bastard?" Russell muttered. Why had Han picked him? And why leave him in a coma for thirty-nine years?

With a sigh, Russell wandered over to the bookcase to plug the sat phone in to recharge it. Life had improved since he'd acquired the new solar-powered generator. The wires from the generator ran through the thin ceiling and up the nearby massive tree to the panels he'd installed on top of the oak tree's sturdy branches. He popped a bottle of synthetic blood into his new microwave, then levitated to hang up his crossbow and quiver.

His gaze returned to that spot. *Don't think about her.* He dropped to the ground, retrieved the warm bottle from the microwave, and paced about the cave as he drank.

He would do some laundry. That would keep him busy. He set his bottle on the table, then grabbed a bucket and went to the river to fill it up. There he spotted the imprint in the sand from where she'd stepped into the river and back onto the shore. There had been a cat woman in his bat cave. The thought made him smile.

What the hell was he doing, grinning like an idiot? He tossed the bucket down and strode away. "She's not my problem."

He dragged a stool up to the table and went to work cleaning his handguns. The ritual was always the same, and it relaxed him, helped him focus. *Not my problem,* he repeated to himself as he went through the motions.

He had only one problem. Killing Han. And what then? His gaze slid back to where Jia had stood the night before. *Not my problem.* But didn't she have the same problem he did? Would it hurt to keep her informed? What if he went to Tiger Town to give her an update?

With an abrupt move, he stood, knocking over his stool. He paced about the cave, but it seemed like the walls were closing in on him. He finished his bottle of blood, then checked on his stash of synthetic blood. One ice chest was empty; the other still had six bottles. The ice had melted, leaving a pool of water.

Good. Something to do. He threw on his coat and leather gloves, grabbed a knife and two buckets, then teleported to the edge of a glacier in the Himalayas. As a Vamp, he could tolerate cold better than most mortals could, but even so, the instant change to subzero temperatures was like slamming into a brick wall. He went to work at vampire speed, and within a few seconds, he'd chipped off enough ice to fill his buckets.

Back in his cave, he emptied the ice into the second ice chest and pulled out the stopper so the melted ice could drain into a bucket. This was the water he used for brushing his teeth. Sometimes he warmed it up to use for his shower.

As he pulled off his gloves, he checked his watch. Five hours had passed since he'd awakened. Five hours that he'd not talked to another living soul. *Since when did that ever bother you?* His gaze shifted back to Jia's spot. Damn her for making his solitude seem so . . . solitary.

The sun would have set at Zoltan Czakvar's castle in Transylvania. Even though Russell had enough blood to last a few more days, it wouldn't hurt to have more. He loaded his empty bottles into the first ice chest, dropped the fully charged sat phone into his coat pocket, then grabbed the ice chest and his quiver and teleported to Zoltan's castle.

The second he landed in the armory, an alarm went off, the pitch designed so that only vampires and shifters could hear it. Thanks to Zoltan's head of security, Howard Barr, the castle now boasted the best in high-tech security. Ironic, Russell thought, since he wasn't sure Zoltan needed security anymore.

After eight hundred years of being a vampire, Zoltan had accidentally re-mortalized himself two months ago by drinking too much of the Living Water from the hidden valley of Beyul-La. As far as Russell could tell, Zoltan was taking the change fairly well. He was so damned happy with his new wife, newly adopted son, and baby on the way that he constantly had a dopey grin on his face.

Russell stifled a groan. He wasn't going to begrudge Zoltan his newfound joy. After eight hundred years, the guy deserved a break. And he'd always been a good friend. He'd been the one to help Russell adjust to being undead. He'd taught him how to use his new skills, and after Russell had gone AWOL, Zoltan had generously allowed him to take whatever supplies he'd needed from the castle without reporting him to Russell's old boss, Angus MacKay.

It was different now that Howard Barr was at the castle. The Kodiak bear shifter worked for

Angus, so everything Russell did or said on these premises was reported.

Russell set the ice chest and quiver on the table. When the alarm abruptly stopped, he glanced up at the newly installed camera. No doubt Howard knew exactly where he was. Any second now, the nosy were-bear would come charging down the spiral staircase to butt into his life and ask him a million questions.

With vampire speed, Russell filled his coat pockets with ammo. Then he set the box of arrows on the table and pried off the lid.

Footsteps pounded down the spiral staircase. "Russell." Howard ducked to keep from knocking his head on the low stone archway.

"Howard." Russell grabbed a handful of arrows and stuffed them into the quiver.

"I wasn't expecting you," Howard said as he approached. "You usually wait two full weeks before returning."

Russell shrugged and added more arrows to his quiver.

Howard planted his hands on the table, leaning toward him. "I heard you saw the dragon shifter, Xiao Fang, last night."

Russell paused, then put the lid back on the arrow box. No doubt J.L. had reported immediately to his boss, and it hadn't taken Angus long to spread the word.

"How was he?" Howard asked.

"He looked okay." Russell returned the box to its place on a shelf. "Han was giving him an archery lesson. Patting him on the back like a proud papa."

"Sick creep," Howard muttered.

"Exactly."

"Look, the next time you see Xiao Fang, give J.L. or Mikhail a call. They'll come instantly and bring some shifters with them. We'll help you get the boy out of there."

"I work alone."

Howard gave him an annoyed look. "I know you want to kill Han all by yourself, and you're welcome to it, but this is a young boy we're talking about. From what I hear, he could start shifting any day now. We need to get him away from Han as quickly as possible."

Russell slipped the quiver over his shoulder and reached for the ice chest.

"Wait." Howard strode over to the shelf where he kept the sat phones. "Take a new phone with you so you can call."

"I have a phone."

"I gave you that one two months ago." Howard selected a new phone. "Take this one. It's fully charged."

"So is mine."

"What?" Howard blinked. "How—"

"I'm going to the kitchen now—"

"Wait!" Howard stepped closer, his eyes narrowing. "I noticed something odd when Mikhail and I went back to Beyul-La to pick up the supplies. One of the solar-powered generators was missing. And a microwave." He crossed his arms over his chest, tilting his head with a wry look. "Any idea what happened to those items?"

Russell returned his wry look. "Not a clue." He teleported to the castle's kitchen.

He unloaded the empty bottles from the ice chest and tossed them into the recycle bin. Then he helped himself to a Bleer from the fridge. He was halfway through the mixture of beer and synthetic blood when Howard charged into the kitchen and screeched to a halt.

Russell glanced at his watch. "It took you longer than usual. Been eating too many donuts?"

Howard glared at him. "I'll take your hasty departure as a sign of guilt. I always suspected it was you, so I never reported the missing stuff to Angus."

Surprised, Russell set his Bleer bottle on the counter. "I appreciate that."

"We would have never defeated Lord Liao or won that last battle without your help." Howard gave him a frustrated look. "Whether you like it or not, we're on the same side."

"I work alone." Russell turned to open the refrigerator.

With a sigh, Howard lumbered toward the kitchen table. "I was alone for years, and it sucked."

A vision of Jia flashed across Russell's mind, but he pushed it aside and started loading his ice chest with bottles of synthetic blood. "Is Zoltan here?"

"Mikhail teleported him to his townhouse in Budapest." Howard sat at the kitchen table and reached for his box of donuts. "The monthly coven meeting started about twenty minutes ago. It may be awhile before they get back."

Russell paused with the ice chest half full. "Why would Zoltan go to a vampire coven meeting?"

Howard bit into a donut. "He's still Coven Master of Eastern Europe."

"But he's no longer a vampire."

Howard shrugged. "As far as I can tell, no one wants to believe it. The villagers went ballistic when he broke the news to them. That's why I'm still here doing security. Zoltan's in the weird position now where someone might try to kill him for *not* being a vampire."

Russell frowned as he finished loading the ice chest. "Why can't people be happy for him? It took the guy eight hundred years to get some joy in his life."

"I know." Howard took another bite from his donut. "But the villagers are dependent on the tours that come twice a week. Busloads of people come here to see a real vampire castle and spend money in town. If rumor spreads that Zoltan isn't really a vampire—"

"They could lose their cash cow," Russell concluded.

Howard snorted. "You could put it that way." He stuffed the last of his donut into his mouth. "At last month's coven meeting, Zoltan broke the news to all the Vamps and told them they would have to vote on a new Coven Master this month."

"Makes sense." Russell piled some ice on top of the bottles in the chest, then closed the lid. "I'll be on my way then."

Howard sat up abruptly. "They're back. That was fast."

Zoltan materialized close to the kitchen counter with Mikhail, an old vampire friend from Russia.

The sour look on Zoltan's face brightened when he saw Russell. "I didn't know you were coming tonight. How are you doing?"

"I'm fine." Russell shook hands with the only Vamp he called friend. "Thank you for keeping the fridge full of synthetic blood. I know you don't need it anymore." He handed a Bleer to Mikhail and a regular beer to Zoltan.

"Thanks." Zoltan's frown returned as he wrenched the top off the bottle. "I need a drink."

"The coven meeting was over fast," Howard observed. "What happened?"

"Don't ask." Zoltan collapsed into a chair at the kitchen table and gulped down some beer.

"What's wrong?" Howard pushed the box of donuts toward Zoltan. "Didn't they vote for a new Coven Master?"

Zoltan shot an annoyed look at Mikhail. "The vote was unanimous."

Mikhail scowled back. "Don't blame me. I can't be Coven Master of Eastern Europe. I live in Russia."

"Close enough," Zoltan muttered. "You could have volunteered."

Mikhail snorted. "I have no patience for all the whining that goes on at Coven Court. I would declare everyone guilty and fine them a million euros for wasting my time."

Zoltan sighed and reached for a donut.

"So who is the new Coven Master?" Howard asked.

Zoltan took a bite and mumbled, "They voted for me again."

Russell scoffed. "But you're not a vampire."

"They don't care!" Zoltan waved the donut in the air. "They know I could still live forever, so apparently I'm stuck with the job for all eternity!"

Howard grimaced. "They're willing to let a non-vampire judge them at Coven Court?"

Zoltan groaned. "Lazy bastards. I should do like Mikhail said and fine them all a million euros." He gave the Russian a wry look. "You're not off the hook. I'll need someone to teleport me to all the meetings."

Mikhail grunted, then gulped down some Bleer. "Why don't you just let me turn you back into a vampire? Don't you miss being able to teleport?"

"I do miss that." Zoltan nodded. "But not enough to give up the days I can have with my wife and family. And stuff like this—" He eyed the donut in his hand. "This is damned good." He popped the rest into his mouth.

Howard sat back with a smirk. "Now you're talking."

Mikhail shook his head. "If we're done for the night, I should get back to Moscow. Pam's working—"

"I need a lift back to Tiger Town," Zoltan interrupted him.

Mikhail gave him an annoyed look. "What am I, your taxi service?"

Zoltan shrugged. "You wouldn't have to cart me around if you'd taken the Coven Master job."

Mikhail groaned and drank more Bleer.

"I'll take you." As soon as the words were out

of Russell's mouth, he flinched. What the hell was he doing?

Even Zoltan looked surprised. "Oh. Thanks, Russell."

"I'm out of here then." Mikhail vanished, taking his bottle of Bleer with him.

Russell swallowed hard. He couldn't back out now. He was going to Tiger Town. The thought of seeing Jia again made his heart beat faster. *Dammit.* What was wrong with him? It wasn't like the princess would be happy to see him. She'd probably slap him again.

Zoltan stood. "Can you give me a few minutes? I need to grab my bag from upstairs."

"That's fine." Russell picked up the loaded ice chest. "I need to take my supplies home first."

"Home?" Howard eyed him curiously. "You've never mentioned a home before. Where is it?"

Shit. Now he was saying too much. Without another word, Russell teleported back to the bat cave. Using vampire speed, he put away his new supplies. The faster he moved, the faster his heart pounded. Since it was a warm August night, he decided to leave his coat behind. He put on a clean T-shirt, then quickly washed his face, brushed his teeth, and combed his hair.

What the hell are you doing? This wasn't a date. He was just going to check in on Jia to see how she was faring. That was all. It was well after midnight in Tiger Town, so she was probably asleep. Or she might not even be there. She might have already escaped.

The thought of her trekking through the forest

in the middle of the night made his chest tighten. He quickly teleported back to pick up Zoltan, then took him to Tiger Town. Zoltan had called his wife to let her know he was on his way, so she was waiting for him in the courtyard.

Zoltan dropped his duffel bag on the stone pavement and ran toward Neona. She laughed as he whirled her around in a circle.

Russell looked away, annoyed that after two months of marriage, the two were still acting like newlyweds. To his surprise, he spotted Rajiv at the top of the stairs that led down the riverbank. The were-tiger was focused on something in the distance.

"I thought you'd be asleep." Russell approached him.

Rajiv turned and greeted him. "Any luck finding Han tonight?"

"No." Russell motioned toward Zoltan. "I gave him a lift."

"That's good." Rajiv turned back to gaze at the road that led south. "Someone's coming."

Russell narrowed his eyes. "Looks like a truck. Isn't it late to have visitors?"

Rajiv glanced toward him with a brief smile. "We're out in the middle of nowhere. For those of us who can't teleport, it takes a long time to get here."

Russell nodded and shifted his weight.

Rajiv gave him a curious look. "Was there something you needed? Did you want to talk to Jin Long?"

"No, no. I'm fine." Russell glanced north to

where the royal residences were situated. "Just wondering . . ." He shifted his weight again. "Is your cousin all right?"

"Jia?" Rajiv looked surprised. "Sure. She seemed fine at dinner."

So she was still here. Russell's pulse accelerated.

Rajiv studied the approaching truck to the south. "I'll see what's going on." He started down the stairs to the riverbank. "So long."

"Later." Russell glanced again toward the houses built on the north side of the courtyard. Zoltan and Neona had already disappeared down an alleyway to their home.

He teleported to the edge of the courtyard, then moved quickly and quietly through the maze of houses. Jia's home should be easy enough to spot. It would be the one with guards out front.

Jia paced back and forth in her room, growing increasingly agitated. It looked like she had no choice but to go with Plan C, but just thinking about it filled her with dread. Surely there had to be another way, but she'd racked her brain all day, and this was the best she could come up with.

Her backpack was ready to go. She'd packed an extra set of clothes and the rest of her knives. A rolled-up cotton quilt was strapped to the bottom of her backpack so she could use it for catnaps. Her favorite four knives were in place, either in her boots or attached to her legs.

It was just her fear that was making her hesitate. With a growl of frustration, she whipped the knife from her right boot and hurled it at the silk banner on the wall. A hit, dead center between the man's legs.

Damn. Even her aim was off. *Get a hold of yourself.*

All day long she'd strategized and come up with three plans. It would be easier to escape late at night after most were-tigers were asleep, so she'd waited a few hours after sunset to put her plans into action.

Plan A: telling the guards she wanted a late-night snack from the palace kitchen. She would conceal her backpack beneath a bulky cape, then, while the guards thought she was on her way to the kitchen, she would make a run for it.

A hundred yards to the north, there was a trail that wound downhill from the bluff to the riverbank. Her uncles, Rinzen and Tenzen, had a canoe stashed nearby in some bushes, since they loved to go fishing. She would take their canoe across the river and head toward the nearest of Han's camps. Earlier in the day, she had sneaked into Rajiv's office in the palace to study his map and take notes on all the locations of Han's campsites.

Plan A hadn't worked. Even though she'd assured the guards she would be right back, they had insisted on accompanying her. She'd had no choice but to go to the palace kitchen and pretend to be enjoying some almond cookies. She'd tried to tempt the guards with some strong, homemade Tiger Juice, thinking they'd be easier to handle if they were drunk, but they had refused.

An hour later, she'd tried Plan B. Just a quick trip to the outhouse, she'd assured the guards. No need to accompany her. But they had insisted.

Now she was stuck with Plan C. It was the best plan, actually, but she'd saved it for last, hoping to avoid it. Her hands had trembled as she'd unwound the bolts of red and gold embroidered silk. With the ends tied together, the two lengths of material made a rope about thirty yards long. Since the fabric was smooth and slick, she made a knot every three feet to give her a handhold and foothold.

Plan C was simple. Tie one end of the silken rope to the heavy beam that crossed her room's ceiling. Then toss the other end out the back window so that it fell over the edge of the bluff. She would climb down the rope, then head north to her uncles' canoe.

You can do this. She tied a knife to the end of the silk rope, then tossed it over the heavy wooden beam that traversed the ceiling. Standing on top of a chest, she tied off the rope and returned the knife to her left boot.

Her knees wobbled as she climbed off the chest. Dammit. Only three feet off the ground, and she was shaking. How on earth would she climb down a thirty-yard rope?

She shook her head, trying to keep the memory from coming back, but it seeped into her mind, eager to torture her and paralyze her with fear. Thirteen years ago, her father had rushed her out the back door of their home and set her on a low branch of a tree. His deep voice edged with tension, he'd instructed her to climb as high as she could. She had. Like most were-tigers, she'd been adept at climbing. But she'd never imagined that high in a tree, she would see her parents and older brother captured by Master Han and slaughtered.

She clenched her fists, chasing the memory away. *You can do this.* She slipped on her backpack. The door and front window were closed and bolted. She'd placed a second chest by the back window so she could climb out. With trembling hands, she gathered up the silken rope and tossed it out the back window.

Her hands started sweating as she climbed onto the chest and sat on the windowsill. She wiped her hands on her pants, then clutched the silken rope. With a shaky breath, she eased out the window and landed on the bluff.

So far, so good. There was a narrow ledge of land here between the house and the cliff. *Don't look down.* Her heart thundered loudly in her ears.

With the silken rope clutched tightly in her hands, she backed up slowly toward the edge of the cliff. Panic seized her, and she stifled a cry. She couldn't let the guards hear her.

When her feet slipped off the edge, she fell till her arms snapped straight and took the weight. Unfortunately, her hands started sliding. She hissed in a breath, feeling a moment of sheer terror till her hands stopped at a knot. Her shoulders strained, and she desperately struggled to catch the rope between her feet so she could find another knot. She found one and pressed her boots on it to relieve some of the tension on her arms.

Her breaths came out in pants, and sweat beaded her brow. *You can do this.*

She slid her right hand down to the next knot, then quickly grabbed it with her left hand. Her feet came loose, and she dangled from her arms again till she found the next knot with her feet. *Don't look down.* She squeezed her eyes shut and took long, slow breaths.

"Going somewhere?" a man's voice whispered close by.

With a squeal, Jia flinched and her hands slipped.

"Careful." The man looped his arms around her and pulled her close.

The second she hit his rock-hard chest, she felt an instant surge of relief. Russell was back! He must have changed his mind and decided to work with her after all. And here he was rescuing her. Again!

He was hovering in the air with nothing to hold onto, but he seemed so at ease. Totally strong and confident. When he smiled at her, her heart leaped for joy.

"Russell," she breathed.

"Yes?"

"You've come to help me escape?" She wrapped her arms around his neck. "Thank you! I know we'll make a great team!"

Chapter Four

What the hell? Russell stiffened. Why did this woman always misinterpret his actions? Was she being blinded by her eagerness to succeed? No doubt she was desperate to have someone who was on her side, but why couldn't she understand that it wasn't him?

He tightened his grip on her. *Just a few seconds,* he thought, *let me hold her for just a few seconds.* Her face was nestled in the crook of his neck, her breath warm against his skin. His chest swelled at this proof that she was happy to see him. But she was only happy because she thought he'd come to help her.

Shit. He was going to disappoint her again. And she would probably slap him again. After a quick glance at the open window above them, he teleported to the interior of the room, taking Jia with him.

She stumbled back as she materialized, then glanced about the room with a confused look. "Why are we here?"

"Isn't this where you live?" He'd noticed the two guards out front before sneaking around to the back and discovering the silk rope stretched taut through the back window.

He pivoted, inspecting the small room. It was surprisingly plain for the home of a princess. There were two chests, one low table, and two square pillows to sit on. The only decoration was a screen across one end of the room, and the only color was the bright red rope she'd tied around a ceiling beam.

"We can't stay here," she whispered, casting a nervous glance at the door. The walls were thin, so she was probably afraid the guards would hear. With an excited grin, she grabbed his arm. "Let's go to your secret hideout!"

He hesitated, aware that his response would wipe the hopeful look off her face. "No."

Her smile wobbled, then returned full force. "Then we're going straight to work, investigating Master Han's campsites?"

"No. I'm not taking you anywhere. I only came to see how you were doing."

Her hands slipped off his arm, falling limply at her sides as she stumbled back a few steps. Her face went pale, all expression wiped clean. Even the sparkle in her eyes turned dull and lifeless.

Russell's chest tightened. He might as well have stabbed her. No, this was even worse. As a were-cat, she had nine lives. She would survive a stabbing. What he had done was inflict injury to her soul.

He backed away. "I shouldn't have come. I'll go now."

"Wait."

When her eyes flashed with anger, he felt a surge of relief. Her fighting spirit was still there.

She stepped toward him, her teeth gritted. "We need to talk." She lifted her hand, and he caught her by the wrist.

"What . . . ?" She tugged at his grip, but he held fast. "Why—"

"You were going to slap me."

She snorted. "I said *talk*. But I think I like your idea better." She pulled her other hand back, and he nabbed that wrist, too. "What—"

He lifted her hands over her head and turned her like they were doing a country-western dance. Then, with her arms crossed, he pulled her back against his chest.

"Let me go!" She struggled to get free, but he held her closer.

"Ssh," he whispered in her ear. "You don't want the guards to hear."

"Maybe I should call them in to beat the tar out of you."

"I would just teleport away."

"Coward."

He drew in a hissing breath. "Princess."

"Don't call me princess."

"Don't call me coward."

"If the shoe fits." She stomped on his foot, but he merely winced and pulled her tighter against him.

She grew still. He closed his eyes briefly, relishing this position. He'd enjoyed it last night, too. Even with the backpack she wore, her body seemed to fit perfectly against his, smaller, but snug and sheltered, as if she were a blade and he, the sheath. He lowered his head till his nose grazed her hair, and the floral scent of her shampoo filled his senses.

A shudder ran down her body.

Was he offending her by holding her like this? He knew he should release her, but it felt so damned good. *Just a few more seconds.* "My apologies for grabbing you. I thought you were going to slap me."

She shook her head slightly. "I was only going to point at the rope to prove how desperate I am to escape."

"I see," he murmured against her soft hair.

"Why won't you take me with you?" she whispered.

"I work alone." *And I don't want you to get hurt.*

"But I can help you." She turned her face to try to see him, and his mouth accidentally brushed against her brow.

He lifted his head, and she looked away. He felt her rib cage expand as she took a deep breath. Would it hurt to take her to a few of Master Han's camps? She would be an extra set of eyes.

But she would get in the way, he argued with himself. He would get distracted, and that would put them both in danger.

He eyed the silk rope she'd made to escape. She was clever, resourceful, and brave. Excellent with knives. How could he find fault with her for wanting to succeed? Especially when her goal was the same as his?

"We want the same thing," she whispered, echoing his own thoughts. "Please take me with you."

He swallowed hard. It was getting damned hard to refuse her. "You could get hurt."

"So could you. I'm willing to take the risk. I won't be a burden to you, I promise."

He squeezed his eyes shut. *You could be her hero.*

A knock sounded at the door and he jumped back, releasing her.

"Jia?" Rajiv called from the front porch. "Are you asleep?"

Her eyes wide with horror, she lunged forward and grabbed Russell by his T-shirt. "They mustn't find you here!"

"I'll just go."

"No! I still need to talk to you."

Meaning she still wanted to convince him to take her with him. "I can—"

"Hide!" She ran over to the screen, pushed it back, and motioned for him to come.

As he approached, his gaze landed on the white banner with the figure of a man painted on it and a knife firmly embedded in his groin. "What the—"

She gasped. "My favorite knife! I almost left without it. How could I be so forgetful?"

He gave her an incredulous look. "I'm a little more concerned about your aim."

She winced. "I was . . . distracted."

"Remind me never to distract you."

"Jia?" Rajiv knocked on the door again.

"Just a minute," she called back. "I-I was

asleep." She dashed across the room and furiously pulled the rope back through the window. Loops of red and gold silk pooled onto the floor.

With a snort, Russell yanked her favorite knife from the wall, then levitated up to the beam and sliced the material free.

"Thank you!" she whispered, bundling up the fabric in her arms.

He dropped quietly to the ground and helped her gather up the rope and carry it to the small area behind the screen.

"Don't leave!" she warned him. She dropped her backpack on the floor by his feet, kicked off her boots, then stretched the screen across the room.

He sat on the floor, surrounded by mounds of gold and red silk. It was darker here, since the screen blocked the moonlight that filtered through the open window. Even so, he spotted a thick, quilted pallet folded and stashed in the corner. Was that her bed? Then this small area had to be her bedroom. He winced, imagining Rajiv's reaction if he caught a vampire in the princess's bedchamber.

Jia's soft footsteps crossed the room to the door, then Russell heard the scrape of the bolt. "Is there something wrong, Rajiv?"

Heavier footsteps entered the room, and the door closed. "Everything's fine," Rajiv answered. "I just wanted to give this to you."

"What is it?" Jia asked, and Russell shifted closer to a gap in the screen. Unfortunately, all he could see was Rajiv's back.

"Another gift from the Grand Tiger of South Korea," Rajiv explained. "It must be very expensive, since he sent it with a courier."

"Oh." Jia didn't sound overly thrilled.

"The courier told me he had a tough time getting it through customs, so it delayed his arrival here," Rajiv continued. "The Grand Tiger insisted that you receive the gift today, so the courier begged me to bring it straight to you. Apparently, you're supposed to receive a gift every day until your betrothed arrives."

Betrothed? Russell sat back. Jia was engaged? To a Grand Tiger? He closed his eyes, no longer wanting to see, and wishing he didn't have to hear.

"They really shouldn't go to so much trouble," Jia murmured.

"It is a bit much," Rajiv agreed, "but look at it this way. They're definitely serious about the marriage. And they're trying hard to impress you."

"I suppose," Jia mumbled.

A sick feeling gnawed at Russell's gut, and he twisted his hand around a clump of red silk. What the hell had he expected? She was a princess after all. And to think he'd come so close to taking her with him into danger.

"Open it," Rajiv urged.

There was a creaking sound of a lid being lifted, followed by Jia's gasp.

Rajiv whistled. "That's got to be worth a fortune. And you know what? It would look perfect with the bracelets from your mom. Let's see." A chest opened.

"It's late," Jia protested.

"Come on, I want to see you look like a princess." There was a pause and some rustling sounds, then Rajiv said, "I wish Grandfather could see you now. I wish he could see the wedding."

"I know." Jia sighed. "I miss him, too."

"You should probably make your wedding gown from all that red and gold silk they sent you yesterday," Rajiv said. "I have a feeling that's why they sent it."

Russell scoffed silently as he tossed the material away. She had used an engagement present for her escape?

"I'll let you get back to sleep now," Rajiv said, and his footsteps crossed to the door. "See you tomorrow."

The door shut, then Jia's steps rushed to the door and she slid the bolt.

Russell eased to his feet and opened the screen a few feet. When Jia turned to face him, his heart stilled for a moment. Even in her plain clothes, she looked every bit a princess. The moonlight shone around her, gleaming off thick, raven-black hair, smooth, flawless skin, and large, golden cat eyes. A long necklace of gold and jade encircled her neck, and a jade pendant of a tiger nestled between her breasts. More gold and jade decorated the cufflike bracelets around her wrists.

He leaned back against the wall as his heart slumped.

She stepped toward him. "I'm sorry you had to hear that, but it doesn't change anything."

"You think not?" He crossed his arms over

his chest. "You're engaged. To a Grand Tiger. A wealthy one."

"No. Not at all." She took the necklace off and dropped it back into its box. "His son. The prince."

Of course. No grasping old geezer for Jia. She was going to have the dashing young prince. A sliver of anger sliced at his gut.

"I haven't agreed to it." She shut the box.

"You're accepting the gifts."

She gave him an annoyed look. "He's coming to meet me in two weeks. If I don't like him, I'll return the gifts and tell him to get lost."

"You've never met him before?"

"No. I didn't even know about the engagement till yesterday. Grandfather arranged it when I was ten. I'm only going along with it for now out of respect for my grandfather."

Russell shifted his weight. "So if you like the guy, you're going to . . . go through with it?"

She shrugged. "I don't know. All I know is I need to find Han and kill him before the prince arrives. I have thirteen days now."

Russell snorted. So she expected him to help her, then deliver her back here in time for her wedding. "You have no business out in the jungle fighting Han's soldiers."

Her eyes simmered with anger as she ripped the bracelets off her wrists. "Do you see these? They're all I have left of my parents. I will see my family avenged. Whether you help me or not."

"Not."

"Wait." She dropped the bracelets into an open

trunk, then dashed toward him. "Pay no attention to my anger. It makes me say foolish things. I know very well that you are my best chance at succeeding. Please." She grabbed his T-shirt in her fists. "Take me with you."

He slowly pried her hands loose. "You're a princess. A betrothed princess. I can't put you in danger."

"If you don't help me, I'll have to do it on my own, and that would be even more dangerous."

He winced inwardly. That much was true. He gently squeezed her hands. "Stay here. You have family and a future. Enjoy your life. I'll take care of Han, and when I'm done, I'll bring his golden mask to you and lay it at your feet."

She looked up at him, her eyes glistening with tears. "I know you would. I believe you, but . . . I need more."

"I'm sorry." He released her and teleported away.

Chapter Five

I am Xiao Fang. One of the last of my kind. Centuries ago, there were many of us. We roamed the earth. We ruled the skies. Men feared us.

Now I fear man.

Three months ago, I breathed fire for the first time. Soon I will shift for the first time. I wish I had my wings now so I could escape. And fly home.

With a black pen, I slowly draw a Chinese word on a sheet of white paper. The man with the golden mask has given me several black markers and reams of paper. He has given me children's books with pictures and words. Each day, I am to learn how to write a new word, he says, so we will be able to communicate.

As a dragon shifter, I cannot speak. My throat is designed for fire, not words. The women who raised me in Beyul-La spoke Tibetan and Chinese, so I understand those languages. They taught me how to write a few words. Two of them had the gift of communicating with winged creatures, so they could read my thoughts, as I could read theirs. Queen Nima and Winifred. They were like mother and sister to me. And then there was Norjee, the mortal boy who could talk to me in my mind. I called him my brother.

I finish writing the word, then set it next to the other papers I have written. They all say the same thing.

Home.

I pace about the small room. We are in a new place now, completely underground. Last night, someone tried to kill the man with the golden mask—Master Han, he calls himself. He teleported me here, where he claims we will be safe. He will protect me from the evil vampires and shifters. I should trust him, he says. He will let no harm come to me, for I am special.

I am a prisoner. I have all the food I could want. I have clothes and a warm bed. But the door is always locked. When I am allowed to wander about the camp, I am closely guarded.

Some of the guards take pity on me. During the day, when Han is not awake and watching, they bring me freshly baked bread. One officer named Wu Shen gave me a roll of tape, so I started taping my written pages on a wall in my small room. I have four rows now that stretch across the wall. With nothing else to do, I start a fifth row. Soon the wall will be completely covered with the same word.

Home.

I have been to many different camps in the last two months. The guards are always the same. They wonder why Master Han wears a mask. During the day, when Han locks himself up for his death-sleep, it is safe for them to speculate. Some say he wears the mask to hide a hideously disfigured face. Disease or fire, they say, and it must have happened before he became a vampire. Some claim he is simply ugly as a reflection of his evil soul. Others argue that cannot be, for no one is more evil than the demon Darafer, and he is fair of face.

I believe Master Han wears the mask to hide his many faces. There is the face he adopts for me. Kind, caring, gently spoken. He wishes to keep me safe. He will take care of me. His words are always warm, but his eyes are cold. I am unsure whether to trust him.

There is the face he uses when he addresses his army. He is fearless, masterful, in charge. When I see it, I believe he is strong. I am tempted to trust him.

Then there is the face that reacts whenever there is trouble from the evil vampires and shifters. He claims they are persecuting him for no reason. They want him dead. He doubles the guard and goes into hiding. When I see this, I believe he is weak. I know not to trust him.

When his soldiers are defeated, he screams in rage and his men cower, for he will seize a man and take him into his private room for feeding. We can hear the man scream before he grows quiet. Then Han returns with the dead body, ripped to shreds and sucked dry. When I see this face, I fear him.

I complete the fifth row of papers taped to the

wall just as I hear the lock being turned. I have no windows in this underground lair, but I sense it is nighttime. Han visits me every night, so I step away from the wall and steel my nerves.

The door opens. He stands in the doorway, and the candlelight in my room makes his golden mask gleam. He enters, and the guards close the door.

His cold eyes inspect me while he speaks softly, his voice laced with kindness. "How are you today, son? Did you sleep well? Do you have enough to eat?"

I bow my head in greeting, wishing he wouldn't call me "son."

"Did you learn to write any new words?" He glances toward the wall, and his body stiffens.

I feel the anger growing inside him, and I step back.

"Why do you persist in this nonsense?" His hands curl into fists as he turns back to face me. "Why can't you do as I ask? I take good care of you. I told you to trust me!"

He lifts a hand as if to strike me, and I flinch. This is the angry face that I fear. I have seen men die when Han is like this.

His fist shakes, as if he is fighting for control. Then, with a growl, he attacks the wall, ripping the papers down. "How many times do I have to tell you? Your home is gone! I'm all you have left now." He turns to me, his eyes glowing with rage. "If you want to live, you will trust me."

Tears sting my eyes. I am tired of being alone, tired of being afraid. I am tempted to give in. Give up. He will be kind to me if I give up.

My head hangs in shame, and my gaze falls on the torn papers scattered across the floor. *Home.*

How can I give up my home, my heritage? Anger burns in my chest and simmers through my veins. I am dragon. I belong with my own kind. My dragon brother and sister, Huo and Chu, are still in Beyul-La. More eggs are waiting to hatch. I am the oldest. I will be their leader.

I snatch a paper off the floor and show it to Han. *Home.*

He rips it from my hands. "Your home is gone!"

A tear rolls down my face as I grab another paper and lift it to my chest. *Home.*

"You stubborn—" Han growls, then walks away a few feet. His hands clench and unclench, then abruptly he turns to me. "Fine. I'll take you there. You can see for yourself."

My heart lurches with hope. He'll take me home?

He grabs hold of my arms, and everything goes black.

When we land, my nostrils fill with the familiar scent of home—crisp mountain air, pine trees. The sky is clear, lit up with a trillion stars and a moon almost one-third full.

But no one has come to greet me. We have landed by the central fire pit, and it is cold. I spin about, surveying the valley. The houses are destroyed. My breath catches in my chest. Where are the warrior women of Beyul-La? This has been their valley for thousands of years. They would never give it up. They have a sacred pact with the dragons.

"The women are gone," Han says. "If any of them are still alive, then they abandoned you."

I shake my head and run toward the sacred mountain. The women will be in there. Norjee will be there, along with Huo, Chu, and the eggs. I look up, expecting to see the top of the sacred mountain covered with snow.

It is gone. I stumble to a stop. How? How could a mountain disappear?

"It happened after we left," Han says as he approaches me. "I brought you here so we could rescue your dragon brothers and sisters. When the evil vampires and shifters trapped us inside the mountain, I knew it wasn't safe, and I teleported you out. I was injured. A knife in my back from one of the evil ones. But still I managed to get you out in time."

I gasp for air. I have a vague memory of being trapped inside with screaming soldiers. But what happened to the women? To Huo and Chu and the eggs?

"The evil ones blew it up." Han stands beside me, pointing at what used to be the sacred mountain. "Look at it. Nothing left but a pile of rubble. No one could survive that. Those bastards murdered my soldiers. Everyone inside the cave died. The women of Beyul-La. The dragons."

I stumble back as if I have been struck across the face.

"You would be dead, too, if I hadn't saved you." Han turns toward me. "Your home is gone. The dragons are dead. You are the last of your kind."

My body shakes so hard that I crumble to my

knees. *The last of my kind.* How can this be? How can I bear it? My brother and sister gone. The eggs gone. Norjee gone. My mortal mother and all the women who raised me—gone.

I am alone. *Alone,* the word echoes in my mind, and I grasp my head in pain. I open my mouth to cry out, but no sound can emerge.

Alone. Alone. My skin grows hot. Heat gathers in my chest, then sizzles up my throat. Smoke escapes from my nostrils. I want to scream fire.

"I'm sorry." Han reaches out to touch my shoulder but quickly jerks his hand back.

The heat of my skin has burned him.

"You should have trusted me," he growls. "It would have spared you the pain of having to see this."

I curl up, hugging my knees to my chest, resting my head on my knees. Last of my kind. I can live for five hundred years. I will be alone for a long time.

"Your home is with me now," Han says. "I will take care of you."

Is there any point in resisting? My despair runs deep. I might as well give up.

He lies, a voice slips into my head. It is soft, but insistent. *He lies.*

I lift my head. Is someone speaking to me? *Who are you? Where are you?*

Movement in the sky catches my attention, and I see a large bird land on the branch of the nearest tree. It is an owl. Queen Nima's owl!

Where is my mother? I ask the owl. *Where are my brother and sister? Are they truly dead?*

The queen left before the mountain was destroyed, the owl answers. *She took Huo and Chu with her. And the eggs.*

I scramble to my feet, my heart beating fast. *Where are they?*

Far away where they will be safe, the owl tells me. *After you were taken, two of the eggs hatched. The vampire woman, Emma, bonded with the babies and took them far away so they would be safe.*

I am not alone. Tears run down my face and cool my hot skin.

"I know this must be upsetting for you," Han grumbles. "Let's go back now. To your real home." He reaches out for me, but I step back.

Is Norjee nearby? Or any of the women? I ask the owl. *Can you find them for me?*

I believe they left with the tiger shifters. The owl cocks his head. *If I ask the eagles, they might know where the tigers live.*

Find them, I urge the owl. *Find Norjee. He can talk to you. I am being held in an underground camp. I know not where it is. I will call the birds that live close by so they can tell you where I am located.*

The owl rustles its wings. *It has been boring since everyone left. I am proud to be of service again.*

Thank you, I tell the bird as it flies away.

"Let's go home." Han grabs my arm. "I hope you learned your lesson, that you can trust me."

I nod my head, my shoulders slumped as if I have surrendered. But inside I am filled with hope. I will escape. I am dragon.

And I am not alone.

Chapter Six

The following day, Jia initiated Plan D. Since she was finding it too difficult to escape the guards, she would convince her cousin to call them off. She spent the day in the palace, playing the role of the delighted bride-to-be. For hours, she worked in the kitchen, helping the cooks, pestering them with questions, and practicing elaborate dishes to impress the prince. Then she brought the red and gold silk, neatly folded, to the court seamstresses and asked for their assistance in making the most beautiful wedding gown ever.

The women twittered with excitement as they discussed different patterns and headpieces. Jia pretended to be enthralled by it all, and soon, the whole of Tiger Town was gossiping about her betrothed's upcoming visit. When the next gift arrived by courier, everyone gathered around to see what the prince had sent her. A lovely pearl necklace. Jia ended up having to put it on for everyone to see. All the villagers agreed that the prince would fall madly in love with their princess the second he saw her.

Jia endured all the talk with a plastered smile on her face. She could barely eat a bite all day, but the court ladies interpreted that as wedding jitters. In truth, the prospect of marriage to a total stranger was making her stomach churn. And the repercussions if she turned him down were making her head ache.

Back in her room, she took the necklace off. Her mission remained unchanged. Escape, find, and destroy Han. Finding and killing Han would be a challenge, but the escape part would be easy if Rajiv called off the guards.

Unfortunately by that evening, the guards were still there. After dinner, Tenzen and Rinzen taught a martial arts class in the courtyard, so Jia decided to join them. The class was mixed gender now, but when Jia had begun the class at the age of eight, she'd been the only female. Her grandfather had allowed it, thinking the physical activity and focus would help her recover from her grief. He hadn't realized she'd started formulating her plan for revenge.

Her uncles considered her more of an assistant now than a student, so she helped them. Anything to convince Rajiv that she was so content with her life right now that she no longer planned to escape.

There was one new student whom she enjoyed teaching, a seven-year-old mortal named Norjee. She could relate to the boy, since, like her, he'd witnessed death and destruction at a young age. He'd been adopted by his aunt Neona, one of the warrior women of Beyul-La, and her new husband, Zoltan. The family was living here in Tiger Town, since Beyul-La had been destroyed.

According to Neona, Norjee felt responsible for the kidnapping of his dragon friend, Xiao Fang. Since Norjee had inherited the gift of communicating with winged creatures, he and Xiao Fang had become close, calling each other brother. Norjee's guilt rested heavily on his young shoulders, making him fiercely determined to master martial arts so he could help rescue his friend. Jia assured him that Xiao Fang had looked healthy when she'd seen him two nights ago. Even though she gave Norjee an encouraging smile, inside she also nursed some guilt. Because of her failure to kill Han, the dragon boy was still captive.

Even more reason she had to succeed. She glanced over her shoulder to see if the guards were still at the edge of the courtyard. They were. Since it was now dark, torches had been set up around the perimeter of the courtyard. Parents were congregated in small groups, chatting with each other and watching their children practice. Just as she spotted Norjee's parents, he landed a roundhouse kick to her hip.

"Oof!" She jumped back, and Norjee grinned at her.

She smiled back. "Show-off. That's what I get for not paying attention."

He stiffened suddenly, his grin disappearing as he scanned the sky overhead.

"Norjee? We were talking about paying attention."

He didn't seem to hear her. He pivoted, looking frantically about.

"Norjee, what's wrong?"

"The owl! I hear the owl!" He ran across the courtyard just as an owl swooped down and landed on top of one of the tiger statues that guarded the stairs leading up to the palace.

Jia followed him, and soon his parents joined them.

Neona reached out to softly stroke the bird's wing. "It's my mother's owl. He's found us."

"He's come a long way," Zoltan said.

The owl cocked his head, concentrating on Norjee.

After a moment, Norjee glanced at his parents. "He says Master Han brought Xiao Fang to Beyul-La last night."

"What happened?" Neona asked, and her son turned back to the owl.

Jia ran over to her uncles to ask them to stop the class and bring Rajiv and Jin Long. Soon everyone was gathered around the tiger statue, waiting to hear the news.

"The owl is weary from his long journey," Norjee said. "He has gone without food since last night."

"I'll bring him something," Jia offered and rushed up the stairs to the palace. In the kitchen, she tossed some rice and boiled chicken legs in a wooden bowl, hoping the owl wouldn't mind his meat cooked. As she ran back, she realized she hadn't been followed. Her guards had remained with the crowd around Norjee.

"I hope this will be all right." She set the bowl on a step, and the owl fluttered down to peck at it.

Apparently, Norjee had already related the owl's story, for some of the men were asking him questions.

"You say Xiao Fang doesn't know where he is being held?" Jin Long asked.

Norjee shook his head. "He told the owl it was underground, but he didn't know where."

"None of the thirty camps that we know about are underground," Rajiv said. "This must be a new place."

"I'll try calling Russell." Jin Long pulled out a sat phone. "If he still has the same number."

"Xiao Fang is going to ask the birds nearby to spread the word about him," Norjee said, his eyes bright with excitement. "When the news reaches here, I'll be able to tell you where he is!"

"This is wonderful!" Neona hugged her son. "Then we'll be able to go rescue him."

"I can go with you, right?" Norjee asked.

Neona exchanged a worried look with her husband, and Zoltan shook his head.

"It would be a battle against Master Han—" Zoltan began.

"But I have to go!" Norjee cried.

While Norjee's parents tried to dissuade him and Rajiv asked him more questions, the whole scene became loud and chaotic. Villagers were excited about this new way to locate the dragon shifter, but they worried about going to war against Master Han. Jia's guards were in the midst of it all, arguing with their neighbors and forgetting to watch her.

Slowly she backed away, debating whether she

should flee. If she stayed here and the news arrived about Han's location, the were-tiger men and Vamps would go to fight him. The last time they'd battled Master Han, she hadn't been allowed to participate. Chances were they still wouldn't let her fight. No, if she was going kill Han, she'd have to do it on her own. Now.

She ran to her house and changed into her hunting clothes and boots. Her heart racing, she strapped on her knives and slipped on her backpack. She peeked out the front door, half expecting her guards to be there again.

They weren't! Headed north, she sprinted along the bluff till she found the path that wound down to the riverbank. All she had to do was cross the river in her uncles' canoe, and she would be on her way to finally completing her mission.

Russell was hidden on a high bluff, watching camp number twelve, when he felt a buzzing in his pocket. The sat phone? It had been two months since he'd last received a call. He pulled it out and whispered, "What?"

"Russell? This is J.L. Something's come up at Tiger Town. I thought . . ."

His words faded as Russell stiffened with alarm. Had something happened to Jia? Had she escaped? Was she wandering about the forest alone? Or had she attempted to repel down that cliff again and fallen? A vision leaped into his head—Jia lying on the ground with broken bones, blood seeping from her head.

Not my problem, he told himself, but the vision kept replaying in his mind. "I'll be right there."

Two seconds later, he materialized in the courtyard of Tiger Town. Immediately, he scanned the noisy crowd, looking for Jia. He spotted her guards, Rajiv, J.L., Zoltan, and Neona. The townspeople were jabbering about birds and the dragon shifter. No mention of Jia. No sight of her, either.

J.L. waved him over, so he strode toward the tiger statues that guarded the stairs to the palace.

"We have news," J.L. began, motioning to an owl that was eating from a bowl on the stairs. "This is Queen Nima's owl from Beyul-La. It saw Master Han and Xiao Fang last night. Han was showing the boy how the valley is destroyed and trying to convince him that the warrior women and all the dragons are dead."

So the news had nothing to do with Jia. Russell didn't want to acknowledge the relief that swept through him. Instead, he concentrated on what J.L. had just said. "Han is trying hard to gain the boy's trust. That's a good sign. It means the boy is resisting."

Neona grimaced. "It was cruel of Han to tell Xiao Fang that all the other dragons are dead. Thank God the owl was there to tell him the truth."

"So the dragon shifter can communicate with birds?" Russell asked.

"Yes," Zoltan replied and motioned to a young boy. "Norjee can, too. He's the one who gave us the information from the owl."

"Xiao Fang said he and Han are in a new camp,

one that is entirely underground," J.L. added. "He's going to ask the nearby birds to spread the news of his location, and hopefully, that news will eventually reach us here."

A bird grapevine? Russell wasn't sure it would work. It wasn't like the birds could relay the latitude and longitude. Their directions might end up somewhat vague in translation. Still, it was worth a shot. "You say Han has gone underground?"

"Yes," J.L. replied. "No idea where."

"If we could just find the general area," Rajiv said, "then my uncles could sniff him out. They can pick up a vampire's scent from three miles away."

"I'll do some eavesdropping," Russell offered. "Maybe I can figure out the location of this new camp. See you later." After the others thanked him, he strode back through the crowd.

He was going to have to step up his game. If the Vamps and were-tigers discovered Han's location first, they would attack, and he might miss his chance at killing Han himself. There were others equally determined to kill Han. Like Jia.

He scanned the crowd once more. Where the hell was she? He moved to the top of the stairs that led down to the riverbank. From here, he could see her house at the edge of the bluff. No rope hanging from the window. No movement on the riverbank or among the houses on the river. Everyone was behind him in the courtyard.

A movement caught his eye. To the north and barely discernible, there was a canoe crossing the river. One occupant. It had to be her. A strange spurt of pride erupted in his chest, and he smiled. Jia had done it. She'd managed her escape. Clever, courageous girl.

Foolish girl. His smile faded. How did she think she was going to find Han on her own? How could she endanger herself when she had family and a whole town who loved her? Why couldn't she be happy playing princess? A *betrothed* princess.

He glanced back at Rajiv. One word and he could end Jia's great escape. His chest tightened at the thought of disappointing her once again.

But he couldn't let her do this. He would talk to her, convince her to go back on her own. Then she wouldn't have to endure the humiliation of being caught and dragged home. He focused on the far side of the river, selecting a place to teleport. No doubt she would be angry when he appeared. She might even slap him.

A little pain was worth it if he could keep her safe.

The thought gave him a small shock. Why did he care what happened to her? What was this woman doing to him that she occupied his thoughts so much?

He shook his head. *She's not my problem.*

Her canoe reached the shore.

"Dammit," he muttered and teleported.

Jia was a few feet away, her back turned to him as she heaved the canoe up onto dry land. Her boots had gotten wet when she'd disembarked, and now they squished with every step she took. On her back, she had a pack with a bedroll strapped to the bottom. Her long hair was braided and swayed each time she gave the canoe a tug.

"Going somewhere?"

With a squeak, she spun around to face him. "Russell!" She pressed a hand to her chest. "Good God, you scared me." She took a deep breath, then her eyes widened and she eased back a few steps. "Don't you dare . . ."

He moved toward her. "What?"

She held up a hand to stop him. "Don't come any closer. I know not to trust you now. I won't let you teleport me back home."

"Then get back in the canoe and paddle yourself home."

"I will not! I'm heading west, and you won't stop me."

"I can—"

"No!" Her eyes simmered with anger. "I've come too far. So help me, if you stop me now, I will shift and rip you to pieces."

"You can shift now?" Russell glanced up at the moon that was less than half full.

She glowered at him. "I'll shift in two and a half weeks. And then I'll hunt you down. You won't be able to hide from me. I'll track you down and—"

"Wait." Russell held up a hand. "Can you really track a vampire by his scent?"

"Yes." She lifted her chin. "I can track just as well as my uncles. I can do everything the men do, but they won't let me."

Russell winced. "I'm sure it must be frustrating—"

"You have no idea. There's no one telling you what to do. You're . . ." Her eyes shimmered with tears. "You're free."

Free? Didn't she realize his obsession was like a

prison? He couldn't be free until he killed Han. "Jia." He stepped toward her. "They'll be worried sick about you. You can't endanger yourself. You're a princess."

Her eyes flashed. "Don't call me that."

"For God's sake, Jia, you have family that loves you. Don't you know how fortunate you are? I would give any—" He stopped midword, not wanting to think about all the people he'd lost.

She gave him an entreating look. "If you understand the importance of family, then let me do this."

He swallowed hard. "And the wedding? Have you forgotten you're engaged?"

"I'll decide if I want to do that later. For now, I'm doing what I have to. Just like you."

He walked away a few steps, considering what to do. If he took her back, he would hate himself almost as much as she would. But he couldn't let her venture off on her own. If something happened to her, how could he live with that? He already had the guilt of so many deaths on his shoulders. How could he handle another death, especially when it was her—an innocent, brave, and beautiful young woman whose only crime was that she loved her family too much to let their deaths go unpunished?

Take her with you, an inner voice urged him. *No.* He shook his head. It would be a disaster. She would make him . . . care. *You already do.*

No! He rejected that immediately. No more thoughts about feelings. He had no feelings. His heart was dead. He lived only to kill Han. He needed to track the bastard down in whatever hole he was hiding in—

He stiffened with a sudden idea and spun toward her. "You can sniff out a vampire?"

"Yes." She shrugged. "But only if I'm within a few miles of him."

"What if he's underground?"

"If he's not surrounded by tons of rock, I should be able to." She tilted her head, watching him warily. "What are you thinking?"

"You might . . . be useful."

Her eyes widened. "Then you'll team up with me? We can be partners?"

"Maybe." He held up a hand to keep her from getting too excited. "I'm not sure if this is a good idea. Your cousin would want to kill me."

"I won't let him." Jia strode toward him, a smile blossoming on her face. "Can we start tonight?"

"I need to test your abilities first."

She nodded. "I can do it."

"That remains to be seen. I'll teleport you three miles away from my secret hideout. Then I'll go there and wait one hour. If you don't find me, the deal is off. I'll find you and teleport you home."

She winced. "And if I do find you?"

"We'll be a team."

Her grin returned full force. "I'll find you. You'll see."

He had to be out of his freakin' mind. Russell reached for her to teleport, but she surprised him by throwing her arms around his neck and nuzzling her face against his chest.

"What are you doing?" He grabbed her by the upper arms and tried to ease her back, but she tightened her grip around his neck.

"I have to know your scent." She rubbed her nose against his shirt. "Lean over, please."

He leaned forward slightly, and she buried her nose in the crook of his neck. Her fingers delved into his hair, loosening the strands from the ponytail so she could get a good sniff.

"I can't track down any old vampire I might detect," she whispered against his neck. "It has to be you."

His hands tightened on her arms. Already his groin was reacting. How on earth was he going to work with this woman, a betrothed princess, when he longed to hold her in his arms?

Her breath was warm and sweet against his neck. All he had to do was turn his head and he could kiss her. Would she let him? Would she curl up against him like a tiger kitten and purr?

He shoved that thought away. This was business. Only business.

"I'm ready." She glanced up at him, smiling.

I'm screwed. His dead heart squeezed in his chest. What the hell had he done? Her smile was the most beautiful thing he'd seen in ages. He gathered her close so he could teleport, trying not to think about how good her body felt pressed against his own. As soon as he got to his bat cave, he'd have to take a cold shower. And then he would wait. Would she find him?

No, she would fail the test. She had to. Then he could teleport her home and return to his normal life. He would regain his sanity. He had to.

For he had a strange desire to go completely mad.

Chapter Seven

Fia took a deep breath to calm her nerves. She was alone now, surrounded by dense forest, and the clock was ticking. Before leaving her, Russell had given her his watch with a timer set to go off in one hour. He claimed he would be able to hear the alarm even if she was ten miles away. When her time was up, he'd find her and teleport her back home.

Arrogant jerk. He'd acted like she was sure to fail. He'd even shown her how to turn on the alarm in case she got scared and wanted to give up early. His parting words—"Watch out for snakes"—had clearly been meant to frighten her.

Unfortunately, it was good advice. Rajiv had progressed to his second life after a cobra bite.

She took another deep breath. She was not giving up. She'd roamed many a forest in the dark of night without getting scared. Of course, she was usually in tiger form when that happened. And she was rarely alone, since all the were-tigers of Tiger Town shifted and hunted together.

In spite of that, she had successfully sniffed out Han's camp in Myanmar by herself. So she could do this, too. She had her knives, her determination, her excellent night vision, and her nose.

But she had a problem. The air was so still and muggy that she was having trouble catching Russell's scent. If she could just get a breeze from the right direction . . .

She glanced at the watch's glow-in-the-dark face. Four minutes up already. A rising swell of panic crept up her chest.

Quickly she swung her backpack off and retrieved the red silk bag containing her mother's bracelets. She hadn't worn them before for fear they might gleam in the moonlight and cause her escape to be seen. "Mom, Dad, I need help. Be with me, please."

She clasped the bracelets around her wrists, the right one just above Russell's watch, and, as usual, they gave her a sense of comfort. Her family loved her. They were depending on her. Their were-tiger blood ran through her veins. She had their skills, their power. She just needed to trust in it.

After slipping the backpack on, she closed her eyes and focused all her attention on the smells surrounding her. The new growth and decay of the forest. The scent of animals, some asleep in their burrows, others roaming about. Slowly, she rotated. *Trust your instincts. The tiger will know.*

The scent was so faint that she wasn't sure if she was imagining it, but it was all she had to go on. She headed northwest. No doubt Russell was testing her past the limit of her ability. He had to be over three miles away. The undead creep had probably set her up to fail.

Every five minutes she stopped and rotated, sniffing the air carefully. Her gut feeling remained the same. Northwest.

After twenty-five minutes, she knew her instincts had steered her right. His scent was coming in clearly now. With a grin, she quickened her pace.

Ten minutes later, she came across a stream. *Yes!* This had to be the one that ran through Russell's cave.

"Take that, vampire. You'll have to work with me now." She hurried upstream, and his scent grew stronger.

It was a surprisingly nice scent for a vampire. The bad ones like Han usually smelled of human blood. After all, she thought with disgust, you are what you eat. With a shudder, she recalled the stench of Lord Qing, one of Han's deceased vampire lords. He'd smelled of rancid blood, greasy hair, and centuries-old unwashed skin.

Jin Long and the other good Vamps she knew had a cleaner, more sterile smell. Something to do with the synthetic blood they drank, she guessed. That and they believed in bathing.

Russell's scent was similar, but somehow earthier. Maybe it came from living in a cave in the middle of a forest. The coppery scent of blood was overshadowed by the fresh smells of pine, oak, and moss. His hair had carried the scent of a melted mountain glacier. And his skin had smelled like . . . man. A strong, virile man in his prime, powerful and . . .

She scoffed at herself. There was no point in dwelling on his handsome face or glorious muscles. Or how her heart had raced when she'd snuggled up against him. She could never be interested in a vampire. How could she forget that it was a vampire who had killed her brother and parents?

Besides, Russell had no interest in her other than her nose. If she didn't prove her skill at sniffing out bloodsuckers, he'd drop her off in Tiger Town without a second thought. The heartless jerk. She'd tried twice in the past to trust him, and both times, he'd let her down.

He didn't seem to know how much he'd hurt her. Most probably, he didn't care. It had been her fault for wanting to believe in him, for imagining him as some kind of hero who understood and shared her need for vengeance. After years of pursuing her mission all alone, she'd longed for someone to help her shoulder the burden. Someone who would understand the pain that still tormented her. Someone who would acknowledge her strength and skill without trying to lock her up in the palace to play princess.

With a sigh, she realized she'd wanted Russell to be the one. He was the only one she'd ever met who was as dedicated to killing Han as she was. And he was so wonderfully strong and capable that she couldn't help but be impressed by him. Deep down in her heart, she wanted him to be equally impressed by her. They needed each other in order to succeed. She'd wanted to believe that so much that she'd ignored his constant warnings. *I work alone.*

"Not anymore. We'll be a team now, whether you like it or not." She winced, knowing he would reply *not*.

Eventually, the stream disappeared into a pile of rocks. What had Russell said? The stream went through a rock tunnel for a mile or so? She had to be close.

She glanced at the watch. Fifteen minutes to go. The terrain was hillier now, and she breathed heavily as she scrambled up a steep hill. At the top, she stopped and sniffed. His scent was strong. She was closing in.

Her heart pounded, imagining his surprise when she arrived at his secret hideout. But what if he was disappointed? He might look for any reason to break up their partnership. In that case, she needed to make sure she proved valuable to him. No matter what happened, she couldn't allow herself to be a burden.

Russell paced in the bat cave, alternately congratulating and cursing himself for leaving Jia three and a quarter miles away. At first, he'd assured himself it was a good strategic move to test her to the max, but now he acknowledged he was full of shit. The ugly truth was he had set her up to fail.

What else could he have done? Every time he pulled her into his arms to teleport, he was tempted to hold her longer than necessary. Every time he looked into her eyes or saw her smile, he felt a tug at his undead heart. He couldn't allow this to continue. Feelings would distract him, make him weak. Weakness would cause him to fail.

But what if he needed her tracking abilities? If he did, then her failure would ultimately bring about his own. And if anything happened to her in the forest, he didn't know if he could forgive himself. Already he had the deaths of too many people on his shoulders.

Dammit. Was he putting Jia in danger just to avoid a severe case of lust? After teleporting to his cave, he'd taken a cold shower, and it hadn't helped. His groin reacted every time he recalled the way she'd cuddled up against him and nuzzled his neck. She was so damned sweet and soft. And so alone out there in the dark forest.

"Ow." He winced as his foot rammed into a table leg. Normally, he could see well in the dark, but he wasn't paying enough attention. Already she was distracting him.

He turned on his sat phone to see how much time had passed. Fifty minutes. She had ten minutes to go. He strained his ears but couldn't hear the alarm. She hadn't given up early.

A sense of respect filled his chest with warmth. His Jia was brave. Clever and resourceful.

His Jia? What the hell—

A noise interrupted his thoughts. He stiffened, listening closely. Someone or something was moving through the woods and not being quiet about it. Was it Jia, purposefully making noise to ward off predators?

He quickly turned off the phone. The ceiling above his kitchen and table area was very thin and porous—nothing more than a thin layer of tangled roots. Any light in the bat cave might shine through a bit, so he was being careful to keep the cave dark. She had to find him by scent alone.

He paced some more. Checked his phone. Eight minutes to go. His nerves tensed. What if she found him? What if he got to see her pretty smile every night? And he would be able to hold her and talk to her. Maybe even . . .

He shook his head. She was engaged to someone else. *You can't have her.* The warning message flared from his brain but fizzled out before it reached his heart. To hell with it all. He wanted her to find him.

The thrashing sounds outside grew closer. *Please be Jia.*

He teleported aboveground, then levitated high into a tree so he could see who or what was approaching.

His phone buzzed. Even though it was set at its lowest volume, he grabbed it quickly so the sound wouldn't be heard. "What?" he whispered.

"About time," J.L. grumbled. "I've been trying to call you for twenty minutes."

Russell glanced down at his secret hideout. "I was out of range."

"Yeah, I figured that. Here's the deal. We've been searching for Jia for over forty minutes. It looks like she's run away. Have you seen her?"

"Why would she be out here?" He scanned the land below as the noise grew louder.

There! His heart lurched in his chest.

She emerged from a copse of slender young trees, headed quickly for the massive oak tree that grew close to the top of his cave. He winced. The ceiling was too thin to support—

Her foot broke through the tangled roots, accompanied by a feminine squeal. Her leg slid into the cave up to her midcalf.

"What was that?" J.L. demanded. "Did I hear a scream?"

"It's nothing. The mating call of a . . . water buffalo. Later." Russell hung up and jammed the phone into his pants pocket. Then he teleported to solid ground close to Jia.

Her back was to him, and she was squatting on her left foot, her hands on the ground to keep her balance as she struggled to pull her right foot free.

He caught the scent of fresh blood. "You're injured."

"Russell?" She twisted toward him, her face brightening with a big smile. "I did it! I found you!"

"Is your leg hurt?"

"It's no big deal. I'll still be able to work."

"The ground is too thin there. Don't move."

"I know." Her voice lowered to an embarrassed mumble. "I'm stuck, and I can't get up."

His mouth twitched. "Stay put. I'll get you."

"Like I'm going anywhere," she muttered.

He levitated, stretching out horizontally so he could reach her. "Grab on to me."

"I surprised you, didn't I?" With a grin, she looped her arms around his neck. "You didn't think I could do it."

He rose higher till her leg pulled free. His body swung back into a vertical position, bumping gently against her. Once again she was in his arms, and it felt so good. This partnership was going to kill him.

She hugged his neck. "I did it! We're a team now."

"Yes." He winced as his groin tightened.

When she leaned back to look at him, her smile withered away. "I was afraid of that. You're disappointed."

"I'll manage." *Don't get hard. Don't get hard.* Unfortunately, the more he admonished his perverse manhood, the more it defied him.

"I can tell you're angry. You're scowling at me. To be honest, I'm a bit angry with you, too."

"What for?" Could she feel the bulge?

She gave him a wry look. "It's blatantly obvious."

Damn. He glanced down.

"You left me more than three miles away. You wanted me to fail."

"Oh, that." He exhaled with relief. "Yeah. I did."

She snorted. "Well, at least you're honest about it. You made it very hard for me."

Hard. For her. He gritted his teeth. "You're welcome to slap me if you want." Maybe then he would come to his senses.

"You may find this hard to believe, but I don't go around slapping people all the time."

He arched his brow in doubt.

"You're the exception." Her eyes glimmered with amusement. "I'll try to restrain myself in the future."

"Thank you. I'll try not to be exceptional."

She grinned. "I think we're going to make a great team."

His heart squeezed in his chest. She seemed genuinely happy to be with him. Her smile had a way of lighting up her face, making her eyes twinkle and her lips look soft and luscious. Seconds ticked by as he stared at her mouth.

Slowly her smile faded. "Russell?"

"Yes." He lifted his gaze to her eyes. Her beautiful golden eyes.

Time stretched out as they looked at each other. The air between them grew thick and heavy, almost electric. He could feel the sizzle wherever her body was pressed against his.

Her gaze lowered to his mouth, and he leaned forward.

Beep, beep, beep.

He jerked his head back. The alarm on his watch went off. *Shit.* It was loud enough to wake the dead. Or the Undead. He'd put the alarm on its highest volume, thinking she would be miles away when the allotted hour was up.

She fumbled with her hands behind his neck. "How do I turn it off?"

"Let me see it." He turned his head just as she leaned forward to look over his shoulder. His mouth brushed against her cheek.

Immediately she pulled back, breaking the contact.

"That was an accident."

"I know." Her face flushed pink.

He gritted his teeth. What had happened to that

sexy moment when he'd thought she'd wanted him to kiss her? Had he only imagined it?

She avoided looking at him. "Maybe you should put me down."

"The ground beneath us would collapse. Hang on a second." He teleported her down into the bat cave. The damned watch continued to beep, filling the cave with a loud echo.

With her feet on solid ground, she let go of his neck. In the dark, he slid his hand along her arm till he hit metal. "What is this?" he said over the noise of the alarm.

"One of my mother's bracelets. I put them on to encourage myself."

A pang of guilt nagged at him. "I'm sorry I left you so far away." He felt past the bracelet and found his watch. "I was worried something would happen to you."

"You worried about me?" she asked just as he punched the button to turn off the alarm.

The cave was suddenly silent, her question hanging in the air unanswered. He berated himself for admitting too much as he unfastened the watch, then slipped it into a pocket.

"Stay put till I get some lights on." He lit two oil lamps close to the kitchen area.

She looked around the cave, her mouth curling into a small smile. "I love what you've done with the place."

His answering smile faded when he felt his heart squeeze once again. *Don't fall for her,* he warned himself. *You can protect her and admire her, but don't start caring about her.*

He moved to the table to gather his weapons, and when she joined him there, he noticed her slight limp. "Are you sure you want to do this? You're injured."

"It's just a scratch." She removed the knife from her right boot and set it on the table. "I'll clean my ankle in the stream and be good to go."

He pulled a stool toward her. "Sit."

"You're making too much of this."

"Sit." As soon as she sat, he hunched down and pulled off her boot.

"I can do it myself."

"Your sock is still damp." He pulled that off as well. "I'll give you some dry ones so your feet won't chafe."

"You don't need to do that."

"Why not?" He looked up at her. "You want sore feet?"

She heaved a sigh. "I know you didn't want this partnership, so I won't allow myself to be a burden."

Did she think he was looking for an excuse to be rid of her? She must not realize how attracted he was. Or how, in the last moments, he had desperately wanted her to pass the test.

He rolled up the hem of her pants, trying not to think how delicate her ankle looked or how soft her skin was. "You're not a burden. You're a partner. That means for the success of our mission, we must keep each other's health and safety in mind. If you're injured or in any way incapacitated, you have to let me know."

"All right."

He examined the bloody scrape that started at her ankle and extended a few inches up her calf. Another pang of guilt nicked at him.

She stiffened suddenly. "What is that? You have Han's mark on your arm?"

With a muttered curse, he glanced at the tattoo on the inside of his right wrist. "It's nothing."

"All of Han's men have that mark. I've seen it on a bunch of soldiers who were in the clinic at Tiger Town. It means 'slave'—"

"It means nothing. Now stay put so you don't get any sand in the wound." He filled a bucket from the stream, then poured water over her ankle and foot.

"How did you get it?" she asked softly. "Did he capture you? Force you to work for him? Were you under his control?"

"No!" Russell scowled at her. "He never controlled me."

"Then why do you have his mark? Why do you want to kill him?"

"I don't explain myself." Ignoring her frustrated look, he grabbed a towel and his first-aid kit from the bookcase. In a few minutes, he had the wound treated and wrapped.

"Thank you," she mumbled.

Guilt jabbed at him once again as he returned his supplies to their rightful place. He handed her a pair of dry socks.

"Thank you," she repeated.

"Don't—" He clenched his jaw with exasperation. "Don't thank me. You wouldn't have gotten injured if I hadn't put you through that stupid test."

"I don't mind proving myself."

"You could have been injured or attacked." He slipped a knife into each of his boots, then buckled on his sword belt. "I kept telling you not to wander about the forest alone at night, but then I intentionally put you into the exact same danger I warned you against. You should have slapped me when you had the chance."

She gave him a curious look as she pulled on his socks. "Are you always this hard on yourself?"

He paused in the middle of fastening his watch on his right wrist. Normally it did a good job of concealing the damned tattoo. She was already seeing through him, asking questions. If he wasn't careful, she would get completely under his skin.

He put on his coat. "Let's get to work."

"I guess the answer is yes," she muttered as she pulled on her boots.

He groaned inwardly. If he was being hard on himself, it was only because the mission was hard. Physically, he was in great shape for keeping her safe, but socially, he was sorely out of practice. He filled his pockets with ammo and weapons, wondering if he could manage to be charming. Probably not. With a sigh, he levitated up to the ceiling to grab his crossbow and quiver.

She glanced up. "Sorry about the hole."

He dropped back to the ground and attempted a wry smile. "You mean the new moon roof? Maybe it will increase the property value."

She sat back. "Oh my gosh. Are you attempting humor?" When he winced, she grinned. "You can't sell this place."

"I know. I don't actually own it." He shook his head. Major fail on the charming issue. "Besides, no one would want it."

"I would. I think it's beautiful."

He scoffed. "It has no plumbing."

"It has running water." She pointed at the underground stream. "You've seen my house. No electricity, no plumbing. This isn't so different. I'll be quite comfortable here."

His mouth dropped open. Did she think she was going to live here? She must not realize that he was suffering from a severe case of lust. But she had to know that betrothed women didn't shack up with other men. It would ruin her reputation and drive him insane. How could he live with her without touching her?

Obviously, he needed to somehow forget he was attracted to her. *Willpower,* he told himself. No unnecessary touching. No more lame attempts at being charming. He would work with her each night, then before dawn, he would teleport her back to her house in Tiger Town. But he better not mention that now, or they would spend the rest of the night arguing instead of working.

He sat on a stool next to her. "Before we get started, I think we should set some ground rules." When she nodded, he continued, "Rule number one: our partnership is strictly for business. Our mission is to find Han and kill him."

"I agree." She slipped her knife back into her boot.

"Rule number two: our method of operation. We'll start off with the assumption that Han's underground bunker is somewhere near one of his established camps. I'll teleport you to each camp, then you will use that supernose of yours to track him down."

"Agreed."

"Rule number three: establishing rank. I'm in charge. You will follow my orders without question."

"Excuse me?"

"You'll obey my orders—"

"Why?"

He frowned. "I am not accustomed to explaining myself."

She gave him a wry look. "Try."

"I'm the commanding officer—"

"No. We're partners. That means we're equal."

He gritted his teeth. "We are not equal in battle experience. If we come under attack, the situation could become deadly in less than a second. There will be no time for discussion. Your best bet at survival will be to do precisely what I tell you. Does that explain it?"

"I . . . suppose."

"Then you agree."

She scowled at him. "Okay, you big bully."

He scowled back. "Rule number four: I am not a bully. I will do everything in my power to keep you safe, even at the cost of the mission."

Her eyes widened. "You mean you would lose a chance to kill Han in order to save me?"

"I already have." When her eyes softened, he stood abruptly and swung the crossbow and quiver over one shoulder. "It's a simple matter of logic. You deserve to live. Han doesn't. He can always be killed another day."

"Right." She tilted her head, studying him. "One might get the impression that you cared."

"Only about safety. Are you ready to go?"

"Not quite." She slipped off the stool. "Rule number five—"

"I'm in charge. I do the rules."

"Number five," she repeated, regarding him seriously. "If something happens to me, if I'm mortally wounded, I need you to make sure my body stays intact. Don't let them hack me to pieces."

He grimaced. "I'm not going to let them hurt you."

"I know you intend to protect me, but if something goes wrong, and I'm dying, promise me you will not take me to Tiger Town."

He stiffened. "Of course I'll take you there. Neona is a healer."

"No!" She grabbed the lapel of his coat. "Promise me you will bring me here."

"You would die here."

Her eyes glinted with a fierce look. "I know."

His heart stuttered in his chest. "Dammit, woman, you *are* suicidal. I should take you home now."

"No!" She seized his coat with both hands. "I'm as afraid of death as anyone. I won't try to make it happen. But if it does, promise me you will bring me here and watch over me until I wake up to my second life."

"It's not going to happen. I won't let it."

"Promise me." She gazed up at him, her eyes simmering with emotion. "I want to trust you."

He swallowed hard. "You can trust me."

"Thank you."

How could he not reassure her when she was looking at him so desperately? He cupped the back of her head and kissed her brow. "Let's get to work."

Chapter Eight

Tia checked her backpack, hoping to conceal the fact that her nerves were all in a jumble. During the last ten minutes, it felt as if she'd careened through every possible emotion. Fear that if she didn't find Russell in time, he would take her back to her prisonlike room in Tiger Town. Pain when her foot had crashed through his ceiling. Panic with the realization that she was stuck. Joy at having passed the test to become Russell's partner. Curiosity over the tattoo on his wrist. And most recently, the anxiety of asking him to watch over her if she was mortally wounded.

But out of all the emotions she'd experienced, one continued to haunt her. A strange, tingling feeling that she'd never experienced before. When he'd held her in his arms and they'd gazed into each other's eyes, it had seemed like time had screeched to a halt and the world had suddenly constricted to a tiny point that had contained only her and Russell. She'd felt breathless and dazed, yet somehow achingly aware of him. His every breath, every movement. His eyes, his hands, his mouth.

She had wanted him to kiss her.

A vampire. She cast a sidelong glance at him as he downed a bottle of synthetic blood before their departure. God help her, she was attracted to a vampire. She'd known from the first night she'd met him that he was handsome. She'd admired his physique and determination. She'd respected his expertise. Teaming up with him had been the logical choice, since it gave her the best chance at successfully completing the mission she'd worked on for thirteen years. But now she wanted to kiss him? There was nothing logical about that. She had to be losing her mind.

Sure, there were a few good Vamps, but she could never forget that it was a vampire who had killed her parents and brother. Rajiv had also lost his parents to a vampire. For generations, vampires had been the sworn enemy of the were-tigers. Vampires hated shifters because they were not susceptible to mind control. And unlike a naïve human, who normally had no idea that vampires existed until it was too late, a were-tiger could instantly identify a bloodsucker by his scent. In most cases, whenever the two met, one was going to die, and since vampires knew that cat shifters had nine lives, they had a nasty habit of hacking a were-tiger into pieces so he couldn't come back.

And now she was hopelessly attracted to a bloodsucker. *No, not hopelessly,* she corrected herself as she removed her mother's bracelets. She could never dishonor her family by falling for the wrong kind of man. Somehow, she would put this attraction aside. Vengeance for her family had to come first.

Stay with me, Mother. Give me strength. She returned the bracelets to their red silk pouch and stuffed them into her backpack beneath her spare knives.

Russell finished his bottle and wiped his mouth with the back of his hand. "After we leave the bat cave, we might get another call from J.L. They know you're missing in Tiger Town, and they're looking for you."

Jia swung her backpack on. "I'll tell them I'm with you, if you don't mind. Then they'll know I'm safe."

Russell snorted. "I doubt they consider me very safe."

She winced. Rajiv might go into a tiger tizzy if he knew she was hanging out with a vampire whom she secretly wanted to kiss.

Most were-tigers her age were already well versed in kissing. Between the ages of fourteen and sixteen, they each shifted for the first time. It was an important benchmark in a were-tiger's life and called for a celebration that continued for the three nights of the full moon. It was during that party that the young adults usually received their first kiss.

Unfortunately, in Jia's case, none of the local boys had wanted to risk kissing her. Their parents had warned them that she was a princess and stealing a kiss from her would bring the wrath of her grandfather, the Grand Tiger, upon their household.

So, in all of her twenty-one years, Jia had only received an occasional peck on the cheek from family members. How many times had she lain awake at night imagining her first real kiss? She was convinced it would be hot and passionate, for the man's desire for her would be so overwhelming that he would risk the Grand Tiger's anger just to kiss her.

Never had she imagined that her first nonfamilial kisses would come from a vampire. And how embarrassing that they had both been accidents! Last night, Russell's mouth had accidentally brushed her brow; tonight, her cheek. Clearly it had meant nothing to him, for he'd quickly admitted it had been an accident. Her heart had shriveled with humiliation.

It was all wrong. The man she'd dreamed of had always been wildly romantic, with a burning, uncontrollable desire for her. And he had certainly never been a vampire.

But now, Russell had surprised her by kissing her on the forehead. On purpose. Why on earth would he do that?

She glanced at him again as he turned off the lamps. Had the kiss been nothing more than his reaction to her display of emotion? Or did he feel more than sympathy? There had been a few moments when she'd suspected he cared about her. Like when he'd doctored her foot. But then there were other times when he seemed brusque and distant.

It would be better if he didn't care. If she hoped to resist this attraction, she would need him to remain distant.

As he turned off the last lamp, the cave plunged into darkness. It was time for them to go, which meant he would teleport her out. Any second now, he would reach for her and pull her into his arms. Instantly, her heart started pounding. Her skin tingled with anticipation.

Good God, was her attraction hopeless after all?

"Ready?" he asked softly, and her skin prickled with goose bumps.

His night vision had to be better than hers, for she couldn't really see him; she could only sense his presence in front of her. She extended her hands till her fingertips grazed his chest. As she rested her palms on him, his chest expanded with a deep breath.

He stepped closer, one of his boots slipping between her feet. His hands slid beneath her backpack. "I have to get a good grip on you so I don't lose you. You'll need to hold onto me, too."

"I understand." She wondered why he felt compelled to explain something she already knew.

When she smoothed her hands up to his shoulders, he pulled her closer till she bumped against his chest. Even through his bulky coat, she could feel the softness of her breasts pressed against his rock-hard chest.

"Rule number one," he muttered, his grip on her tightening.

She swallowed hard. "What about it?"

"Strictly business," he gritted out.

"Oh." The strange, tingly hyperawareness returned, and she could feel the pressure of his hands, the strength of his arms, the hardness of his chest, the softness of his breath against her brow, and the scent that belonged only to him. How was she going to resist this man? He was all wrong, but he felt so right.

Everything went black. As soon as they landed, he released her abruptly and strode away. She regained her balance and looked around. They were on top of a hill, with a clear, starry sky overhead. Scrubby trees, only shoulder-high, grew at an angle from being constantly buffeted by the wind. The moon, almost half full, shone down, painting the bushes silver and outlining Russell's silhouette where he stood on the edge of a bluff overlooking a valley.

When she joined him, he pointed across the valley at the lights flickering on a high cliff. "That's one of Han's favorite camps. He has control of all the land and villages within a hundred-mile radius. I'll teleport closer so I can see inside. I've never seen any guards on this bluff. You should be safe here to do your sniffing."

"Okay."

"I'll be back as soon as possible. We have—" The phone buzzed in his pocket, and he made an impatient noise as he pulled it out. "Let's get this over with." He punched a button. "What?"

Jin Long's voice was loud enough for Jia to

hear. "Why aren't you answering your damned phone?" he demanded. "And don't give me any bullshit about a water buffalo. They don't squeal like girls. Do you have Jia with you?"

Russell looked at her, and she mouthed, *"Water buffalo?"* The corner of his mouth curled up. "Yeah, she's with me."

"What—" Jin Long sputtered. "Why did you take her?"

Russell shrugged. "Why not?"

"You can't do that," Jin Long growled. "Bring her back now!"

"No."

"You told them I was a water buffalo?" Jia asked, but she forgot to be indignant when he smiled at her. God help her, the man had dimples. He should smile more often.

"Russell—" Jin Long switched to English. Jia couldn't understand him, but his tone was certainly angry.

Her mouth twitched when Russell lowered the phone and glanced at his watch with a bored expression.

Then Rajiv's voice cut in, speaking in Chinese. "What are you doing, Russell? You can't kidnap a princess!"

Russell switched back to Chinese. "I didn't kidnap her."

"Then why is she with you?" Rajiv demanded. "Did you threaten her—"

"Enough!" Jia ripped the phone from Russell's hand. "Rajiv, stop yelling at him. I'm here of my own free will."

"You need to come home now," Rajiv ordered. "If Russell won't teleport you, I'll send Jin Long—"

"No, I'm not coming home until I complete my mission."

"Jia, I don't want you doing this," Rajiv insisted. "It's too dangerous—"

"Russell will keep me safe. He wants to kill Han, too, so it makes perfect sense for us to team up."

"What about your engagement?" Rajiv asked.

She glanced at Russell, who was not looking at her but was still standing so close that she knew he could hear every word. "Killing Han has been my mission for thirteen years. Nothing is going to stop me."

Rajiv sighed. "All right. I'll make a deal with you. Come home, and I'll let you go with Rinzen and Tenzen to track Han."

Now Rajiv was taking her seriously? But even with this new offer, she knew she had made the right decision. "I appreciate it, but I'm sticking with Russell. He has skills that our uncles don't have. And I firmly believe he is my best chance at success."

"But you don't even like him," Rajiv protested. "The last time I saw you with him, you slapped the hell out of him."

Jia groaned inwardly. Only once in her life had she slapped a person, and everyone seemed to be stuck on it. Even Russell was watching her now with a wry look on his face. She turned her back to him and lowered her voice. "I get along with him fine now."

"I don't want you working with him," Rajiv grumbled. "I'm not sure he can be trusted."

A spurt of anger shot through her. "How can you say that? He's saved your life more than once. And he saved mine the other night."

"I know," Rajiv gritted out. "But he's not . . . stable."

"He's as steady as a rock!" she argued. "I trust him with my life, and so should you. Now I have work to do, so I'll call you later. Bye." She punched the Off button and turned to give the phone back to Russell.

He didn't take it. He was staring at her like she'd grown another head.

"Something wrong?"

"No." He grabbed the phone and vanished.

She'd defended him. She'd fussed at the Grand Tiger and head of her family on his behalf. In spite of his astonishment, Russell cautioned himself not to misinterpret the situation. Her defense was probably nothing more than an indication of her desperation to succeed. He was a means to an end. He signified the successful killing of Han. But what if he meant more to her than that? She'd said she trusted him with her life. *Steady as a rock.* She believed in him.

How could he resist her now?

Rule number one, he reminded himself. Focus on business. After teleporting onto a roof in Han's camp, he listened in on conversations. Nothing new was going on, so he teleported back to the bluff where Jia had remained. Her nose hadn't detected any vampires in the area other than him. Without further ado, he grabbed her and teleported to the next camp.

An hour later, they had investigated eight more encampments with no results. Because of their close proximity to some of the camps, he used hand signals to communicate with her. Other times, he leaned close to whisper in her ear. She was growing increasingly tense each time he teleported her to a new place, but he figured it was disappointment over their lack of progress.

"There are thirty camps in all," he whispered in her ear when he slipped his arms around her once again. "And no guarantee that Han is hiding anywhere near them. Locating him could take us several nights."

She nodded. "I understand."

Why did she sound so breathless? "Are you tired? Do you need a break?"

She shook her head. "I'm fine. Let's get on with this."

"All right. The best spying place for the next camp is high in a tree."

Her hands clamped down hard on his shoulders. "What?"

"Don't worry. If our combined weight is too much, I'll just levitate." He teleported to a thick branch, positioning Jia next to the trunk.

She gasped when the branch dipped.

He levitated while helping her grab onto the trunk. Then he grasped another branch to pull himself forward so he could scan the interior of the campsite. It was much the same as the previous nine camps—a few soldiers barely doing the minimum.

"Do you smell anything?" He turned to Jia.

Her eyes were squeezed shut, and she was hugging the trunk tightly, her grip so hard that her knuckles were white. Perspiration beaded her forehead, and her breathing was fast and shallow.

"Jia? Are you all right?"

Her face was deathly pale, and her cheek pressed hard against the bark. "D-don't mind me. Go on with your business."

He recalled finding her hanging from the silken rope outside her house in Tiger Town. Her eyes had been shut then, too, and her face pale. "You're afraid of heights."

Her eyes flickered open. "Is it that obvious?"

He nodded. "Yeah."

She winced. "Do what you need to do. I'll be fine."

He took hold of her upper arm. "I'll teleport you out of here."

Her eyes widened. "Don't take me back to Tiger Town."

"Why would I do that?"

"Because—" She grimaced. "I look like a scaredy-cat."

His mouth twitched. "We all have issues."

"I can't imagine you being afraid of anything."

A memory flashed through his mind of the night soon after he'd awakened as a vampire, when he'd learned that all of his men had died in Vietnam without him and all of his loved ones in the States were gone. He understood fear too well. Even if he lived for an eternity, he never wanted to experience another night like that.

"I'll teleport you down to the ground." He eased around behind her so he could get a better hold on her.

She trembled, her fingers digging into the trunk. "I hate that you're seeing me like this."

"It's all right." He burrowed a hand between the tree trunk and her waist, the bark scraping his knuckles. "You should have warned me. I thought were-cats were good climbers."

"I was. Then . . . I wasn't."

"What happened?"

She shook her head slightly, her cheek still glued to the tree.

"I have a good hold on you." With his right hand, he squeezed her upper arm. With his left arm, he tightened his grip on her waistline, pressing her back against him. "Let go of the tree now. I have you."

Still clutching the tree, she slowly moved her head back till it rested on his shoulder. "It happened thirteen years ago."

That was how long she'd wanted to kill Han. "How old were you?"

"Eight. My father was the leader of our village, and he refused to bow down to Master Han."

Russell winced. "Han attacked?"

She nodded her head. "Dad told me to hide in a tree as high as I could climb. I saw him and my mother and brother killed. And hacked—" Her voice broke.

Russell squeezed her tighter and tilted his head so his cheek rubbed against her brow. Eight years old? Far too young to witness something that horrific. "I'm sorry."

"The ground below me was full of terror. I stayed in the tree till the next night, when Grandfather came with a troop of soldiers. They had to carry me down. Since then, I've been afraid of heights."

"I understand." How terrified she must have been trying to climb down that silken rope. His poor, brave Jia.

"I didn't want to tell you. I know you're looking for a reason to be rid of me. Who would want a coward—"

"You're not a coward. You're the bravest woman I've ever met."

She turned her head toward him, her eyes wide with shock. "Then you . . . don't want to be rid of me?"

"No. You're my . . . partner." He kissed her brow.

With a sigh, she released her grip on the tree, and he teleported her down to the ground.

What the hell was he doing kissing her again? He released her and quickly stepped away. "See if you can catch Han's scent."

"Right." She inhaled deeply, clearly trying to calm her nerves. Then she closed her eyes and rotated slowly, sniffing at the air.

With her eyes shut, it was safe for him to study her. She was a natural beauty, her face sweet and oval-shaped, her skin clear and luminous, her hair thick and shiny, her body slim and graceful. It was so tempting to take her into his arms and kiss her. A real kiss. On the mouth. But how could he, when she was engaged?

He clenched his fists tightly, then released them. *Rule number one. Strictly business.* It was a good thing she was engaged. It served as a constant reminder that he couldn't get involved with her. He couldn't afford to care.

She opened her eyes and shook her head. "I'm not catching anything. But then . . . " She bit her lip.

"What?"

She blushed. "It could be that I'm too . . . aware of your scent and not able to smell past it."

"Oh." He winced. "I guess we vampires all smell pretty much the same."

"Not . . . really."

"I don't stink quite as bad as the others?" When she shook her head, he scoffed. "Well, that makes me feel special."

Her mouth twitched. "You don't stink. But it is getting hard to ignore you."

What the hell did that mean? He glanced at his watch. "If I leave for three minutes, will that be enough?"

She nodded. "I think so."

"I hate leaving you alone here. How about one minute?"

"Two."

"Deal." He noted the time and teleported back

to the bat cave. Halfway through a bottle of blood, he stopped with a jerk. What if Jia was hungry? Or thirsty?

He grabbed a sack and teleported to Zoltan's kitchen. After taking a few bottles of water from the fridge, he stole some breakfast bars from the pantry. A can of mixed nuts. A bag of chips. And a container of instant noodles.

"Russell?" Howard charged into the kitchen. "What—" His eyes narrowed as Russell emerged from the pantry. "What are you doing with human food?"

"Later." Russell heard Howard yelling just before he teleported back to the bat cave, where he deposited the food he'd stolen from Zoltan's pantry. He checked his watch. Five seconds to go. He selected a breakfast bar and bottle of water, then returned to Jia's side.

"Oh, thank you." She smiled at him, and his heart squeezed. She dropped the bar into a pocket and opened the water for a long drink.

"Did you smell anything?"

"No." She twisted the top back on. "Let's keep working."

Russell took her to ten more camps, leaving her alone at each site for a minute so she could sniff without any interference from him. Still no luck. With dawn approaching in an hour, she was yawning and visibly having trouble staying awake.

"I think we should call it a night," Russell told her. "I'll take you home and pick you up tomorrow night after sunset."

"What?" Her eyes widened. "You can't take me back to Tiger Town."

"It's your home. You'll be more comfortable there."

"No!" She shook her head. "I can't go back. They—they might lock me up. Or hide me somewhere you can't find me."

"I can always find you."

"And what if Rajiv orders my guards to fight you? I don't want you having to fight other were-tigers."

He stiffened. "I wouldn't hurt any of your kind."

She touched his arm. "I know that, but I'm not sure Rajiv does. He . . . he doesn't trust you right now. He might have Jin Long teleport me across the world."

Russell winced. That was a possibility. He could lose several nights tracking her down instead of Han.

"Besides," Jia continued, "you told me you wouldn't take me back."

"No, I didn't—"

"You implied it. When I was hugging the tree."

He scoffed. "If I don't take you home, Rajiv will have every right to be furious. A princess like you shouldn't be cooped up alone with a vampire."

"Don't call me princess. And it doesn't matter if I'm alone with you. I know you're not going to bite me."

"Your reputation would still be ruined." When she rolled her eyes, he groaned in frustration. "You'll be trapped in the bat cave all day with nothing to do. I won't be able to teleport you anywhere. I'll be in my death-sleep."

She shrugged. "I'm just as tired as you are, after working all night. I'll get some sleep, too."

His eyes narrowed. "There's only one bed."

"I have a bedroll with me. I'll make do."

He gave her an exasperated look. "You can't sleep in the same cave with me. Your family will want to kill me."

"No, they won't. It's not like we're going to do anything. Remember rule number one? This is strictly a business relationship."

"Do you expect your fiancé to believe that?"

She waved a dismissive hand. "No one will believe we've done anything. You'll be in your death-sleep all day."

For some reason the idea that he was completely harmless ticked him off. "You can't shack up with a man when you're engaged!"

She lifted her chin. "I can with a dead man."

He stepped closer. "There's a huge flaw in your thinking."

"I think not."

"I think so. The sun won't rise for another fifty minutes." He pulled her close and whispered in her ear, "I'm not dead yet."

Chapter Nine

A shudder skittered down Jia's spine, and she pushed Russell away before he could notice his effect on her. "You said you wouldn't take me back. You're a man of honor, so I know you'll keep your word."

He snorted. "Another flaw in your thinking." His gaze raked over her with a bold look. "Are you sure you want to be alone with me?"

She swallowed hard. He was purposely trying to unnerve her. Did the rascal think he could frighten her enough that she would beg to go home?

Never. Even though he was a bloodsucker who could overpower her in a second, she would not give in to fear. Her face grew warm as she recalled how he'd kissed her forehead once again. Whether it had been merely sympathy for her tragic past or the possibility that he might actually care about her, she wasn't sure, but she felt positive that he would never harm her. "I trust you. Now take me to . . . our hideout."

He watched her intently, his eyes taking on an odd gleam. "Fine. Let's do it." He pulled her back into his arms and teleported.

When they arrived, he released her abruptly, then lit a few oil lamps. He levitated up to hook his crossbow and quiver on a clawlike root in the ceiling. "You might regret your decision. There will be no privacy for you."

She glanced toward the far end of the cave where the bathtub was located. No chamber pot in sight. Thank goodness she'd relieved herself in the forest ten minutes earlier while he'd been checking out a camp. She could wait till he was in his death-sleep before doing it again. "I suppose you wash your face and hands in the river?"

"Actually I use this." He showed her a bucket of water positioned beneath an ice chest spigot. "I pack chunks of a Himalayan glacier in the chest to keep my food supply cold. I use the melted ice for washing my face and brushing my teeth."

"Oh." No wonder she'd picked up that scent on him earlier. She noted the plastic bin sitting atop a nearby wooden crate. Small containers of soap and shampoo were neatly arranged in the bin, along with a tin cup holding his toothbrush. He was rather neat and tidy for a guy who lived in a cave.

As he emptied his pockets onto the table, she noticed that the knuckles on his left hand were coated with dried blood. It must have happened when he'd tried to pry her loose from the tree trunk. "You're injured."

He glanced at his hand. "No big deal. It'll heal during my death-sleep."

"It was my fault—"

"Don't worry about it." He showed her the sat phone. "Do you know how to use this? You should call your cousin to let him know you're all right."

"I will."

He glanced up at the hole in the ceiling. "You'll probably have poor reception in here, but I'll fix that tomorrow night. Be sure to call during the day. If you call while J.L. is awake, he could use your voice as a beacon and come here to take you away."

"I understand." She removed the knives from her boots. "Since you're warning me, that must mean you're okay with me staying here."

He scoffed. "It means I want to keep the bat cave a secret." He took the sat phone over to the bookcase and plugged it in to recharge it. "You're the one who insisted on coming here. Who am I to keep a princess from getting what she wants?"

She gritted her teeth. "Don't call me princess."

"It's what you are." He unbuckled his sword belt and dropped it on the table with a loud clunk. *"Princess."*

Was he picking a fight? She yanked her knives from her belt and tossed them on the table. "If I always got what I wanted, Han would have died years ago. And my family would still be alive."

Russell closed his eyes briefly, then opened them. "You're right." He strode toward the ice chest and removed a bottle of blood and another one of water. "I apologize for my lack of social skills. I'm used to being alone." He loosened the top of the water bottle, then handed it to her.

As she accepted it, she realized his picking on her had been his way to create distance between them. Most likely, he was not comfortable with her invading his space. "I appreciate you letting me stay here. I'll try not to get in your way."

He popped his bottle into the microwave. "Don't worry. In forty-five minutes, I won't be aware of anything you're doing."

That was true, but she would definitely be aware of him all day. She took a sip of water. "You have electricity?"

He nodded and motioned to the wires snaking up through the dirt ceiling. "A solar-powered generator."

She smiled. "Your cave is more advanced than my room at home."

He didn't answer; he just concentrated on unbuckling his watch. As it came off his right wrist, she noticed the tattoo. No wonder it had taken her a few days to see it. His watch did a good job of hiding it.

Curiosity swelled inside her. None of the other good Vamps had Han's mark on them. How did Russell get it? How did he become a vampire?

She fiddled with her water, screwing the top on and off. "So do you . . . like being a vampire?"

He scoffed, then removed his bottle from the microwave. "I am what I am. No point in thinking about it."

"Why do you want to kill Han? What did he do to you?"

He paused with the bottle halfway to his mouth. "Han deserves to die." He took a long drink, guzzling down most of the bottle.

"I told you my reasons. Why don't you tell me yours?"

He clunked his bottle onto the table and gave her an annoyed look. "I don't explain myself."

"I'm your partner. You can talk to me."

"I don't need therapy." He took off his bulky coat and threw it onto the second table. "And I don't need a partner except for business."

She bit her lip. Why did he keep trying to push her away? "We are partners. You agreed to it. Is it too hard for you to be a little friendly?"

"Yes."

She snorted, then leaned over to remove the knives strapped to her calves. "Aren't you the life of the party."

He glanced at the clock on the microwave. "You'll have to endure my company for thirty-six more minutes." He motioned toward the bathtub. "Before I pass out, should I rig up a sheet for you?"

"No, I'll be fine."

He arched a brow. "You don't mind bathing in front of me?"

Was he trying to frighten her again? "You don't scare me. All I have to do is wait till you're dead, and I'll have all the privacy I could want. I could prance about the cave naked, and you would never know."

His jaw shifted. "Fine. Then what about my privacy? You'll be awake while I shower."

She glanced over at the tub. "Y-you're going to shower now?"

"It generally works best for me to bathe while I'm still alive." He smirked. "I warned you there would be no privacy. Shall I take you back home?"

"No." The rascal was still trying to unnerve her, but she'd show him. She lifted her chin. "Why would a little nudity disturb me? I've been shifting at the full moon since the age of fourteen. Everyone of age in the village shifts. And we all strip beforehand." She sighed dramatically. "I have seen more naked men than I ever care to recall."

His eyes narrowed. "Is that so?" He leaned toward her. "So do you plan to watch?"

"Of course not! Why would I even be interested?" She tried in vain to keep her face from growing warm. "I don't know what the big deal is. I mean, the male anatomy is basically the same, no matter who."

"All right, then. Since it's no big deal . . ." He reached a hand over the back of his head, grabbed the neck of his T-shirt, and pulled it off.

She gulped. While it was true that she'd seen her share of nude were-tigers, the men were generally on the lean side. Their muscles didn't make all those bulges and dips across the stomach. Their chests weren't so wide, and their shoulders didn't look like they were chiseled from marble.

He tossed his T-shirt onto the table, then unbuckled the belt to his pants.

She looked away, pretending to watch the river. "Is there anything to eat?" Her voice came out in a squeak.

"You're hungry?"

Was that the sound of a zipper? *Don't look at him.* "Are there any fish in the stream?"

"I have some food here. Do you like chips?"

She heard the rustle of a package being ripped open.

"Turn around if you dare."

The rascal. "I love chips." She turned back to the table. *Only look at the chips.* She rotated the bag on the table so the open end faced her. *Don't look at the way his unzipped trousers are hanging low on his hips.*

"There's more water in the ice chest." He whisked his belt through the loops and dropped it on the table.

"Thanks." Good God, she could see some of his underwear. She rammed a few chips into her mouth. "Why do you have people food here?"

He kicked off his shoes. "I stole them from Zoltan's castle in Transylvania."

"Oh." She grabbed another chip. Red underwear. Dark red. "So do you entertain here often?"

He shot her an annoyed look, then pulled off his socks. "You're the only other person who's seen this place."

"Ah." Cotton underwear. Snug fit. Snug enough she could see the distinct outline of a rather large—

"Noodles?"

She jumped. "What?"

"Do you like noodles?" He set a tublike container on the table in front of her. "You could make this for dinner." He motioned to the bookcase. "Use the bowl there to heat up some water. Do you know how to use a microwave?"

"Yes." Her face grew warm. Had he noticed her looking at his underwear? Surely not. She'd been fairly stealthy about it. "The palace in Tiger Town has electricity, and the kitchen is fairly modern."

"Good. You can also heat up some river water if you want a hot bath. I usually prefer a warm shower, but . . ."

Her eyes widened as he moved closer to her. *Don't look down.* "What?"

"What color is my underwear?"

"Re— I hardly noticed."

"In that case"—the corner of his mouth curled up—"I'll be taking a cold shower."

Her mouth dropped open. Oh God, he'd noticed.

He grabbed an empty bucket and headed toward the underground stream.

Her cheeks blazed with heat as she nervously organized all the stuff on the crowded table. A *cold* shower? Did that mean he had a *desire* for her? The very idea made her heart race.

This was bad. Really bad. She would never have insisted on living with him if she'd suspected this. Vampires and were-tigers didn't get involved. They were enemies, not . . . lovers. She'd been shocked enough to realize her own attraction, but now the problem was twice as bad.

Or maybe not. She slid a quick glance at him. He was levitating to fill the bucket suspended over the tub with water. Cold water meant he was fighting the attraction. It also explained why he pushed her away so often. Although he occasionally slipped up and kissed her.

She shook her head. There was no point in panicking over this. She could be misinterpreting the situation. Maybe he wasn't attracted to her at all but was simply trying to frighten her into returning to Tiger Town. She glanced at him once again and gulped. His trousers had fallen to his ankles, and he kicked them aside.

With a flurry of activity, she neatly stacked his discarded T-shirt, belt, watch, and sword belt on his coat on the second table. Then she arranged his weapons and ammo next to his coat. On the other end of the table, she set her knives and her backpack. All the while, she could hear sloshing noises from the far end of the cave.

Don't look. She filled the plastic bowl with some of her bottled water, then stuck it in the microwave. While it heated, she studied the instructions on the tub of instant noodles. It looked like Japanese and English, neither of which she could read.

"How much—" She glanced his way and gasped. He was standing naked in the bathtub with his back to her while he soaped up his body. Rivulets of soapy water meandered down his broad back, dipping into the curve of his spine and sliding over a gorgeous rump. He reached up to pull the chain on the bucket overhead, and muscles rippled across his back.

Damn. Even his rump was muscular. Water poured from the bucket, dousing his head and sluicing down his body.

The microwave beeped, and she started with another gasp. She couldn't let him catch her watching. Quickly she removed the bowl of heated water. After peeling the top halfway off the tub of noodles, she spotted a line that probably indicated how much water to pour in. With that done, she pressed the lid back down. How long would it take?

She pulled a stool up to the table and split the set of wooden chopsticks that had come with the tub. She could still hear some noises from the far end of the cave, but she didn't dare look.

Was it a mistake to insist on living with Russell? But what else could she do? If she returned home, Rajiv would forbid her from working with Russell, and it would be terrible if she publicly disobeyed her cousin. He would lose face. The royal family would be shamed. Her reputation would be destroyed.

Of course, her reputation could already be ruined if the villagers discovered what she was doing. Rajiv was probably telling them that she was visiting family. He'd never admit that the royal princess was alone in a cave with a vampire. A naked vampire.

Footsteps approached, but she kept her gaze glued to the tub of noodles.

"You cleaned up." He stopped by the table and grabbed the bottle of blood he'd left there. "You didn't need to."

"I don't mind." She caught a glimpse of white and ventured a peek. He had a towel wrapped around his hips. His skin still looked damp, and droplets of water dripped from his shoulder-length wet hair.

He finished his dinner, then dropped the

empty bottle into a plastic crate alongside other bottles. "I drained the water out of the tub. I can put in some fresh water for you."

"I can do it," she insisted. "I don't want to be a bother."

He grabbed another towel off the bookshelf and rubbed his hair dry. The muscles on his back shifted and bunched. "You're not a bother," he said quietly.

When he turned toward her, she quickly focused on her dinner, tearing the lid off and stirring the noodles with her chopsticks.

"Are they done?" He sidled up next to her and peered at the tub. "I think they need to soak a bit more."

"They'll be fine." She cast a sidelong glance at his towel. Why was he standing so close? "I like them firm." She scooped up a few noodles and shoved them into her mouth.

"Good?"

She nodded while she ate.

He leaned closer. "No limp noodles for you?"

She nearly choked and grabbed the water bottle for a quick drink.

He smiled. "I'll fill the bathtub for you."

She ate in silence while he made several trips with his bucket from the river to the tub. By the third time he leaned over to fill the bucket, she imagined his towel falling off.

Oh God, what was happening to her? He was a vampire.

He dropped the bucket on the sandy riverbank

and nudged it with his foot. "Anything else you need before I kick the bucket?"

She shook her head and concentrated on her supper. Or tried to. When he inhaled sharply, his broad chest expanded in a way she could hardly ignore. "Is something wrong?"

"First . . . warning." He shrugged his massive shoulders. "I'll be dead in about five minutes."

She swallowed hard. What could she say? *See you later*? *Have a nice . . . nap*? "You can feel it coming?"

"Yes." He wandered into the river and sloshed the sand off his feet. "I'll see you at sunset."

She was about to respond when he vanished. She jumped to her feet, then spotted him slipping underneath the blanket on his bed. He tossed his towel to the foot of the bed, then leaned back, pulling the blanket up to his chest.

Apparently, he did his death-sleep in the nude. He lifted an arm, bending it at the elbow and resting the hand behind his head.

He has a lovely profile, she thought as she watched him gaze up at the rock ceiling. And the bicep of his raised arm made her mouth run dry. His chest expanded again, and he shut his eyes.

She inched closer. Was he dead?

"Are you going to watch me die?" he asked softly.

She winced. "Does it hurt?"

He opened his eyes and gave her a wry look. "What do you think?"

"I . . . guess it hurts."

He nodded. "You get used to it. Half dead is better than full dead."

"You're not half dead. When you're alive, you're very alive."

A corner of his mouth curled up. "Are you a *Pollyanna*?"

The last word had been in English, so she didn't understand. "What is that?"

"Someone who sees good in things." His small smile faded. "Even when there is none."

Was he referring to himself? Did he not know he was a good man? His chest expanded suddenly, and he lowered his arm as a pained look crossed his face.

She rushed toward him. "There is good in you. I know it."

He gave her a look of astonishment, then exhaled slowly as his eyes flickered shut.

He was gone. Jia's chest tightened. She'd never seen a vampire fall into his death-sleep before. It was more dramatic than she'd realized. And so sad that they had to endure it over and over for as long as they lived.

She touched his neck. No pulse that she could detect. His hair brushed against her fingers, soft and still damp. Dark whiskers shaded his chiseled jaw. There was a tiny scar on his left cheekbone. He must have been injured before becoming a vampire.

She turned his right hand over and smoothed her fingers over his tattoo. The Chinese word for "slave," though she couldn't imagine Russell ever being anyone's slave. "How did you get this? What happened to you?"

Her gaze shifted to his handsome face, and she groaned at how little she knew about him. "Why do you live all alone in a cave? Why aren't you in America with your family? What did Han do to you that you have to kill him?" She sighed. "Why do you have to be a vampire?"

No answer, of course. *He'll be back,* she assured herself. *He'll wake up at sunset.* But he might never answer her questions.

Sunlight filtered through the new hole in the roof, illuminating the kitchen area. Quickly, she examined Russell's face and arms. No burn marks. It would be awful if the hole she'd made caused him any harm. But his bed was safe in a dark alcove with a solid rock ceiling overhead.

Back in the kitchen area, she tossed the cold tub of noodles into the trash bin and wiped down the table.

A whole day stuck in Russell's cave. She was too hyped up now to sleep, so she wandered about, familiarizing herself with her new home. Russell had some clean clothes and towels stashed on the shelves of his bookcase. The top shelf held a CD player, a stack of CDs, and some books.

Most of the books were in English, but she spotted one that she could partly read. *Chinese for Dummies.* The translated title made her smile. Russell was no dummy. The CDs were also about learning Chinese. She imagined him here all alone, practicing night after night. He spoke fairly well. His pronunciation was off sometimes, but it was kinda . . . cute. And sexy. He was a man who didn't let the need to learn a foreign language get in the way of his mission.

On the bottom shelf, she found a carved, wooden box. The latch appeared old and rusted. She brought the box to the table and ran her fingers over the woodwork. Roses and small birds had been carved in a primitive but beautiful style. Homemade.

She fingered the latch. *Curiosity killed the cat,* she chided herself. It was wrong to snoop around in Russell's things.

But was he the type of guy who would ever confide in her? Mister "I don't explain myself" would never talk. Snooping was the only alternative left to her.

She snorted. Her excuse sounded lame, but what the heck? He was dead at the moment and would never know.

The box creaked as she opened it. Nothing but a lumpy, old, dirty rag. Grimacing, she folded back the edges of the oilcloth. There were two pistols inside. Old, she could tell, but she had no idea how old. Revolvers. She touched a shiny barrel. Russell was keeping them in excellent condition. They reminded her of the old pistols she'd seen in American cowboy movies.

She glanced over at Russell. "Are you a *cowboy*?" It was one of the few words she knew in English. She and her grandfather had loved watching American cowboy movies.

With a smile, she imagined Russell riding on a horse alongside John Wayne. She closed the box and put it back on the bottom shelf.

What to do now? She noticed his discarded

trousers on the ground next to the tub. To show her gratitude, she would do his laundry. She gathered up his dirty clothes and towels, then dumped them into the tub he'd filled with water. After adding some soap, she swished them around.

"I might as well do mine, too." She glanced over at Russell. He'd never know. She stripped and tossed her clothes into the tub.

Ten minutes later, she had the laundry rinsed and hanging on the drying racks. She opened the spigot on the tub to let the water drain.

"Time for my own bath." She grabbed the bucket and began refilling the tub. The river water was cool, so she microwaved some water to make it warmer. Each time she passed Russell's bed, she glanced at him. Still dead and completely oblivious that she was crossing back and forth completely naked. For the fun of it, she started striking a pose each time she passed by.

After her bath, she slipped on some clean panties and a camisole. She brushed her teeth and left her toothbrush in the tin cup next to Russell's. She stared at the two brushes awhile.

She took a deep breath and retrieved the sat phone so she could call her cousin.

"Jia!" Rajiv's voice sounded fuzzy. "Are you all right?"

"Of course."

"I can hardly hear you."

"I'm fine!"

"But you're—" Rajiv's voice faded out, then came back. "—Russell."

"He's dead right now. I might as well be alone."

"Where are you?"

"In a cave. I don't really know where."

"I sent Rinzen and Tenzen—" Rajiv's voice crackled. "Once they find you—"

"You didn't need to do that. I'll be fine."

"It's not fine. You're a member of the royal family, engaged—" More crackling noises. "What you're doing is not acceptable, and you know it."

Her face grew warm. "I know you're upset. I'm sorry."

"The only thing saving you right now is that no one but me, Jin Long, and your uncles know what you're doing. I told everyone that Jin Long teleported you to my brother's village in Thailand. Jin Long actually went there to convince my brother to play along."

"Thank you."

Rajiv snorted. "Don't thank me. It's not like I wanted to do this. If I had my way, you'd be home safe and sound, not trapped in some cave with a crazy vampire."

"He's not crazy. And I'll come home as soon as the job is done."

Rajiv's voice faded, then came back. "—home before your betrothed arrives. I asked the ladies to go ahead and make your wedding gown."

She winced. How could she even think about getting married now? "I'll call you tomorrow. Bye." She hung up and plugged the phone back into the charger. This was not the time to worry about the future. She had a mission to accomplish first, and only eleven days left to do it. For now, she needed her rest.

She turned off all the lamps. With a yawn, she unhooked her bedroll from her backpack. Where to sleep? The kitchen area was too bright now that the sun was shining straight through the hole. She wandered across the cave. The ground was too damp by the tub where she'd done the laundry. And too sandy close to the river.

She looked at the bed. Russell was taking up only half of it, and he certainly wasn't going to be rolling about. She walked up to the empty side and pressed her hand against the makeshift mattress. Three layers of sleeping bags were a lot more comfortable than her thin bedroll on the hard ground. And there was even a spare pillow.

Gingerly, she sat on the bed. No reaction from Russell. How could he react? The poor guy was dead. She jiggled the bed, then leaned over to peer at his face.

Nothing. His face was relaxed, the thin lines that usually lined his brow completely gone. His jaw was no longer clenched in concentration, his mouth no longer thinned with irritation but soft. He looked peaceful and almost . . . sweet.

She scoffed. What was she thinking? He was a vampire.

There was no way she was getting under the blanket when he was naked, so she stretched out on top and used her bedroll as a blanket. Just a little catnap, then she'd get up and he would never know she'd shared his bed.

She rolled over, snuggling her face into the pillow. It was really quite comfortable in the vampire's lair.

Some time later she heard a sound, but it hardly registered. She moaned and rolled onto her back.

Two hands grasped her shoulders, and she jerked awake. It was dark in the cave. She'd slept past sunset?

Oh God, no! Russell was awake! She tried to get up, but he pinned her back down.

It was hard to make out his body in the dark, but not his eyes. They were glowing red. His grip on her tightened as his fangs shot out.

A growl rumbled low in his throat. "You should never sleep with a vampire."

Chapter Ten

He was scaring her. Hell, he was scaring himself. In the three years that he'd been a vampire, he'd managed never to bite a person. Thanks mostly to Zoltan, who always had a supply of synthetic blood just a short teleport away. But then, in those three years, he'd never wakened with a woman in his bed, especially a beautiful woman like Jia.

The second he'd taken his first breath, he'd caught her scent. Woman, sex, and food all rolled into one luscious body that was warm and ready for the taking. Immediately, his eyes had turned red. His dick had grown hard.

Her blood was coursing through her body, the scent rich and intoxicating. The added fragrance of were-tigress unleashed a primitive hunter inside him. His fangs shot out, and he was gripped with a need to attack and conquer.

His fingers dug into her shoulders as he fought for control. No doubt she'd be left with some bruises, but it was better than a shredded neck.

"Russell," she breathed. "I'm sorry."

She was sorry? He was the monster here. With a growl, he shoved himself away and reeled out of bed. He stumbled to the ice chest in the dark and drank half a bottle cold. The blood eased his hunger, and the chill cooled the raging beast inside him. Unfortunately, his erection showed no sign of slacking off.

"Russell, are you all right?" her soft voice came from the bed.

God, he wanted her. He wanted to take her into his arms and make love to her. She was so brave and clever. Sweet and beautiful. She defended him, believed in him, trusted him. Or she had until he'd scared the shit out of her. "I apologize for losing control," he said.

"You didn't lose control. You stopped—"

"I frightened you."

"I shouldn't have been in bed with you. I meant to only take a nap, but—"

"It's not your fault I'm the way I am." He set his bottle down and strode to the bookcase where he kept his clean clothes.

"I doubt it's your fault, either. You didn't ask to become a vampire, did you?"

"No." Was she still defending him, even after he'd come close to biting her?

"Was it Han who changed you?"

He ignored the question and pulled on a pair of briefs. "I'll go topside for about ten minutes so you can have some privacy." He lit a lamp and glanced over his shoulder at the bed, careful to keep the bulge in his underwear from showing.

She was standing beside the bed wearing panties and a flimsy-looking top, her long hair wild and loose around her shoulders. His fingers curled at the thought of stroking the black silk of her hair, fondling the white silk stretched taut across her breasts. His vision turned red once again, and he blinked, turning away.

"I'll be back soon. Then we'll get to work." He grabbed his bottle of blood off the table and teleported aboveground.

Jia dressed as quickly as she could, all the time chastising herself for failing to wake up before Russell. Now he felt like a monster, and she felt guilty for bringing that look of shame to his face. All her life she'd been told by the villagers that if you pull a tiger's tail, expect to be scratched. No doubt a similar scenario held true for a vampire. Sleep with him and expect to be bitten.

She wandered back to the bed, recalling the shock of seeing his fangs and red glowing eyes. But then she'd felt him tremble as he'd fought for control, and she had wondered—Did he want her simply because she was there? Or did he truly want her?

He returned, wearing only his underwear, and she turned away to check on the drying laundry while he dressed.

"Here. Eat." Without looking at her, he set a breakfast bar and bottle on the table.

"Thanks." While she ate, her gaze kept wandering back to him. Dressed in trousers, socks, and shoes, he had a towel draped over his bare shoulders. He shaved and washed his face. His hand paused over the tin cup that held both their toothbrushes, then he went ahead and brushed his teeth without a word.

He was just as silent as he finished dressing and arming himself. Not once did he look in her direction. She winced, wondering if he planned to be this cold and distant for the rest of the night.

When she had all her knives sheathed, she announced, "I'm ready."

"Let's go." He reached for her shoulders, then stopped and grabbed her by the waist instead.

"You think I'm bruised."

His jaw shifted, but he avoided looking at her. "I know you are. Hold on to me."

The second she looped her arms around his neck, he teleported her.

For five hours, they teleported from one campsite to another. At each camp, he left her alone for precisely two minutes so she could sniff without any interference from his own scent. No sign of Han. That should have been frustrating, but she found the awkward tension between her and Russell even more disturbing. Finally, she'd had all she could take.

When he put his hands around her waist to teleport once again, she pushed him back. "How do you know I won't bite you?"

He blinked and finally looked at her. "What?"

"I'm a man-eating tiger."

He scoffed. "Don't waste my time. We have work to do."

"Don't piss me off. I could eat you for dinner."

He gave her a wry look. "You eat men?"

"It's what tigers do."

"You don't eat people. You are a person most of the time. It would be cannibalism."

"So you think I know right from wrong when I'm an animal?"

He paused, then nodded. "Yes."

"You trust me not to bite you?" She smoothed a hand down his cheek to his neck. "Even when I'm feeling ravenous?"

"Are you hungry? I could take you to the bat cave. Or Zoltan's place."

She swatted Russell's chest. "You see? Even when I threaten you with bodily harm, you're still thinking about how to take care of me."

He scowled at her. "So?"

"So I trust you, you idiot. I know you won't harm me. Just like me, you know right from wrong, even when your fangs are out. So cut out the remorse routine, and let's be friends again."

"You call your friends 'idiot'?"

She shrugged. "If the shoe fits."

His eyes narrowed. "Fine. We're friends, princess."

"Don't call me princess."

He smirked. "Bite me."

"Maybe I will, *cowboy*." When he stiffened, she continued, "That's right. I found your cowboy pistols."

He gritted his teeth. "You have no right snooping around my stuff."

"Are you really a cowboy?"

"I don't explain myself."

"Well, that's a shame, 'cause I really like cowboys."

He stilled, his gaze growing more intense. "Is that so?"

Her skin tingled. "Yes."

He stepped closer. "And are you really . . . hungry?"

She wasn't sure if he was talking about food, but she nodded. "Yes."

"In that case . . ." He grabbed her by the waist and teleported.

"**A**re you crazy?" Howard whispered as Russell inspected the contents of the refrigerator in the kitchen at Zoltan's castle. "Rajiv is furious. He says you kidnapped his cousin and refuse to return her."

"You don't have to whisper," Russell told the huge were-bear. "She doesn't understand English." He glanced over at the kitchen table, where Jia was sitting next to Howard's wife. "But she does seem to like your donuts. I think that's six she's eaten so far."

"What?" Howard looked back.

"How come you know about this?" Russell asked. "Do the MacKay employees do nothing but gossip like a bunch of old hens?"

Howard snorted. "It's not every day that a Vamp kidnaps a were-tiger princess."

"She's not kidnapped." Russell removed a package of meat from the fridge. "What's this?"

"New York strip steaks." Howard frowned at him. "Elsa and I are having those for supper."

Russell gave him a wry look as he set the package on the counter. "You need all five?"

"I have a big appetite," Howard grumbled. "And Elsa is eating for three."

"Three?"

"Yep." Howard beamed proudly. "Twins. We found out about a week ago." He winked at his wife.

Damn, everyone was having children. "Congratulations." Russell translated the news for Jia, and she grinned while congratulating them both in Chinese.

"She's so sweet," Elsa said, patting Jia's arm. "I wish I could talk to her."

"So do I," Howard muttered. "Then we could find out if she's actually been kidnapped."

"Does she look frightened or abused in any way?" Russell cringed inwardly, recalling the bruises he'd left on her shoulders. "She's just a little hungry. There's not much to eat in the bat cave."

Elsa gasped. "You're making her live with bats?"

"There aren't any bats," Russell protested. "It's actually very nice . . . as far as caves go."

Elsa rose to her feet. "What has she been eating? Is there any way to cook there?"

Howard snorted. "I have a feeling he has a solar-powered generator and a microwave."

Russell shrugged. "She needs more than instant noodles and chips."

"Of course she does." Elsa hurried over to the fridge and shooed them out of the way. "She'll have dinner with us. Steak, and I'll make some salad." She selected a variety of greens and veggies from the fridge and piled them on the counter. "And we'll nuke three potatoes. They're in the pantry."

"I'll get them." Russell strode into the large walk-in pantry.

Howard followed him. "So you're not going to return her?"

"She doesn't want to go back," Russell explained as he scanned the shelves, looking for potatoes. "She wants revenge, just like me. Han killed her brother and parents, and she's helping me track him down. It's a business partnership, that's all."

"Really?"

Russell stiffened at the dubious tone of Howard's voice. "Yes, really. You can tell Rajiv and Angus and everyone else you gossip with that I will keep her safe. In fact, before we leave, I'd like to get an extra sat phone and an antenna I can install outside the cave for better reception. Then she can call Rajiv every day to assure him that she's all right."

Howard frowned. "You're not forcing her to do anything she doesn't want to?"

"No, quite the opposite. I'm helping her do exactly what she wants."

Howard nodded. "Okay. I believe you." He headed out the door, then paused, glancing back. "You do know, don't you, that she's engaged?"

"I know." Russell found a basket of potatoes and picked out the three biggest ones.

"The fiancé is a wealthy were-tiger prince," Howard continued. "Rajiv wants the wedding to go through."

"So?" Russell shot him an annoyed look. "You think I would mess that up for her?"

"I don't know. You just squeezed a raw potato in half."

With a muttered curse, Russell tossed the mashed potato into the nearby garbage bin, then selected another one.

"You like her," Howard said quietly.

Russell shook his head. "Nothing will interfere with my mission. Once Han is dead, I'll take her back to Tiger Town and leave China forever."

"Famous last words." When Russell scowled at him, Howard sighed and patted him on the back. "Believe it or not, I know what you're going through. I lived for revenge once, too." His gaze drifted to his wife, who was rinsing salad greens in the sink. "A life of hatred is worthless compared to a life filled with love."

Chapter Eleven

After three more hours of hunting Han, dawn was approaching, so Russell teleported Jia to the last campsite they would check that night.

While she had enjoyed her dinner with Howard and Elsa, he had spent that time teleporting more food supplies to the bat cave and setting up an antenna in the tree next to the solar panels. Now when Jia called her cousin, she would get decent reception.

"Since this is our last stop, I'd better . . ." Jia motioned toward a thick clump of bushes.

"Right. I'll be up the tree over there." Russell pointed to a tall tree, then teleported to the top of it so he could look inside the camp.

He was surprised by what he saw. The soldiers were armed and rushing into position as their officer barked out orders. They peered over the battlements, as if expecting an attack. Russell scanned the surrounding area but spotted nothing except Jia emerging from some bushes. What had happened to put these soldiers on alert?

The sat phone in his pocket buzzed, and he checked the caller. Rajiv. The Grand Tiger might know what was going on, but Russell knew better than to take the bait with Jia nearby.

He teleported down to her. "Something's got the soldiers agitated. They're staying inside the barricade for now, so you're probably safe out here to do your sniffing. Even so, I'm worried about leaving you alone."

"It'll take me only a minute," she assured him. "I'll be fine." When his phone buzzed again, she gave him a questioning look. "You're not going to answer?"

"Not here." He touched her shoulder. "I put my number into your sat phone in case you need to call. Don't answer your phone unless it's me. Howard may have passed your number on to J.L. or Rajiv. They still think I kidnapped you, so if you call them at night—"

"Jin Long will try to rescue me," she finished his sentence. "I know how they are. Go on, so I can sniff around." She removed a knife from her belt. "I can take care of myself."

His mouth curled up. "I know."

She smiled back. "You're the only one who does know. Everyone else thinks I'm a helpless princess."

"You are a princess."

She swatted him. "Go away, cowboy. You're interfering with my nose."

"I'll be back soon." He teleported to the glacier in the Himalayas. The instant blast of freezing wind nearly knocked him off his feet. Needles of sleet pricked at his exposed face and hands, and he gritted his teeth as he called Rajiv.

"The sun will rise soon," Rajiv told him. "I want you to teleport Jia back home so she can spend the day here."

"And then what?" Russell replied. "Will you let her go with me tomorrow night? Or do you plan to lock her—"

J.L. materialized beside him and gasped. "Holy shit!"

Russell smirked. "I knew you'd show up."

J.L., dressed in trousers and a T-shirt, wrapped his arms around himself and shuddered. "What the hell is this? Antarctica? Where's Jia?"

"Someplace a lot warmer."

"What's going on?" Rajiv demanded on the phone.

"I took a little trip before calling you," Russell explained. "We're high in the Himalayas."

"N-not funny," J.L. said, his teeth chattering.

"You're not with Jia?" Rajiv asked. "Where is she?"

"She's working," Russell said. "At the last campsite we checked, the soldiers were on alert. Any idea why?"

"Angus and Emma have returned to Tiger Town with a bunch of the guys," J.L. said, bouncing on his feet in an attempt to stay warm. "We attacked a camp tonight and took all the soldiers prisoner. There are thirty more supersoldiers in the clinic now getting returned to normal."

"And Emma brought Winifred with her, the warrior woman who can talk to dragons and birds," Rajiv added. "We're hoping Winifred and the owl can figure out where the dragon boy is being held captive. And then we'll know where Han is, too."

"In other words," J.L. shouted over the whistling cold wind, "we've got everything under control. You don't need to endanger Jia any more. Angus wants you to return her."

Russell snorted. "I don't work for Angus. And neither does Jia."

"You have no right to put her in danger!" Rajiv yelled over the phone.

"I won't let anything harm her!" Russell shouted back. The frigid temperature was stiffening his fingers to the point of pain. "You have my word as a Marine. I will keep her safe."

"If you don't, you'll have an army of were-tigers hunting you down!" Rajiv hung up.

Russell sighed, his breath frosting the air.

J.L. grimaced. "Why are you helping that poor girl with her obsession with revenge? Just because you're obsessed too doesn't give you the right to endanger her. You're bloody crazy."

"Is it crazy to think she should be allowed to accomplish something she feels passionate about? Am I crazy that I don't believe in locking her up in a princess prison for the rest of her life? She has the right to be herself and find her own destiny!"

J.L.'s eyes widened. "You see yourself as her champion?"

Russell winced. "She doesn't need a champion. She's stronger, smarter, and braver than any of you realize. We're in a business partnership. I need her help as much as she needs mine."

J.L. inhaled a hissing breath as another shudder racked his body. "We all need the were-tigers. They're our best ally. If we don't stop Han and Darafer, they'll keep taking over more and more territory and killing more humans. The alliance with Rajiv will be totally fucked up if anything happens to Jia—"

"Nothing will happen! I'll keep her safe. Now get out of here so I can return to her and keep my promise."

J.L. muttered a curse, then vanished.

Immediately Russell teleported back to Jia.

Five soldiers had gathered around her in a semicircle, while she faced them, her back to a tree. Two had pistols pointed at her; the other three, swords. Russell's initial shock quickly morphed into rage, first at the soldiers, then at himself. He was the one who had left her alone.

Jia threw a knife at the nearest soldier holding a pistol, then dove to the ground to roll as bullets meant for her tore up the tree. Her knife thudded into the shooter's chest, and he collapsed. Meanwhile, with vampire speed, Russell wrenched the pistol from the other soldier's hand and punched him. He dodged a sword, clobbered the first swordsman, then spun around to land a kick on the second swordsman's head. One soldier lay dead on the ground; three others were unconscious.

The last soldier had his sword lifted overhead,

ready to swipe it down onto Jia. She rolled toward him, whipped out another knife, and plunged it into his leg. He cried out, dropping his sword. Russell leaped on him and snapped his neck.

The soldier fell half on top of Jia, splattering her with blood. Russell pulled him off and she jumped to her feet, breathing heavily as she pulled out another knife.

"Are you all right?" Russell asked.

She looked frantically about. "It's over?"

"Yes. Are you injured?" He inspected her quickly, but she appeared unharmed. The blood on her clothes wasn't hers.

She glanced at the knife in her hand, then grimaced as she rammed it back into its sheath. "I had to kill again. I hate that."

"That's a good thing."

She frowned as her gaze lingered over the two dead bodies. "How can you say that?"

"If you actually enjoyed killing, you'd be a sick bastard." He plucked her knife from the soldier she'd killed. "You want this back?"

She wrapped her arms around herself and shook her head.

Russell wiped the knife clean and pocketed it. Then he retrieved the one embedded in the last soldier's leg. The design of these knives might be traced back to Tiger Town, so they couldn't be left behind. He quickly scanned the area to see if they'd left anything that might identify them. Three of the soldiers were still alive, so he dove into their heads and erased their memories of the last hour.

"We should go before they wake up." He turned

toward Jia and noticed she was visibly shaking. What an idiot he was that he'd bragged just moments ago that he could keep her safe.

He pulled her into his arms, and her trembling body nearly killed him. This was all his fault. He'd known the soldiers were on alert.

She grasped his coat in her fists. "Take me home."

His heart sank. "To Tiger Town?"

"No." She blinked with surprise. "I meant . . . our home. The cave."

He stared at her a moment, his chest squeezing so hard he couldn't breathe. Then he gathered her close and teleported.

They landed in the kitchen area in the dark. He stepped back, planning to light some lamps, but she held on tight to his coat. A shudder racked her body.

"Don't . . ." She leaned against him, her brow resting on his chest. "Just a little bit longer."

He wrapped his arms around her. How many times over the last few days had he held her and thought to himself, *Just a little bit longer*?

She nestled her cheek against his chest. "I can't seem to stop shaking."

"That happens sometimes afterward, but you were strong and brave when you needed to be." He rubbed her back, recalling how panicked he had felt after his first skirmish in Vietnam. How heavily the knowledge that he'd killed other human beings had weighed on him. But tonight he had killed with no remorse, feeling nothing but rage that they had dared attack Jia.

What a cold, heartless monster he had become.

She shivered again. "I was so outnumbered. I thought I was going to die."

Guilt ripped at his heart. "I shouldn't have left you alone."

"I told you to go."

He shook his head. "I screwed up. I won't leave you alone again."

"Then how will I sniff out—"

"I don't give a damn." He held her tighter, his right hand cradling the back of her head. "I'm not leaving you alone."

With a small shock, he realized the full import of what he'd just said. Somehow, in the last few days, Jia had become more important to him than his quest for revenge. "I promised everyone I will keep you safe, and I will."

She looked up at him, then touched his cheek. "I can hardly see you."

"I know." She couldn't see what a monster he was. Somehow, miraculously, she still believed in him. He cupped her face and wiped her tears with his thumbs.

She rested the palm of her hand on his cheek. "Thank you for charging to the rescue."

"Anytime." He kissed her brow. He continued to caress her cheeks with his thumbs, then slowly his thumb inched over to her mouth. Softly, he rubbed the pad of his thumb over her lips. Her mouth opened.

An invitation. His groin hardened, and his vision went red.

With a gasp, she stepped back. "You must be hungry."

"No, I—"

"Of course you're hungry. You used a lot of energy in the fight." She fumbled along the table till she reached the ice chest. "Let me get you a bottle."

"I'm not going to bite you."

"I know that." She pulled a bottle from the ice. "Do you need it warmed up?"

"This will be fine." He opened the bottle and took a long drink of cold blood to cool off the onslaught of desire. "I'll light a few lamps." He set the bottle on the table and soon had two lamps lit. Glancing down, he winced at the bulge that persisted in his trousers. He looked back at Jia, but she was totally focused on the bloodstains on her tunic.

"What a mess. I'd better wash this before it dries." She removed her boots and socks, then waded into the river, where she pulled off her tunic.

He sipped more blood as he watched her, still tinted pink from his glowing red eyes. She leaned over, vigorously scrubbing at her tunic. No doubt she wanted to erase the bloodstains, along with the terror of tonight's skirmish, but her action was affecting him differently. Her movements made her breasts jiggle and agitated the water enough to dampen the camisole she wore. Her nipples hardened as the cool river water soaked through the thin silk.

He turned away. His groin and his vision would never return to normal as long as he was ogling her. He took off his coat and put away his weapons, then grabbed an extra blanket from the bookshelf. As he passed the bed, he snatched his pillow, then continued walking to the far reaches of the cave.

"I'll sleep here," he announced, tossing the blanket and pillow on the ground. "You can have the bed."

"I can't do that." She stepped onto the riverbank, wringing the water out of the tunic. "It's your bed."

He glanced toward her and groaned. Her wet pants and camisole were glued to her body, showing every dip and curve. "It doesn't matter where I sleep. I'll be dead. I could sleep on a bed of nails and not know it."

"Well, if you insist." She stretched out her wet tunic on the nearby drying rack.

"I insist." He grabbed a clean towel off the rack and draped it around her shoulders.

"What—" She glanced down at herself and gasped. "Oh my God, I'm . . . sorry." Her cheeks turned pink as she clutched the edges of the towel together.

"Go back to the kitchen so I can shower. And no peeking like last night."

She huffed. "I didn't—" Her cheeks blazed a hotter shade of pink. "Of all the crazy things . . ." She marched back to the kitchen area and slipped his coat on.

Did she think that made things better? She was in his home, wearing his clothes. This was torture.

A cold shower, that's what he needed. With vampire speed, he filled the tub and overhead bucket, then stripped and showered. He glanced over at Jia a few times, but she was steadfastly ignoring him, eating chips and studying one of his books.

He'd come so close to kissing her. If his red glowing eyes hadn't startled her, he would have kissed her. Hell, he might have done more.

She's engaged, he told himself for the hundredth time. He'd promised he would keep her safe. That meant safe from him, too. She had a prince waiting for her. He couldn't screw up her chance for a happy future.

He grabbed a clean towel off the rack to dry himself, then put on the underwear that Jia had washed the night before. *She's engaged,* he reminded himself again. He couldn't kiss her. Shouldn't even think about her.

"Don't mind me." He strode toward the table. "I just need to brush my teeth before going to bed."

Her eyes widened at the sight of him in his underwear, then she quickly looked away. "No problem. Just pretend I'm not here."

His gaze landed on the tin cup with their toothbrushes resting side by side. *We are pretending,* he thought. Pretending they were only business partners. Pretending they didn't want more. Who were they kidding?

Rule number one was shot to hell.

He was asleep. Dead, to be precise, but she didn't like to think about Russell that way.

She'd stayed in the kitchen, ignoring him, but with every second that the sun had inched toward the horizon, she'd been achingly aware of him. His breathing had grown more labored and tinged with pain. Each time he'd exhaled, she'd wondered if it would be his last breath.

And then it was. Silence.

Her heart squeezed in her chest.

The cave became lighter as more sunlight filtered through the roof. But across the cave, in the furthermost corner, it was dark and quiet.

She turned off the lamps, then removed his coat. Her cheeks grew warm as she recalled how transparent her wet camisole had been. She'd been so intent on getting rid of the bloodstains that she'd never thought about how exposed she would look in wet clothes.

At the time, putting on his coat had been the only remedy she could think of. She'd brought only two sets of clothes with her, and the clean ones were on the drying rack next to the bathtub. There was no way she could walk over there when he was showering.

But now he was dead. He couldn't tease her about peeking. Couldn't tempt her with the way he held her and stroked her face.

"Russell." She approached him for a closer look. His hair was still damp, the ends curling. He looked so sweet and peaceful, not at all like the raging warrior who had plowed through three soldiers in about three seconds.

She brushed his hair back from his brow, then smoothed her hand down his face. With a finger, she rubbed the little indentation where he had a dimple when he smiled. It was surrounded by prickly whiskers.

She touched his lips. It had happened again. She'd wanted him to kiss her.

With a sigh, she straightened. The attraction was growing, but this couldn't be love. Not with a vampire. She was merely reacting to his proximity. And his masculinity. And the way he believed in her. And protected her. The way he looked at her with those hungry eyes. The way his hands sometimes lingered at her waist longer than necessary when they teleported.

She shook her head. It would be best not to think about him. So she spent the next thirty minutes doing laundry, then taking a hot bath.

Before going to bed, she needed to assure her cousin that she was alive and well, so she called him.

"Are you all right?" Rajiv asked. "I sent Jin Long to get you, but Russell pulled a trick on him—"

"What do you mean?" Jia glanced over at Russell while she heard about his little trip to the Himalayan mountains. Her mouth twitched. So that's where the rascal had gone. "Is Jin Long all right?"

"Yeah. He's happy now that Winifred is back."

"Oh, that's good." Jia smiled, recalling how smitten Jin Long had been with the warrior woman Winifred.

"She came with Angus and Emma and a bunch

of MacKay employees," Rajiv continued. "Tiger Town is full of Vamps and shifters again. You should come back to see everyone."

Jia bit her lip. "Did they bring the dragon babies with them?"

"Yeah, you wouldn't believe how much they've grown."

"And Freya?" Jia asked about Winifred's sister, who had actively pursued Rajiv. "Did she come?"

"She stayed in England. Apparently, she has a job now with her brother. And a new boyfriend."

Jia winced. "I'm sorry. I know you liked her."

"I was flattered that she liked me, but I always knew there couldn't be more to it than that." Rajiv sighed. "I'm in the same boat you are, Jia. I have to marry a were-tigress. And a princess, most likely. She'll definitely have to be approved by the Council of Elders. I can't bring dishonor to my family or my position. And neither can you."

A jab of guilt needled Jia. She'd resented her cousin's interference in her life, but in reality, he was just as trapped as she was. "What about love?"

"There's no reason why we can't find love with our chosen mates," Rajiv assured her. "This prince of yours is trying very hard. He sends a gift every day. Today, it was a framed portrait of himself. The court ladies all agree that he's very handsome. If you just give him a chance, I know you could be happy."

Jia sighed, not wanting to think about it. "So why did Angus and everyone come back?"

"Winifred can communicate with winged creatures, so we're hoping she and the owl can figure out where Xiao Fang is being held. And then we would know Han's location, too."

"I see." Jia wondered who would find Han first. It needed to be her and Russell.

"Tonight we attacked one of Han's camps and took all the supersoldiers prisoner," Rajiv continued. "They're in the clinic now so we can return them to normal."

"That's good." News of the attack must have spread, Jia thought. It would explain why the soldiers at the last campsite had been so eager to kill anyone in the area.

"Angus wants to attack a different camp every night," Rajiv explained. "It will deplete Han's army and eventually lure him out of hiding."

She nodded. "It's a good plan."

"It is. You should come back here so you can be part of it."

She glanced at Russell. "I think our plan works well, too."

Rajiv let out a groan of frustration. "I don't like you living with him. Something could happen—"

"He's doing his best to keep me safe."

"Promise me, Jia, if you're mortally wounded, you'll make him bring you back here."

"I'm not going to die, Rajiv."

"There's something . . . I don't think Grandfather ever told you. He was so adamant about keeping you innocent. And of course, we always assumed you'd never get mortally wounded as long as you were living at Tiger Town. You would always be safe here."

Jia frowned. "What is it?"

"When were-cats die and progress on to the next life, they . . ."

"Become more powerful? I know that." Being able to shift at any time was a great advantage.

Rajiv groaned. "There's more. When they wake up, they . . . they have an overwhelming desire to . . . mate."

She blinked. "Mate?"

"Yes."

She snorted. "That's crazy. You're on your second life, and you don't have a mate."

"Well, I . . . it doesn't matter," Rajiv stammered. "The need is so strong that you find someone . . . or take care of it yourself."

She made a face. "Is that what you did?"

"I'm not talking about it! I'm just warning you. You'll need to come home."

She scoffed. "I don't have a mate there. Besides, it's not going to happen. I have no plans to die." Overwhelming need to mate? How laughable. She'd never even kissed a man. She wouldn't know an overwhelming need to mate if it bit her on the ass.

"You shouldn't be there alone with Russell," Rajiv insisted.

Her mouth dropped open. That's why Rajiv was so worried. He was afraid she and Russell would . . .

Her cheeks blazed with heat. "There's nothing between us. It's a business partnership."

"Jin Long thinks he may have some feelings for you," Rajiv said. "You need to call us immediately so we can rescue you if you ever see Russell's eyes start glowing red."

She stiffened. "Why? I know he's not going to bite me."

"Red eyes don't just mean hunger. It also means lust."

Her breath caught. *Lust*?

"You haven't seen it, have you?"

"No, not at all." She covered her mouth. What was she doing? She'd never lied to her cousin like that before. "I should get some sleep now. I'll call tomorrow."

She hung up and paced around the cave. Soon her steps led her to Russell.

She'd already suspected he desired her. Now she had proof. But the more she thought about it, the more she realized he'd done a good job of behaving himself. He'd never actually confessed or attempted to seduce her. In fact, he usually kept her at a distance.

It was her behavior that was questionable. For even though she knew she was living with a vampire who desired her, she didn't want to leave.

Chapter Twelve

I remain a prisoner of the man with the golden mask. I hang my head in false surrender whenever he visits me, but deep inside my dragon heart, I am filled with hope. Even though the sacred mountain of Beyul-La has been destroyed, the warrior women still live. Norjee lives. The other dragons live. I am not alone.

And soon I will be free.

A few days have passed since I talked to Queen Nima's owl. By now, I believe the owl will have found the village of were-tigers. Norjee and Winifred will be able to communicate with him. They will seek to discover my location. They will not give up on me. Although they are mortal, Winifred is like a sister to me. Norjee is my brother.

I have tried calling the local birds, but I am not certain that I am reaching them from this underground prison. I need to be aboveground, where they can see me and know where I am. Only then can they spread the word of my location.

Today I have removed the papers taped to my wall. The same word is written on all of them. *Home.*

Beyul-La is gone, but as long as my family lives, I have hope that someday I will have a home again. It is this hope that stops me from destroying the papers. Before, when I taped them on the wall, I was trying to show Master Han what was in my heart. Now I wish to conceal my true feelings.

I stack the papers neatly under my cot, hidden behind some books where Master Han will not see them. If he sees my hope, he will keep me hidden forever.

I thumb through one of the books Master Han has given me to help me learn how to write. Since my throat cannot produce words, Han wants me to write well in Chinese so we can communicate. I look for words that will please him, and I find two.

Surrender. Submission.

Fire simmers in my chest. I can never surrender. Nor will I submit. My hand refuses to write those words.

I find another one that I can write and that will meet Han's approval. With my black pen, I copy it carefully. I use a piece of the tape Wu Shen gave me to stick it on my wall.

Gratitude.

The man with the golden mask will think I am grateful for the bed and food I have received. He might even think I am grateful that he pretends to care for me, that he pretends to be my father.

I am grateful for his lies so I know not to trust him.

I take a deep breath as the lock turns in the door. I have already received my evening meal, so I know it is time for Master Han to make his nightly visit.

The door creaks open, and he enters. The candlelight from my writing desk makes his golden mask gleam. I bow my head in greeting.

He repeats what he says every night. "How are you today, son? Did you sleep well? Do you have enough to eat?"

I nod and take my empty food tray to the guard at the door. I can see the stairs at the end of the hallway. It is tempting to run, but there are more soldiers upstairs. I would not get far. If only my wings would sprout. If I could make it aboveground, I could fly away.

Is that why Master Han keeps me below ground?

"You've learned a new word." He steps closer to the wall and nods with approval. "*Gratitude*."

Angry fire simmers in my belly. Should I be grateful I am a prisoner? I could blast fire at Han and all his soldiers. I could make them writhe in agony while I escape.

My skin grows hot with disgust. I have killed before. Sometimes I wake, drenched with sweat, for the memory seeps into my dreams and burns the brand of murderer onto my soul. I breathed fire on Lord Liao and his soldiers when they sought to bring the demon, Darafer, back from hell.

My actions solved nothing. Darafer still came.

He was the one who captured me and brought me to Han. He boasts that I will kill again but from now on, he and Han will choose my victims. I will be trained to submit, Darafer tells me. It is only a matter of time, and he has time at his command.

I turn away from the door and the guards outside. I will not kill in order to escape. I will never kill again. For if I did, I would belong here with Han and Darafer. I would be like them. I would have surrendered to evil.

I can never surrender. Nor will I submit.

"I have good news for you." Han walks up to me and pats me on the back. "It's been quiet the last few nights, so I thought we'd resume your archery lessons."

Then we would go aboveground? I nod and give Master Han a smile.

My spirits rise as he leads me up the stairs. We cross the main guardroom. The soldiers jump to attention and bow low as Master Han passes by. There are only a few officers who dare to look upon his golden mask.

Four guards rush up the last staircase and crank open the heavily sealed door. They dash outside, then one returns to report that all is clear.

Han selects a longbow and quiver of arrows, then hands them to a soldier. We ascend the stairs and emerge into a small cave. Five guards wait at the cave entrance, and five more surround us as we leave the cave.

I breathe deep of the fresh night air. The moon above is half full. When it becomes full, will I shift for the first time? Will my wings burst from my back?

I look around, my eyes quickly adjusting to the dark. We are in a semiarid region of hills and giant boulders. At the base of the hill, a dirt road extends into a dark horizon. A target has been set up across the road.

As we descend the hill, the guards spread out, leaving Han and me centered a short distance from the target.

"Do you remember the proper stance?" Han hands me the bow.

I turn my left shoulder to the target and plant my feet apart. I extend my left arm straight, my hand fisted around the bow.

"Very good." Han hands me an arrow.

For a second, I consider slamming the arrow point into Han's chest. But he is wearing the thick black armor over his chest. And I will not kill again.

I notch the arrow into the bowstring, pull back, and take aim. The arrow flies and hits the edge of the target.

"Not bad, son!" Han pats me on the back. "You'll get better with practice." He hands me another arrow.

"Master." A soldier runs toward us and bows. "A truck is coming."

The guards gather around us, their swords ready. Dust swirls on the dirt road as the truck zooms toward us. It comes to a halt and two men emerge—the driver and Wu Shen.

Han waves his hand to disperse the crowd of soldiers around us. They step back as Wu Shen dashes toward us.

"Report," Han says.

Wu Shen bows quickly, then says, "I bring bad news. Camp number three failed to report in this morning. I took a unit of soldiers there, and it was empty."

Han stiffens. "They deserted? I will hunt them down and kill them!"

Wu Shen shakes his head. "There were signs of a battle. Two dead soldiers and bloodstains on the ground. I believe the camp was attacked by the same group of vampires and shifters that have been plaguing us for months. Most probably, the survivors were taken prisoner."

Han draws in a hissing breath and clenches his fists. "Those evil bastards! How dare they attack me!"

I step back. I have seen Master Han kill in a fit of anger. I hope he will not kill Wu Shen. The officer always looks kindly at me and asks if there is anything I need. His eyes have been sad lately. I heard the guards outside my door talk about him. He had two sons who served Master Han, and they both died at Beyul-La.

"I also received word that another camp was attacked last night," Wu Shen continues. "There was a skirmish outside the barricade, and two soldiers were killed."

"Dammit!" Han spins around, shaking his fists in the air. "Why do they keep persecuting me?"

I step back again. Everyone is watching Han with worried faces, afraid of what he will do. No one will notice if I call the birds.

I send out a distress signal far and wide. A

hawk is first to respond. Then a pair of eagles. A host of smaller birds arrives and circles far overhead.

I am dragon, I tell them. *I am Xiao Fang. Remember my name and location. Spread the news as far as you can fly. The warrior women of Beyul-La are looking for me. They will understand you.*

I hear the birds chirping overhead. They are discussing which ones will go in different directions.

"We should kill those bastards!" Han continues to rant. "Where are they hiding?"

"Your vampire enemies have teamed up with the were-tigers," a soldier says quietly.

"Then find the were-tiger village," Han orders. "Assemble the troops. I will give you three days to prepare. We will attack on the fourth night and destroy their village!"

Wu Shen inhales sharply. "The were-tiger women and children live there."

"Good!" Han yells. "That will teach them to mess with me!"

My skin crawls with fear. I do not want other shifters killed. And what if the warrior women are living in the were-tiger village? What if Norjee is there? I look up at the sky. *Find the were-tiger village! Warn them they are in danger!*

The birds swirl in a giant circle overhead, chirping and squawking.

Then they stop. No movement. No sound.

I blink. How can they stop in midflight? I look frantically about. Han is frozen, his fists lifted in the air. Wu Shen has stopped talking, his mouth open in the middle of a word. All the soldiers are motionless, frozen in time.

I cringe inside. I know only one entity who can control time. I want to run, but my feet will not budge. Something is stopping me. My hands move. They clench into fists. Unlike the others, I am aware, so I know what is coming.

I see him in the distance, strolling casually toward us. He is dressed in his usual fashion, all in black with a long black coat. His eyes gleam in an inhuman way, the green glowing in the dark.

As much as I loathe Master Han, I know he is weak. He takes delight in causing fear and pain, for it makes him feel less weak. To him, being a villain is like a game, and his victims are little toys. He plays at being evil.

Darafer embodies evil.

The demon approaches me, his mouth curling up on one side with a twisted smile. "What are you doing, dragon boy?"

I lower my head.

"Did you think I wouldn't notice?" He steps closer. "You think I can't hear you talking to your friends?"

I lift my head as fear swells inside me.

Darafer points to the sky. "You can blame yourself for this." With a wave of his hand, every bird overhead plummets from the sky. One thud after another, the birds hit the ground till the earth is covered with death.

A wheezing sound of pain wrenches from my throat. How many birds have died because I spoke to them?

Darafer seizes my shirt and glares down at me. "Maybe you can fool Han, but remember this, dragon boy. You will never fool me." He releases me with a push.

My feet are still stuck, so I fall back on my rear. I am surrounded by dead birds.

How will I contact the owl again? How can I let the warrior women and Norjee know where I am?

Darafer waves his hand, and everyone jumps back to life as if time had never stopped.

Wu Shen resumes his talking but pauses after a few words and looks around. His eyes widen at the sight of Darafer.

"What's with all the dead birds all of a sudden?" a soldier asks, nudging one with his boot.

Han stiffens, turning toward Darafer. "Do you realize two of our camps were attacked last night?"

The demon shrugs. "You're in charge of training the soldiers. I just make them."

"Then make me some more!" Han yells. "My army used to be a thousand strong, and now it's down to three hundred!"

The demon zooms toward Han and grasps him by the throat. Han's guards move toward him, but with a flick of his wrist, Darafer sends them all flying back a hundred feet.

"You left me in hell for seven months," Darafer growls. "You thought you could take over the world without me, didn't you? You pathetic worm. While I was gone, you lost over half of your army." He pushes Han back.

Han stumbles, then makes a quick bow. "As

your humble servant, I beg your assistance in making more supersoldiers."

"That's more like it." Darafer crosses his arms and gives Han a disdainful look. "Remember who's the boss around here, and we'll get along fine."

"Yes, my lord." Han bows again.

"I have grown more demon herb," Darafer says. "And I am producing the potion. It should be ready by tomorrow night. Round up more volunteers, and I'll mutate them."

"Thank you, my lord." Han bows. "I will do as you say."

"See that you do. And take the dragon boy below ground before he talks to more birds." Darafer turns away from Han and smiles at me. "You will submit to me, too, Xiao Fang. It's only a matter of time."

My heart sinks with despair. If I cannot reach my friends, how will they rescue me? If I cannot warn the were-tigers of an impending attack, will they and my friends die?

"I'm watching you," Darafer says, then vanishes.

Fire burns in my belly, and hot tears sting my eyes. For even if I manage to get away from Master Han, how can I hope to escape a demon?

Even as fear threatens to overwhelm me, I cling to a truth that must ever remain constant.

I am dragon. I can never surrender. Nor will I submit.

Chapter Thirteen

When Jia awoke, the cave was dark, except for an oil lamp lit in the kitchen. She sat up, alarmed that she had slept so late. Russell was sitting at the table, quietly cleaning his guns.

She scrambled out of bed. "You should have woken me up."

"You looked tired. And you had a rough time last night." He concentrated on his work, barely glancing her way. "An hour delay isn't the end of the world."

"But we don't have any time to waste." She reported what Rajiv had told her about Angus and his employees attacking a camp every night until they lured Han out of hiding. "We need to find Han before they do."

"Agreed." Russell stood. "I'll go topside for a few minutes so you can dress."

She quickly relieved herself in the stream, then dressed and braided her hair.

Russell teleported back in and reassembled his

handguns at vampire speed while she ate a breakfast bar. Then he put on his coat and armed himself.

She sipped some water, then cleared her throat. "Do you have my knives from last night?"

"Yes." He retrieved them from his coat pocket and set them on the table in front of her. "Are you sure you want to do this? I can always zip through the camps alone if you need a night off."

She recalled his reference to the rough time she'd had last night. Was that why he'd let her sleep late? When she thought about it, she had acted terribly shaken afterward.

"I'm all right." She noticed he'd cleaned the knives for her. "I knew from the start that this could be dangerous. I'm still as committed as ever." She glanced up and met his gaze. "We're partners."

His eyes searched hers.

What would it take to turn those eyes red and glowing? She shoved the thought away and quickly sheathed the knives. "We should get to work."

"Good." He levitated to get his crossbow and quiver.

"Why do you use arrows when you have so many guns?" she asked.

"They're quiet, so they don't announce my presence."

"Do you ever use your cowboy pistols?"

"No, they're antiques." He swung the crossbow and quiver over his shoulder. "I would never take them into battle."

"Then why do you have them? It's not like you to keep anything unpractical around here."

With an annoyed look, he extended a hand to her. "I don't explain myself. Let's go."

With a sigh, she walked up to him and placed her hands on his shoulders. "I've known you five days now, but I hardly know you at all."

He took hold of her waist. "That knowledge is not necessary for the completion of our mission."

She snorted. "You know all about me. You know how my family died. You know what kind of life I live. You even know about my fear of heights."

"I know you're engaged."

She swallowed hard. "I never officially agreed."

His hands tightened on her waist. "Your cousin expects you to go through with it."

She frowned. "We're not talking about me. It's you I don't know anything about."

"I don't explain myself."

She swatted his shoulder. "You're the most stubborn, exasperating man!"

His mouth curled up. "And that's all you need to know about me." He teleported, taking her with him.

After a few minutes of studying the campsite, he declared nothing was going on.

"I can't smell anything." She gave him a wry look. "Other than you."

"Is it that bad? I shower every night."

She shrugged. "It's not bad at all."

He gave her a dubious look. "I don't smell like a sack of blood?"

"You do a bit, but you also smell like the cave and your soap." *And a gorgeous hunk of man.* "So why do you want to kill Han?"

He scoffed. "You thought you could just sneak that in?"

"It was worth a try."

"I have my reasons."

"Which are?"

"I don't explain myself."

She rolled her eyes.

He grinned and took her to the next campsite. Same story there. Nothing happening.

"So why do you have the cowboy pistols?" she asked.

He gave her a bland look. "Are you going to nag me all night?"

She shrugged. "Maybe." What she really wanted to ask was, why did his eyes turn red? Did he truly desire her as a woman? But since she didn't dare ask, she was pestering him about everything else. "Are you really a cowboy? Do you know John Wayne?"

"He's dead." Russell made a face. "But then, so am I."

"You're not dead."

"Undead," he muttered. "Whatever the hell that means. I'm dead half the time."

"You mean alive half the time."

His mouth twitched. "If you say so, Pollyanna."

"So why do you have the cowboy pistols?"

With a frustrated groan, he pulled her into his arms. "How do I shut you up?"

Kiss me. "Talk to me."

"I don't explai—" He stopped when she placed a finger on his lips. His eyes darkened, and he grabbed her wrist to move her hand. "You should stay away from my mouth. I have fangs, you know."

"I like to live dangerously."

His eyes turned red. He released her abruptly and walked away.

She'd done it! Just by touching his mouth? Her skin tingled at the thought that she could so easily affect him. Who was she kidding? He affected her, too. Her heart was pounding, and there was a strange, fluttery feeling in her stomach.

But was it fair to torment him this way? "I'm sorry."

He kept his back to her. "The pistols belonged to my great-grandfather, Johann Hankelburg. They're Colt Single Action Army revolvers, issued to him in 1873. After his service, he settled in Colorado and started a small ranch. The Big H, he called it, for he had dreams of making it big. Over the years, the ranch grew."

"So you come from a long line of cowboys," Jia said.

Russell nodded. "It became a tradition for the eldest son to serve in the military. My grandfather fought in World War I; my father in World War II. The pistols were handed down to each of them. Before I left for my first tour of duty in Vietnam, my father took me to my great-grandfather's grave, and we buried the pistols there by the headstone. He told me I had to survive, no matter what, so I could come back to get them."

"And you did," Jia said softly.

Russell sighed. "I came back undead."

"So you've been a vampire since the Vietnam War?" That had to be about forty years, Jia thought.

When Russell didn't answer, she tried another question. "Why did your father bury the pistols? He could have just waited for you to come back."

"He had lung cancer. He wasn't sure how long he'd be around, and he was worried . . ." Keeping his back to her, Russell shifted his weight and raked a hand through his hair. "My younger brother, Markos, was having some trouble. Drugs. My dad was afraid he'd take the pistols and sell them. They're worth a lot of money."

Jia stepped closer. "And your father is gone now? What about your mother?"

Russell turned toward her, his eyes no longer red. "All I have left are the damned pistols." He shrugged like he didn't care, but the tears in his eyes made her heart ache.

Did he have no family at all? "Is your brother gone, too?"

"Markos actually straightened out. He joined the Marines a few years after I did. Even did a tour in Vietnam." Russell took a deep breath. "He was always trying to follow in my footsteps. I guess he did. He's listed as MIA, just like I am."

"I'm sorry." So Russell was all alone. She was tempted to tell him he wasn't alone, that she would be with him, but how could she make such a promise?

Russell shrugged. "So are you going to stop nagging me now?"

She smiled. "I'll give you a short reprieve."

"That's decent of you." He held out a hand. "Let's get going."

She walked up to him. "I'm sorry if I made you sad."

"You didn't. I plan. I strategize. I'm undead. I don't do feelings."

"Of course you do."

"Not if I can help it. They're a distraction. They make you weak."

She huffed. "I disagree!"

"Imagine that," he muttered dryly, taking hold of her waist.

"Feelings make you strong." She grabbed hold of his shoulders. "I would have never managed what I've done if it hadn't been for the way I feel about my parents and brother."

"Those feelings have led you into danger. They could get you killed."

"And you're not trying to kill Han because of feelings?" She thumped Russell on the chest. "You don't keep those pistols because of feelings?"

His hands tightened on her, but he remained silent.

"You have your pistols. I have my mother's bracelets. We're holding on to the only things left from our families." Her eyes burned with tears. "Because we loved them."

He closed his eyes briefly and drew in a long, shuddering breath. "Let's go."

"That's all you have to say?"

"I don't explain myself." He teleported, taking her with him.

"Stay down." Russell crouched behind a large boulder with Jia.

She looked around. "I don't recall coming to this campsite before."

"We haven't. There's no good cover here for spying." He'd brought her to the northernmost camp, close to the Tibetan border. There were no trees to hide behind, just dry, barren ground with a few scattered rocks and boulders.

Since the land was unsuitable for farming, the population was sparse. With no people to control, Han rarely visited this outpost. But it had occurred to Russell that it also made a good area for him to hide in.

Peering around the boulder, Russell spotted a truck emerging from the wide gate. Another truck followed. And another.

Were they deserting the campsite? "I need a closer look." He glanced at Jia. "Will you be all right here?"

She nodded. "Be careful."

The concern in her eyes was hard to bear. She was killing him with all her talk about feelings. What did she expect from him? She was engaged. As soon as their mission was done, she'd marry her prince and go far away. He'd probably never see her again.

And even if he could win her heart, what did he have to offer her? A cave he didn't own? The stuff inside the cave wasn't his. He'd borrowed or stolen most of it. The ranch in Colorado was gone, sold years ago while he'd been stuck in a coma in a cave in Thailand. He had no home to take her to. No family. He was a penniless vampire vagabond.

He had to be honorable to Jia. Honor was about the only thing he had left.

"I'll be right back." He teleported into a dark, shadowy spot outside the barricade, then levitated enough to peer over the top.

The soldiers were packing up and leaving. Russell spotted the officer Wu Shen supervising. Wu Shen had helped them before. When Darafer had taken Dougal's wife prisoner, the officer had sneaked into Tiger Town to let them know where she was. It had been his way to repay them for rescuing some of his family members who had been forced to work at Darafer's demon herb farm. Darafer had turned them into living zombies.

Russell teleported into the camp, hiding in the shadow between two buildings. Wu Shen stepped back as another transport truck drove through the gates.

"Captain, sir?" Russell called out softly in Chinese.

Wu Shen turned, then his eyes narrowed. He barked out more orders to a nearby group of soldiers, and as they hurried away, he strode toward the shadow where Russell was hiding.

"What are you doing here?" Wu Shen whispered.

"I was going to ask you the same thing," Russell said.

Wu Shen snorted. "You should leave before I order my men to capture you."

"I would just teleport away. What's going on?"

Wu Shen's eyes flashed with anger. "Why

should I tell you anything? You and your friends killed my sons at Beyul-La."

Russell stiffened. "You had sons there? In the cave?"

"Yes. The cave you blew up."

Russell winced. "It's true we trapped them in there. But the plan was to knock them out, then use the cave as a clinic to change them back to normal. We intended to save them."

Wu Shen grew pale. "Why didn't you?"

"The trapped soldiers panicked before we could knock them out. They tried to blast their way out with grenades and brought the mountain down on themselves."

A pained look crossed Wu Shen's face. "This is true?"

"Yes. Whenever possible, Angus and his guys take your soldiers prisoner. They have two clinics where they're able to undo the mutations and turn the soldiers back to normal. The goal has always been to kill Han, not the mortals who were tricked into serving him."

Wu Shen sighed. "I believe you. I've known for some time that you've been taking soldiers prisoner. There are signs of a struggle, but never any bodies."

"I'm sorry about your sons."

Wu Shen nodded. "My boys were lured in with the promise of becoming superhuman. They believed Han, believed that he could take over all of China—even the world—and they would live like kings." He snorted. "I never trusted Han, but

I resigned my position with the Chinese army so I could become an officer here and watch over my boys."

"I'm sorry." Russell winced inwardly, recalling how many of Han's soldiers he'd killed with the attitude that they'd asked for it. Over the last few days, he'd seen Jia's reaction to killing, and it had opened his eyes to how cold-blooded he'd become.

Wu Shen turned away, his shoulders slumped.

"Can you tell me where Han is hiding?"

He shook his head.

"Then tell me where they're keeping the dragon boy prisoner."

With a frown, Wu Shen turned back to Russell. "I wish I could help you, but the boy is in the same place as Han."

"Is he all right?"

"He's doing well, but he's terrified." Wu Shen grimaced. "Darafer would terrify anyone."

"You know you're working for some cruel bastards."

"If that's all you came to say—"

"We need your help."

"If I'm caught, I'll be killed. If I try to leave, I'll be killed. I'm as trapped as my boys were in that cave."

"If we can kill Han, the soldiers will be free. No more will have to die."

Wu Shen nodded slowly. "My boys sold their souls to Darafer, so now they're in hell. I might as well join them there."

"What can you tell me?"

"I received orders from Han earlier this evening. Soldiers from each camp are to move southeast, where the army will assemble. New recruits will be mutated tomorrow to increase the army's size. I've been given three nights, starting tonight, to prepare the army and move them into place. On the fourth night, Han will teleport there to lead the attack."

"Where is the attack?" Russell asked.

"The main village of were-tigers." When Russell drew in a sharp breath, Wu Shen nodded. "I suggest you evacuate the women and children. And prepare for battle."

Chapter Fourteen

When Russell arrived with Jia, the courtyard of Tiger Town was bustling with activity. Angus and about thirty of his employees were there. Most of the were-tiger villagers were lurking about, curiously watching the proceedings. They greeted Jia's sudden appearance with cheers and waves.

Russell gave her a wry look. "They're glad to have their princess back."

Rajiv ran up to them and gave Jia a hug. "Thank God you're back." He nodded at Russell. "You did the right thing."

"We have bad news." Russell waved Angus and his men over and switched to English. "I just talked to Wu Shen. Han's army is preparing to march on Tiger Town."

"What?" Rajiv turned to Jia and asked in Chinese, "Han is coming here?"

"Yes." She nodded. "We need to evacuate the women and children."

A series of gasps echoed around them, then a

flurry of whispering as the news spread among the villagers.

"This is rotten timing," Rajiv muttered. "Your fiancé is supposed to arrive in a little over a week."

Jia winced. "Can we postpone his visit?"

Rajiv sighed as he looked around Tiger Town. "We'll wait to see how the battle goes."

"How long before Han arrives?" Angus asked in English.

"He plans to lead the attack in four nights," Russell replied. "This isn't like Beyul-La, in the middle of the Himalayas. There are roads here, and his army has transport trucks, so they'll be moving faster."

Angus nodded. "I'll call in reinforcements. About a hundred of the soldiers we saved over the last year have promised to help." He turned to J.L. and Dougal. "Can ye contact them?"

Dougal nodded. "My wife kept a record of all their names and villages."

"If we divide the villages up, we can reach most of the soldiers tonight," J.L. said, and the two Vamps dashed to the clinic.

"We have three nights to get prepared," Russell said. "Wu Shen said they would be mutating new recruits tomorrow."

"Any idea how many?" When Russell shook his head, Angus continued, "Over the last six months, we've taken eighty soldiers prisoner. Thirty more last night. We figure Han has close to three hundred."

Russell frowned. Even with the hundred rescued soldiers, Angus could pull together a force of less than two hundred. "You should continue attacking Han's camps for the next three nights. We need to deplete his army as much as possible."

"Agreed," Angus said. "We'll start after we evacuate the women and children."

Something nagged at the back of Russell's mind. He was forgetting something. Something Wu Shen had said.

Angus turned to Rajiv. "How quickly can ye coordinate the evacuation? I'll lend you as many Vamps as I can for teleporting."

"I'll take care of it." Rajiv bounded halfway up the stairs in front of the palace and called in Chinese for the villagers' attention. They gathered around the base of the stairs, complaining.

"We don't want to leave!" an elderly man shouted.

Rajiv lifted his hands, but the grumbling increased.

"You can't make us leave our homes!"

Jia rushed up the stairs to be by her cousin's side. When Russell followed her, he was jostled by angry were-tigers.

"You all heard the news," Rajiv announced. "Han's army is coming here."

"It's those vampires' fault," an old woman yelled, glaring at Russell. "They came here, and now we're in trouble."

Another woman pointed at Russell. "Why was this vampire with our princess? I thought she was with Your Eminence's brother in Thailand."

Rajiv exchanged a worried look with Jia.

"She was!" Russell replied. "But when I learned

that Tiger Town was in danger, I picked her up on the way here. I knew she would want to be with you."

Jia slanted him a grateful look before addressing the crowd. "I will do everything I can to help."

"Then send the vampires away!" the old woman shouted. "If they leave, Master Han will leave us alone."

"That's not true," Rajiv said. "Han and his vampire lords have plagued us for many years, long before we met the good Vamps."

"There's no such thing as a good Vamp!" An elderly man shook his fist.

"My grandfather, the Grand Tiger, lost three of his sons to Han and his evil vampire lords." Rajiv motioned to his cousin beside him. "Lady Jia and I both lost our parents to vampires. How many of you have suffered and lost loved ones because of Master Han?"

The were-tigers grumbled.

"Since we met the good Vamps, all three of Han's evil vampire lords have been vanquished," Rajiv continued. "Russell here killed Lord Ming. With help from Jin Long, Jia and I were able to kill Lord Qing. The captive dragon shifter killed Lord Liao. Han is the only one left. We are so close to being free from them forever! Bear with us just a little longer."

"But we have to leave our homes," a woman whined.

"Yes," Rajiv told her. "It is the best way to keep you and your children safe."

"It shouldn't be more than a week," Jia added.

"Most of you have relatives in the other colonies. Just spend a few days with them until it's safe to come back. Think of it as a small vacation."

"That's easy for you to say," another woman muttered. "You haven't met my mother-in-law."

Everyone chuckled.

Rajiv smiled. "You have my word. Han will soon be dead, and the vampire menace that has plagued our people for forty years will be over!"

The villagers cheered.

"All men with fighting experience should remain to defend our town," Rajiv told them. "The rest of you, pack only what you need for a few days, then come to the palace. Lady Jia and I will help you get sorted into groups, according to which colony you wish to go to. Then the good Vamps will take you there."

The villagers rushed off to their homes to pack.

The warrior women, Neona and Winifred, rushed up the stairs. "Can we help?"

"Yes, thank you." Jia took the two women into the palace.

"You did well," Russell told Rajiv.

He snorted. "I never expected to become the Grand Tiger." With a sigh, he headed up the stairs. "I hope I don't let them down."

"You won't." Russell followed him. "I never realized until now how much some of the were-tigers dislike vampires."

"Yeah, we had a bad history with them before you guys came along." Rajiv gave him an embarrassed look. "I apologize for accusing you of kid-napping Jia. I know she probably begged you to take her. She's lived for revenge for so long. I kept procrastinating, hoping she would get over it."

Russell nodded. "She's very . . . determined."

Rajiv arched a brow. "You mean stubborn? Anyway, I appreciate you keeping her safe. Rinzen and Tenzen are still in the forest hunting for you. If I call them, will you teleport them back? They're excellent warriors, so I need them here."

"I can do that."

"Thank you." Rajiv glanced at the open palace door and lowered his voice to a whisper. "Jia might insist on being here for the battle, but I don't want her in danger. Do you have a safe place you can take her?"

Russell nodded. "I can—"

A bright flash in the sky interrupted them.

"What the—" Russell lifted a hand to shade his eyes from the glare.

A glowing ball of light was falling from the sky and seemed headed straight for the courtyard. The people there dashed to the edge, watching and shouting with great excitement.

"Jia!" Rajiv yelled. "Come see this!"

Jia, Neona, and Winifred emerged from the palace and gaped at the sky.

"I've seen this before." With a grin, Jia clasped her hands together. "When Dou Gal's wife was captured. They helped us rescue her."

"They?" Russell asked.

Rajiv nodded, smiling. "They can help us."

"Who are they?" Neona and Winifred both asked.

As Russell watched, the bright light suddenly

split into seven balls of fire that shot down to the courtyard, then hovered just inches above the pavement. Each fireball assumed the shape of a man, holding a sword extended to the sky. Six of the fiery men were in a line, while one stood in front. With a whoosh, the fires extinguished, receding up the men's bodies till only their swords were left ablaze.

Russell shook his head, hardly believing his eyes. In the courtyard below, there was hushed talk about angels. Some of the villagers fell to their knees and bowed.

The men in question wore pants and sleeveless tunics of royal blue. Their upper arms and wrists were banded in cuffs of gold. Their chests were covered with golden armor, and their heads were crowned with slender gold circlets.

What the hell? Russell raked a hand through his hair. "Who are these guys? Do they always make such a grand entrance?"

Jia nodded. "When they want your attention, they do."

In unison, the seven men turned their swords of fire, pointing them down to the ground. They lowered their arms, and when the tips of the blades hit the pavement, the fires extinguished.

"I must greet them." Rajiv ran down the stairs.

Russell and Jia followed him, then Angus joined them.

The six men in line sheathed their swords while the man in front spoke. "Greetings, dear souls. I am Briathos, commander of the Epsilons, fifth unit of God Warriors."

"I bid you welcome." Rajiv bowed.

"We're glad to see you again," Angus added. "Ye've been a great help to us in the past."

"What exactly did they do?" Russell whispered to Jia.

"They sent Darafer back to hell," she whispered back.

Russell snorted. "Too bad they didn't keep him there."

Briathos turned his head toward Russell and gave him a curious look.

Russell raised a hand in greeting. "Hey, guys. I'm guessing you know where Han is. Tell me, and I'll get rid of him. Then you can banish Darafer again, and we'll be done with all the bad guys within an hour. Tiger Town will be saved, and you can go back to heaven to . . . play your harps. Everybody will be happy. What do you say?"

Briathos continued to study him, while the Epsilons behind him exchanged looks.

"Russell," Rajiv whispered. "You don't talk to angels like that."

Russell scoffed. "I'm still trying to believe they're real." The more he looked at the so-called angels, the more detailed they appeared, but there was something off about them. They seemed to shimmer in and out of focus, as if they weren't quite there.

Briathos turned to Angus. "Approximately two hours ago, there was a rupture in your Earth time. As always, these phenomena must be investigated. We have come to report our findings. The demon Darafer stopped time and killed a great number of birds in order to frighten the dragon shifter, Xiao Fang. We will continue to monitor Darafer's actions. That is all." He bowed his head. "We bid you good evening."

"What?" Russell stepped forward. "That's it? Aren't you going to do something?"

Briathos arched a brow.

"Why are you carrying around those awesome weapons if you're not going to use them?"

Briathos sighed. "There is always one like this. You remind me of Dougal Kincaid."

"I'm Russell."

"Yes, I know. Allow me to explain—"

"You know me?"

"Yes. In His infinite wisdom, the Heavenly Father has bestowed the gift of free will upon His children. Because of that decree, we are not allowed to interfere in the course of human events—"

"Well, I can believe that!" Russell interrupted. "'Cause a lot of crap has happened to me over the years, and where the hell were you?"

Briathos frowned. "We cannot interfere unless someone's free will has been violated to the point they are forced into evil."

"My free will was violated when Han put me into a coma for thirty-nine years. My free will was violated when I became a vampire!"

"Yes," Briathos agreed. "But remember this, Russell Ryan Hankelburg. You did not become evil."

Russell gulped. This angel guy seemed for real. "What about Xiao Fang? He's being held prisoner. Isn't that a violation of his free will?"

"The boy remains strong," Briathos said. "He has not been forced into evil. We are watching the situation, and the second Darafer crosses the line—"

"Why do we have to wait?" Russell yelled. "Tell me where Han is, and I'll rescue the boy."

"All will be revealed in due course. Prepare yourself. Your time is near."

"I'm ready now! I've been ready to kill Han for two years! The bastard took everything from me!"

Briathos regarded him sadly. "You still have more to lose. But even more to gain."

"What does that mean?" Russell demanded, but Briathos and his band of angels vanished. More to lose? He glanced at Jia. God, no. He couldn't let anything happen to her.

She stepped closer to him, her face pale. "Han put you in a coma for thirty-nine years?"

He winced. In his anger, he'd said too much.

"Jia." Rajiv waved her over. "We must hurry with the evacuations."

She touched Russell's arm. "We'll talk later, okay?" She turned and accompanied her cousin up the stairs to the palace.

Russell watched her go, his gut twisting into knots.

"'Twill all work out," Angus assured him. "When Han comes with his army, ye'll have yer chance to avenge yerself. And when the God Warriors send Darafer to hell, there will be no one left here who will want to call him back. We will finally have peace."

"I hope so." Russell started up the stairs. There

was something still bugging him, something he'd missed. He replayed the conversation with Wu Shen in his mind. The officer had recited Han's orders quickly and precisely. What was there to be confused about?

With a jerk, Russell came to a halt. Wu Shen had received those orders tonight. He couldn't teleport, so he must have taken one of those trucks to see Han. When Russell had talked to Wu Shen, the sun had been set for about an hour and a half.

Russell charged up the stairs and into the palace. Rajiv and the women were taping up signs on the wooden pillars, a different sign for each of the were-tiger colonies. "Rajiv, do you have a map?"

"In my office." Rajiv pointed to a hallway to the right. "First door."

Russell ran into the office and spotted the big map on the wall with all of Han's campsites marked. He located the northernmost one where he'd been earlier that night.

Within driving distance, he thought. Han was hiding close to that camp. Probably within an eighty-mile radius.

"I have you now, you bastard."

Chapter Fifteen

For two months, I have believed that it is possible to escape Master Han. When the moon is full, perhaps this month or the next, I will shift into dragon form for the first time and gain my wings. Somehow, I will escape this underground prison, and as soon as I see the sky, I will fly away.

But last night, I saw Darafer make all the birds plummet to their deaths. What if he does the same to me? I know Master Han is dangerous and I should fear him. But I fear the demon even more.

When Lord Liao and his guards formed a circle to bring the demon back from hell, I shot fire at them to stop them. The flames burned the vampire lord and his guards, but they had no effect on Darafer at all. I have no defense against him.

In the morning, I hear the soldiers grumbling. They wait until Master Han is hidden away in his death-sleep before they dare to complain. They have orders to shovel all the dead birds into a pile so they can be burned.

I mourn for the birds and wonder if the eagles have left behind little ones. Are the eaglets in a nest, hungry and calling for parents who will never return?

My hope is waning. The only comfort I can find is the knowledge that the other dragons survived. They will live on. The remaining eggs will hatch. Queen Nima will raise them well. They will fly and breathe fire for five hundred years.

As for me, I hold on to the truths I repeat to myself every day. I am dragon. I can never surrender. Nor will I submit.

I used to think those truths would set me free. Now I fear they will cost me my life.

Breakfast and lunch trays are brought to me, but I do not eat. In desperation, I consider breathing fire upon the soldiers in order to escape. But I cannot bring myself to harm the soldiers, who have been good to me.

After lunch, half of the soldiers prepare to leave. I hear them grumbling about a long drive to Darafer's secret enclave, where he is growing the demon herb. They have to be there to guard Master Han during the ceremony. Tonight Darafer is changing more mortals into supersoldiers.

A spark of hope ignites inside me. Master Han and half of his soldiers will be gone tonight. Darafer will be occupied, too, at the ceremony. If I set this place on fire, the remaining soldiers will be busy putting out the flames, and I can make my escape.

I pace my room, waiting for sunset. Waiting for the man in the golden mask to leave. When my dinner tray arrives, I eat. I need my strength tonight.

Master Han knocks on my door and enters. "How are you today, son? Did you sleep well? Do you have enough to eat?"

I bow, hoping I will never hear those words again.

"Are you ready to go?"

I stiffen at his question. Does he know I plan to escape?

Master Han extends a hand toward me. "Come. I want you to attend the ceremony with me."

Panic flares inside me, a spark of fire simmering in my belly, and I step back.

Han keeps his arm stretched out. "You didn't think I would leave you here alone, did you? We're family now. We will go together."

I shake my head and retreat another step.

His extended hand curls into a fist. "Come here."

Hot tears burn my eyes. My feet refuse to move.

With a whoosh, Master Han swoops toward me and grasps me by the arms. "Don't think you can defy me. I've been good to you so far. That could change in a second."

The spark in my belly withers away, and I bow my head. I will not escape tonight.

"That's my boy." Han pats me on the shoulder.

Everything goes black as he teleports me away.

When we arrive, I look around. The moon is half full. The sky is clear. The land is green. A field stretches out before us, line after line of carefully tended green bushes. Workers move between the plant rows, their shoulders slumped, their eyes devoid of life. Like me, they are trapped by a power greater than them.

A thick forest surrounds the field. I am tempted to slip away into the trees, but Han does not release his grip on me until his guards encircle us and escort us to the end of the field. Wu Shen is waiting there with about thirty soldiers. They have brought the mortal volunteers who will be changed.

A stage has been erected at the end of the field. Wu Shen's soldiers position the mortals in a row facing the stage, then they form a line behind the mortals. They are armed with swords, and I fear they will strike any volunteer who changes his mind. Wu Shen orders the mortals to kneel.

Master Han leaves me with his guards as he inspects the mortals. "This is it?" he yells. "There are less than fifty. I need at least a hundred!"

Wu Shen bows. "My apologies, master. This was all we could gather on short notice."

Han marches down the row of kneeling mortals, eyeing them with disdain. "Some are too old. Or too sickly to be soldiers."

"That is why they volunteered," Wu Shen says as he follows Han. "They want the potion that will give them superstrength so they can be healthy again."

Han clenches his fists. "They should come for the honor of serving me!"

The mortals bow down, their foreheads touching the ground. I suspect they have been warned not to anger Master Han.

With a deafening crack of thunder and flash of lightning, Darafer suddenly appears on the stage. I have seen Darafer arrive quietly and stealthily, so I know his theatrics are designed to illicit fear. And they do.

The workers in the field run to hide in the forest. The mortal volunteers tremble with terror. Some sneak looks at the soldiers behind them. The soldiers grip the handles of their swords.

Wu Shen comes to stand beside me. He glances at Han's guards, who are still close by, then asks, "Is this your first time to see the ceremony?"

I nod.

On the stage, Darafer waves his hand, and with another crack of thunder and bright flash, a black cauldron appears beside him.

During the crack of thunder, Wu Shen leans close and whispers, "I will try to help you."

I look at him, surprised, but he is watching Darafer as if nothing happened. I follow his example and keep my face expressionless even though my heart is pounding.

Master Han climbs onto the stage and bows to Darafer. "Your servant, always."

The demon gives him a twisted smile. "Together we will rule the world." He turns to inspect the mortals. "Tonight, you will join us on our noble quest. No longer will you be mere mortals. Your strength, speed, and agility will be greater than you ever imagined. You will live longer and be superior in every way. While I will be a god among men and Master Han will be emperor, you will be kings. Are you willing?"

The mortals say yes. They are willing.

Darafer lifts his arm, and a golden chalice suddenly appears in his hand. He dips it into the cauldron. "By drinking my potion, you will be transformed. You will be so powerful that no mortal will be able to defeat you. In exchange for this gift, we require only two things. The first requirement: you will give your complete obedience to Master Han and myself. Are you willing?"

The mortals murmur yes.

"I should warn you that disobedience will be severely punished," Darafer says, and he turns his head toward Wu Shen. "Is that not true, Officer?"

Wu Shen stiffens. His face grows pale. "Yes, my lord."

"How is it that the Vamps and shifters know of our impending attack on the were-tiger village?" Darafer asks.

Wu Shen steps away from me. "They have been attacking our camps in order to lure Master Han out of hiding. If they are preparing for a retaliatory strike, it simply means they believe their strategy will work."

"Is that so?" Darafer's eyes take on a greenish glow, and I fear for Wu Shen.

I step toward him, but Wu Shen lifts a hand to stop me. With a sad look in his eyes, he shakes his head slightly.

"Did you think I wouldn't know?" Darafer shouts. "This is what happens to those who betray me!" He shoots an arc of lightning at Wu Shen, who is instantly engulfed in flames.

I stumble back. I close my eyes to block out the sight, but I can still hear Wu Shen's cry of agony. I can still smell the stench of burning flesh. My stomach roils, and I fall to my knees. I make wheezing sounds as I gasp for breath.

"That brings me to the second requirement," Darafer says calmly.

I open my eyes and see that the mortals are upset and mumbling among themselves. Wu Shen's body is no longer on fire, but it lays there black and lifeless.

"Silence!" Master Han shouts, and the mortals grow quiet. Their eyes are wide with fear.

Darafer lifts the chalice high. "Once you drink of my potion, you will become powerful. And your soul will belong to me. Are you willing?"

The mortals hesitate.

Behind them, the soldiers draw their swords.

"I am willing!" one cries and runs toward the stage. "I will serve you, my lord."

Others rise and edge toward the stage.

I cannot bear it. There will be more soldiers who will follow the evil commands of Han and Darafer. More men who will go to hell when they die, their souls forever bound to a demon. I look at Wu Shen's dead body, and rage ignites inside me. Fire burns in my belly and races up my chest to my throat.

No more! My thoughts scream in my head. Even if it costs my life, no more!

I spring to my feet and dash wildly toward the field of demon herb. Fire erupts from my throat, and soon the field is ablaze.

"No!" Darafer shouts, and with a wave of his arm, the fire dies out.

But it is too late. The bushes are black and dead like Wu Shen.

In an instant, Darafer is in front of me. His eyes are glowing, his face harsh. He strikes me so hard that I fly back and land on a burned bush.

"Don't kill him." Han zooms toward us and yanks me up by the arm. "We need him. If a village dares to defy us, he can burn it to the ground like he did this field. He'll be our weapon of terror."

They expect me to kill for them. I try to pull away, but Han slaps me, then grabs me in an iron grip.

"You will suffer for this," he growls and teleports me away.

Chapter Sixteen

"It looks deserted," Jia said as she peered around the boulder. Russell had brought her back to the camp where he'd talked to Wu Shen the night before. "You think Han is hiding around here somewhere?"

"I'm sure of it." Russell was crouched beside her. "I'll check the camp out. You stay here and do your sniffing, okay?"

She nodded, and he teleported into a dark shadow beside the camp's wooden barricade. He levitated to peer over the wall, then climbed over.

Jia closed her eyes a moment to concentrate on her sense of smell. No vampires or humans in the vicinity. Only the scent of Russell nearby. While she waited for him to return, her thoughts shifted to Tiger Town and the impending battle.

A great deal had been accomplished last night. All the women, children, and elderly had been evacuated. After the Vamps had finished teleporting the evacuees, they'd started bringing in

Han's cured ex-soldiers, who had offered to help. Over a hundred of them were now in Tiger Town. After being changed back to normal, they were no longer supersoldiers. They knew they were at a disadvantage fighting Han's army, but they were determined to rid their homeland of Han once and for all.

Meanwhile, the call had gone out to more Vamps and shifters around the world. They would be arriving tonight. Angus MacKay hoped to gather an army of two hundred.

Russell had remained in Tiger Town to help, even though Jia had known he was anxious to get back to tracking Han. As dawn had approached, Rajiv had convinced her to spend the day in Tiger Town, partly to help with all the work and partly to keep her reputation intact. Too many were-tigers were watching. Russell had understood and, after promising to return for her this evening, he'd teleported back to the bat cave for his death-sleep.

She'd missed him. And she'd been so relieved when he'd arrived at her house a few minutes after sunset. His excitement had been contagious. Tonight, he claimed, they would complete their mission. Han was hiding somewhere near this camp. An eighty-mile radius, Russell insisted. He and Jia had a chance to prevent the battle of Tiger Town from ever happening, for tonight they would find Han and kill him.

After teleporting her to the bat cave, Russell had quickly explained the plan to her. With gloves on his hands to keep from getting burned, he'd given her a thick silver chain. "When we find Han, loop this chain around him to keep him from teleporting away. Then I'll stake the bastard."

At first Jia had objected. For thirteen years, she'd envisioned herself as the one to plant the stake in Han. Why should Russell have the honor?

"My need is greater," he'd replied.

"Greater than losing my family?"

"I don't explain myself." When she'd raised a hand to swat him, he'd continued, "We'll be killing him together, so half the honor will go to you."

She made a noise of frustration now as she waited behind the boulder. Why did Russell want revenge so badly? Last night, in anger, he'd admitted that Han had put him in a coma for thirty-nine years. She suspected there was a lot more to the story than that.

Russell materialized beside her. "The camp is completely deserted."

"Didn't Wu Shen say something about a ceremony tonight to change more soldiers? What if Han is there?"

"I have no idea where the ceremony will take place. I do know Han's hideout is around here. Once we find it, we can wait till he returns."

Jia frowned. "It could be hours before he returns."

"It could be hours before we find his hideout." Russell patted her shoulder. "Don't worry. Once we find his hideout, we've got him. If he doesn't show up tonight, we'll kill him tomorrow night."

Jia nodded, her heart pounding. Thirteen years of planning and training, and it was finally happening. Not only would she have her revenge but killing Han now would also keep him from attacking Tiger Town. She could save all her friends and family there. But why was it so important to Russell?

"We'll teleport five miles out and do a loop around the camp. Ready?" He grabbed her shoulders.

"Wait. I—" She took a deep breath. "If I'm going to help you kill someone, I deserve to know why."

Russell gave her an impatient look. "You know why. He killed your family."

"Yes, but what did he do to you?"

"You're wasting our time."

"He put you in a coma for thirty-nine years. What else happened?"

Russell gritted his teeth. "I don't explain."

She swatted his shoulder just before he teleported her away. When they arrived, they looked around. Dirt, rocks, a few scraggly, parched trees.

"Can you smell anything?" he asked.

She couldn't but didn't want to tell him. "I'm going on strike until you talk to me."

He groaned. "We don't have time for this. We have a lot of territory to cover."

"Then you'd better start talking."

He scowled at her. "You're driving me crazy."

"Ha! You've been driving me crazy for a week!"

"You've known me for only a week."

"Exactly."

He crossed his arms, glaring at her.

She crossed her arms and glared back.

"I'll take you back to Tiger Town." He reached for her. "The partnership is over."

"No!" She jumped back. "You need me to find Han. Come on. Tell me what he did to you."

"Dammit, woman!" Russell reached for her again. "Why do you need to know?"

She moved out of reach. *I need to understand you.* She gave him an entreating look. "Please."

His arm dropped to his side, and he stared at her a few minutes before letting out a resigned groan. "You know what he did. He put me in a vampire coma for thirty-nine years."

"Why? Why did he leave you like that for so long?"

Russell snorted. "I've been wanting to ask him that since the minute I woke up." A pained look crossed his face. "While I lay there in a cave like a helpless lump of meat, everyone I cared about died. My parents died believing both their sons were dead."

Jia swallowed hard. "I'm sorry."

With a sigh, Russell turned away from her. "I was on leave in Phuket when I received the news that my brother was missing in action. I made plans to go to Saigon to see what I could find out, but something happened." He shook his head. "I don't remember. I just remember waking up in a cave in Thailand."

"You don't know how you got there?" Jia asked.

"No. But we know it was Han's cave. Inside, he'd put hundreds of men into vampire comas and encased them in clay. They were laid out in a huge cavern like a burial ground of terra-cotta warriors. I was the only one who survived. For some reason, Han had separated me from the others. I was in a small cave by myself."

Jia tilted her head, considering. "He took extra care with you. He must have thought you were special."

Russell turned back to her with an exasperated look. "If I was so bloody special, why did he leave me for so long? While I was there, my men in Vietnam were drawn into an ambush. Every one of them slaughtered! If I had been with them, I might have—"

"You can't blame yourself for that," she interrupted.

"I should have been with them!" he shouted. "And I should have gone home. I was gone so long, my wife—"

Jia gasped. "You're married?"

"I was. She had me declared dead." Russell waved a dismissive hand. "She waited seven years before remarrying. I don't blame her. I checked up on her when I finally made it back to the States. She has children and grandchildren. She's happy. She's better off thinking I'm dead."

Jia winced. "I see."

"But she had a daughter." Russell's eyes glimmered with tears. "Our daughter. I was scheduled to go home to meet her after she was born, but I never made it. She grew up without me and died of breast cancer at the age of forty." His hands clenched into fists. "I never got to meet her!"

Jia's chest constricted as she felt his pain, and she pressed a hand to her heart. "Oh, God."

"Now you know." He blinked away tears. "I lost my daughter. My parents. My brother. My men. My mortality. Even the fucking ranch is gone. I lost everything, thanks to Han."

"I'm sorry." With tears in her eyes, she ran up to Russell and placed her hands on his face. "He didn't take everything. You still have your honor and courage. You're still a good man."

He snorted. "Does a good man kill for revenge?"

"A good man seeks justice." She gave him a tremulous smile. "A good woman does, too."

A corner of his mouth curled up, and he cradled her face with his hands. "Jia, what are you doing to me?"

"I'm trying to be a good partner." She patted his shoulder. "We'd better get back to work."

He studied her quietly a moment, then kissed her brow. "You're the best partner a man could hope for."

As her heart swelled, he teleported her to the next spot.

Two hours later, Russell was finding it increasingly hard to focus on the mission. Each time he took Jia into his arms to teleport, he held her longer than necessary. Whenever she closed her eyes to concentrate on sniffing, he found himself watching her, memorizing every curve and line of her face. If they killed Han tonight, the partnership would be over. Tiger Town would be safe, and she would return home and prepare for her betrothed's arrival in a week.

Was this his destiny—to always lose anyone he cared about?

Frowning, she opened her eyes and pointed to the west. "There's something about three miles that way. It smells like burned feathers and death."

Dead birds? "Didn't the God Warrior say Darafer killed a bunch of birds to scare Xiao Fang?"

Jia nodded. "We must be close."

Russell teleported her west until he, too, could smell the stench of death. Using that as a beacon, he zeroed in on a pile of burned bird carcasses. They were stacked waist high.

"Oh, my gosh." Jia covered her nose and mouth. "There must be over a hundred of them."

"Can you smell Han?"

She shook her head. "It's hard to smell anything but death."

Russell looked around. The land was hillier, but still desolate. Large boulder formations. There was a dirt road leading east with tire tracks on it. Beyond the pile of birds, he spotted something big, covered with a camouflage tarp. He zoomed over and discovered a hidden army truck.

Han's hideout had to be close by. It was underground, but there had to be an entrance somewhere. He checked underneath the truck. Nothing but dirt.

He glanced back at Jia to make sure she was all right. She was waving at him.

He dashed over, and she pointed at footsteps leading uphill toward a boulder formation. He spotted what looked like a cave.

"Be ready." He drew his sword. "Stay behind me."

With a nod, she yanked a knife from her belt.

He approached the cave silently from the side, then paused, his back to the boulder by the entrance. A quick peek told him they'd found the right place. Inside the cave was a small structure made of rusted sheet metal. A camera was positioned over the door.

"We'll teleport just inside," Russell whispered. "Then they won't know we're coming."

She bit her lip. "What if Han isn't there? If he finds out we know about his hideout, he won't come back."

"We'll have to question the soldiers, then I can erase their memories." He gave her a wry look. "Try not to kill any of them."

She snorted.

"You could always slap them. You're good at that."

Her mouth twitched. "Thank you."

"For what?"

"Relieving some of my stress."

"Let's go." He sheathed his sword so he could hold her, then he focused on the metal door.

They materialized just on the other side at the top of a partially enclosed stair landing. He peered around the edge of the wall. Below them was a guardroom. One guard was seated at a desk, his arms folded on top, cushioning his head as he snored away. The other four guards were immersed in a card game, sitting on the floor around a low coffee table.

Russell drew a knife from his coat pocket, then teleported down to the card game. He slammed the knife hilt into one guard's head, knocking him unconscious, then yanked another guard up, his knife poised at the man's throat. "Don't move. Don't shout," he warned the guards.

Meanwhile, Jia ran down the stairs and pointed her knife at the remaining guards. The whole act had taken only seconds, and the guard at the desk continued to snore.

The guard with the knife at his throat was breathing heavily, but he remained silent.

One of the other guards raised his hands in surrender. "Are you here for the dragon boy?"

"Xiao Fang is here?" Jia asked. "Where?"

"Three flights down in the dungeon," the soldier replied. "Han locked the kid up in a cage."

Russell eyed the soldiers with suspicion. "Why are you being helpful?"

The soldiers exchanged weary looks, then the second one said, "Han slapped the kid around and said he'd starve him for a week. We'd rescue him ourselves if we could."

"Why haven't you?" Jia asked.

The first soldier sighed. "How can we betray Han? He'll kill us, and then our souls will go to hell."

"Yeah," the second soldier muttered. "If you piss Han off, he takes you into his private room and sucks you dry."

The first soldier nodded. "If he doesn't kill

us that way, then we'll end up dying for him in battle."

Russell glanced quickly around the room. There was only one door. "Where is Han?"

"He was hungry, so he teleported to a nearby village," the first soldier said. "He always kills anyone he feeds from because he has to remove the mask."

"Yeah," the second soldier agreed. "No one is allowed to see his face and live."

"What's wrong with his face?" Jia asked.

The soldiers shrugged.

Russell wondered briefly if Han had been scarred or mutilated before becoming a vampire. "We'll take the boy and wait for Han to return. I suggest you guys take the truck outside and leave."

The first soldier snorted. "Where can we go that Darafer can't find us? We're doomed."

"Go to the were-tiger village," Jia suggested. "There is a doctor there who can return you to normal. You'll no longer belong to Darafer."

"Really?" The second soldier exchanged a hopeful look with his comrades.

"We'll leave right away." The first soldier eased to his feet and handed Jia a ring of keys. "So you can unlock the boy's cell."

Russell released his grip on the soldier he'd been holding. The men grabbed the truck keys off the table and helped get the sleeping and unconscious guards up the stairs and out the door.

Jia gave Russell a worried look. "Should we trust them? What if this is a trap?"

"We'll find out soon enough." Russell drew his sword and eased open the other door. It led to a stair landing. No one in sight. He hurried down the stairs with Jia close behind.

"I can smell Han," she whispered. "I think he lives down here."

They moved quietly along a corridor lined with doors. At the end of the hallway, Jia paused in front of a heavy door. "This is Han's room. His scent is strong here."

Russell tried opening the door, but it was sealed shut. "He must teleport in and out."

She leaned close, sniffing. "He's not here now."

"Let's find the boy then." Russell headed down a narrow flight of stairs.

The third floor below ground was dimly lit with only one tube of fluorescent lighting, which tended to flicker. The air was thick and stale, the stone floor coated with dust. The area wasn't large. One wall was stone, with manacles fastened into it. Probably for chaining a prisoner to the wall for a good whipping. There were bloodstains on the wall and floor.

The opposite wall contained four small prison cells. They were dark, but Russell spotted something huddled against the back wall of the second cell.

"Xiao Fang?" He sheathed his sword, then put his hands on the bars. His skin sizzled, and he quickly let go. Silver. With a wince, he flexed his seared fingers. Han had put the boy in a silver cage to keep any Vamps from teleporting in or breaking through.

"Are you all right?" Jia asked.

"Yeah." He reached in his pocket for some heavy gloves. "Unlock the door."

Jia tried one key after another on the heavy padlock. "Xiao Fang, is that you? We've come to rescue you."

As Russell slipped on his gloves, he saw the huddled mass straighten. It was the boy, standing at the back of the cave. "It's all right," Russell reassured him. "We'll take you to Tiger Town. Neona is there. And Winifred. You can talk to her, right?"

The boy eased forward slowly. When he came into view, Russell winced at the bruises on the kid's face. There was a cut along one of his cheekbones and dried blood on his swollen lips. The poor kid was probably afraid to trust them.

Jia unlocked the door and swung it open. The boy took a hesitant step forward.

She smiled at him. "I'm a shifter, too. A weretiger. I teach martial arts, and one of my students really wanted to rescue you himself. His name is Norjee, and he calls you his brother."

A wheezing sound escaped from Xiao Fang. He ran straight to Jia and wrapped his arms around her. She held him tight and looked up at Russell with tears in her eyes.

Russell's heart expanded. He hadn't known he could still feel this much joy. He tousled the boy's hair. If only he'd rescued the boy a week ago when he'd had the chance. But he'd opted for revenge instead. He'd chosen hate over love. Never would he make that mistake again.

"How touching," a muffled voice announced from the top of the stairs.

Russell spun around as he drew his sword. "Stay behind me," he whispered to Jia and the boy.

Han stood at the top of the stairs, dressed in a red silk robe. The fluorescent light flickered off his golden mask and the golden sheath attached to his belt. "I've been waiting for you to find me, Russell."

"You . . . know me?" Russell frowned. There was something familiar about the way Han said his name. And the golden sheath was at least a foot long. That had to be one badass dagger.

Han chuckled. "Of course I know you. You bear my mark. I chose you."

"You left me to rot in a cave for thirty-nine years."

Han waved a dismissive hand. "You didn't rot. The other men did, but I was very careful with you." He descended the stairs slowly. "I checked on you every three months. About once a year, I would feed you a few drops of my blood to keep you healthy."

"Healthy? I was in a coma! For thirty-nine years."

Han shook his head. "An insignificant amount of time when you can live forever. But I was quite shocked and disheartened when I discovered you were missing. After all, you belong to me."

"Never," Russell growled, lifting his sword. "I'm killing you tonight."

Han shook his head. "There have been so many times when I could have killed you. Did you never wonder why I didn't?" He paused on the bottom step. "When we took you and your foolish friends captive, I made sure no harm came to you. Even when you killed Lord Ming, I made no move to stop you."

A sick feeling settled in Russell's gut, but he ignored it. Han was just playing some sort of mind game. "You're a bastard. You deserve to die."

"Why? Because I have the balls to take over the world? You will rule the world with me, Russell. As my underling, of course, but still, it is your destiny to be by my side."

The man was out of his mind. Russell flexed his gloved hand on the hilt of his sword. If he charged at Han, the bastard would teleport away. He needed to trap him somehow. He could loop the silver chain around Han, or . . . a better idea came to mind.

"Xiao Fang." Han motioned toward the jail cell. "Get back in your cage where you belong."

Jia held tight to the boy. "He will not."

Han walked toward them, his hand resting on the hilt of his weapon. "You're a gutsy woman, I'll give you that." He slid the dagger out with a soft, metallic scrape. "But I could teleport behind you in a second and slit your throat."

With tears in his eyes, Xiao Fang pulled away from Jia and eased back toward the prison cell.

"No," Jia whispered.

"You heard the master." Russell sheathed his sword, then grasped the bars of the prison door with his gloved hands, opening it for the boy. "In you go."

"What?" Jia gave him an incredulous look.

Xiao Fang backed away, his battered face crumbling with despair.

Han chuckled. "Excellent."

With a mighty heave, Russell wrenched the

prison door loose and zoomed toward Han, slamming the silver bars into him and pinning him against the wall.

Han cried out, dropping his dagger. His silk robe smoldered where the bars touched him. Smoke curled around the bars as the silk burned away and the silver sizzled against Han's skin.

"You're going to die," Russell growled, pressing the prison door harder into Han. "You destroyed my life. I lost everyone I loved because of you."

"Not everyone," Han hissed. "Stop it, Russell."

The way the bastard kept saying his name was infuriating. "Stop acting like you know me!" Russell reached up and ripped off the mask.

He froze. All breath was sucked out of him as he stared at the familiar face. No burns or scars. A face much like his own. The mask tumbled from Russell's hand.

"Hey, bro," Markos said in English. "Miss me?"

Russell stumbled back, the prison door falling to the floor with a clatter.

"I told you we belong together." Markos looked down at his burned skin and winced. "I understand why you've been angry. We'll just call it even now, okay?"

Russell shook his head, not believing what he was seeing and hearing.

"He's not Asian?" Jia asked in Chinese. "Russell, what's going on? Why aren't you killing him?"

With an amused smirk, Markos answered her, "You expect him to kill his own brother?"

Jia gasped.

Russell glanced back at her. Her face had gone white with shock.

She pressed a trembling hand to her chest. "Your brother killed my family?"

Russell's stomach twisted. Oh God, how could she ever forgive him? How could she ever look at him again?

"What is this?" Markos asked, watching him curiously. "You care about her?" His eyes narrowed. "I didn't expect to have competition for you."

Russell gritted his teeth. "Leave her alone."

"Or what?" Markos smirked as he pulled a second knife from his sleeve. "Can you really kill your brother?"

Russell drew his sword but hesitated, and in that second, Markos teleported behind Jia and plunged his knife into her chest.

"Game over!" Markos shoved her onto the ground. "I win. And you're mine."

With a roar, Russell charged, his sword aimed at his brother's heart.

Markos teleported away.

Russell collapsed onto his knees in front of Jia. His head fell back and he screamed his rage to the heavens.

Chapter Seventeen

Russell pressed his hand against Jia's wound, but the blood continued to seep out. Panic ignited inside him. "I'll take you to Tiger Town. Neona can—"

"No," Jia whispered, her eyes shut tightly against the pain. "You promised you would let—"

"I can't let you die!"

Her eyes opened, and the desperation he saw there nearly killed him. "Take me home. To the cave. You promised."

"I promised I would keep you safe, and I failed you." Tears blurred his vision. "My brother killed your family. He's killed you! How can you bear to look at me?"

She gripped his coat with her fist. "You have never failed me. Honor your promise. Take me . . ." Her hand fell limply to the ground.

"Jia!" He felt her neck. Her pulse was still there, but weak. She'd lost consciousness.

The boy was crouched beside them, his breaths

coming in soft wheezes, tears streaming down his bruised face. Russell wasn't sure what kind of terror the boy had survived, but he knew the kid shouldn't be left alone, even for the few seconds it would take to teleport Jia to the cave. And he didn't dare leave her alone. What if Han came back and chopped her into pieces like he did with her family?

Not Han, he corrected himself. Markos. His little brother was a mass murderer. Russell's stomach roiled, and bile crept up his throat.

He swallowed hard, mentally pushing aside all thoughts of his brother. No time for it now. Jia needed him. So did Xiao Fang.

"Don't worry. You're safe now," he assured the kid as he carefully picked Jia up. "I'm going to call Jin Long to come get you and take you to Winifred. We have to go to the surface for the phone to work. Can you follow me up the stairs?"

The boy nodded and jumped to his feet.

Russell went up the stairs, trying hard not to jostle Jia, while the boy followed close behind. They crossed the empty guardroom and ascended the last flight of stairs. The guards had left the door wide open in their hasty departure.

As they emerged from the cave, the boy pivoted, looking around nervously, as if he feared Han or Darafer would show up to ruin his escape.

After easing to his knees, Russell cradled Jia in his lap as he managed to remove his coat. He lay the coat on the ground, then placed Jia on top. She moaned.

"Stay strong," he told her as he pulled the sat phone from his coat pocket.

"Come," he said, motioning for Xiao Fang to follow him. He rounded a boulder, keeping Jia partially in sight as he punched in the number. Jin Long answered on the second ring.

"I need you here now!" Russell told him. "I have Xiao Fang with me. Hurry! We're wait—"

J.L. materialized beside them and grinned when he saw the dragon shifter. "Thank God! Come on. I'll take you to Winifred."

Xiao Fang made a wheezing sound as more tears rolled down his cheeks. He surprised Russell by wrapping his arms around him and hugging him. Then he jumped at J.L., latching on to him.

J.L. patted the boy's back. "Where's Jia?"

Russell clenched his fists and kept his face blank. "Close by."

"I smell blood." J.L.'s eyes narrowed on Russell's bloodstained clothes. "Did you fight with Han?"

Russell's stomach threatened to heave. If the dragon shifter told Winifred everything that had happened, everyone would soon know who Han really was. And they would also know that Russell had failed in his promise to keep Jia safe. "Han escaped. Leave now before he comes back."

J.L. nodded and teleported away, taking Xiao Fang with him.

Russell dashed back to Jia and gently took her into his arms. "Sweetheart, we're going home now."

He teleported to the bat cave and lay her on the bed. On the way to grab a stack of towels, he tossed his coat on the ground. It was coated with blood. Her clothes were drenched with blood. It made his fangs ache and his stomach churn with hunger. But with every hunger pang, his gut clenched with nausea. All this blood was a constant reminder of his guilt. He'd failed to protect Jia. She would die, murdered by his own brother.

He pressed one of the towels against her wound, and she moaned.

"Jia." He brushed her hair away from her brow, then cursed himself for leaving a smear of blood on her face.

Her eyes flickered open. "Russell?"

"Yes."

"You were right. It hurts to die."

"I'm so sorry. I promised to protect you, and I—"

"No." She reached a hand toward him, and he clasped it with his own. "You're a good man."

"I failed you. I hesitated—"

"That's why you're a good man. An evil man would not hesitate to kill his brother."

He winced. "I can't believe he . . . it makes me want to puke. How can you bear to look at—"

"Shh." She squeezed his hand. "You are not your brother. You're my . . . my partner. My cowboy."

His phone buzzed. He glanced at his coat, where the phone rested in the pocket. "That's probably Rajiv. He must know by now that you were stabbed. We should let him know—"

"No! Don't answer it." Jia coughed, and blood drizzled from her mouth.

He released her hand so he could wipe her face with a towel. "They'll be frantic with worry."

"Don't answer. They'll take me away. They'll try to save me."

"That's what I should be doing."

"You're doing what I asked you to. Thank you." She bit her lip. "There's something I should tell you. When I wake up, I might behave . . . strangely."

"What do you mean?"

"I-I might . . ." She winced. "Whatever I do, please don't let it bother you."

He snorted. "I don't care what you do as long as you come back."

"I will come back." She squeezed his hand. "And I'll be stronger. Better than ever."

Tears burned his eyes. "I think you're perfect now."

Her mouth curled up slightly with a smile before thinning again in pain. "I'm cold. Will you hold me?"

"Yes." He stretched out beside her and wrapped his arms around her. "I'm so sorry. I wish there was something I could do for your pain."

"Talk to me." Her breathing grew more labored. "Tell me what it's like to be a cowboy."

He rubbed his chin against her hair. "It's not as exciting as the movies. You work long hours. Even when the weather is bad. There's never a day off."

"You . . . didn't like it?"

He paused a moment, thinking back on the days he'd spent riding alongside his father. The sun shining. The snowcapped mountains in the distance. "I loved it."

"Maybe . . . you'll have a ranch again someday."

He stroked her cheek with his thumb. How could he? He'd never see the sun again. Or his father. That was all in the past. And as for the future, he was finding it hard to imagine without Jia.

For three years, ever since he'd awakened undead, he'd thought his heart was dead. He'd thought he was incapable of any feeling but hate. He'd had no purpose for his existence other than revenge.

But somehow, in only a week, Jia had changed everything. He wanted a heart now so he could give it to her. He wanted to live so he could be with her. He wanted love instead of hate, joy instead of revenge.

But she wasn't his. She never would be. Her future was with a prince.

His own future seemed suddenly bleak, and his newly awakened heart ached with despair. He might have to commit the ungodly crime of killing his own brother. If so, he would spend eternity with nothing but guilt to keep him company. Once Han was dead and the mission was over, Jia would leave. How could he live without her?

His phone started buzzing again. Rajiv wasn't giving up. The poor guy had to know that his cousin was dying.

Jia stiffened slightly in his arms, then exhaled slowly.

He waited, his heart constricted with pain. Waited to hear another breath, but there was nothing.

"Jia." He continued to hold her. Even though she was gone, he couldn't let go. And now that she couldn't hear him, he would say the words in his heart. He'd wanted to tell her earlier, but how could he, when her future was with someone else?

"Jia, I'm in love with you."

Ten minutes later, Russell paced about the cave, growing increasingly anxious that Jia was still dead. He ignored the hunger pangs, ignored the gnaw in his gut about his brother. Instead, he chose to focus on Jia. How long would it take for her to wake up? He had no idea.

He did figure she wouldn't enjoy waking up in a pool of blood. The smell was getting to him, too, as a constant, nauseating reminder of his failure, so he decided to take action. After warming up some water, he used a dampened towel to wipe her face. He removed her bloody tunic and tossed it on the ground.

Her silk camisole was soaked through. He lifted the hem enough to clean the wound on her rib cage. It was healing! Already the wound had sealed shut. He grinned with this new evidence that she was indeed progressing to her next life.

He slid one of his clean T-shirts over her head and far enough down to cover her breasts. Then he cut the camisole off and dropped it on top of her bloody tunic.

"I'm not peeking," he told her as he slipped her arms into the sleeves. "I know you're engaged to someone else."

His extra-large T-shirt ended just above her knees. He reached underneath to pull off her bloody trousers and underwear. They ended up in the growing pile of soiled clothes on the ground. He washed her arms and legs, then shifted her so he could remove the top sleeping bag. It was stained with blood, but the bags underneath had remained clean.

"There. You'll feel better now." He covered her with a soft blanket.

A hunger pain shot through his stomach, nearly doubling him over. No matter how squeamish he felt, he needed to eat. He stumbled over to the ice chest, pulled out a bottle, and guzzled half of it down. In a few seconds, nausea struck. He ran into the river and heaved till his stomach was empty.

As the water current swept the blood away, he remained in the stream, hunched over with his hands resting on his knees. He panted for breath, too weak to move. Too overwhelmed to function.

His brother was Master Han. He'd tried not to think about it, but the truth was there, making his gut twist with despair. His brother had killed Jia and her family. For over forty years, his brother had ravaged southern China and surrounding countries, terrorizing and killing people.

"Markos." He stumbled upstream and tossed fresh water on his face. "What happened to you?"

His mind raced, zipping through childhood memories, trying desperately to recall any indication that his brother would someday turn into an evil monster. Only two years younger, Markos had been the quiet, studious one. He'd been picked on a bit at school, but Russell had always been quick to punish any bullies. Everyone had soon learned that messing with Markos meant retaliation from the older brother.

Markos had tried to be more physical like Russell, who had been the quarterback on the high school football team. How Dad had loved that. He had never missed a game.

When Markos had tried football, he'd ended up injured in his first game. Cracked ribs and a severely sprained back. He'd had to wear a back brace for two months. And since he'd been unable to do his chores on the ranch, Russell's workload had doubled. Had he complained too much? Made his brother feel bad?

He shook his head. He'd always suspected it had been Markos's reliance on pain pills that had gotten him into trouble with drugs. But Markos had recovered. All kids had their share of problems growing up. They didn't turn into evil vampire warlords. What had happened to Markos? Had the war in Vietnam damaged him beyond repair? Or had becoming a vampire traumatized him? Had he gone crazy with his newfound strength and superpowers?

And what was Russell to do? Would he have to kill his brother? If Markos attacked Tiger Town with his army, there would be plenty of people trying to kill him. The job could be left to Angus or any of his employees. But what if Markos killed one of them? What if he killed Zoltan or Howard? Both those guys had wives who were expecting. Or Markos might kill some of Jia's friends or family.

Russell groaned. Markos was his brother. He had to take responsibility. His brother had to be stopped before he could kill anyone else.

With his decision made, Russell trudged toward the table, where he'd left the half-empty bottle of blood. He warmed it up in the microwave, then tried sipping it slowly. It stayed down.

He stripped down to his underwear, then, using rocks, he anchored his dirty clothes in the stream. The rushing current would wash away most of the blood. He emptied the pockets of his coat and anchored it in the stream, too. Then he gathered up Jia's bloody clothes and the soiled sleeping bag. He couldn't leave them here or aboveground, where the scent would attract predators. So he teleported to another cave hundreds of miles away.

He dropped the bloody load, then looked around. This was the cave where Wu Shen had once taken him, J.L., Howard, Gregori, and Abigail Tucker prisoner. It was here that he'd met Darafer and the three vampire lords. And Master Han.

Han—short for Hankelburg? Russell recalled how the vampire lords had wanted to kill them. Master Han had stiffened after seeing Russell. Shock at seeing his brother on the opposing team? Han had quickly announced that Russell bore his mark. He'd kept his brother alive.

Russell sighed. He didn't see how he could do the same. Most probably, Markos would have to die.

After teleporting back home, Russell showered and put on clean clothes. Jia was still dead. He looked at the clock on the microwave. Twenty-five minutes had passed.

He warmed up more blood and took small sips. His strength was coming back. But what about Jia? She'd lost so much blood. Wouldn't she be weak when she woke up? She would need some good food.

"I'll be right back," he told her, then grabbed a tote bag and teleported to the kitchen in Zoltan's castle.

What would be quick but healthy? He examined the contents of the refrigerator and spotted a Ziploc bag of sliced ham. He grabbed it and a package of sliced cheese. He tossed them into the tote bag, then stepped into the pantry. A loaf of bread, a bag of chips, some bananas, a jar of mixed nuts.

"Russell, what are you doing?" Howard's voice called out. His footsteps were drawing close at a fast pace.

"What I always do. Steal." Russell stuffed some paper plates into the bag. It was full now. "Later."

"Wait!" Howard came to a halt at the pantry door. "I just heard the latest report. Rajiv is frantic. What happened to Jia?"

"She's fine. I need to get back to her."

Howard gave him a worried look. "Is it true what Xiao Fang told them? That Han is your brother?"

Russell's jaw clenched. The news was out.

Howard grimaced. "Holy crap. What are—"

"Don't worry about it. I'll take care of him."

"Listen, you're not in this alone. Will you—"

Russell teleported back to the cave. The last thing he wanted to hear now was sympathy. He checked on Jia. Still dead.

He spread the food out on the table and soon had a paper plate stacked with four ham and cheese sandwiches. He was just opening the bag of potato chips when he heard a soft gasp.

Jia was waking to her second life.

Chapter Eighteen

Jia inhaled deeply as a feeling of euphoria swept through her. She was alive, but so much more alive than before. Every nerve seemed to tingle with heightened sensibility. Even the air she breathed was more refreshing.

She opened her eyes, and her vision was sharper. In spite of the dim light, she could see every crack and crevice in the rock ceiling overhead. Heat surged through her, igniting every muscle with extra strength and more flexibility. Her heart pounded so loud that it deafened her.

The tiger inside her growled, elated with the gift of more power. The heat increased, simmering in her chest like a fire. She kicked off the blanket and sat up.

"Jia, you're back! Thank God."

She glanced to the side. Russell was approaching her, a relieved, happy look on his face. He seemed to be glowing with a golden hue. Were her eyes doing something odd? No matter, for he looked more gorgeous than ever.

"Jia?"

Her heart pounded so loud that his voice seemed to be coming from a mile away. He was asking her something, but it was hard to concentrate, when the fire inside her was creeping up her neck. Sweat trickled between her breasts, and she rubbed her chest. What was she wearing? It looked like one of Russell's T-shirts.

"Jia!" He raised his voice as he stepped closer. "Are you all right?"

Was she? Had the wound healed? She pulled the T-shirt up to look.

"Sheesh." Russell spun about, putting his back to her. "I—" He cleared his throat. "I made some sandwiches in case you're hungry. You should probably eat. Get your strength back. You've been through a lot."

His words made her smile. He didn't realize how strong she felt. She was naked underneath the shirt and fairly clean. All the blood was gone, so he must have washed it away. She felt along her rib cage. Her skin was intact. And tingling.

She recognized the feeling. Her skin was burning and itching, as if she needed to escape her human shell. Even though the moon wasn't full, she was going to shift. From now on, she would be able to shift whenever she wanted.

What freedom and power! With a grin, she yanked the T-shirt off and tossed it aside. It landed by Russell's feet.

He glanced at it, his back still turned toward her. "Do you want some new clothes? There are some clean ones on the drying rack. I can—"

His voice grew dim as her heartbeat thundered in her ears and the fire exploded in her head. She crouched on all fours, digging her fingers into the blanket. A cry escaped her mouth as her body shifted.

"What's wrong?" Russell turned back to her. "Oh, shit!"

Her bones crackled, seeking a new shape. Fur sprouted from her skin. Her skull expanded, her teeth grew longer. Sharper. Claws shot from the end of her fingers as her hands transformed into paws.

"Damn." He stepped back. "I didn't realize you were going to—"

She threw her head back and roared. Power surged through her, fueled by the inner fire. Never had she felt so alive.

"Okay." He watched her warily. "I guess you don't need any clothes right now. How about some food?"

Her muscles rippled, begging to be used. She pushed off the bed with a graceful leap and landed, knocking Russell over with her front legs. She settled half on top of him, pinning him to the ground.

He grimaced. "That was impressive."

She flexed the paw that rested on his chest, and when her claws emerged, she sliced open his shirt a few inches.

His eyes widened. "Nice claws." He lifted a hand to pat her head, but when she grinned, he jerked his hand back. "Nice teeth."

She growled low in her throat.

He gulped. "By the way, when I mentioned

food, I wasn't referring to myself." He motioned to the table. "Sandwich?"

She eased closer to his face.

He stiffened. "Jia? You're in there, right? Those are your eyes. They were glowing before, but they look more normal now."

She butted her forehead against his, then turned to the table. Stretching up, she placed her front paws on the table and gobbled down the sandwiches.

He scrambled to his feet. "That was fast. I'll make some more."

The heat inside her ratcheted up till she felt she would combust. She ran into the stream and settled up to her neck in the cool water.

He smiled. "I've heard that tigers like water." He moved behind the table to make more sandwiches. "You had me worried there for a second. I thought I might have to teleport away."

Even in the stream, she was still on fire. Her skin tingled, signaling her body was ready to shift back to human form. She closed her eyes and let it happen. Maybe the fire would go away once she was back to normal.

The shift didn't hurt this time. With a whoosh, her bones adjusted and her fur receded. Grinning, she opened her eyes. Was shifting going to be that quick and easy from now on?

"That was amazing." Russell watched her with a stunned look. "How do you feel?"

She was still crouched in the stream up to her neck. "I feel wonderful. So strong and . . ." She sucked in a breath, suddenly aware of how the water current was sweeping across her skin. It felt so good. As if all her nerve endings were being caressed. The burning sensation receded from her head and moved down her body.

"The sun will rise in about twenty minutes. I brought plenty of food to get you through the day." He motioned to the new stack of sandwiches he'd just made. "Are you hungry?"

"I'm fine." She shivered as the rushing water sent tingles up her arms and down her spine. The fire burned in her belly, but her skin was pebbled with goose bumps. How could she feel hot and cold at the same time?

She unbraided her hair and leaned her head back to wash it. As she arched her back, the water tickled her breasts.

With a gasp, she sat up. Her nipples had hardened. The fire inside her moved between her legs, scorching her with a sudden need. A hunger.

She squeezed her thighs together, hoping to squelch the fire, but the flames grew hotter. What was happening to her? She crossed her arms, hugging herself, but that only made her breasts ache to be touched.

"Is something wrong?" he asked.

"I-I'm fine." Was this what Rajiv had warned her about? An overwhelming desire to . . . Her breath hitched as she looked at Russell. God help her, she did want to mate.

He tilted his head, studying her. "You don't seem fine."

The sizzling sensation between her legs was growing stronger. The heat unbearable. Pressing her thighs together just made her more sensitive. More desperate. A whimper escaped her mouth.

"You look like you're in pain." He grabbed a towel and walked toward her. "Maybe you should lie down. Get some more rest."

She stood up, the water waist high, her long hair concealing her breasts. "Russell."

"Come on out." He stopped at the river's edge and stretched the towel out between his arms. "I won't look."

"But I want you to." With a sudden move, she shoved her hair behind her shoulders.

He stiffened, his eyes flashing red before he turned his head.

A thrill of victory shot through her. He wanted her. And she needed him. He would know how to quench the fire inside her. But she needed to hurry. He would go into his death-sleep when the sun rose.

She strode toward him, and the movement of her thighs brushing against each other made her want to scream. She had to mate. She wasn't sure how, but Russell would know. He would help her through this.

She ripped the towel out of his hands and tossed it aside.

"What are you—?" He turned back to her. His gaze swept over her quickly, and his eyes turned a darker, more intense red. "Jia—"

She placed her hands on his chest. "Russell."

He stepped back. "Do you want a . . . sandwich?"

"No." She kept moving toward him, and he retreated till he bumped into the table. "I want you."

"But—"

"I need you." She smoothed her hands over his T-shirt, then slipped her fingers into the hole she'd made earlier with her claws and ripped the shirt in two.

"Sheesh! You can't—I have a limited number of shirts, you know." He hissed in a breath as she caressed his bare chest.

His skin was so smooth, so deliciously sculpted over his chest and abs. He was a beautiful man, and he would be her mate. If she could just figure out how to go about it.

A kiss. Didn't people kiss before mating? She grabbed him by the shoulders and went up on her toes to plant her mouth firmly against his.

He reeled back, but she leaned forward, puckering her lips and pressing hard against his mouth. When her breasts touched his bare chest, she gasped.

He seized her by the upper arms and moved her back. "What the hell has gotten into you?"

The kiss hadn't done much for her. But she'd definitely liked the feel of her bare skin against his. Obviously, they both needed to be naked. She unbuckled his belt.

He grabbed her wrists. "Jia! We can't do this."

"Of course we can." She struggled to undo the button at the waistband.

He lifted her hands up, away from his trousers. "You're engaged."

"I don't care." She jerked her hands away and pulled down his zipper.

"I care! I'm not—shit!" He stiffened when she

yanked his trousers and underwear down to his thighs.

She gasped as his manhood sprang free. It was thick and swollen. The longer she stared at it, the bigger it seemed to grow. And the more she throbbed and burned between her legs. "I've never seen a man look like this."

"I should hope not," he muttered, reaching for the waistband of his underwear.

Before he could cover himself up, she curled a hand around him. His manhood jerked against her palm.

He hissed in another breath. "Dammit, Jia. I'm not doing this. Not when you're engaged."

She shoved him toward the bed and he stumbled, his trousers falling to his ankles.

"Would you stop—" He leaned over to make another grab for his underwear, but she took advantage of his position by planting her hands on his rump and giving him a hard push.

He sprawled on the bed, grunting when his swollen groin hit the surface. Quickly, he rolled onto his back, but she was just as quick to grab his trousers and underwear and yank them off completely.

"What the—" He started to sit up but fell back when she lifted his legs onto the bed. "Jia—"

She jumped on top, straddling him on her hands and knees. "I need you. And I know you want me. Your eyes are red. Rajiv warned me what that meant."

Russell gritted his teeth. "Of course they're red. I'm seeing you naked. But that doesn't mean we should—"

"I have to." She glanced down at his manhood. It was erect and pointed right at her belly. "Will that really fit inside me? It looks too big."

He snorted. "Have you forgotten what it means to be engaged to someone else?"

She inched forward on her knees till his erection was in line with her private parts. "How do we do it?"

He grabbed her shoulders, holding her back. "You're a virgin, right? Why are you doing this?"

"I need—" She lowered her hips till the tip of his erection grazed against her. A blast of sensation shot from her core, and she shuddered. Oh God, if she didn't mate, she felt like she would burn to death. "I have to do this! Help me, please."

"You can't—" He grasped her hips to stop her. "You're going to hurt yourself. You can't just . . . fall on the sword. You have to be ready."

She gave his so-called sword a dubious look. "Isn't it ready? How much bigger can you get?"

"I'm talking about you. There are certain steps that should be followed to make—"

"What steps?"

"Well . . . generally speaking, you would start off with some kissing."

She rolled her eyes. "We did that. What's the next step?"

He scoffed. "That wasn't a kiss."

"Of course it was."

"Two mouths colliding don't make a kiss."

"Next step!"

He frowned at her. "Touching."

She dragged her hands down his chest. "Okay, done."

"I would have to touch you, too."

"Can we just get on with this?" She clasped his manhood in her hand and positioned herself over it.

"Wait!"

"What now?"

"You need to be . . . ready." He sat up and slid a hand between her legs.

She shuddered at the feel of his probing fingers. "Oh, God, Russell, help me." She grasped his shoulders and moaned when moisture seeped from her core.

He closed his eyes briefly, scowling as if he was angry with himself. "You're ready."

She pressed against him, crying out with relief as he guided her to the right place. Shudders racked her body as she felt him sliding inside her, deeper, until he hit a barrier.

"Is that it?"

He clenched his teeth. "We should stop now so you'll still be—" He gasped when she sat down hard. "Shit."

The burst of pain made her cry out, but then she sank further and further, taking more of him inside her. Oh, God, yes, this was what she needed. She hugged him tight, pressing her breasts against him.

"I'm on fire, Russell. Can you feel it?"

"Yes." His hands skimmed up her back.

She rocked gently against him. "What do I do?"

"You're doing good."

Her hands slipped to his neck and entwined in his hair. "I'm so glad you were here. That it was you."

His hands tightened on her, then with a groan, he suddenly rolled her onto her back. His manhood slipped almost completely out, but then he plunged back in, making her gasp.

He stroked her breasts, then took a nipple into his mouth. She arched her back, moaning from the sweetness of it. Again and again, he thrust into her. Harder and harder till she was gasping for air, swirling in a sea of sensation that grew stronger and stronger.

Just when she thought she was going to drown, the sensations shattered. She cried out, holding onto him tight. With a shout, he pumped into her, then collapsed, holding his weight on his elbows.

His fangs shot out. With a groan, he rolled onto his back.

She pressed a hand to her chest, waiting for her pounding heart to calm. She squeezed her thighs together. The sweet throbbing was still going on.

She'd done it. She'd mated for the first time. A laugh bubbled up her throat. The fire was gone, and she felt so strong and free.

Russell rose from the bed and strode toward the ice chest. Keeping his back to her, he stuck a bottle of blood into the microwave and waited for it to warm up.

She rolled onto her side to admire the sight of his back and buttocks. "Thank you."

He stiffened, but didn't turn around, didn't say a word.

Was he angry with her? She sat up. "Are you all right?"

He removed the bottle and took a sip. "The sun will be up in a few minutes. After I'm dead, you should call your cousin to let him know you're all right. Xiao Fang told him you were wounded, so I'm sure he's been worried."

She winced. She would have to admit that she'd progressed to her second life. And Rajiv would want to know if she'd mated. He would not be thrilled that the were-tiger princess had mated with a vampire. Especially when she was engaged.

Was that why Russell was refusing to look at her? Did he feel guilty? It wasn't his fault. She was the one who had practically forced him.

She gasped. Oh God, she had forced him. He'd tried over and over to stop her, but she hadn't listened. She'd been totally engulfed in a feverish need to mate. "Russell, I—"

"Get some rest." He tossed the empty bottle into a plastic bin. "We can talk when I wake up." He strode to the far end of the cave where he'd left a blanket and pillow.

He wasn't going to share the bed with her? Her heart sank.

"Goodnight." He stretched out and closed his eyes.

Tears stung her eyes when his breathing stopped. "I'm so sorry."

He had every right to be angry. He'd tried to stop her. He'd reminded her that she was engaged. And she had ignored his objections.

Rajiv would be angry, too. She'd have to explain to him that she didn't care if her engagement fell through. She didn't know the were-tiger prince. As far as she was concerned, he could jump in a lake.

But Russell . . . She walked over to him and adjusted his blanket. She did care about him. He was the one who believed in her, the one who filled her thoughts and pulled at her heart. It would kill her if she lost his friendship. Or lost his respect.

A tear rolled down her cheek. "Please don't hate me. You're my . . . my partner. My cowboy. I need you." Her heart squeezed in her chest with a painful realization. She needed him to love her.

Because she loved him.

Chapter Nineteen

When Russell woke up that evening, he found Jia asleep in the bed, wearing one of his T-shirts. There were signs that she'd been busy during the day. His clothes and coat, which he'd left soaking in the stream, were washed and drying. All the laundry had been done, and the cave cleaned up.

He lit an oil lamp, then retrieved a bottle of blood from an ice chest. As he sipped his breakfast, he wandered over to the bed to watch her sleep. He wasn't sure what to make of what had happened. It seemed like she'd been driven by some need beyond her control. Had death traumatized her to the point that she'd had to confirm her life by having sex? Why the sudden desire to rid herself of her virginity?

How on earth was he supposed to give her up now? He'd tried to resist her. He knew better than to sleep with a woman who was engaged. But in the end, his desire had won the battle. His love for her was greater than his sense of honor.

He guzzled down the rest of his bottle and dropped it into the plastic crate with the other empty bottles. There was a primitive caveman inside him that had urged him to take her and stake his claim, as if she'd been a prized possession. And that same caveman wanted to destroy any competition.

He took a deep breath and forced his mind out of caveman mode. Jia was a strong, independent woman, and he loved that about her. The fact that he couldn't bear to give her up was his problem. All he could do was be honest with her and try to convince her that life with a penniless vampire would be better than living in a palace with a were-tiger prince.

Shit. He was so screwed.

Even so, falling in love with her had been the best thing to happen to him in years. It made him feel hopeful and alive, instead of dead and full of hate. But he wasn't sure how she felt. Last night, she'd seemed desperate. For him? Or just for sex?

He heated up some water and took a hot shower. He wasn't in any hurry to wake Jia up. Not when he was afraid of what he might hear. Besides, there was no point in hunting for Han tonight. He would remain hidden until tomorrow, when it was time to lead his troops into battle.

As Russell toweled off and dressed, he considered what to do with his brother. He needed to be alone with Markos so he could talk some sense into him. So the second he spotted Markos tomorrow night, he would teleport behind him, catching him by surprise so he could kidnap him.

Without Markos there to lead the army, the soldiers would probably hesitate to attack Tiger Town. They might even desert. From what Russell had seen from the guards last night, their morale was low. They no longer wanted to die for Han and risk going to hell.

Once he and Markos were alone, they would decide the outcome of the battle. There was no need to put anyone else in danger. Russell sighed, not wanting to think about that final confrontation. Would Markos surrender and give up his plan to rule the world? Somehow Russell had to convince him to stop. If not, he would be forced to kill him.

His heart constricted in his chest. *God, help me. Spare me from that pain.* Hadn't he been through enough?

There was a rustling sound from the bed. Jia was waking. She blinked at him sleepily, and his heart squeezed again. Was he going to lose her, too?

"I'll go topside for a few minutes to give you privacy." He grabbed a sword and the sat phone, then teleported out to do a perimeter check. Nothing but a few small animals that ran away as he approached.

He wondered how preparations were going at Tiger Town, but he didn't dare call one of the Vamps, since they might teleport to him and learn the location of his hideout. So he called Howard in Transylvania.

"Guess who's here," Howard said. "Last night, Angus had Neona, Norjee, and Xiao Fang teleported here. Neona agreed not to take part in the battle, since she's expecting."

"That's good. How is Xiao Fang?"

"He's coming along," Howard replied. "Neona has healed his injuries, and he's talking to Norjee quite a bit. He hasn't said much about his captivity, though. He keeps asking if Jia is all right. He says she was stabbed."

"Tell him she's fine. Her wound is completely healed."

"That's a relief. The poor kid is afraid to be happy. He's worried that Darafer will find him."

Russell winced. That was a possibility. "Is there any way to get rid of Darafer?"

"We're not able to kill him," Howard grumbled. "As far as I know, only the Heavenly Father and archangels can destroy him. The God Warriors can banish him back to hell, but it takes seven of them. And they can only do it if he breaks the decree of free will."

Russell sighed. Even if he solved the situation with his brother, Darafer would remain a problem. "What's going on at Tiger Town?"

"Angus has gathered an army of two hundred. As soon as the sun sets here, Mikhail is supposed to teleport me there."

"Any sign of Han's army?" Russell asked. "Do I need to spend tonight tracking them?"

"No. You can relax. Queen Nima's owl is watching the army and having other birds report to Winifred, so Angus knows where the army is. He expects them to arrive at the Mekong River tomorrow afternoon. We figure they won't attack until after sunset, when Han shows up."

"Tell Angus that as soon as I spot Han, I'm kidnapping him. That should keep the army from attacking."

There was a pause, then Howard said, "You should stand down, Russell. Don't get involved. He's your brother—"

"That's why I have to do this. I can't allow him to kill another person."

Howard groaned. "I get that, but I don't want you to do something you'll regret. You'll have to live with the consequences forever."

"I know. Later." Russell hung up and stood still as despair threatened to engulf him. Did he have to lose everyone he ever loved?

With a heavy heart, he teleported back into the cave.

Jia was sitting on the bed, dressed in her second set of clothes and braiding her hair. "Hi." She smiled at him, then glanced away, her cheeks turning pink.

Great. Things were going to be awkward. "How do you feel? You look . . . beautiful, but then, you always do."

Her blush deepened. "I'm fine."

"Do you have enough food here to eat? When the sun sets in Transylvania, I could steal some of Howard's donuts for you."

That made her smile. "I'm fine, really. Just . . . embarrassed."

"There's no need to feel bad." Having sex with

him was embarrassing? Dammit. He plugged the sat phone in to recharge. If she apologized or called it an accident, he might lose it.

"It was my first time to die and come back." She slipped off the bed and wandered toward the table. "I wasn't sure what exactly would happen. I didn't expect to shift."

"No big deal." He grabbed another bottle of blood from the ice chest and wrenched off the top. Not that he was hungry, but he had to keep busy or he might rip something apart. "You're a were-tiger. You shift. No need to apologize for it." *Not when I love you the way you are.*

"I . . . hope I didn't scare you."

He shrugged and took a sip of cold blood.

She winced. "Rajiv warned me I might behave . . . strangely."

"You mean like a sex goddess?"

Her mouth fell open. "No! I mean, he said I might feel an overwhelming desire to mate, but I'd never mated before, so I didn't think—"

"You knew?" He plunked the bottle down on the table. "You knew that would happen?"

"I'm sorry! I didn't—"

"Don't—" He clenched his fists. "Don't apologize."

"I didn't think anything would happen!" She stepped toward him. "I'm sure it was shocking for you, but it seems to be a completely normal occurrence for were-cats. Think of it as a cultural thing."

Anger shot through him. "A *cultural* thing?"

"Yes." She waved a dismissive hand. "It's just

something that happens when a were-cat progresses to the next life."

"Well, thank God you had a convenient dick nearby!"

With a gasp, she stepped back.

Dammit! He slammed two handguns down on the table along with his cleaning supplies, then sat on a stool to get to work.

"Russell?"

He ignored her as he dismantled the first gun. This was worse than he had thought. She'd simply been driven by an innate need to mate. He'd just been expedient. It hadn't meant anything personal to her at all. No wonder she was embarrassed. She'd used him. And now she intended to go on with her life, her second life, as if nothing had happened.

"Russell?"

He cleaned the handgun at vampire speed. Tomorrow night, he'd end things with his brother. She would have the revenge she wanted. And then she would be free to marry her prince.

"Russell!"

He glanced up. Damn, she was staring at him with tears in her eyes. Maybe she was taking it personally after all. He set his tools down. "What's wrong?"

"I—" She closed her eyes with a pained look. "I made a mistake."

Damn. Why didn't she just cut his heart out and throw it into a blender? "I thought our night together was a cultural thing. Now it's a mistake."

She winced. "That's what you think?"

He jumped to his feet. "I don't know what the hell to think!"

She bit her lip. "I made a mistake when I acted like last night wasn't important. I made light of it because I was trying to hide my shame."

"You're ashamed that you slept with me?"

"No! I'm ashamed of the crime I committed." She squared her shoulders. "I abused you. You tried several times to stop me, but I ignored your wishes. I— I forced you to mate with me, and I—"

"Forced?"

"Yes. I know it's unforgivable, but I hope—"

"Forced?" He skirted the table to stand in front of her. "You're forgetting something really big."

Her gaze lowered to his groin. "I don't think so."

He scoffed. "I'm referring to the fact that at any point last night, I could have teleported away. I stayed because I wanted to."

She blinked. "But you kept trying to stop me."

"Because you're engaged. Not because I didn't want you." He stepped closer. "Did you force me to kiss your breasts and suck on your nipples?"

Her mouth dropped open.

"Did you force me to push you onto your back so I could thrust deeper inside you? Did you force me to have the biggest damned climax of my life?"

She stared at him, her eyes wide. "Y-you wanted to mate?"

"Yes! So you can stop apologizing or feeling ashamed. I did exactly what I wanted to do. It's what happens when a man falls in love."

"You mean—"

"Yes! I'm in love with you."

She gasped, her hand covering her mouth.

He shifted his weight. Now that his heart was out, she would toss it into the blender by reminding him that she planned to marry someone else.

A tear rolled down her cheek, and she moved up close to him. "I was so afraid I had abused you. I couldn't bear the thought that you would hate me."

"Never. I love you."

She gave him a wobbly smile as more tears came down her face. "That's good. Because I love you."

He stiffened, his breath caught in his chest. "You . . . ?"

"I finally realized it last night, but the feeling was already there. That's why I insisted on being with you when I died." She reached up to touch his cheek. "If I was going to need a mate, I wanted it to be you. It could be only you."

Something hard but fragile seemed to shatter in his chest, and he cupped his hand around the back of her neck to pull her into a kiss. The sudden move caught her by surprise, so her mouth was open. He took advantage, molding his lips to hers and slipping his tongue inside.

She stiffened, most probably still surprised. He cradled her head in his hands so he could devour her mouth. God, how he needed her. His chest tightened. His groin swelled.

Her hands smoothed over his shoulders and around his neck. Soon her mouth was moving with his, her tongue was stroking his. They kissed till they were breathless and panting against each other's lips.

He rested his brow against hers. "That's a kiss."

"I think I like kissing after all."

When he opened his eyes, she was tinted pink.

She grinned. "I love it when your eyes turn red. It makes me feel so powerful."

"You are powerful. You could destroy me with a single word."

Her fingers delved into his hair. "What word would that be?"

"Good-bye."

Her eyes widened. "Then we'll never say it. It would destroy me, too."

He pulled her close for another kiss. She held him tightly, kissing him back. Her body pressed against him, and his groin grew hard. After ravishing her mouth to the point that she was limp and breathless, he planted kisses along her cheek to her ear.

With a moan, she tilted her head.

He sucked her earlobe into his mouth, then whispered, "I want you naked so I can kiss you everywhere."

"Oh." She shivered. "Well, if you insist." She tugged at his T-shirt, but he pulled it off before she could rip it in two.

"Wait." She grabbed his hands when he reached for his belt. "I want to undress you."

"Well, if you insist," he repeated her words. "Then I'll undress you."

"Deal." With a grin, she unbuckled his belt.

With vampire speed, he unknotted her belt and

took off her tunic. Then he undid the drawstring on her trousers and dropped them to the ground. She was down to her panties and camisole before his trousers were unzipped.

She gave him a wry look. "Are you in a hurry?"

"Once I have you naked, I'll go as slow as you like."

Her golden eyes gleamed. "Well, if you insist."

"I do, princess."

"Cowboy." She tugged his trousers and underwear down, and his swollen manhood popped out. "Oh, hello. I remember you."

"You're going to talk to it?" He kicked off his shoes and trousers.

She stroked him with her fingers. "I may do more than talk."

"Well, if you insist." He swooped her up to carry her to the bed. When he sat her down, he pulled the camisole up and over her head. Her breasts bounced free, round and firm, topped with plump, pink nipples.

"Last night happened too fast," he murmured as he cupped her breasts and felt their weight against his palms. "I wasn't able to give you the attention you deserve."

He brushed his thumbs over her nipples and they pebbled. "Look at that. How pretty they are." He leaned down to run his tongue over the pebbled skin.

She shivered, then slid her hands up his arms to his shoulders. "I love touching you. You're so beautiful."

He snorted. "Guys aren't beautiful."

"You are." She smoothed her hands down his chest to his abdomen. "So many muscles."

"So many curves." He grazed his fingers along the curve of her waist and hips.

"So soft, but wonderfully hard." She curled her hand around his erection.

He sucked in a breath as she gently stroked him, then rubbed her thumb over the crown. With a groan, he removed her hand. "That's enough."

She frowned. "But I like touching you."

"I'm about to explode." He kissed her hand. "I want to be in charge for a while. I'm going to make you writhe and scream with pleasure."

"Really?" She gave him a dubious look, then her mouth twitched. "Well, if you insist." She lay back onto the bed and lifted her arms overhead. "All right, cowboy. Let's see what you can do."

He tapped the end of her nose. "Your wish is my command, princess."

"Don't call me princess."

With a smile, he hooked his fingers into the waistband of her panties and pulled.

She shifted her hips, lifting them up tantalizingly as he dragged the panties over her rump and down her legs. Now that she was stretched out naked on the bed, he took his time to study her. She had the lithe, muscular build of an athlete, but all the luscious curves of a beautiful woman.

Her nipples hardened and her hips squirmed a bit. "Why are you just looking at me?"

"I like what I see. You're beautiful. And you're already writhing."

She snorted. "Because you're making me nervous. Where's all this pleasure you promised me?"

"I'm getting there." He stroked the bottom of her feet.

She pulled them away. "That tickles."

"Ah." He grazed his fingertips along her ankles. "Does that tickle, princess?"

"Yes." She kicked at him.

He moved up her calves and tickled the back of her knees. "And this?"

"Yes." She stopped him by bending her legs at the knees, then gasped when he shoved her knees apart.

Now he could see the pink folds of her sex, and his groin grew harder.

"Why are you staring?"

"Does it disturb you?" He grazed his hands up her thighs.

Her legs trembled, and moisture glistened on her folds. He breathed deeply, catching the scent of her arousal.

"Russell, do something. This is starting to drive me crazy."

Smiling, he stretched out beside her. "Are you ready to writhe with pleasure?"

"Yes!"

He planted kisses down her neck as his hand smoothed down her belly. By the time his mouth reached her breasts, his fingers were delving into the black curls that covered her mound.

With a moan, she lifted her hips, pressing against his hand. He smiled to himself, loving how assertive and free she was. He teased her nipple with his tongue and was rewarded with another moan.

"Russell," she breathed as her hands raked through his hair.

He drew her nipple into his mouth and sucked. A few hard pulls, then he glanced up to see her reaction as his hand slipped between her legs. She was wonderfully slick with moisture and already swelling. Her eyes flew open when he pinched her clitoris.

"What . . . oh my . . ." She gasped as he gently massaged her.

He kissed a trail down to her belly as he stroked her. Soon she was panting and pressing against him. He nuzzled her black curls with his nose, then slipped his fingers between her slick folds. One finger slid inside, then two. So hot and wet.

With a groan, she writhed her hips. He settled between her legs and gave her clitoris a lick. She cried out, her legs thrashing.

What a wild one she was. He grasped her buttocks to keep her still so he could drag his tongue over her folds, then between them. Moisture seeped out, and he sucked it into his mouth. Her body squirmed. He tightened his grip and clamped his mouth onto her clitoris. A few quick flicks with his tongue, and she screamed. Her body jerked, then her sex throbbed against his face. He inserted two fingers, and she screamed again. Her vagina contracted, squeezing his fingers and making his dick ache.

He couldn't wait any longer. He slid into her.

With a cry, she wrapped her arms and legs around him. Her fingers dug into his shoulders.

The caveman in him broke free, and he slammed into her over and over. "You're mine," he growled. "Mine."

His climax hit like a strike of lightning. He squeezed his eyes shut but saw bolts of light flash through the darkness. He lost control, pumping wildly into her, then he crashed beside her, gasping for air. His fangs shot out, but thankfully he was too knocked out to do anything with them.

Slowly, he became aware of her panting breaths and trembling body. He pulled her close and rested his chin on top of her head. His fangs receded.

"Russell," she breathed against his chest. "Is it always going to be like that?"

"I don't know. Give me about ten minutes, and we'll find out."

She snorted. "Are we going to mate all night long?"

"If you insist."

She laughed and hugged him tight. "I insist."

"Your wish is my command, princess."

She scooted up so they were face-to-face. "I'm worried about my home and my people. Han is attacking Tiger Town tomorrow."

"I know. I'll take care of him."

"What are you going to do?"

"Kidnap him. Take him some place where we can have a . . . talk."

She frowned. "What if he just teleports away?"

Russell sighed. "I may have to knock him out and tie him up with silver."

"I'll help you. Take him inside the palace. I'll wait for you there with the silver chain."

"You don't have to—"

She put a finger on his mouth to hush him. "I'm going to be there for you. We're partners."

"I'd rather you stay here, where it's safe."

She scoffed. "Don't worry about me. I can shift whenever I want now. Besides, we made a deal."

"We did?"

She nodded. "That we would never say goodbye. So you have to take me with you."

He brushed her hair back from her brow. "If anything happens to you, I'll never forgive myself."

"What could happen? Even if I die, I'll come back. And then I would be even stronger." She gave him a pointed look. "Can you handle that?"

He smiled. "Yes, princess."

She smiled back. "Don't call me princess."

He kissed her nose.

She rested a hand on his cheek. "I'm going with you because I love you."

"I know." Unease settled in his heart. No matter what she said, it would still be dangerous. "I love you, too."

Chapter Twenty

The following night, right after sunset, Jia arrived with Russell in Tiger Town. The courtyard was full of Vamps, shifters and Han's ex-soldiers, all waiting for the battle to begin. Angus was at the top of the stairs that led down to the riverbank. From there, he had a good view of the Mekong River and Han's army, gathered on the other side.

"Howard was supposed to tell Angus about our plan to kidnap Han," Russell told her. "I'll check with Angus to make sure he knows."

Jia nodded. "I'll be waiting for you inside the palace."

"All right." He squeezed her hand before turning to leave.

She watched him go, her heart heavy. For thirteen years, her plan to destroy Han had been inspired by hatred and the need to avenge her family. But now that she'd fallen in love with Russell, vengeance no longer ruled her heart. Now she wanted to kill Han so she could spare Russell the pain of murdering his brother.

He might resent her for butting in, but she was willing to face his anger if she could protect him from harm. What else could she do, as much as she loved him?

She weaved through the crowd, then, in her room, she changed into a simple robe that tied at the waist. Instead of her boots, she put on some slippers. This way, she could fling off her clothes in a second in case she needed to shift. She wedged a knife under the sash and hid two more in the deep pockets of her bell-shaped sleeves. Tied to her sash was the silk pouch that held the silver chain.

Outside again, she hurried through the crowded courtyard, headed for the palace. When Russell teleported his brother to the throne room, she would loop the silver chain around Han to keep him from escaping.

Halfway up the stairs to the palace, she heard Rajiv calling her name. She turned to see him bounding up the steps.

"Jia! Are you all right?" He stopped beside her, his gaze looking her over carefully.

She'd called him during the afternoon to assure him she was fine, but when he'd pressed her for more information, she'd changed the subject to the upcoming battle. The last two nights with Russell had seemed too precious and personal to discuss on the phone. She'd wanted to treasure her time with Russell without dealing with any outside interference. "I'm perfectly fine. You can stop worrying."

"But you were stabbed. Xiao Fang told us about it."

"The wound has healed." She motioned to the palace. "I need to wait inside. Russell is going to teleport Master Han to the throne room. I'm supposed to help—"

"You're going to fight Han again?" Rajiv looked aghast. "He nearly killed you before."

"I'm stronger now—"

"He did kill you, didn't he?" Rajiv grabbed her arm and looked closely at her eyes. "I can sense more power in you. You're on your second life, aren't you?"

"Yes."

"Dammit!" Rajiv released her and turned away to clench his fists. "Russell said he would protect you. I should clobber—"

"It's not his fault! He was in shock. He'd just found out that Han is his brother."

"He should have brought you here! Leah could have patched you up, and Neona could have taken away the pain. Dammit, Jia, why didn't you do as you were told? And how could Russell just let you die? I'm going to kill—"

"He did what I asked him to! Believe me, he wanted to bring me here, but I insisted."

Rajiv took a deep breath, then lowered his voice. "Did you mate with him?"

She lifted her chin. "Yes."

Rajiv let out a howl of outrage so loud that half the crowd in the courtyard turned to look at them.

"We'll talk about it later," she said quietly.

"Did you forget that your fiancé is arriving in a week?" Rajiv hissed between gritted teeth.

"We can contact him after the battle—"

"It's too late. He's already left Korea. He and his entourage are sailing to Hong Kong on the royal yacht."

Jia groaned. "Fine. I'll reject him in person then."

Rajiv scoffed. "You're refusing him?"

"Yes. I'm in love with Russell."

Rajiv gave her an incredulous look. "You're giving up a were-tiger prince for a vampire who has nothing?"

A spurt of anger burst inside her. "He has honor and courage. And I refuse to give in to the old prejudices of our people. How many Vamps are here now, willing to risk their lives to protect our home?"

"I know very well that there are good Vamps. They're like family to me. But many of our people, especially those in outlying colonies, have no experience with good Vamps. They equate death and destruction with vampires, and they are not going to understand. A were-tiger has never mated with a vampire before—"

"There's a first time for everything," Jia interrupted. "Now, if you will excuse me, I have to go to the palace to help Russell defeat his brother. How do you think he's feeling right now?"

She turned and marched up the stairs. When she reached the top, she heard Rajiv calling for Tenzen. As she opened the door, her cousin and uncle joined her.

Rajiv held the door open for her. "We're not going to let you do this alone."

Her heart swelled. Rajiv was still on her side. "Thank you." Now Master Han would have three tigers to contend with.

With a pair of binoculars, Russell scanned Han's army on the far side of the river. He estimated about two hundred soldiers: most on foot and a few officers on horseback. No sign of Darafer, and so far, he hadn't spotted Markos, either.

"Ye doona have to do this," Angus muttered. "We're prepared to fight."

"I'm not letting another person die because of my brother."

"Ye're no' alone in this. I could station some guys in the throne room."

"Have them wait outside the door. I need to talk to Markos first. If I can convince him to surrender . . ." Russell's voice faded with doubt.

With a sigh, Angus patted him on the back. "Have ye spotted him yet?"

"No." Russell lowered the binoculars. The moon was almost three-quarters full and bright in the night sky. He had expected to catch the gleam of his brother's golden mask. "When did the army arrive?"

"About two hours before sunset," Angus replied. "Rajiv was in charge. Every time they approached the river, he ordered his men to fire at them."

Russell glanced at the male were-tigers who

were armed with rocket grenade launchers. No wonder Han's army was staying put. The minute they attempted to cross the river, they would be easy to pick off.

He spotted a small group behind the army, all dressed in black, making them hard to see in the dark. With the binoculars, he focused on them. They were heavily armed, and the one in the middle was wearing a black Kevlar vest and a hood concealing most of his head.

Russell's heart beat faster as he waited for a telltale gleam of gold. *Look this way, Markos. Let me see your mask.*

The man lifted his head to gaze at the sky. Nothing but black inside the hood.

A black mask. Of course. Russell's chest constricted with a mixture of relief and dread. "I found him."

"Really?" Angus asked. "Where?"

"The group in the back, all dressed in black. Han is in the middle."

Angus narrowed his eyes. "I hope ye're right. A surprise attack only works the first time."

"I know." Russell handed the binoculars to Angus while he focused on Markos. Always before, he'd seen Master Han through a dark lens of hatred, but now that his eyes were open, he saw things he'd missed before. The way Han stood, the gestures with his hands, the tilt of his head. *Markos.*

Russell closed his eyes briefly, trying to shut out the pain, but of course, it didn't work. There was no help for it. *God help me.* He teleported behind his brother, grabbed him before anyone had time to react, and took him to the palace throne room.

Jia and Rajiv had the silver chain stretched out, each of them holding an end, and they immediately jumped at Han to wrap the chain around him. He struggled, but Russell held him tight from behind.

"I'll knock you out if I have to," Russell warned him.

"Russell?" Markos grew still. "No need for the silver. I'll stay. I've been wanting to talk to you."

Russell released his brother as Jia and Rajiv looped the chain around him a second time.

Markos grunted as the silver burned the silk material of his sleeves. The Kevlar vest protected his torso. "I said I would stay. Don't you trust me?"

"No." Russell shoved his brother's hood back, then ripped off the black mask and tossed it on the floor.

Even though Russell knew what to expect this time, it still made his heart clench to see his brother's face. Markos's eyes and hair had always been a darker brown than his own. But the shape of his jaw and nose were almost identical. They were the same height, same build. They'd grown up in the same house with the same parents. So why had they become so different?

Russell searched his brother's eyes, trying to find the younger brother he knew.

Markos gave him a wry look, then glanced at

the were-tigers. Tenzen had his sword drawn. Rajiv passed the ends of the chain to his cousin, then drew his sword.

With a smirk, Markos turned his attention to Jia. "You again. Tell me, did it hurt to die?"

She yanked the chain tighter, so that it sizzled against his arms.

He winced, then shot Russell an annoyed look. "These damned cats. You kill them, and they just keep coming back."

Jia narrowed her eyes. "When you killed my parents and brother, they didn't."

"Oh?" Markos gave her an inquisitive look. "Did I hack them into itsy-bitsy pieces?" He shrugged. "Too bad I can't remember. There have been so many, you know."

With a hiss, she pulled a knife from her belt. Rajiv took a step closer with his sword.

"Shut the fuck up," Russell muttered. "Before my friends decide to kill you."

"Your *friends*?" Markos snorted, then angled his head toward Jia. "So, is she your pet kitten? Do you make her purr?"

Russell seized his brother by the neck. "Shut up, or I'll kill you myself."

"Is that why I'm here?" Markos sneered. "Don't tell me my noble brother has turned into a lowly executioner."

Russell released him with a shove. "I brought you here so I could talk to you."

"Great!" Markos cleared his throat and switched to English. "So, are you over your shock yet? Last time, you looked like you were going to barf."

"I feel sick every time I think about my brother being a mass murderer."

"Aw, does it offend your noble sensibilities? Get over yourself, Russell. You were a soldier, too. We were mass murderers by profession. How many villages did you wipe out?"

Russell gritted his teeth. "It was war. How you handle the aftermath is up to you. As far as I'm concerned, I have done nothing to be ashamed of. I was fighting for freedom. And for my country."

"So am I." Markos's mouth curled up with amusement. "But now, the country doesn't belong to some corrupt government in Washington. This country is mine!"

Russell scoffed. "It was never yours. You stole it."

"To the victor go the spoils." Markos's face grew harsh. "You were an officer. You never knew what it was like to be a grunt, and to have an idiot officer over you treating you like expendable meat. I wasn't going to take it anymore! I'm in charge now!"

"And now you consider your soldiers expendable? How many more have to die for you, Markos?"

He shrugged. "They volunteer. They want the superhuman abilities that come with serving me. And they want to be a part of my greatness. Why should I deny them?"

His greatness? Russell groaned inwardly. His brother was more than an asshole. He was certifiable. Illusions of grandeur and no conscience about the death and suffering he caused.

Markos grinned. "I'm going to take over the world. Not bad for a farm boy from Colorado, huh?"

"You think Dad would be proud of you?"

Markos's smile faded. "That idiot. He always acted like you were Mr. Perfect. Ha! You'll be working for me now."

"You're delusional."

"Not at all." Markos waved a dismissive hand. "I know exactly how you are. You always had to be the leader, the noble protector. And you expected the helpless little brother to follow."

"I did what I was supposed to do. I was older than you."

"So I was doomed never to be in charge?" Markos sneered. "Why do you think I kept you in a coma for so long? I knew I wanted you to rule by my side, but I couldn't risk you taking over. So before waking you up, I had to make sure I had everything under *my* control. Now *I'm* the one with more experience. *I'm* the older one now."

Russell stepped back as if he'd been hit. "You . . . you destroyed my life over a fucking case of sibling rivalry?"

Markos shrugged. "How does it feel to be the lowly one? It really sucks, doesn't it?"

"Do you know what happened while I was in a coma?" Russell clenched his hands into fists. "Our parents died. I lost my wife. I lost my daughter! Even the ranch is gone!"

"Why do you care about puny mortals, when we can live forever? And why bother with a ranch when we can rule the world?" Markos snorted. "This is why I have to be the boss. You think too damned small!" He took a step toward Russell, but Jia yanked him back. "Cut it out!" he yelled at her in Chinese.

"Leave her alone," Russell growled.

Markos switched back to English. "Is she really that special to you? I'll make sure she lives. Just like I took care of you. The minute I realized how powerful and immortal I was, I knew I was destined for greatness, and I had to share it with you. I started planning for you. I experimented with hundreds of people to master the technique of long-term vampire comas. When I learned you were on leave in Phuket, I searched until I found you. You were so happy to see me that it was easy to take you by surprise."

Russell's stomach churned with disgust. "You should have left me the hell alone."

"No! We belong together. I want you by my side while I take over the world."

Russell shook his head. "Your army is depleted. They no longer want to fight for you. Half of our army is made up of soldiers who deserted you and want to kill you. It's over, Markos."

His brother's eyes flashed with anger. "It's not over! I'll make you second in command. And I have Darafer—"

"Do you really think you can trust a demon? He's probably letting you do all the work so he can kill you—"

"No! He needs me. And I need you, Russell. You have experience with my worst enemies—these shifters and vampires. You know how they work. With your help, we can defeat them."

Russell glanced over at Jia, who was watching carefully but probably not understanding much of their English. Rajiv understood, though, and his grip flexed on his sword as if he was eager to use it. Next to him, Tenzen was also ready with a sword.

"These are my friends," Russell said. "Do you expect me to betray them?"

Markos snorted. "Are you going to betray your own brother? Now that you know who I am, you have to join me."

"I have to convince you to stop. It's over, Markos."

"Stop saying that! Russell—"

"Enough," a voice spoke from behind a large column. Darafer stepped out, dressed in his usual black attire, his hands resting in the pockets of his long black coat. "Your army grows restless, Han. How about I kill all these people and take you back?"

Tenzen and Rajiv jumped back to keep both Darafer and Han in their sight. Rajiv kept his sword pointed at Markos, while Tenzen aimed his at the demon.

Russell stepped back, his hand going to the knife wedged under his belt. He glanced over to Jia and motioned toward the door with his head. With the arrival of Darafer, the level of danger had just skyrocketed, and he wanted her out of here.

She bit her lip, then shook her head.

"I'm not leaving without my brother," Markos told the demon.

Darafer sighed. "Have you been listening to him? He's not interested. In fact, if you don't surrender, he probably intends to kill you."

"He's my brother!" Markos yelled. "He would never kill me."

Darafer smiled slowly, his gaze shifting to Russell. "Are you sure about that?"

"Then help me, Darafer," Markos said. "Make him join us."

The demon sneered. "The last time I forced someone, I ended up back in hell, and you never got me out."

"A mistake on my part, I admit that." Markos inclined his head. "Only you can make more supersoldiers. But remember how Wu Shen betrayed us. We need a second in command whom we can trust. If you bite my brother, he'll do whatever you say. He'll even kill the angels if they show up."

Darafer shook his head. "He can't kill an angel any more than he could kill me."

"He could attack them, and that would distract them enough that you could escape," Markos insisted. "You know we need him. He could get Xiao Fang back for us."

"That much is true. The dragon boy trusts him." Darafer cast an amused look at Russell. "What do you think? Are you ready to join your brother, or shall I give you a little . . . encouragement?" His eyes turned black.

Russell pulled his knife out. "Try it, asshole." He shot a look at Rajiv. "Get Jia out of here now!"

Rajiv ran toward his cousin and jerked the silver chain out of her hands. "Go!"

The chain fell to the ground, releasing Markos just as Darafer morphed into a large black wolf.

Russell lifted his knife as the wolf slowly advanced.

Tenzen ripped off his tunic and shifted into a tiger.

"Get out!" Rajiv pushed Jia toward the door, then he shifted.

She pulled off her robe.

"No!" Russell yelled when she shifted.

All three tigers advanced on the wolf. Growling, Darafer snapped at one of the tigers, and it jumped back.

Markos grinned. "Now this is interesting."

Russell tried to keep up with which tiger was Jia, but the three large cats were dashing around Darafer, trying to keep him isolated. "Jia, stop! Don't do this."

"Eenie, meenie, miney, moe, catch a tiger by its toe," Markos chanted. "You know if he bites one, it'll turn evil." He laughed. "We could have an evil tiger on our side. Wouldn't that be cool?"

The thought that Jia could be bitten made Russell frantic. He jumped between the tigers and Darafer. "You want me, asshole?"

Darafer growled and leaped toward him.

A tiger jumped on him from the back, raking its claws down a hind leg. Darafer spun about, his jaw gnashing.

"No!" Russell plunged his knife into the wolf's shoulder.

Darafer snapped his jaws down on Russell's arm.

"Yes!" Markos pumped the air with his fist.

Russell winced as pain shot up his arm, followed by a surge of anger so strong that it knocked him on his ass.

Darafer changed back to his human form, dressed in black, with no sign of a wound. "You're mine now," he hissed at Russell. "Kill the one you love. Use that knife with my demon blood on it so it will burn like hell. Do it!"

Russell's grip tightened around the bloodied knife as he scrambled to his feet. Red-hot rage flooded him, and all he could think about was murder. *Kill the one you love.*

Jia. He glanced over at the tigers. Which one was she? The three tigers were huddled up close. No doubt she was in the middle, and the two males were trying to protect her.

"Yes!" Markos grinned. "Kill her, Russell!"

Kill the one you love.

With a roar, Russell dashed forward at vampire speed and rammed the knife into his brother's heart. A look of shock crossed Markos's face just before he crumbled into a pile of dust.

Darafer laughed. "Well, that saves me from having to kill him later."

The knife tumbled from Russell's hand as he realized what he'd done. The rage inside him exploded, and he threw his head back, roaring to heaven. One of the tigers moved toward him.

A bright light suddenly burst in the throne room, and the seven God Warriors appeared with their swords ablaze with fire.

"Attack them!" Darafer yelled at Russell as the

seven angels moved to surround him. "Stab them now!"

"For breaching the decree of free will, you will be banished back to hell," Briathos announced.

The seven God Warriors lifted their swords of fire and began to chant.

"Damn you!" Darafer broke through their ring, but they moved to encircle him once more. "I'm not going alone!" Just as his form wavered, he grabbed a tiger by the hind leg. Whoosh, he disappeared, taking the tiger with him.

"No!" Russell shouted. With Darafer banished, the effect of the demon bite was immediately erased. All the rage was gone, but now he was filled with abject fear.

Which tiger had Darafer taken with him to hell?

The two remaining tigers shifted back to human form, their faces stricken with horror. Tenzen. And then Rajiv.

"No!" Russell collapsed to his knees. He screamed again deep from his soul.

Jia was gone.

Chapter Twenty-one

The palace door burst open, and Connor, Dougal, and Howard dashed inside.

"We heard screaming." Connor stopped short when he noticed the God Warriors.

Russell remained on the floor, his thoughts whirling, unable to accept what had just happened. His gaze shifted to the pile of dust that had been Markos, then to the silk robe on the floor that Jia had taken off before shifting. Both of them were gone. Both in hell? His heart clenched with pain, and he was tempted to rip some shit apart and scream until his head burst.

Markos had probably gotten what he deserved, but that didn't make it any easier to live with. Russell had known he might be forced to kill him, but he'd clung to a hope that he could somehow save his brother. And Jia . . . he hadn't saved her, either. When he imagined what she might be going through right now, he felt like his heart would explode. He had to help her, but how could he, when she was in hell?

"What happened?" Howard demanded.

Rajiv fell to his knees in front of Jia's discarded robe and gathered the silk in his arms. "Jia . . ."

Dougal looked about. "Is she injured? Where is she?"

"Darafer took her to hell," Russell whispered. His gaze fell on the knife still coated with demon blood. Would that get him into hell? God help him, he deserved to go there. He'd killed his brother. He'd failed Jia.

Or maybe not. Maybe he could still help her. He reached for the knife.

Briathos kicked the knife across the room. "Dear soul, you will be no help to her dead."

Russell's pain shifted into rage, and with a shout, he leaped to his feet. "How could you let Darafer take her?" He grasped Briathos's tunic in his fist and jerked the angel toward him. "How could you screw up like that? I thought angels were supposed to be perfect!"

Connor and Dougal pulled Russell back, but he shoved them away.

Briathos regarded him sadly. "We are not perfect. Only the Heavenly Father can make that claim."

"So Darafer has been banished?" Dougal asked. "What happened to Han?"

Russell glanced at the pile of dust, and bile rose up his throat. He rammed his fist against his mouth and swallowed hard.

"Markos Hankelburg is dead," Briathos reported quietly. "Russell killed him while under Darafer's control. We arrived to send the demon back to hell, but as he was vanishing, he grabbed Jia and took her with him."

Dougal and Connor glanced at the pile of dust, then at Russell.

Howard reached out to touch Russell's shoulder, but Russell stepped back. How could he accept sympathy when he was the murderer?

"I'll let Angus know," Connor said as he headed out the door.

"I'm so sorry about Jia," Dougal told the weretigers in Chinese.

"We haven't lost her," Russell insisted. "We'll get her back!"

Rajiv and Tenzen rose to their feet. Since their trousers were ripped to shreds from shifting, they tied their discarded tunics around their waists by knotting the long sleeves.

"Is she still alive?" Rajiv asked Briathos.

The leader of the God Warriors nodded. "Yes. I will give you more information soon." His face went blank, and his body shimmered like a reflection upon water.

"When?" Russell waved a hand in front of Briathos's face, but there was no response. "Hello? Are you there?"

"He has joined the Heavenly Host," another angel explained.

"He's telling them what happened?" Howard asked.

The angel shook his head. "They already know. We are in constant communication. The council of archangels called an emergency meeting and asked Briathos to attend."

"They wish to extend their apologies for this unfortunate situation," a second angel added.

"Unfortunate?" Russell gritted his teeth. "What's happening to Jia? Is she being tortured?"

"Most likely she will be treated well," the first angel replied. "Lucifer only resorts to torture when he has something to gain from it. In this case, he would gain nothing but the wrath of the Heavenly Father."

The second angel nodded. "The Father does not approve of demons taking His children alive against their will."

Russell snorted. "Well, that's big of Him!"

"Calm down." Dougal touched Russell's shoulder.

"Jia's in hell!" Russell clenched his fists, wishing he could hit something. "I've got to help her!"

Rajiv tilted his head, studying him. "You're in love with her."

"Yes, dammit!" Russell's eyes burned with tears. "I have to save her, but I don't know how."

"'Twill work out." Dougal gripped his shoulder harder. "Believe me, I know what ye're going through."

Russell took a deep breath and blinked the tears away. He'd never felt so damned helpless. "Tell me what to do," he begged the angels. "Can I take her place?" After all, he was headed for hell anyway for killing his brother.

"The archangels have begun their meeting," the first angel said. "Briathos is giving his report."

"He's in heaven?" Howard glanced at the shimmering angel. "I can see him here."

"To interact in your world, we take on these human forms that you see," the first angel explained. "But they are merely projections—"

"Enough!" Russell yelled. "How do we save Jia?"

"The archangel Gabriel has decided on a course of action," the second angel announced. "First, a message will be sent to Lucifer, demanding the return of the live mortal."

"And that will work?" Russell asked.

"Perhaps," the second angel replied. "Perhaps not. Lucifer enjoys the havoc caused by his demons."

"This sort of occurrence is not without precedence," a third angel commented. "We had trouble banishing the demon Rasputin back to hell. He was planning on taking members of the Russian royal family with him."

"But we were able to stop him," a fourth angel added.

"The mortals kept trying to stop him," a fifth angel chimed in. "But because he was a demon, they were unable to kill him."

"What about Jia?" Russell demanded. "What if Lucifer refuses to return her?"

Briathos turned solid once again. "The meeting has adjourned. Gabriel sent a message to Lucifer. We will have a reply in due course."

"How long is that?" Russell asked. "And what if Lucifer says no?"

"Do not fear. We are preparing for that," Briathos assured him. "Gabriel is asking the Heavenly Father for permission to invade Lucifer's domain."

"Ye're invading hell?" Dougal asked. "Ye can do that?"

"It is not done often," Briathos admitted.

"I believe the last time was a thousand of your earth years ago," the second angel added.

"If you go, take me with you," Russell said.

Briathos winced. "That is not recommended. If you die in battle there, your soul could end up trapped in hell forever."

Russell took a deep breath. "I'll risk it if it means saving Jia."

"So will I," Rajiv said, then translated for Tenzen, who also vowed to go.

"When will we know?" Russell asked.

"All will be revealed in due course," Briathos replied.

Russell grimaced. "What the hell does that mean?"

"That pissed me off, too," Dougal muttered.

Briathos sighed. "It means it is hard to tell you a certain time. Our time is different from yours. A few hours for us are days for you. It could be a week."

"A *week*?" Russell clenched his fists.

"For you," Briathos said. "The good news is that it will be only a few hours for Jia, too. We will return when we have news." Briathos and his unit of God Warriors vanished.

Russell rammed his fist into a column. He would go crazy in a week.

Ten minutes later, Russell was sitting on the floor in the palace, leaning against a column that he'd pummeled into submission.

Rajiv took a seat beside him. "Don't blame yourself. It was my fault. I should have taken her outside."

Russell shook his head as more tears burned his eyes. "I kept telling her I would protect her, but what did I do for her? First I failed her when she was killed. And now she's been taken to hell."

"She told me that she mated with you."

Memories of their two nights together rushed through Russell's mind. He dragged a hand with bloody knuckles through his hair. "I don't blame you if you're angry. I shouldn't have done it, but God, I love her so much."

"I figured as much," Rajiv admitted. "When Darafer shifted into a wolf to bite you, your first thought was for her safety. Then you let him bite you to keep him from attacking—"

"Don't," Russell interrupted him. "I still failed her."

Rajiv sighed. "When my parents were murdered by Lord Qing, my brother and I moved here to live with Grandfather. And then Jia came here after her parents were murdered. She's like a sister to me. If you go to hell to rescue her, I'll be there with you."

Russell nodded, then hefted himself to his feet. "We'll get her back somehow."

Howard peered through the door. "Come on out, guys. Angus wants to see you."

Russell and Rajiv followed Howard down the palace steps and across the courtyard. It was crowded and noisy with people trying to talk to Russell, but he barely noticed. Angus was at the top of the stairs that led down to the riverbank. Han's army was still across the river, agitated and restless. No doubt they were wondering what had happened to their leader.

Angus motioned for Russell and Rajiv to join him. "I heard what happened, Russell, and I wanted to let ye know how sorry we are that ye had to—"

"I'm fine," Russell muttered.

Angus gave him a dubious look. "I also wanted to warn you that once we announce that the war is over, there will be celebrating. It will be a cruel sound for both of you. The war with Han is over and Tiger Town is safe, but the cost was too high for either of you."

Rajiv nodded, his face harsh with grief.

"I'll let you do the translating into Chinese." Angus lifted a bullhorn and turned it on. "Attention all those who are gathered here this evening."

Voices hushed on both sides of the river.

"There will be no battle tonight," Angus continued. "Master Han is dead, and the demon Darafer has been banished back to hell." He passed the bullhorn to Rajiv, who repeated the announcement in Chinese.

Behind them in the courtyard, cheers rang out. Han's ex-soldiers hooted and clapped, while the were-tigers broke into a joyful rendition of the Tiger Dance. Soon a chant began to echo throughout Tiger Town. *"Han is dead! Han is dead!"*

Russell clenched his fists hard as more tears burned his eyes. The last of his family was dead by his own hand, and it was cause for celebration.

Han's army across the river grew noisy as they adjusted to the fact that they were now free.

Angus took the bullhorn back, and after he made a few loud, blaring sounds, the noise on both sides of the river quieted down. "Attention, soldiers across the river. We wish you no harm. You may go home in peace. If you would like to break the bond that Darafer holds over you, we have a medical procedure that can return you to normal. The ex-soldiers you see here have all been freed from the pact with Darafer. If you wish to be set free, lay down your weapons and come to us."

Rajiv translated the announcement, and the ex-soldiers in the courtyard cheered when they were referred to.

Russell watched the army across the river to see what they would do. A few of the officers on horseback rode away. A handful of foot soldiers drifted off into the woods. But the majority of the army tossed down their weapons and waded into the river, heading for Tiger Town.

"Congratulations." Howard patted Rajiv on the back. "Your town is safe. And the war is over."

"It's not over," Russell growled. "Not till we have Jia back."

"You're right." Howard gave him a worried look. "We'll get her back. I'll go with you."

Russell snorted. "You can't go. Your wife is expecting. You can't risk it."

"We will all be going with you, lad," Angus said quietly.

Howard punched him on the shoulder. "See what I've been telling you all along? You're not alone, Russell. You never were."

The tears that had threatened to fall finally slid down Russell's face.

Chapter Twenty-two

Night after night passed with no word from the God Warriors. Russell's impatience grew increasingly hard to bear. All he could do was constantly remind himself that time was different in heaven and hell. Jia's captivity in hell could be as short as an hour, but even that seemed too long. What if she was suffering? Or afraid?

Each day before dawn, Russell returned to the bat cave for his death-sleep. The other Vamps and shifters were staying in the area, either at Tiger Town, Zoltan's castle in Transylvania, or Kyo's mansion in Tokyo. Everyone kept smiling and telling him that Jia would be all right, that she would be saved, but their forced cheerfulness was driving him crazy.

And so he escaped whenever he could. He did his death-sleep on the sleeping bags and pillows where her scent still lingered. He removed the bracelets she loved so much from her backpack and set them on the table where he could see them. They kept him company while he cleaned his guns and drank his meals.

For the first four nights, he stayed busy. All of the ex-soldiers at Tiger Town needed to be teleported home. Then all the were-tigers that had been evacuated needed to be brought back. The clinic was overflowing, since over a hundred new supersoldiers were receiving the treatment to turn them back to normal. Russell helped the other Vamps set up tents in the courtyard and along the riverbank.

Dougal's wife, Leah, was in charge of the medical team, and they were in constant need of supplies, so Russell helped the other Vamps teleport medical supplies and extra food in. He even helped the were-tigers cook, since they needed to produce several hundred meals every day.

On the fifth night, he teleported to Tiger Town, but there was still no news from the God Warriors. He helped Rajiv repair and paint the column in the palace that he'd abused with his fists. He visited Jia's room, thinking it would comfort him to see where she had lived and slept, but the room was full of gifts from her fiancé, the wealthy prince. Jewelry, embroidered silk robes and slippers, porcelain vases and tea sets. All sorts of things that he couldn't afford.

He teleported back to the bat cave and paced about. She loved him. He had to believe that. And he had to believe that he could save her. That meant he needed to prepare for a future with her. Would she be willing to marry a vampire? He was dead half the time, so he had only half a life to share with her. He smiled to himself, recalling Jia's tendency to be a Pollyanna. She would insist that he wasn't dead half the time, but alive. And even better, he could live as long as she. As a were-tiger, she could live about five hundred years.

But how would they live? He had no job, no money, and no real residence. He couldn't envision taking her back to Colorado. His life there was over. In fact, he'd been declared dead. And Jia would be miserable so far away from her people.

No, she needed to stay here in China, where she had friends and family. Perhaps Rajiv would let him buy some land next to Tiger Town?

Russell picked up one of Jia's bracelets and ran his fingers over the hammered gold and inlaid jade. She was a princess. He needed to provide well for her.

His gaze wandered about the bat cave. The microwave and solar-powered generator had some value, but he couldn't sell stuff that he'd stolen. He'd always intended to give them back once his mission was over.

The now familiar pang struck his chest once again. His mission was over. He'd found Master Han. And he'd killed him. The revenge he'd wanted for so long had ended up a double-edged sword. He'd stabbed his brother through the heart, only to cut himself to the core. He'd fallen in love with Jia, only to lose her.

He shoved the depressing thoughts away and tried to focus on a happy future with Jia. How to finance it? His gaze landed on the wooden box on the bottom shelf of his bookcase. The Colt Single

Action Army Pinch Frame revolvers handed down to him from his great-grandfather.

Since they dated from 1873, they were valuable. He set the box on the table and unwrapped the oilcloth to examine the pistols. Could he give up the only thing he had left from his family?

What family? he thought with a snort. It was actually a relief that his parents were dead and would never know that their youngest son had become a murderous vampire warlord. Or that their oldest son had killed him.

Home was gone. The past was over. He could never go back. Better to sell the pistols to provide for a future with Jia. Maybe Zoltan would be interested in them or know where he could sell them.

He slipped one of Jia's bracelets into his coat pocket, grabbed the box of pistols, and teleported to the armory of Zoltan's castle. It was dark inside, but he knew his way around. He set the box on the table, then headed up the spiral staircase to see if Zoltan was home.

To Russell's surprise, the door was locked from the outside. *Oh right,* he remembered, *there are guests staying here.* Zoltan had invited a bunch of the guys and their families so they could meet his wife, Neona. If there were children about, he had probably thought it best to keep the weapons locked up.

Russell teleported to the kitchen and discovered Shanna Draganesti and another woman there, stacking homemade cookies on a large tray.

He recognized Shanna right away, since he'd stayed at the Draganesti townhouse in New York a few times during his first year as a vampire.

Back then, he'd been employed by Angus's company, MacKay Security & Investigation, so most of the trips had been for business, such as the battle to defeat the villain Casimir.

But his first trip had been a mere month after being transformed, when he had wanted to check on his family. After learning that his daughter was dead, he'd spent the rest of the night in the townhouse kitchen drinking Blissky. Shanna and Roman had joined him, and he'd always been grateful for the compassion they'd shown.

The other woman here in Zoltan's kitchen was probably a wife of one of the other Vamps, but there were so many of them now, he couldn't keep them straight.

"Russell!" Shanna smiled at him as she slipped on oven mitts. "How wonderful of you to stop by."

"Good evening." He nodded his head at the other woman. "Ma'am."

"Call me Heather." She extended a hand toward him. "I'm Jean-Luc's wife."

"Nice to meet you." He shook her hand. "Is Zoltan around?"

"He's in the courtyard." Shanna removed two pizzas from the oven. "Everybody's there for the party."

"Please say you'll join us," Heather said as she filled a huge ice chest with juice boxes and bottles of beer and Bleer.

Russell shifted his feet. "I don't really feel like celebrating."

Heather winced and exchanged a look with Shanna.

"We're so sorry about your brother and Jia," Shanna murmured.

Russell shrugged. "I don't blame you for wanting to party. The villains are all in hell, where they belong. The war is over."

"True, but it's not really over till we get Jia back," Heather said. "All the guys intend to help."

Russell swallowed hard. As much as he appreciated everyone's support, he didn't want any of the men with wives and children to be at risk. "That's not necessary."

"It is." Shanna sliced the pizzas. "We're all family."

"And everyone will want to see you," Heather added. "Tonight's a big night for me and some of the other wives. Neona has offered us some of her Living Water. Tonight I take my first sip."

"So you'll be able to live as long as your husband without becoming a vampire?" Russell asked.

Heather nodded. "I'm starting the process tonight, along with Toni, Lara, and Olivia. Our husbands are relieved they won't have to transform us."

Russell could well believe that, since the act would require draining their wives of every last drop of blood.

Shanna sighed. "It was very hard on Roman when he had to change me."

Heather gave her a curious look. "You could become mortal again if you drink some of the Living Water."

Shanna frowned as she gathered some bags of

chips onto another tray. "I've been giving it a lot of thought. On the one hand, I could have my days back with my children. But on the other hand, I feel like I would be denouncing my life as a vampire, as if it's not good enough. I can't do that to Roman."

Heather nodded. "It's a tough decision."

Shanna smiled. "I've learned to be happy with my situation. How about we get this food up to the party?" She picked up the two trays of pizza.

Heather motioned to the ice chest stuffed with juice boxes, beer, and Bleer. "Could you carry that for us, Russell?" She picked up the tray of chips and another tray of cookies.

Russell groaned inwardly as he hefted the heavy ice chest up the stairs. When he reached the great hall, he could see the front doors of the castle were open. The chatter of adult voices and squeals of children filtered in from the courtyard.

"We brought food!" Shanna announced as she passed through the door, and she was greeted with cheers.

"And we have a guest!" Heather glanced back at Russell when he hesitated just inside the door. "Come on."

He gritted his teeth. More smiles and happy faces when all he wanted to do was rescue Jia. More pats on the back with a sympathetic look. If a greeting card company made cards that said, *Sorry you had to murder your brother,* he would have dozens of them by now.

Deep inside, he knew he shouldn't be annoyed that these people cared. He just hated the sympathy right now. He hated feeling helpless when Jia was in danger. And most of all, he hated the waiting.

His stomach churned as he followed Shanna and Heather down the steps into the courtyard. White lights had been strung up along the battlements and around the central stone fountain to give the place a festive look. A few floodlights made the place safe enough for the children to run around in. Two long buffet tables were already half covered with trays of food. Shanna and Heather added their trays as a horde of noisy children gathered around.

To the side, there were a dozen round patio tables with chairs, making the courtyard look like an outdoor restaurant. A crowded restaurant. A lot of the Vamps and shifters Russell had met during his first year of working for Angus were here. And they were all smiling and waving at him to come over.

Dammit. He hated that these guys were going to risk themselves. All their wives and children were here. They had too much to lose.

Angus and Emma were at a table, each holding one of the were-dragon babies they had adopted. The twins were only about two months old, but since dragon shifters aged twice as fast, they looked a bit older. Jack and his wife, Lara, were at the same table with their baby. A girl, Russell guessed, by the pink dress.

Roman Draganesti rushed over to the buffet tables to help his wife hand out food to all the kids. He gave her a loving smile. "The family just keeps growing."

Shanna smiled back. "I know. Isn't it wonderful?" She waved at Russell, motioning for him to put the ice chest down by the tables of food.

He set it down, and immediately the children swooped in like a horde of locusts and grabbed all the juice boxes. So many kids. He stepped back. Would he be able to have children with Jia someday? He supposed their children would be the first half-vampire, half were-tiger kids in the group. They'd probably be prone to biting. And if they were half as noisy as these kids, they could probably wake the Undead.

Suddenly one of the older kids hugged him.

"Xiao Fang." Russell noted the dragon shifter was looking much better. The boy grinned at him, then dashed off with another boy. That had to be his friend, Norjee.

Russell smiled, watching the two boys scamper about. That was one thing he could be proud of doing—rescuing Xiao Fang.

Another one of the older children ran toward the stone fountain in the middle of the courtyard. "Let's finish our game!" He covered his eyes and started counting.

The other children squealed and darted around the courtyard, looking for places to hide.

Howard pulled two bottles out of the ice chest and handed Russell a Bleer. "Have a seat. Enjoy the party."

Russell shook his head. "I don't want you guys going to hell with me."

Howard took a sip from his bottle. "Well, that's our decision, don't you think?"

"You have wives and children. How can you risk dying in hell?"

Howard shrugged. "Any of us could die at any time. Not that I'm being flippant about it, but we know that whatever happens to us, the children will always be loved and taken care of. We're family." Howard gave him a pointed look. "You're part of the family, too."

Russell snorted. "I'm not good at family. I just killed my brother." He wrenched open the Bleer and took a long drink.

Howard gave him one of those sympathetic looks that he hated, so Russell changed the subject. "Where did all these kids come from? I don't even know who they are."

"Well, that's because you've been living like a hermit for the past two years." Howard motioned to the blond boy at the fountain, who had counted up to forty-seven. "That's Roman's son, Constantine. He's seven."

Russell recalled meeting Tino over two years ago. "He's grown a lot."

"You know Xiao Fang and Norjee." Howard pointed at the two boys who were crouching by the fountain on the opposite side from where Tino was counting.

Russell smiled. It was a good strategy, and one he'd employed often as a kid. Not hiding at all but positioning yourself so close to home that you could reach it before getting caught.

A girl ran up to Howard. "Help me, Uncle Howard. Mom and Dad went back to the kitchen to get some Blardonnay."

Howard grinned as he opened the ice chest. "You can hide behind here."

She kneeled down.

"This is Sofia, Roman and Shanna's daughter," Howard explained. "How old are you now? Five?"

She nodded. "Don't let Tino see me."

Howard chuckled, then pointed at a flagpole. "See the two little ones who think they're actually hiding?"

Russell couldn't help but smile at the two toddlers who were sitting behind the pole. The little girl had black curls, and the boy a shock of red hair.

"Those two are inseparable," Howard said. "Ian's little girl and Robby's little boy. They'll both turn two in the fall. Oh, they have company." Howard laughed as two more young children crowded behind the pole. "Those are the Panterra twins, Eric and Adriana. They've just turned two. They all know each other from being at Dragon Nest Academy."

"And those?" Russell pointed to the chapel, where an older girl was hiding with two younger ones.

"The Echarpe kids. Bethany's about ten now, and the twins are four. And over there, Phineas and Brynley are chasing after their twins. Ben and Gwen have graduated from walking to running at full speed."

"You keep up with all of this?" Russell gave the were-bear a wry look. "You must like kids."

Howard nodded and aimed a happy look at his wife. Elsa was sitting at one of the tables, deep in conversation with Neona. "Elsa's helping Neona design a big nursery here in the castle. Zoltan wants me continue to work here as head of security, so it looks like we'll have our twins here."

"That's good." Russell spotted Connor at the entrance to the castle, helping a little redheaded toddler scramble up the stairs. "I guess that's Connor's son."

"Yeah." Howard chuckled when the boy grabbed at his father's kilt. "I heard the Scottish guys complaining that they have to wear underwear under their kilts now. The little ones keep tossing their kilts up. That one is Gabriel. He's a year and a half."

At the mention of the name Gabriel, Russell tensed. He was sick of waiting for news from the angels. He wanted Jia back now. "I brought some antique pistols with me. I . . . I'd like to sell them if any of the guys would be interested."

Howard tilted his head, considering. "Zoltan has a collection in the armory. I think Jean-Luc has a collection, too, though he's more into swords."

Just then, Tino shouted, "One hundred. Ready or not, here I come!" He looked about and grinned at the four toddlers lined up behind the flagpole.

Meanwhile, Norjee and Xiao Fang touched home and laughed when Tino scowled at them. Sofia crept away from the ice chest and inched along the tables.

When Tino's back was turned, she made a mad dash for the fountain. He spotted her and gave chase, finally tapping her on the shoulder.

"You're it!" Tino announced, then winced when his sister stomped on his foot.

Howard chuckled. "Where are the pistols?"

"In the armory."

Howard nodded. "I'll get the keys and the guys and meet you there."

Russell teleported inside the armory, turned on the light, and finished his bottle of Bleer while he waited for the others to arrive. Soon he heard the door unlock and footsteps coming down the stairs.

Zoltan patted him on the back. "It's good to see you."

"*Bonsoir, mon ami.*" Jean-Luc shook his hand. "I hear you have some antique pistols?"

"Yes." Russell removed the pistols and set them on the table. "Colt Single Action Army Pinch Frame revolvers. My great-grandfather received them in 1873. They have consecutive serial numbers, double digit."

"*Formidable.*" Jean-Luc picked one up to examine it.

Zoltan looked at the other. "Why would you part with these?"

Russell shrugged. "They're from the past. Right now, I'm more interested in having a future. With Jia, I hope."

Howard nodded. "We'll get her back."

"I'll give you two hundred thousand," Jean-Luc said.

"Two-hundred fifty," Zoltan countered and smiled when Jean-Luc gave him an annoyed look.

"Sold," Russell said quickly. He liked the

thought of the pistols being here in Zoltan's castle, where he could look at them whenever he liked. "I have an account at your bank in the village, if you would transfer the money there."

"Sure. Not a problem," Zoltan replied.

"I'd like to spend some of it right away." Russell took Jia's bracelet from his pocket. "I want to have a necklace made that matches this."

"Impressive." Jean-Luc took out his cell phone and started taking photos. "I know a jewelry designer in Paris who could do it. I'll send him the photos."

"Thank you." Russell smiled to himself. Now he would have a wedding present for Jia that was as good as any from the were-tiger prince. "I also need some wedding rings."

Howard chuckled. "You're in a hurry."

"You're in luck." Zoltan grinned. "I'll take you to the jewelry store in the village."

Two hours later, Russell returned to the bat cave. He set Jia's bracelet on the table next to its twin, then placed the box of wedding rings next to them. Now he needed to buy some land from Rajiv. It was near dawn, so he would wait till sunset before returning to Tiger Town.

When Russell awoke, he realized this was the sixth night since Jia's kidnapping. Maybe Briathos and the God Warriors would return tonight with news. He quickly dressed, guzzled down some blood, and teleported to Tiger Town.

Although the courtyard was crowded with

tents, it was eerily quiet. The treatment to turn the supersoldiers' DNA back to normal worked best when they were unconscious.

Down by the river, the were-tigers were in groups, talking in hushed voices as they pointed at and admired a row of four black SUVs. Standing next to each SUV was a guard dressed in a black suit.

"Hey, Russell." J.L. walked up to him, a bottle of synthetic blood in his hand. "You got here fast. You must have heard the news."

"What news? Did Briathos return?"

J.L. shook his head and motioned to the SUVs. "The were-tiger prince and his entourage arrived about an hour ago."

Russell groaned. And Jia wasn't here to tell the precious prince to get lost. He doubted Rajiv would do it. As far as he knew, Rajiv might want the wedding to go through. "Where are they?"

"In the palace." J.L. finished his bottle of blood. "Rajiv is hosting a banquet in their honor."

Russell tamped down a surge of anger. It seemed that the prince was still the preferred choice for Jia's husband. "Then we should go." He marched toward the stairs.

"Wait." J.L. followed him. "It's an official were-tiger affair. I don't think we're invited."

Russell snorted. "Think again." He needed to meet this prince.

Chapter Twenty-three

"You'll need to make a formal greeting," J.L. warned him when they reached the double doors to the palace. "If you don't show your respect, it'll be taken as an insult."

Russell snorted as he heaved open one of the doors. He didn't mind being polite to Rajiv, but the prince was another matter.

"Don't speak until you've been spoken to. Follow my lead," J.L. whispered before stepping quietly into the throne room.

Russell followed, trying not to recall the awful events that had happened here. Right over there, he'd killed his brother. And there was the spot where he'd realized Jia was gone.

The room looked different now, bright and sparkling with candlelight. Tall brass candelabras were positioned between each of the red painted columns, and two more flanked the throne that sat on the dais at the far end of the room. Candlelight gleamed off the golden tigers that decorated the ornately carved wooden throne.

Along the perimeter of the room, red silk banners hung from the ceiling, each ending with a golden tassel. On the banners, embroidered tigers were either crouching or leaping. On the floor, a series of low tables had been lined up to make one long banquet table. A red silk table runner with gold tassels extended down the length of the table, although it was barely visible for all the food. There were enough platters of meat and bowls containing vegetables and sauces to feed twice the number of guests present.

Rajiv, dressed in a purple silk robe, sat on a floor cushion at the head of the table. His long black hair had been pulled up into a topknot, encircled with a gold ring and pierced with a long hairpin in the shape of a golden tiger. Twelve guests were at the table, six on each side, all sitting cross-legged on red silk cushions.

To Rajiv's right sat a young man with a gold crown on his head and an entitled smirk on his face. That had to be the prince. Russell fought an urge to wipe the smugness off his face, and not with a silk napkin. The rest of the people on the right were probably his entourage. The last in line was a woman. Russell assumed that the further down the line a person sat, the lower his rank. Behind the seated guests, six men in black silk robes were standing and eyeing him and J.L. with suspicion.

Russell smirked. How many bodyguards did the prince need? He had to be a wimp.

To Rajiv's left sat his uncles, Rinzen and Tenzen, plus four more elderly gentlemen. All the guests had stopped eating to look at the intruders.

Russell felt a tug on his trouser leg and noticed that J.L. had knelt. So this was the formal greeting? With an inward groan, he knelt. Then, to his surprise, J.L. planted his hands on the stone floor and bowed forward till his forehead touched the ground.

Damn. No way was he prostrating himself before Jia's fiancé. He glanced at Rajiv, who looked tense but was keeping his face expressionless. There was no help for it, Russell realized. Rajiv was a future in-law, so Russell couldn't embarrass him in front of his own kind. Gritting his teeth, Russell bowed low.

"I bid you welcome," Rajiv said.

"Your kindness is beyond measure, Your Eminence," J.L. said. "Please forgive our ill-mannered intrusion. We merely wish to pay our respect."

Russell rolled his eyes. Enough with the groveling. He started to stand but noticed that J.L. was still sitting on his knees, so he followed suit.

"Allow me to introduce you to my esteemed guest." Rajiv motioned to the right. "This is Prince Kim Mi-nam of South Korea. Your Highness, these gentlemen are Wang Jin Long and Russell. They are both Americans."

The prince sniffed. Russell was tempted to cure the prince's sniffles, and not with a tissue.

Rajiv gestured toward the Vamps. "Would you care to join us?"

The prince stiffened and set his chopsticks

down with a loud clunk. "You intend to share this table with vampires?"

Rajiv gave him a conciliatory smile. "Don't worry. They won't be eating any of the food."

"That is not the point," the prince growled. "They're loathsome, filthy creatures."

Russell gritted his teeth. He was tempted to wash out the prince's mouth, and not with soap.

Rajiv's hand gripped his chopsticks so hard that his knuckles turned white. "These are my dear friends and trusted allies. Perhaps you have heard of our troubles? For over forty years, my people have been plagued by Master Han and his three vampire lords. Many of my people were hunted and slaughtered, including my parents and the parents of your betrothed."

The prince shrugged. "We have heard the horror stories of Master Han and his three lords, but that sort of loathsome behavior is hardly surprising for vampires."

Rajiv's smile looked forced. "Then you may be surprised to learn that there are good vampires. Jin Long helped me kill one of the vampire lords, Lord Qing. Russell killed Lord Ming, and just recently, he killed Master Han. With that one brave act, he succeeded in doing what my people have been unable to do for forty years. And by killing Han, he stopped an army from attacking my village. To me and my people, these men are heroes."

The prince grunted and regarded Russell and J.L. with disdain. Russell met his gaze, giving him a look of challenge. *Which would you like first, Prince? A black eye or a broken nose?*

Rajiv lifted a hand, and a servant approached. "Please bring two cups and a bottle of Blissky for our new guests."

As the maidservant rushed off, Rajiv gestured to the food. "Please enjoy the meal. Let me pour you a drink." He lifted a teapot and filled the prince's cup.

The were-tigers started eating again. Russell and J.L. scooted to the end of the table, where they sat cross-legged. Russell watched everyone carefully and noticed that Rajiv's gaze was drifting often to the pretty young lady in the prince's entourage. She was quietly focusing on her plate in front of her.

The maidservant placed two cups in front of Russell and J.L., then filled them with Blissky, a mixture of synthetic blood and whisky.

"I must say, I am terribly disappointed that Lady Jia is not here," the prince grumbled. "Surely she knew we would be arriving soon."

"I apologize," Rajiv murmured. "It couldn't be helped."

"Why will you not tell me where she is?" the prince demanded. "I could have my men fetch her."

Rajiv smiled. "I appreciate the offer, but that will not be necessary. We hope to have her back soon." He exchanged a look with his uncles. The other men on his side of the table shifted uncomfortably and fiddled with their food. Obviously, none of them wanted the prince to know where Jia was.

"A toast to Lady Jia." Russell lifted his glass,

and everyone drank. "So, Rajiv, can you tell me who everybody is?"

Rajiv looked relieved to have the subject changed. "You know my uncles." He motioned to the four older gentlemen. "These are esteemed members of my Council of Elders."

"I have already introduced my entourage, but I will do so again." With an annoyed look, the prince nodded to the people on his side of the table. "My father's secretary of state, the leader of our Council of Elders, my personal secretary, my head of security, and Lady Yi-soo."

"If I might be so bold as to inquire, why is there a noblewoman traveling with you?" Rajiv's gaze lingered once more on the young lady.

Prince Mi-nam waved a dismissive hand. "Her title is merely honorary. In truth, she is little more than a servant."

Lady Yi-soo kept her head bowed, but her cheeks turned pink.

Rajiv's jaw shifted. "Then I am even more curious as to why she is here."

The prince glanced down at her with a scornful look. "My father insisted on it. She is to serve as Lady Jia's personal bodyguard and tutor. Lady Yi-soo is skilled in martial arts and fencing. And she will be teaching Lady Jia our language and glorious traditions. Surely Lady Jia will not wish to be an embarrassment to our royal court?"

Rajiv gritted his teeth. "Of course not."

Russell wondered what the prince would look like with his golden crown wrapped around his throat.

J.L. cleared his throat. "Then Lady Yi-soo can understand us? She speaks Chinese?"

"Of course," Prince Mi-nam answered for her. "She is fluent in several languages. She was allowed to attend school with the other royal children."

"*Other* royal children?" Rajiv asked.

The prince shrugged. "My father has sired over fifty children, but they need not concern you. I am the eldest legitimate son and therefore heir to the throne. The illegitimate children inherit nothing, so you needn't fear that Lady Yi-soo will be a threat of any kind to your cousin. As my wife, Lady Jia will become the Grand Tigress and receive all the honor and wealth due to her station."

Rajiv's eyes narrowed.

Russell amended his vision. Instead of wrapping the prince's golden crown around his neck, he imagined cramming it down the bastard's throat.

"Are you saying Lady Yi-soo is illegitimate?" Rajiv asked quietly, glancing at her.

She set her chopsticks down as her cheeks bloomed a brighter pink.

The prince snorted. "Is this really worth discussing? Do you wish to cause her further embarrassment? Believe me, she already knows her place."

Rajiv hissed in a breath.

Russell slammed his cup down on the table. "Is it one of your glorious traditions for the Grand Tiger to be unfaithful to his wife?"

The prince huffed. "My father's private life is hardly any of your concern."

Anger simmered in Rajiv's golden eyes. "It is our concern if you intend to follow in his footsteps."

The prince gave him an incredulous look. "Your Eminence, surely you understand the true nature of an arranged marriage. My betrothal with Lady Jia has been enacted for the sole purpose of creating an alliance between our two kingdoms. It is a political union, nothing more. Like my father, I will look elsewhere—"

With a growl, Russell jumped to his feet. "You bas—"

"Stop," J.L. hissed in English as he grabbed Russell's arm. "Let Rajiv handle this."

Russell pulled away. "I need to clobber him."

The prince cleared his throat. "I understand English, too."

"Then understand this," Rajiv announced. "I will not allow my cousin to enter into a faithless marriage. She deserves better than that."

Prince Mi-nam snorted. "Come now. You're a Grand Tiger just like I'll be someday. We're not allowed to marry for love. It is only natural for us to—"

"I realize I will have to marry according to my position," Rajiv interrupted, "but I will make every effort to ensure my marriage becomes a union based on love. I will treat my wife with respect and honor, remaining faithful to her each day, so that in time I might earn her love."

The prince rolled his eyes. "We can live for hundreds of years. How could you remain faithful for centuries?"

"How could I not be faithful when there is love?" Rajiv asked. "My grandfather was faithful to his wife. My parents were faithful to each other. That is *our* tradition. My cousin will not accept less."

Prince Mi-nam huffed with indignation. Russell was ready to punch the prince's lights out, but he felt a surge of pride over how well Rajiv had handled the matter. Obviously, he and Rajiv felt the same way about marriage. And it looked like Lady Yi-soo did, too. She was gazing at Rajiv with tears in her eyes.

A sudden flash of light filled the room, and Russell turned to see Briathos materializing by the door.

"What the hell?" Prince Mi-nam scrambled to his feet and rushed to stand behind his bodyguards.

Russell snorted. He was a wimp, all right. "Not hell. More like heaven." He turned to the God Warrior. "Any news? How is Jia?"

Briathos bowed his head. "Greetings, dear souls. An hour has passed since—"

"You mean six days!" Russell yelled.

"Yes." Briathos gave him a wry look. "We are aware of how much time has passed on Earth."

"What has happened?" Russell demanded. "Did Lucifer let her go?"

"Lucifer?" Prince Mi-nam asked.

"It's a long story," Russell growled, then asked Briathos, "well?"

The God Warrior shook his head. "Lucifer has refused to release her. The archangel Gabriel is gathering an army of five hundred God Warriors. We have permission to invade hell."

Russell nodded. "I'm coming with you."

"*Hell*?" Prince Mi-nam asked, his voice rising.

Russell shot him an impatient look. "Yes, hell. When I killed Master Han, the God Warriors came to banish the demon Darafer back to hell. Unfortunately, he took Jia with him."

"Lady Jia is in hell?" the prince asked, an incredulous look on his face. "That's impossible! People aren't taken to hell."

"Oh, really?" Russell gritted his teeth. "I'll take you. You can help us rescue her."

The prince scoffed. "Don't be ridiculous. I'm not sure I even believe this ludicrous story."

"It is true," Rajiv told him. "Lady Jia was kidnapped by a demon and taken to hell."

"We will assist with her rescue," Tenzen said, motioning to his twin, Rinzen.

"Me, too," J.L. added.

Briathos regarded them sadly. "Your courage is to be commended, but I must warn you once again of the grave danger. If you are killed in hell, you run the risk of your soul being trapped there forever."

Russell nodded. "I understand. I'm still going."

Rajiv walked down the length of the table to join Russell. "I will go with you."

"But Your Eminence," one of Rajiv's elders protested. "You mustn't go. It is too dangerous."

Rajiv rested a hand on the elder's shoulder. "Before we leave, Jin Long will teleport my brother here. If something happens to me, Raghu will be the new Grand Tiger. He and his wife just had twins, so the line will be secure."

The elder nodded sadly. "Please be careful, Your Eminence."

Russell glanced back at the prince, who had turned pale. "Well, Your Highness?"

Mi-nam gulped. "I—I could send some of my bodyguards."

His bodyguards stiffened with horrified looks on their faces. One fell to his knees. "Your Highness, please—"

"I will go," Lady Yi-soo interrupted.

Rajiv gasped. "My lady, no—"

"Yes!" The prince waved a hand at her. "She can go. She *should* go! After all, she's Lady Jia's bodyguard." He clapped his hands together as if to make her decision final. "Lady Yi-soo will represent our people in the rescue of Lady Jia."

What a worm. Russell glared at the prince. He would let a woman take his place on a dangerous mission?

"My lady." Rajiv moved to her side. "There is no need for you to endanger yourself."

She rose to her feet. "I have lived my entire life trapped in one wing of the palace. I wish to do this. I need to."

Rajiv stepped closer. "Then fight by my side. I will do my best to keep you safe. You have my word."

Her mouth curled up. "I am an excellent fighter, Your Eminence. I might be keeping you safe."

Smiling, he took her hand. "You have a deal.

Although I would prefer taking you somewhere other than hell."

She returned his smile, her cheeks blushing. "Well, I've always wanted to travel . . ."

"When do we leave?" Russell asked the God Warrior. "What weapons should we bring?"

"Your weapons will not work on demons or the inhabitants of hell, for they are already dead," Briathos replied. "But fear not. We will equip each of you with a sword of fire."

"Awesome," J.L. whispered.

Briathos gavc him a wry look. "The enemy will be using similar weapons on you."

J.L. winced. "There's always a downside, isn't there? But it could be worse." He grinned when Russell gave him a dubious look. "We could be on the wrong side."

Russell snorted, then asked Briathos again, "When do we leave?"

"Gather your men. We will meet you in the courtyard in three of your Earth hours. From there, we will take you to the gates of hell." Briathos's form shimmered, then vanished.

Chapter Twenty-four

Three hours later, Russell stood in the courtyard of Tiger Town, flexing his hand around the grip of his new sword. The blade was powerful, the edge fine and sharp, but overall, the sword was surprisingly light. Perfectly balanced, beautifully wrought, but that was probably to be expected with an angelic weapon.

He studied the engravings on the golden pommel, wondering if there would be fine print that said *Made in Heaven,* but the lettering there made no sense to him. Of course, he slapped himself mentally. Why would he assume the writing in heaven was related to any earthly language?

The blade gleamed silver in the nearly full moon. There, he felt it again. A slight vibration against the palm of his hand.

"Do you feel it?" he asked Angus, who stood beside him.

"Aye," Angus replied, studying the hilt of his sword. "'Tis most peculiar."

"The swords are forging mental connections to each of you," Briathos explained. "Later, in battle, they will respond to you, unleashing fire when you wish it."

"Awesome," J.L. whispered.

"You will need to rely on these swords for your protection," Briathos continued. "Once we are in hell, you will lose all your supernatural abilities. If you are wounded there, let me know immediately. The wound will need to be cleansed with holy water."

Russell winced as he glanced around the crowded courtyard. There were still tents filled with ex-soldiers getting turned back to normal. Those who had volunteered to go to hell were gathered on the steps and entrance to the palace. Vamps like Robby, Ian, Jack, Connor, and Mikhail. Shifters like Howard, Phil, and Carlos. Half shifter Phineas and mortals Austin and Zoltan. Even Vamps like Roman and Jean-Luc, who didn't work for MacKay S&I, had come. They all had wives. Many had children or children on the way. Most had said their good-byes before teleporting here.

A few of the women were here, like Leah and Abigail, since they were working on the medical team. Right now, they were hugging their husbands, Dougal and Gregori. Rajiv was standing close to Lady Yi-soo, and the two were deep in conversation. Other were-tigers were studying their new swords. Briathos and his unit of God Warriors were at the base of the stairs by the tiger statues. And according to Briathos, those who had volunteered to go with Russell would no longer be able to shift or teleport or mentally control anyone. They would be in even more danger than he'd originally thought.

He eased closer to Briathos. "You said there would be five hundred God Warriors?" When Briathos nodded, Russell continued, "Could you guys keep these people here surrounded so they'll be somewhat safe?"

Briathos looked closely at Russell. "Are you concerned for them?"

"Well, sure. They have wives and children. And . . ."

"And?" Briathos asked.

Russell frowned. "I feel bad that they're doing this. I would prefer for them to stay behind."

"Because you always work alone?"

Russell winced. How did the angel know that?

Briathos gave him a wry look. "You were never truly alone. These people care about you. The Heavenly Father loves you. Is it that hard to accept?"

Russell's eyes burned. "Yes, it is. What could be remotely loveable about me? I just killed my brother! If I die in hell, I'll end up right where I'm supposed to be."

Briathos's eyes flashed with anger. "Heed my words, mortal. No one is supposed to end up in hell. The Heavenly Father did not create you to fail."

Russell's breath caught. The angel was right. He couldn't fail. Jia was counting on him. "I will succeed. I have to get Jia out of there."

"You risk your life for the love of Jia. You ask

me to protect these people because you care about them. Therein lies the truth you have refused to see. You are loveable because you love with a pure and selfless heart. And when you are offered love, it is because you are worthy of it."

Russell blinked away tears as his gaze wandered over all the people gathered there. Six nights ago, Angus had told him they would all accompany him to hell, but he still found it hard to believe. They had been rooting for him the whole time he'd thought he was alone. They were his friends. His family. He was blessed.

"News coming in from the Heavenly Host," Briathos murmured, then raised his voice so everyone would hear. "Gabriel and his army have arrived at the gate to hell. It is time for us to go."

"How do we—" Russell started, then everything flashed black.

Suddenly, he was bombarded with high-definition techno-color so dazzling he had to blink his eyes to adjust to it. He was standing with the others in a green valley dotted with bright yellow and purple wildflowers. On either side, snowcapped mountains gleamed under a bright sun. Bisecting the valley was a trickling stream that sounded like music to his ears. A cool breeze caressed his face, filling his lungs with crisp mountain air. He felt a surge of joy and an urge to continue along the stream to the end of the valley, for without a doubt, he knew that would lead him home. He was back in Colorado.

"Wait a minute." He shook his head. "This is hell?"

"Aye." Dougal smiled as he gazed about. "It looks just like the Isle of Skye."

"You mean Colorado," Russell said.

Carlos leaned over, as if he was touching something. "It's my favorite beach in Brazil. Don't you see the waves coming in?"

"You each see your home?" Briathos asked, and they nodded. "And you each have an urge to continue in that direction?" He pointed toward the end of the valley.

"Yes," Russell replied. "What's down there?"

"The gate to hell. It looks pleasant here in order to lure you in. Do not be deceived." Briathos waved a hand, and the landscape shimmered. The mountains faded away. The colors ran together, mixing into a dull, muddy brown. The soft grass beneath Russell's feet withered up and turned to dust. They were left on a flat, desolate plateau under a dingy sky.

It reminded Russell of an old photograph where even the black and white tones had faded into dreary browns. There were no stars, no sun, no birds, no trees. Even the air felt scorched and stale, and the slight stench of sulfur turned his stomach.

"Everything's dead," Angus said.

Briathos nodded. "At one time, a millennia ago, there were dead trees here and there. But the inhabitants of hell started to draw them and admire their stark beauty. Lucifer had them burned away, for nothing is allowed here that can bring comfort to a sad soul."

"So this is hell?" Russell asked. "No life, no joy?"

"Correct. But given each mortal's innate need for joy, the inhabitants are eventually lured into finding it where it should not exist, and sadly, that becomes their only source of joy." Briathos frowned. "They are allowed to torture each other."

Russell swallowed hard. "Are they torturing Jia?"

"Lucifer claims she is being treated well." Briathos sighed. "But we cannot trust his word. Come, this way."

They followed Briathos and his team of six God Warriors and soon arrived at a ridge overlooking a flat plain. A short distance away, there was an enormous walled city, filled with hovels in shades of brown and gray. In the center, a palace of stone loomed, square-shaped and forbidding, with no outside windows or decoration.

Just below the ridge, five hundred God Warriors were gathered, their golden armor and shields gleaming. Light emanated from them so that they looked like stars reflected in a sea of murky brown. In front of them, the gray stone wall extended as far as Russell could see. It was thick and crenellated like the wall of a medieval castle, but there were no guards in sight.

"The wall is unmanned," Russell said. "And the gate is wide open."

Briathos nodded. "It is not designed to keep people out. But once you are inside, you will discover the door is closed and well guarded."

"So it's easy to walk in—"

"But nearly impossible to leave, unless you are in the company of an angel," Briathos said, then turned to face Russell's friends. "The large building you see in the center is Lucifer's palace, where Jia is being held. Gabriel's army will forge a path down the main street, making a tunnel for us to pass through. After we enter the palace and secure Jia, we will rejoin Gabriel's army and make for the gate with all haste. Do not allow yourself to be cut off from the group, or you may find yourself trapped in hell forever."

Everyone nodded, then Briathos continued, "Once we come under attack from demons and the dead, your swords will activate. But remember, you cannot kill someone who is already dead. And as mortals, you cannot kill a demon. A clean thrust through the heart of your enemy will make them appear dead, but they will revive within an hour. That is why we must proceed as quickly as possible."

"Understood," Russell said. If they didn't move fast, the dead would keep coming back.

They followed Briathos and his unit down the ridge to join the army. There, they were surrounded by huge, muscular angels, all armed with multiple weapons, and all grim with determination.

Gabriel gave the order, and with a tremendous shout and blaring of horns, the army charged through the gate. There was little resistance for a mile or so. Dead souls lined the road, throwing refuse and yelling curses. But when Gabriel's army drew near to the palace, a horde of demons flashed onto the scene. Hideously ugly, with red, glowing eyes, they wielded flaming swords and chains with metal studded balls. When the balls whooshed toward them, they lit up with fire.

The God Warriors held up their shields and continued their advance. Angels and demons clashed, their flaming swords slashing through the air, leaving trails of fire in their wake. Clanging noises filled the air as the fiery metal balls hit angelic shields.

More demons arrived, hundreds of them, flashing onto the scene with a puff of sulfurous smoke. Their ranks began to surround the angelic army. As Gabriel pushed forward to the palace steps, his army grew thinner and more elongated. Russell and his friends were no longer deeply surrounded, and at places, they were close to the enemy.

Russell lifted his sword, ready to do battle, and the blade burst into flame. He stabbed at demons as he made his way up the palace steps.

"Oh, no," Briathos said beside him, and Russell followed the angel's line of vision. Here on the steps, they had an excellent view of the main street that led from the gate to the palace.

A huge horde of mortal dead were attacking the angelic army from the rear, pushing them toward the palace. The gate out of hell was now blocked off.

"I thought we entered too easily," Russell yelled over the noise.

Briathos nodded. "Lucifer means to trap us here. If he can get even one God Warrior to join his side, he will consider it a great victory. Come, we must hurry." He charged up the remaining steps, slicing his way through the demons.

Russell and his friends followed, their fiery swords clearing a path to the palace door.

Briathos and Roman yanked the doors open, while Russell, Connor, and Howard stood ready to attack anything that might come out. Surprisingly, there was nothing.

Briathos gave them a wry look. "It is always easy to enter—"

"But hard to leave," Russell finished. Even if he managed to find Jia, it was questionable whether they could escape hell now that the gate was blocked.

"Sheesh, this place is worse than the Hotel California," J.L. said, but when Russell and Briathos gave him a blank look, he muttered, "Never mind."

Behind them there was a huge roar, and they all spun about.

"What is that?" Roman asked.

Another horde of mortal dead charged from the rear, but instead of attacking the angels, they were fighting the demons and other dead inhabitants of hell.

"The dead are fighting each other?" Connor asked.

"It's a rebellion!" Briathos's face lit up with excitement. "A faction from hell has taken our side!"

Russell narrowed his eyes to see who the leader was. "Shit! It's Wu Shen! He's leading Master Han's dead soldiers."

"Yes!" J.L. pumped the air with his fist.

Rajiv grinned at Lady Yi-Soo and gave her a high five.

"This way!" Briathos motioned for them to enter the palace. It was stark and empty, with multiple hallways and staircases leading off the foyer. "We'll divide into seven groups. Each group must have a God Warrior, or you will risk getting lost in the labyrinth of hallways and rooms. The instant a group finds Jia, the God Warrior will contact the others so that we can all assist with the rescue."

The Vamps and shifters quickly divided, and each group took off running. Briathos charged up the staircase on the left. Russell followed, along with Roman, Connor, and Howard. Their footsteps echoed eerily through the palace, lending punctuation to Russell's thoughts.

Hold on, Jia. We're almost there.

There was something going on. Jia could tell from the hushed, excited voices of those around her in the banquet room, but she didn't dare ask. Since her arrival in hell, her strategy had been to draw as little attention to herself as possible.

When she'd first arrived, she'd discovered she'd gone from one throne room to another. Unable to retain her tiger form, she'd shifted back.

Darafer had tossed her on the floor in front of a throne. "Master, I bring you a live hostage."

When she'd looked up, she'd seen a beautiful face with eyes so cold and dead that she'd shivered.

Lucifer had given her an indifferent glance, then leaped off his throne and backhanded Darafer, sending the demon flying back so hard that he'd crashed into a stone wall. "You failed. The kingdom on earth you promised me has not come to pass."

Darafer had prostrated himself. "Forgive me, master. The God Warriors ganged up on me—"

Lucifer had kicked him. "You let those bastards banish you a second time!"

"We can get even with them! They'll come to rescue the girl. And they'll bring those wretched vampires and shifters with them. We can trap them here. Torture them."

Lucifer had straightened, closing his eyes and breathing deeply, as if he'd smelled something sweet. "I will forgive you if Gabriel comes. For millennia, I have wanted to make him suffer."

Darafer had scrambled to his feet. "We'll turn him! We'll make all of them evil!"

Lucifer had cast Jia a dubious look. "I fail to see why they would want to rescue her, but we shall see." He'd waved at two guards. "Take her to a holding cell until I call for her."

As Jia had been led away, she'd almost wished Russell and Rajiv would leave her be. She couldn't bear the thought of them being trapped in hell with her.

Before locking her into a small room, a servant had tossed her a red robe. She'd put it on and paced about. Time had seemed to drag by, but she knew it hadn't been long before her door was opened. The servant and guards had led her down one hallway after another, then up a flight of stairs. Now they were in a large room, lined on one side with windows that overlooked a central courtyard. Two long banquet tables extended down the length of the room, with guests seated on the far right and left sides. They lounged on Roman-style couches.

At the far end of the room, Lucifer had a table to himself, where he lounged and picked at his food as he watched the others. Jia recognized Darafer, who was sitting on the first chaise to Lucifer's right. The other guests were unknown to her, except for Master Han, who was sitting on the last chaise lounge on the left. He gave her a solemn look, then frowned at the platter of meat and fruit in front of him.

Lucifer and Darafer were dressed in crimson robes, their perfectly formed faces and bodies radiating life and power. But the other guests, including Han, were different. Their skin and clothing were in drab sepia tones, as if they were only negative photographic images of their former selves. Jia cringed inwardly. These were dead inhabitants of hell.

She was led to a fourth table at the base of the two long banquet tables and instructed to sit there among some empty chaise lounges. She tried to make herself look inconspicuous in spite of her bright red robe and healthy glowing skin.

A hissing sound brought her attention to the floor. Good Lord, snakes! She pulled her legs up onto the chaise and grabbed the knife from her place setting. As her heart calmed its thunderous beating, she became aware of the hushed, excited voices of the other guests.

"Invasion," one whispered. "Trap," said another.

Her nerves tensed. Had the God Warriors come for her? Were Russell and Rajiv with them?

A servant rushed into the banquet hall and whispered something to Darafer, who nodded with a smirk of satisfaction.

Lucifer scowled at the demon. "If you fail, you will suffer for it."

"The plan is working, master," Darafer insisted. "Gabriel is within your gates, within your grasp. We have the God Warriors surrounded. They cannot leave!"

This announcement caused more excited gossip among the guests.

"Gabriel brought those wretched vampires and shifters with him, too," Darafer continued. "Some of them are the murderers of your guests at tonight's table. Soon we will capture them all!"

The guests snickered and clinked their wine goblets together.

Did that mean Russell was among the invaders? Jia glanced over at Master Han. He wasn't drinking with the others.

Another servant burst inside the banquet hall. "Master, the invaders have entered the palace!"

Lucifer waved his hand, and all the snakes transformed into demons armed with wicked-looking swords. Jia cringed. There had to be fifty of them.

"Bring the girl here," Lucifer ordered, and two servants dragged her down the length of the banquet tables. She passed by several dozen demons, who glared at her with red, glowing eyes, then she was tossed onto the dais. With her heart pounding, she scrambled to her feet. Here, she could see the double doors that marked the entrance to the room. They were closed now, but any second, they might burst open, and Russell might appear.

"Let them come." Lucifer took a sharp dagger from his table and sliced his arm, letting his blood seep down the blade, coating it red. He stabbed his dagger into a peach, and it shriveled into a black glob. "We'll see how well they handle demon blood."

Chapter Twenty-five

"I can hear them inside," Briathos whispered as he paused outside a set of double doors.

"Let's do it." Russell grabbed a door handle, and Roman took the other. Connor and Howard lifted their swords, ready to charge in.

"Hold on." Briathos tilted his head a moment, concentrating. "All right, I've alerted the others. They'll be coming soon. We should wait—"

Russell flung open the door and rushed inside, followed by his friends. They came to a quick halt when several dozen armed demons hissed at them.

Howard winced. "Guess we should have waited."

"Impatient mortals," Briathos muttered as he extended a flaming sword toward the demons to keep them back.

Russell spotted Jia immediately, and a surge of relief spread through him. Even though she was surrounded by demons, she looked well. She immediately grinned, her eyes sparkling, but then she glanced nervously at the guy at the head table. That had to be Lucifer. And there was Darafer, seated at the first couch. A few of the other guests were recognizable—Casimir, Corky, and Rhett Bleddyn—but Russell's gaze shifted quickly to the last couch on the left where a human form was hunched over the table, his head bowed.

"Markos," Russell whispered, and the lifeless shadow that resembled his brother raised his head.

Russell's breath caught. He'd expected to see rage or hatred in his brother's eyes, not shame and despair.

"Markos," he repeated, stepping toward him.

His brother lifted a hand to stop him, then glanced quickly at the armed demons and back to Russell.

A warning? Russell's chest tightened. Was Markos worried about his safety? *Damn*. A wave of anguish struck Russell hard. He'd wanted so desperately to connect with his brother while he'd been alive. It seemed to be happening now, but it was too damned late.

"Aw, a family reunion," Lucifer murmured. "How touching." He motioned to the empty couches positioned along the end table. "Take a seat. Keep your brother company. It's the least you can do after murdering him, don't you think, Russell?"

Bile rose up Russell's throat. The devil knew him by name. And knew his crime.

"Release Jia, the were-tigress," Briathos demanded as he pulled Russell back. "Give her to us, and we will be on our way."

"Why the hurry, Briathos?" Lucifer's eyes narrowed. "Have a seat. Join us."

Briathos gritted his teeth. "I will never share a table with you. Give us the captive."

Lucifer snorted. "Such manners. Really, I expect an angel to be better behaved than that. Can't you see I have guests? They've been waiting for you." He motioned to the seven guests. "What do you think, Casimir? Isn't it marvelous to see Connor again? After all, he's the bastard who beheaded you."

Casimir sneered at Connor. "I'll make him suffer for that."

Connor scoffed. "Ye can try. How fortunate that ye found yer head again. Are ye sure it isna screwed on backwards?"

With a snarl, Casimir leaped to his feet. "You fool, you think you can mock me? You and your friends are trapped here in hell. We will torture you until you beg for death!"

Another guest rose to his feet. "Roman Draganesti, this time when we duel, I will be killing you."

Roman sighed. "Ivan Petrovsky. While it is true that I bested you in a duel, I didn't kill you. You were stabbed to death by those two women there."

Ivan glared at two of the other guests. "Katya, Galina, I have not forgotten. I will make you pay."

Katya lifted a knife. "Try it, asshole. I'll kill you again."

"With pleasure," Galina added, raising her knife.

"Hello, Howard." Rhett Bleddyn sneered at the were-bear as he tested the sharpness of his knife. "Welcome to hell."

Howard glowered back at him. "I see you're right at home here."

"He should be," Corky grumbled, scowling at Rhett. "That bastard slept with me and then killed me!"

Casimir stiffened, giving Corky a stunned look. "You slept with that disgusting werewolf? You were *my* mistress!"

"You were dead." Corky shrugged. "And not all that good in bed, either. Your crooked arm was useless."

Casimir huffed. "It was broken in the Great Vampire War and healed this way in my death-sleep."

Rhett snorted. "You should have broken it again. I'll break it for you."

"Don't bother," Corky hissed. "He prefers to look like a freak."

"Bitch!" Casimir threw a knife at Corky, who'd already thrown her knife at Rhett.

With a cry, Corky wrenched the knife from her chest and plunged it into Casimir. "Bastard!"

"Bloody whores!" Ivan hurled knives at Katya and Galina just as they retaliated.

Within seconds, all six guests collapsed on the tables, dead.

"What the hell?" Russell muttered.

With a sigh, Lucifer lowered his head and pinched the bridge of his nose. "It's so hard to find intelligent help these days."

Howard scoffed. "Anyone with any sense knows better than to side with evil. You're a bunch of losers!"

The demons hissed as they brandished their swords.

"Not a good time to be insulting them, Howard," Roman muttered.

"Aye." Connor raised his sword. "The beasties outnumber us."

"Not for long." Briathos glanced back at the double doors as they burst open.

The rest of Briathos's unit and all the other Vamps and shifters poured into the room.

"Did ye find her?" Angus asked.

"Jia!" Rajiv spotted her and waved.

She stepped toward them, but the demons yanked her back.

"There is no need for us to fight," Briathos said. "Hand over Jia, and we will leave."

"No. You're all trapped here." Lucifer stood, his mouth curling into a crooked smile. "You can resist, and we will torture you and kill you over and over. Or you can give in and join me. Your choice. But either way, you're not leaving."

"That's where you're wrong, asshole," Russell said. "We are leaving. Wu Shen is leading an army of Han's soldiers against you. Even the dead souls in hell are attacking you now."

Markos's eyes lit up.

Lucifer blinked, then turned to glare at Darafer. "What is this? A rebellion in my kingdom?"

Darafer shook his head. "That can't be right.

Those soldiers belong to me. They sold their souls to me!"

"Right," Russell goaded him. "You made a bunch of superstrong humans and brought them here to hell, where they could rebel against your master."

Lucifer's eyes turned black as he glowered at Darafer. "You took their souls for yourself? You have betrayed me?"

"No! He lies!" Darafer grabbed a knife off the table and snarled at Russell. "You think you can mess with me? I'll kill you." He charged toward Russell, but Markos leaped in front just as the demon plunged in his knife.

"No!" Russell shouted, grabbing his brother, who stiffened with a gasp, his hands clutching at Russell's shirt.

Darafer ripped the knife free, but before he could resume his attack on Russell, Briathos rammed the edge of his sword against the demon's neck.

"Drop your weapon," Briathos ordered. "And back away."

As Markos crumbled to the floor, Russell fell to his knees, holding his brother. "Markos. You shouldn't have done that."

"I had to." His brother grimaced with pain. "You're still alive. I'm already gone. It doesn't matter what happens to—"

"Don't say that! You matter to me." Russell's eyes burned with tears as he touched his brother's face. "I'm so sorry, Markos. I never meant to kill you. No matter what you did, I still love you. I wanted to save you."

"I know." Markos struggled to breathe. "My fault. I asked . . . Darafer to bite you. I was wrong."

"I should have saved you somehow." Russell's heart squeezed painfully. "I will save you! I'll take you out of here!"

"Too late . . . for me." Markos's eyes flickered shut. "Be happy." He went limp in Russell's arms.

"No!" Russell held him tight as tears ran down his face.

"Since you love him so much, why don't you stay here?" Lucifer smirked. "He'll be back in an hour, you know."

"Master, let us kill them all," Darafer pleaded.

Briathos kept his sword pressed against the demon's neck. "Release Jia, and we will leave."

Lucifer scoffed. "And where will you go? The gate is blocked."

"Wrong again, asshole." Russell rose to his feet. "Wu Shen and his army are taking the gate."

Lucifer's hands fisted, and he turned to the nearest demon. "Check on it." After the demon vanished, Lucifer pulled a long dagger from a blackened peach. "I think you lie, Russell. This weapon is coated with my blood. Once I have proof of your lies, I will use it on you first."

The demon reappeared and fell to his knees. "Master. Our army is surrounded by God Warriors and rebels. The gate is open, and dead souls are trying to escape!"

Lucifer's face turned red with rage. "My own people defy me?" He glared at Darafer. "My kingdom invaded. My people rebelling. And now, they're escaping!"

"Master, please!" Darafer pleaded.

Briathos stepped back as Lucifer flew toward the demon and stabbed him through the heart with the blood-coated dagger.

Darafer screamed and collapsed onto the ground, where he writhed a few seconds before disintegrating.

The demon was dead, Russell realized. He'd thought only the Heavenly Father or an archangel could kill the demon—but then again, Lucifer had been an archangel at one time.

Lucifer breathed heavily, his teeth gritting as he glared at Briathos. "This is my domain. Get out. Take the girl and go!"

Jia ran toward them. "Russell!"

He grabbed her, hugging her tight. "Jia. Thank God."

Lucifer hissed. "It is me you should thank. Now get out of here!"

"My brother—" Russell started, but Lucifer's eyes turned black.

"He's mine." Lucifer turned to the demons. "As soon as they're gone, close the gate. Quickly!"

After one last look at his brother, Russell linked his hand with Jia's and turned toward the door.

"This way!" Briathos and the God Warriors led the way as they all dashed for the palace doors.

Outside, Gabriel and his God Warriors had the demon army subdued, while Wu Shen's army was guarding the open gate.

Russell paused just long enough to look Jia

over. "Are you all right? I was so worried about you. Those bastards didn't hurt you?"

"I'm great!" With tears in her eyes, she hugged him, then turned to give Rajiv a hug.

"This is Lady Yi-soo," Rajiv introduced the woman next to him as he took her hand. "Let's go!" They ran for the gate.

"Who is she?" Jia asked.

"Long story." Russell grabbed Jia's hand. "Let's go home."

Russell and Jia hurried for the gate. While he'd stopped to make sure she was all right, the other Vamps and shifters had gone ahead and were already passing through the gate. Just as Rajiv, Russell, and the two women drew near, Han's three vampire lords jumped into their path to stop them.

"You dared to kill me!" Lord Qing yelled at Rajiv, then swung a sword at him. "I will have my revenge."

Rajiv jumped back, then Lord Qing turned on Jia. She ducked as his sword swooshed over her head. Russell leaped in front to defend her, but Lord Liao attacked him, and he was forced to fight him off.

Meanwhile, the third vampire, Lord Ming, lunged at Rajiv, slashing with his sword.

Russell stabbed Liao, then turned to help Jia, who was unarmed and still under attack by Lord Qing. She screamed as Lord Qing lunged toward her. Before Russell could reach them, Lady Yi-soo pierced Lord Qing through with her sword.

"Jia!" Russell grabbed her.

Rajiv finished off Lord Ming, then ran toward his cousin. "Jia, are you all right?"

"Yes." She smiled at Lady Yi-soo. "Your friend saved me."

Lady Yi-soo bowed her head. "It is an honor."

Russell realized that all their friends were out the gate. "Hurry, let's go!" He grabbed Jia's hand and ran.

Rajiv and Lady Yi-soo were close behind. The God Warriors followed, then Gabriel held the gate open to let Wu Shen and his army out.

"Are they free now?" Russell asked Briathos. "What will happen to them?"

"Wu Shen and his soldiers will remain here outside the gate until the Heavenly Father decides their fate," Briathos replied. "But since they were coerced by a demon, and then rebelled against Lucifer, I expect the Father will be merciful."

With a loud bang, the gate to hell swung shut.

"You are safe now," Gabriel announced. With a whoosh, all the swords of fire disappeared.

Lady Yi-soo looked at Rajiv and gasped. "You're bleeding."

Rajiv frowned at the cut on his arm.

"Allow me." Briathos cut the sleeve away, then poured a vial of holy water on the wound. "This will cleanse away the evil residue so that it can heal normally."

Rajiv winced. "That stings. Once we get home, I'll shift and it'll be fine."

"But it's still bleeding." Lady Yi-soo untied the sash around her robe, then wrapped the silk tightly around his wound. As she tied it off, her robe began to gape open a bit. "Is that better?"

Rajiv tilted his head so he could see her white silk undergarment. "Yeah, I'm feeling much better."

Russell snorted, and Jia exchanged a smile with him. He pulled her into his arms. "I thought I'd lost you."

She wrapped her arms around his neck. "I thought I'd be trapped there forever. I wanted you to come after me, but I was afraid you would and—"

"Nothing can keep me from you." Russell cradled her face with his hands. "Not even hell."

She smiled in spite of the tears in her eyes. "That's my cowboy."

"Anything for my princess." He wiped away a tear that rolled down her cheek.

She embraced him tightly. "I love you."

"I love you, too."

After a moment, she nodded her head toward her cousin. "I'm gone for an hour or so, and Rajiv finds a girlfriend?"

Russell snorted. "First of all, you were gone for a week. I nearly went crazy."

She blinked. "A week?"

"Six nights. And Lady Yi-soo came with the Korean delegation. Your fiancé is waiting for you in Tiger Town."

Jia's eyes widened. "Oh dear."

"It is time to go back," Briathos announced, and everything flashed black.

Chapter Twenty-six

Jia thought her heart might burst from joy as she gazed around Tiger Town. She was home. Russell was with her. All the Vamps and shifters were safe and grinning as they called their wives on their cell phones.

"The tents are gone," Russell said as he looked around the courtyard.

"What tents?" Jia asked.

"There were tents full of ex-soldiers being changed back to normal," Russell explained.

"The soldiers are most likely on their way home," Briathos said. "While we were gone, a second week has passed by."

Jia's mouth fell open. She'd been gone two weeks? She glanced up at the moon. It was waning. She'd completely missed the full moon.

Leah and Abigail ran into the courtyard, squealing when they spotted their husbands. Were-tiger families embraced their loved ones who had gone to hell to bring Jia back.

She rushed over to them to thank them, but even those few minutes away from Russell seemed too long. She hurried back to him and threw her arms around his neck. "Have I told you recently how much I love you?"

He hugged her tightly. "I'm never letting you go again. That week was too much. I almost went crazy."

"You told me." She kissed his cheek.

Nearby, Rajiv kicked off his shoes. "I'm going to shift now so the wound will heal." He pulled off his shirt and handed it to Lady Yi-soo. "You might want to turn around. Then again, you're welcome to watch."

She scoffed. "I'm a were-tiger, too. I've seen people strip since I was a child."

He smiled slowly as he unbuttoned his trousers. "Then why are you blushing?"

Her face bloomed a brighter pink as she turned her back to him. Within a few seconds, Rajiv was in tiger form. He circled and sat in front of her. The sash she'd tied around his arm slipped down his foreleg, which was now completely healed.

She knelt in front of him to retrieve her sash. Even though it was bloody, she cinched it back around her waist. "I will treasure this as a memento of the great adventure I shared with you."

Rajiv butted heads with her, and with a laugh, she hugged him.

Jia smiled at them, then gave Russell a wry look. "Did you ever think you'd fall for a tigress?"

He grinned. "No. Did you ever think you'd fall for a vampire?"

With a laugh, she nestled her head against Russell's chest. "You were so brave, the way you stood up to Lucifer."

"I was desperate. Did I mention you were gone for six days?"

"Yes, and you nearly went crazy." She kissed him on the cheek again. "Is that better?"

"It's a start." He kissed her soundly.

"I beg your pardon," a male voice said loudly. "Is that my betrothed you're kissing?"

The courtyard hushed.

Russell tightened his grip on her and whispered, "Can I teleport him to Antarctica and leave him there?"

"I have to handle this myself." She pulled away and turned toward the voice.

The prince was at the head of the stairs, close to the palace. He was more handsome than Jia had expected, almost pretty, with his perfect features and opulent silk robes. At one time, she would have been impressed. But recently she'd met a gruff cowboy vampire with torn trousers and ripped abs who lived in a cave, and her vision of the ideal man had shifted drastically.

She wanted a hero who wasn't afraid to get dirty—and even violent if he had to. She wanted a man brave enough to risk invading hell to save her. A man who admired her strengths, accepted her as she was, and honored her wishes. A man who never gave up no matter how much he suffered.

She wanted Russell.

"Good evening." The prince looked her over. "I am Kim Mi-nam."

"I am Jia." She bowed. "I bid you welcome."

The prince inclined his head. "I am pleased that you have finally returned. You appear to be . . . well."

Rajiv shifted back to human form and dragged on his trousers. "Your sister has returned in good health, too, in case you're wondering."

Mi-nam's mouth thinned as he cast an annoyed look at Lady Yi-soo. "Half sister."

"She's royal to us." Rajiv retrieved his shirt from her and put it on. "She helped us rescue my cousin, while you opted to stay behind."

Mi-nam waved a dismissive hand. "Since Lady Jia is safely returned, I see no point in dwelling on the past."

"I see a point," Jia said. "After all, I could have been trapped in hell forever had it not been for these brave people who saved me." She bowed to the Vamps and shifters. "I owe you a great debt of gratitude. I assure you that your acts of selfless courage will never be forgotten."

The prince nodded approvingly. "You know how to be properly grateful. That is commendable."

Was that supposed to be a compliment? Jia narrowed her eyes.

"However," Mi-nam continued, "your public displays of affection toward other men are entirely inappropriate. We will leave tomorrow for Hong Kong, and then our journey by sea will take about ten days. During that time, Lady Yi-soo will instruct you in proper ladylike behavior so you will not embarrass yourself or me at court."

Jia gritted her teeth. The prince was about to

find himself very embarrassed. "Your Highness, I regret to inform you that I will not be leaving—"

"Of course you are! I have waited a week, and I will not spend one more day in this . . . primitive place." The prince glanced around Tiger Town, wrinkling his nose.

Go ahead, insult my home, Jia thought. It made it even easier to reject him. "I will not be going with you—"

"You will!" Mi-nam shouted, then took a deep breath to calm himself. "I realize, my dear, that you have recently suffered a traumatic event. No doubt you crave the company of your family and friends. But, as my betrothed, you are now part of *my* family. And you will do as I say."

Jia's hands clenched into fists. "As I was saying, I will not be going with you, because our engagement is over. I will not marry—"

"You don't have the power to make that decision!" The prince stormed down the stairs toward her. "You think you can reject me? Do you realize how magnanimous I am being to accept you after you've been tainted by your stay in hell?"

Jia gasped.

"Okay," Russell muttered beside her. "Now I really need to clobber him."

"You'll have to wait in line," Jia growled.

"Your Eminence," the prince said to Rajiv as he ignored them both. "You must rein in your cousin. I will be gracious enough to overlook her behavior, given her recent trauma, but—"

"Actually, I agree with Jia," Rajiv interrupted him. "She's not marrying you."

Mi-nam stiffened, his face turning red. "Y-you

cannot be serious. Breaking this engagement will cause irreparable harm to the relationship between our two kingdoms. My father will be furious that you dare to insult me like this!"

"It is an unfortunate situation," Rajiv conceded. "However, I would like to propose a solution that might ease your father's anger. If he would be so kind as to accept me, I would beseech him for the hand of Princess Yi-soo in marriage."

Yi-soo stiffened, her face pale with shock.

Mi-nam gasped. "Sh-she's not a princess!"

"She is the daughter of the Grand Tiger, and she has displayed great nobility of character. To me and my people, she is a princess." Rajiv knelt in front of her. "I realize this is sudden, but I know in my heart that you are the one for me. Will you marry me, Yi-soo?"

She pressed a hand to her chest. "I-I believe my father will approve. He actually bears great love for me."

Rajiv smiled. "I'm not surprised. But what about you, my lady? Can you accept me?"

Tears filled her eyes and she nodded. "Yes." She fell to her knees in front of him. "Yes. With all my heart."

Rajiv took her hands in his and kissed them.

Jia took Russell's hand and grinned at him. Everything was working out perfectly.

"Is that why you reject me?" Mi-nam snarled. "You could have a prince, but you prefer a vampire?" He scoffed. "I suppose I should be relieved the engagement is off. I would hate to have children who would inherit your lack of intelligence."

"You go too far," Russell said quietly as he stepped toward the prince. "Apologize or I'll teleport you home in pieces."

"You dare to threaten me?" Mi-nam waved his hand, and five bodyguards immediately surrounded him.

"Your Highness." Jia pulled Russell back. "It is true that I love this man. But even if I'd never met him, I would not wish to marry you. I mean no insult to you or your people. I simply know that I'm not cut out to be the Grand Tigress of your country."

Mi-nam shrugged. "That much is true."

"I will gladly return all the lovely presents you sent."

Mi-nam inclined his head. "That will be appreciated."

"Actually, the red and gold silk have been made into a gown," Rajiv said. "Perhaps you will allow your sister to wear it at our wedding?"

The prince gritted his teeth. "Half sister. And my father has yet to approve of your wedding."

Rajiv nodded and turned to J.L. "Can you teleport me to Korea tonight so I can get permission?"

"Sure." J.L. smirked. "Since you're in such a hurry."

"I am." Rajiv winked at Lady Yi-soo, then raised his voice. "I call for a celebration! Princess Jia has been rescued, we are back from hell, and Princess Yi-soo has agreed to marry me!"

Everyone cheered. Jia helped the other were-tigers set up tables and bring out whatever food they could find. Soon the tables were loaded with platters of smoked fish and pork, bowls of rice, and baskets of fruit. Jugs of Tiger Juice were opened, along with bottles of Bleer and Blissky. Russell helped the other vampires teleport in wives and children. The were-tiger men began pounding on their drums, and soon the courtyard was full of laughing people performing the Tiger Dance. After a few goblets of Tiger Juice, even the prince was joining in on the fun.

Rajiv disappeared for a few minutes, then returned, bathed and dressed in his finest robes. J.L. called the number Lady Yi-soo gave him, then teleported Rajiv to the palace in Korea. Ten minutes later, they returned with news. The Grand Tiger of Korea had given his blessing.

Another cheer echoed through Tiger Town, followed by more drinking and dancing.

After a few hours, Jia had had her fill. Dancing and drinking with Russell was fun, but she wanted some time with him alone.

"I'm going to the bathhouse," she whispered in his ear. "Come see me in about twenty minutes."

His eyes lit up. "It's a date."

Ten minutes later, Jia was soaking in the giant sunken tub in the bathhouse. Before getting in the tub, she'd scrubbed herself in the shower stall to get rid of any lingering sulfurous scent from hell. She'd brought clean clothes from her room, and the robe from hell had been tossed into the bathhouse's furnace.

Now she relaxed in the hot water, letting all the

fear and anxiety of the last few days drift away from her with the rising steam. Through the thin walls, she could hear the drums still beating in the courtyard. The party was still going strong. She closed her eyes, listening to the far-off sound of laughter.

She was home. She was loved. Life was good.

The door creaked open, and she sat up with a gasp.

Russell smiled at her, then closed the door and shot the bolt. "There. Now we won't be disturbed."

With a smile, Jia sank back into the water till it was up to her chin. "Has it been twenty minutes?"

"No, but I couldn't—damn, that's a big tub. How many people are you expecting?"

"Only you."

"That's good." He pulled off his shirt as he kicked off his shoes. "As I was saying, I couldn't wait any longer. I missed you."

"I missed you, too." It was a joy to watch him strip. His muscles had a way of bunching and rippling with every move.

"Did I mention you were gone six days?" He dropped his trousers.

"You nearly went crazy," she murmured, eying the bulge in his underwear.

"Exactly. I can face the devil if I have to, but I can't face living without you." He yanked off his underwear.

Jia bit her lip, catching a glimpse of his aroused state before he cannonballed into the sunken tub. She sat up to avoid having a tsunami go over her head.

He reached for her, then blinked when she set a bar of soap and a washcloth in his hands. "What's this?"

"It's called a bath, cowboy. Wash yourself. And turn around so I can scrub your back."

"Then I can't see you," he muttered, but he turned around and started soaping himself up.

"You can feel me." She lathered up her hands, then rubbed them up and down the sculpted contours of his back. "Do you know you're beautiful?"

He snorted. "Are you stealing my lines?"

"It's true." She leaned forward till her breasts brushed against his back, then kissed the back of his neck.

"Okay." He tossed his bar of soap across the room. "I'm clean enough." He turned around and grabbed her. "Did I tell you how much I missed you?"

"Yes."

He dragged a finger across her lips. "I'm not sure you grasp the full extent of how much I suffered."

"Oh. Poor baby."

"I thought I'd never see your beautiful face again." He planted kisses across her cheeks and nose.

"I thought I'd never kiss these lips again." He molded his mouth against hers and slipped his tongue inside.

With a moan, she stroked his tongue with her own.

He nuzzled her neck. "Meow."

She grinned. "What was that?"

"I've decided to learn tiger language. Did you understand me?"

"Hmm." She ran her hands through his wet hair. "I believe you said that you missed me. And nearly went crazy."

"Exactly. See how well I'm learning your language?" He flicked his tongue over her ear and whispered, "Rawr."

She giggled.

"Did you understand that?"

"I believe so." She slid her hand down his abdomen until she encountered his erection. "Ah, I was correct."

He moaned when she curled her hand around him and squeezed. "Good God, we communicate well."

"Mmm." She gave him a tug.

"I have something to show you."

"I've already found it."

He chuckled. "Not here."

Everything went black, and then she found herself in a dark place. Dark but familiar. The bat cave.

She smiled when he set her on the bed. "Now I really feel like I'm home."

He stretched out beside her and cupped her breast with his hand. "I love you, Jia."

She wrapped her arms around him. "Make love to me."

He scoffed. "Like I need to be told."

She swatted him, then gasped with pleasure as he drew her nipple into his mouth. Desire flooded her, and her core ached for him.

When he reached between her legs, she groaned, pressing herself against his hand. "Take me."

"Patience." He stroked her harder and faster till she was writhing against him. "Did I tell you how much I missed you?"

"Yes!" Tension mounted inside her till she thought she would scream. "You—you nearly went . . . *crazy*!" Her climax hit hard.

While she was still throbbing, he moved between her legs and plunged inside her.

"You're mine, Jia." He moved inside her. "My princess. My tigress. My love." With a shout, he climaxed and triggered another one for her.

They lay together in the dark while their hearts and breathing slowly returned to normal.

"I was going to show you something." He rose from the bed, and soon an oil lamp illuminated the cave.

She sat up in bed and noticed her bracelets on the table. He must have removed them from her backpack. "You took my cuffs out."

"Yes." He touched one of them. "They reminded me of you. I even talked to them like you were here." He picked up a small box and brought it back to the bed. "This is for you. Well, us."

She opened the box and found three rings. Two plain golden bands and one golden one embedded with small diamonds and topped with a big one. Her mouth dropped open.

"If you don't like them, I can take them back. Let you pick them out."

"Th-they're beautiful." They must have cost him a fortune. She wondered briefly how he could afford it, but then he knelt beside the bed.

"Will you marry me?"

For a few seconds, she considered telling him that she didn't need fancy things, she needed only him. She closed the box.

His face grew pale.

Oh, no, she was scaring him. "Will you put my ring on?" she asked.

A grin burst across his face. "Of course." He opened the box and pulled out the engagement ring. "Then you're saying yes?"

"Of course." Her heart thudded as he slid the ring onto her left hand. She was getting married. To Russell.

He sat on the bed beside her. "After you went to the bathhouse, I talked to Rajiv. He agreed to sell me some land just east of Tiger Town. We can build a house there, and you'll never be far from your family and friends."

Her heart squeezed in her chest. "You didn't want to go back to your home in the States?"

He shook his head. "The ranch there is gone. From now on, my home is with you."

Tears filled her eyes. "Have I told you how much I love you?"

He smiled. "How soon can we get married?"

"Soon." She wondered why he'd bought land from Rajiv. Obviously he wanted to live close to Tiger Town but not in it. He must still have dreams of being a rancher.

She bit her lip. Somehow she would make his dream come true. It would be her wedding gift to him. She just needed a few days to pull it all together. "Let's get married a week from now."

Epilogue

One week later . . .

He was wearing a dress to his own wedding.

There wasn't much that Russell wouldn't do for Jia. After all, he'd gone to hell and back for her. He was more than ready to pledge his undying love and devotion to her in just a few minutes. But this was almost more than he could stomach.

Traditional ceremonial gown for the groom, she had called it, but it looked like a damned dress to him. Gold silk with black trim, official tiger colors, she'd told him. The gown reached his ankles and was tied with a black sash embroidered with golden tigers. And if that wasn't bad enough, he was wearing a ridiculous hat on his head that looked like a miniature black UFO. With beads.

His only consolation was that his three groomsmen, Rajiv, Zoltan, and Howard, had to wear dresses, too. In fact, it was worth wearing the damned dress just to hear Howard grumbling and growling. And the strings of beads hanging in front of his face were not so bad, since they obstructed his view enough that he couldn't see the other guys smirking at him.

He was standing with his three unlucky, gowned victims at the top of the stairs leading to the palace. The large landing was where he would marry Jia, since it could be seen by everyone in the courtyard. Were-tigers from all over China, northern Myanmar, and Thailand had traveled to see Princess Jia marry a vampire, something that had never happened before in their culture. They were crowded into the courtyard, along with all his Vamp and shifter friends.

Jia had followed another were-tiger wedding tradition. Every young girl in the village and every daughter of Russell's friends who was old enough to walk had been designated a flower girl. Heather Echarpe had designed Chinese-styled gowns for them all in a rainbow of colors. Bethany Echarpe and Sofia Draganesti had taken charge, like little generals minding their troops. Each girl was equipped with a basket full of flowery ammunition.

A gong sounded, signaling the beginning of the ceremony, and the horde of young girls was unleashed. They swooshed onto the scene like a monsoon of flitting fairies, raining handfuls of colorful flowers. Soon the courtyard and the guests were covered with petals, and everyone was grinning at how seriously the girls were fulfilling their task.

After the girls ran out of flowers, they sat on the

stairs leading up to the palace, leaving a path free in the middle. Another gong sounded, and it was time for the boys to take over. Russell had adopted another were-tiger tradition that required three boys to bring in the rings, a ceremonial dagger, and a gold sash. Xiao Fang was in the middle, carrying a red cushion with the rings, while on either side of him, Norjee and Tino carried the dagger and sash. They mounted the steps and stood next to Zoltan and Howard.

Another gong, and the three bridesmaids arrived. Neona and Leah came down the aisle, followed by Lady Yi-soo. They reached the top of the stairs, and then the drums began.

Russell's pulse started pounding with the drums. There she was. Jia. A mixture of love, pride, and joy filled his heart. And now he could see why he was wearing a damned dress. Her gown matched his. Even her hat matched his. He was part of the were-tiger family now. This was his home. And his new family.

She reached the top of the stairs, and he took her hands in his. Later, he would have trouble remembering all he said, even though Jia would assure him he'd said his vows correctly. At one point, the were-tiger priest used the ceremonial dagger to prick the palms of their right hands, and then, while they held hands, their blood mingling, the priest had looped the gold sash around their joined hands.

But Russell couldn't recall any pain. All he could remember was Jia's smile and beautiful tiger eyes glistening with tears of joy.

After the ceremony, the were-tigers set up tables in the courtyard and brought out platters of food and barrels of Tiger Juice. For the Vamp guests, there were bottles of Bubbly Blood, a mixture of synthetic blood and champagne. And for all the children, there was fruit punch and cookies.

As the Grand Tiger, Rajiv welcomed everyone and invited them back in a month for his wedding with Lady Yi-soo. When Yi-soo requested that all the flower girls return for a repeat performance, the proud parents cheered.

Roman Draganesti joined Rajiv on the stairs overlooking the courtyard and asked to say a few words. With a glass of Bubbly Blood in his hand, he gazed over the crowd, and everyone hushed.

"I am well over five hundred years old," Roman announced, "but I'd like to tell you tonight that in the last eight years of my life, I have found more happiness than I ever imagined possible. And to think it all began when I bit something I shouldn't have."

In the crowd, men chuckled and women groaned.

"What did he bite?" Russell whispered to Howard.

Howard snorted. "Don't ask."

Roman smiled. "I am happy to report that all the VANNAs have been disposed of."

The women cheered.

"The night I lost a fang should have been a disaster, but it was the most fortunate night of my life, for it was then that I met my beloved wife, Shanna." Roman smiled as he motioned toward his wife. "Since then I have been blessed with two beautiful children. And in the eight years that have passed, I have seen more and more of my friends fall in love and marry and have children."

Everyone in the courtyard cheered.

"My life is so much richer for knowing you all. And my heart is so full of joy that I wanted to share a few words with our newly married couple." Roman turned to face them. "We may be a ragtag group of different species, but we are family. I thank God that we have found each other and that we have persevered through every adversity. Together, we are stronger and truly blessed. May everyone raise their glass in honor of our latest couple, Russell and Jia. Welcome to the family."

Everyone cheered and took a drink.

After an hour of partying, Russell teleported back to the bat cave to pick up his wedding present for Jia. Back in Tiger Town, he found her at their table and handed it to her. "This is for you."

She opened it and gasped. Immediately, a bunch of women crowded around for a look.

"It's magnificent." Jia lifted the gold and jade necklace out of the box.

The courtyard was filled with feminine ooh's and aah's.

Russell removed Jia's black beaded hat and looped the long necklace over her head. "Jean-Luc helped me find a jewelry designer in Paris. I wanted it to match the bracelets from your mother." He glanced down at her wrists, but they were bare. Strange. He'd felt sure she would wear them for the wedding.

Jia touched the necklace. "I will treasure this always. Thank you." She motioned to her uncles. "I have a wedding gift for you, too."

Tinzen and Renzen brought several boxes to their table.

"I didn't expect anything." Russell opened the first box and laughed when he saw a Stetson. "Now, this is more like it." He took off the beaded UFO and set the brown cowboy hat on his head. "How did you get it?"

Jia smiled. "I sent Jin Long on a shopping trip to Texas."

Russell opened the next two boxes and discovered a pair of cowboy boots and a leather tooled belt with holsters.

"Now you can wear your pistols like a real cowboy," Jia said.

Russell winced inwardly.

"And there's more!" Jia announced, grinning. "On the land you bought, I had my uncles build a pen. You are now the owner of a horse and three cows!"

Everyone cheered as Russell stared at Jia in shock. She was setting him up as a rancher. She'd anticipated his plan. "How did you know?"

She gave him a wry look. "How could I not know? You're a cowboy."

He pulled her into his arms. "Thank you." His gaze wandered over the gifts on the table. All this, plus a horse and a few cows? "Jia, how were you able to afford it all?"

With a shrug, she reached for his new leather belt. "Here. Try it on."

He eyed the empty holsters with dismay. "I have to tell you something. I-I don't have the pistols anymore. I sold them so I could buy the rings, your necklace, and the land, and have enough left over to build a small house."

Jia's mouth dropped open. "Y-you sold them?" She pressed a hand to her chest. "But they're all you have left of your family."

"You're my family now." His gaze fell to her bare wrist. "Where are your bracelets?"

She winced. "I sold them to buy your presents and the farm animals."

"Jia! That's all you had left from your mother!"

She sighed. "I wanted to help your dream come true."

"Where did you sell them? I'll get them back."

"You lost your pistols, too."

He waved a dismissive hand. "It's okay. I sold them to Zoltan. I know exactly where they are, and I can look at them whenever I want."

She lifted her chin. "Same thing with my bracelets. I sold them to one of our friends, so I can see them whenever I wish."

"But you can't wear them. I'm getting them back!" Russell looked around the crowd of people, then rushed over to Angus and Emma, who had hired him back a few days ago. They were each holding a dragon shifter baby.

"Congratulations!" Emma smiled at him.

"Thank you." Russell stepped closer to Angus. "Is there a way I can get my next paycheck in advance?"

"Och, funny ye should ask." Angus handed his

baby to Shanna Draganesti, then pulled an envelope from his sporran. "I've been meaning to give this to you."

Russell opened the envelope and stiffened when he saw the amount of the check. It was almost a quarter million. "What the hell?"

"That's yer salary for the last two years," Angus explained. "Ye never officially resigned, so I've always considered you an employee of MacKay S&I. Ye were certainly working all that time."

"But . . ." Russell looked at the check again to make sure he was seeing right. "This is more than two years' wages."

"Aye." Angus nodded. "As far as I can tell, ye never took a day off, so ye worked a lot of overtime. And ye deserved a bonus for going above and beyond the call of duty. If it were no' for you, we would have never defeated the vampire lords and Master . . ." He winced.

"My brother," Russell muttered. "You don't need to pay me for killing—"

"Lad." Angus squeezed his shoulder. "Ye worked hard. Ye earned the money. Take it."

Russell took a deep breath and exhaled. "All right."

"And ye're still working for me." Angus gave him a pointed look. "From now on, I expect reports."

"Yes, sir." Russell saluted.

Angus grinned and slapped him on the back. "Off ye go, lad. Yer bride is waiting."

"Actually, I need to find out who bought Jia's bracelets so I can buy them back," Russell said.

Shanna laughed. "I can help you with that." She handed the dragon baby back to Angus and removed a gift box from her large handbag. "This is your wedding present from Roman and me."

Russell opened it and discovered Jia's bracelets inside. "Y-you're giving them back?"

"I never intended to keep them. They belong to Jia."

Then it was Roman and Shanna who had helped finance the start of his ranch. "Thank you. I don't know how I ever got such good friends."

Shanna gave him a hug. "Enjoy your life with Jia."

"I will." He rushed back to his bride and slipped the bracelets onto her wrists. Her eyes glistened with tears, and he knew with a surge of joy that he'd scored big time.

"How did you get them so quickly?" Jia asked.

"Shanna gave them to us as a wedding present."

Jia blinked away some tears. "We are truly blessed with our friends."

"I know." He wiped away a tear as it rolled down her face. "And I'm blessed to have found you. We'll have a good life. Although I can't promise that I'll always agree with you."

She smiled. "That just means you'll occasionally be wrong."

He snorted. "But I do believe we will have a long and happy life. And I will always love you."

"That's my cowboy."

He held her tight. "My princess."

Acknowledgments

Back when Roman Draganesti lost his fang in *How to Marry a Millionaire Vampire,* I had no idea I had tapped into a world that would last for sixteen books. My heartfelt gratitude goes to all the Love at Stake readers who made the series such a success. Thank you for your notes and e-mails, which give me encouragement. You help me continue to write with joy.

With the end of Russell's story, I'll be bringing the series to a close, a temporary one, perhaps, since I still have a few plans. But right now, I have other ideas calling me, ideas that are demanding to be brought to life. I hope you will join me on some new adventures!

I also wish to thank my agent, Michelle Grajkowski of Three Seas, who always gives me joyful support and encouragement. Many thanks to everyone at HarperCollins/Avon Books—my editor, Erika Tsang, who has been with me since book one; her assistant, Chelsey; the publicity experts,

Jessie, Caro, and Pam; and the art director, Tom, who has created the most exquisite covers.

My critique partners, M.J., Sandy, and Vicky, have also been with me since book one. I don't know how I would have survived the writing of sixteen books without them! Over the years, they have become my best friends, and I am ever thankful for their loyalty, kindness, and compassion.

I am also grateful for my children and my husband. They have always believed in me, even when I doubted myself. They are my rock, my shelter, my joy, and my peace. And finally, since I write about love, I cannot forget to thank the source of love, our Heavenly Father. In my attempts to spread joy and hope and reinforce the value of love, I have felt truly blessed. Thank you all for allowing me to be part of your lives.

SIZZLING PARANORMAL ROMANCE FROM *NEW YORK TIMES* BESTSELLING AUTHOR

KERRELYN SPARKS

WANTED: UNDEAD OR ALIVE

978-0-06-195806-9

Bryn Jones believes vampires are seductive and charming, and that makes them dangerous. So the werewolf princess is wary when she has to team up with the recently undead Phineas McKinney to stop a group of evil vampires, even though he makes her inner wolf purr.

SEXIEST VAMPIRE ALIVE

978-0-06-195805-2

Abby Tucker has dedicated her life to finding a cure that will save her dying mother and needs only two more ingredients. To find them, she'll have to venture into the most dangerous region in the world—with a vampire named Gregori who makes her heart race.

VAMPIRE MINE

978-0-06-195804-5

After 499 years of existence, nothing can make Connor Buchanan fall in love again. Cast down from heaven, Marielle is an angel trapped in human form who hopes to heal Connor's broken heart and earn her way back home. But suddenly she has these *feelings*—for a vampire!

EAT PREY LOVE

978-0-06-195803-8

Carlos Panterra is looking for a mate, and when the shape shifter spies beautiful Caitlyn Whelan, it's like sunshine amidst the darkness. At last he's found the perfect woman, except...she's a mortal. But Caitlyn knows that their attraction is more than just animal magnetism.

STEAMY, SENSATIONAL VAMPIRE LOVE FROM *NEW YORK TIMES* BESTSELLING AUTHOR

KERRELYN SPARKS

THE VAMPIRE AND THE VIRGIN

978-0-06-166786-2

FBI psychologist Olivia Sotiris is in dire need of a vacation. But when a deadly criminal from a case back home tracks her down, it's up to sexy bloodsucker Robby MacKay to save her life.

FORBIDDEN NIGHTS WITH A VAMPIRE

978-0-06-166784-8

Vanda Barkowski is a vampire with a hot temper, and now a judge sentences her to anger management class. Worse, Phil Jones has agreed to be her sponsor, but can she resist her attraction to this forbidden mortal?

SECRET LIFE OF A VAMPIRE

978-0-06-166785-5

No one can throw a vampire bachelor party quite like Jack. But when the party gets out of hand and the cops show up, Jack has some explaining to do to beautiful Officer Lara Boucher.

ALL I WANT FOR CHRISTMAS IS A VAMPIRE

978-0-06-111846-3

Toni's best friend has been locked up in a mental hospital because she said she was attacked by vampires. The only way to get her out is to prove that bloodsuckers really do exist, so Toni takes a job for the undead, but damn sexy, Ian McPhie.

Give in to your Impulses!

These unforgettable stories only take a second to buy and give you hours of reading pleasure!

Go to ***www.AvonImpulse.com*** and see what we have to offer.

Available wherever e-books are sold.

IMP 0811